By Alan Dean Foster

PIP & FLINX ADVENTURES

For Love of Mother-Not
The Tar-Aiym Krang
Orphan Star
The End of the Matter
Flinx in Flux
Mid-Flinx
Reunion
Flinx's Folly

Sliding Scales
Running from the Deity
Bloodhype
Trouble Magnet
Patrimony
Flinx Transcendent
Strange Music

FOUNDING OF THE COMMONWEALTH

Phylogenesis
Dirge

Diuturnity's Dawn

ICERIGGER TRILOGY

Icerigger
Mission to Moulokin

The Deluge Drivers

STANDALONE COMMONWEALTH NOVELS

Nor Crystal Tears
Voyage to the City of the Dead
Midworld
Drowning World

Quofum
The Howling Stones
Sentenced to Prism
Cachalot

THE DAMNED TRILOGY

A Call to Arms
The False Mirror

The Spoils of War

THE TAKEN TRILOGY

Lost and Found
The Light-Years Beneath My Feet

The Candle of Distant Earth

THE TIPPING POINT TRILOGY

The Human Blend
Body, Inc.

The Sum of Her Parts

STRANGE MUSIC

STRANGE MUSIC

A PIP & FLINX ADVENTURE

■ ■ ■

Alan Dean Foster

DEL REY | NEW YORK

Copyright © 2017 by Alan Dean Foster

Published in the United States by Del Rey, an imprint of Random House, a division of Penguin Random House LLC, New York.

DEL REY and the HOUSE colophon are registered trademarks of Penguin Random House LLC.

Hardback ISBN 978-1-101-96760-7
Ebook ISBN 978-1-101-96761-4

Printed in the United States of America on acid-free paper

randomhousebooks.com

2 4 6 8 9 7 5 3 1

FIRST EDITION

Title-page image: © iStockphoto.com

Book design by Dana Leigh Blanchette

TO DEAN ABLES

*Thank you for everything you've done
for everyone . . . including Speckel.*

FOREWORD

■ ■ ■

by Kevin Hearne

Growing up in the '80s, there were plenty of big-name authors to choose from in the sci-fi/fantasy section. (Robots and dragons and quests, oh my!) But when I hit the bookstores, the big-name author whose work I always sought out first was Alan Dean Foster, and it was for a very specific reason: I knew that no matter what kind of story he wrote next, I would be entertained.

Not lectured on politics or kinky social constructs. Not subjected to pages of speculative science or unpronounceable names with apostrophes in them. Simply, delightfully entertained. And since he's written 126 novels and counting, I think that we can safely say Mr. Foster is one hell of an entertainer.

He writes both science fiction and fantasy, and his book *Spellsinger* was the first fantasy I ever read. It was full of talking animals, an idea that obviously appealed to me very much when I began writing the Iron Druid Chronicles, but also tremendous humor and a vocabulary that, once absorbed, allowed my teenage self to score fantastically well on the verbal section of my SATs. To this day, he still uses words I have to look up and I geek out about it.

Foster's first-contact novels are among my favorites. *A Call to*

Arms, the first novel of The Damned trilogy, introduces a composer on a boat in the Gulf of Mexico to not one but three different species who have come to Earth seeking help in a galactic war that has dragged on for centuries. The human talent for war could tip the scales and the composer tries his best to convince the aliens in spite of ample evidence that no, we're quite peaceful really—look, I write music and drink wine! Most amusing to me are the chapters from the alien points of view, where humans are strange and terrifying creatures, and what's more, their music isn't particularly good.

Nor Crystal Tears introduces humans to the Thranx, an insectoid species that eventually forms the Commonwealth with humanity; the founding of said Commonwealth gets its own trilogy beginning with *Phylogenesis,* and Foster wrote numerous standalone books and series set in that universe: *Sentenced to Prism* includes some unusual silicon-based aliens that still make me paranoid about quarantine procedures. One of them is named A Surface of Fine Azure-Tinted Reflection with Pyroxin Dendritic Inclusions, but the human protagonist rudely shortens it to a perfunctory "Azure," which is just the beginning of a long series of miscommunications in a clash of cultures. It's a recurring question in Foster's work: How do we get along with people who are vastly different from us? His novels are full not only of thrilling conflicts but also diverse people living together in harmony, an alluring picture that makes me want to live in those worlds as well as see more of this one. That's why picking up a new Alan Dean Foster book has always been a window to a better place.

It was the Pip and Flinx stories that started it all for me. They feature a red-headed lad, Flinx, who has a telepathic bond with a flying minidragon named Pip. While being quite charming, Flinx also has a roguish streak to him and gets in *so* much trouble. In the second book, *The Tar-Aiym Krang,* Foster points out that "his morals were of a necessity of a highly adaptable nature." If that's not a recipe for shenanigans, I don't know what is. Yet among the hijinks, the banter, and the tense action sequences are moments of poignant introspection as Flinx struggles to find his place in the world and deal with the legacy of his past.

To say that this series was formative for me would be an understatement. The fact that it's still going is a great joy because I never know what winsome treasure I'll find on the next page—the happily named Truzenzuzex is still one of my favorite names to say aloud, ever—and I'll always be indebted to Mr. Foster's imagination for sparking mine and providing countless hours of enjoyable reads.

I got to meet him at Phoenix Comicon a few years back and thank him personally. We'd both been living in Arizona for decades, but our paths had never crossed due to a sad fact of life: My meager salary as a high school English teacher had given me no disposable income to attend cons or signings or indeed do much else. My lot was to eat ramen, grade essays, and write stories about a Druid and his Irish wolfhound in my spare time. But then I wound up getting published by Del Rey—the same publisher as my favorite author!—and an editor arranged a meeting over breakfast. We had waffles in one of the con hotels and I managed not to scream. That was a truly fine day.

And today is a very fine day for you, too, because now you get to discover so many amazing worlds full of fascinating critters and get happily lost in them as I did. From ship-eating fish and Devilopes on the planet of Moth to the Thranx philosoph Truzenzuzex and a species of tunneling bears, you're in for a heck of a ride. Hold on!

STRANGE MUSIC

PREFACE

■ ■ ■

Vashon killed a girl yesterday. She had beautiful flippers.

Except she wasn't a girl, exactly, and they weren't flippers, exactly. But she was beautiful. Her black fur had been made partly iridescent and streaked and spotted fit to turn the head of the most jaded local. And now she was dead.

He would have preferred to have avoided it. Unnecessary deaths too often led to complications. But she had been obstinate in defense of her mistress. Time and silence being of the essence to the operation, the soldiers under his command had been forced to cut her throat. To a Larian, that was the ultimate form of murder. To a human like himself, it was just another throat-cutting.

Nasty business, it had been. But business all the same. Now it was going to pay off. It had better.

And on top of everything else, he was going to have to compose yet another song.

1

■ ■ ■

"There's a whale here to see you."

The pale pink sunsuit covered Clarity Held from neck to feet. Lighter than gossamer, it was akin to wearing a moderate blush. Photosensitive, it did what was necessary to allow the body to produce vitamin D while simultaneously preventing the wearer's epidermis from burning. Brilliant as the work of any jeweler, the slender emerald coils of the dozing Alaspinian minidrag Scrap lay draped around her neck.

Though Flinx wore a similar suit for similar reasons, his was all but transparent. As his olive-hued skin was much darker than Clarity's, he required proportionately less protection from Cachalot's burning tropical sun. The bright yellow star beamed down through a smattering of scattered cumulus that hung like cotton in a baby-blue sky.

Though there was some moderate wave action beneath them, it did not jostle the platform that sustained their home. Hydrophobic construction materials kept it sufficiently elevated so that only the occasional breaking crest splashed against the underside. Small high-efficiency wave generators moored aft of their residence combined with solar coatings and energy storage to provide ample power for their needs irrespective of the weather.

With a sigh Flinx set aside his imported antique fishing pole, careful not to make contact with the thumbnail-size stunbar that hung at the end of the high-test line. So far the day's catch consisted of a pair of tubular *o'otts,* slick with the extruded oil that let them shoot through the tepid water, and a single migratory *thamm.* Not much more than a drifting brown mouth lined with electrified nodules, the *thamm* would be suitable only for the soup pot.

Not much of a fisherman, he told himself. Not even after living on Cachalot for a year. His risible efforts were a running joke among the local dolphins.

A brilliant crimson, blue, and green shape spiraled down to wrap itself around the hoop mast that served as a wind stabilizer for the extended dwelling. Though Pip seemed far more at home on Cachalot than any human, the truth was that to survive here she needed something only humans could provide: a dry surface. Unlike many of the Terran snakes she so closely resembled, she was not a particularly good swimmer. And her formidable arsenal of corrosive neurotoxin was useless for defense underwater.

It served superbly for bringing down native aerial lifeforms, however.

Squinting at the mast, Flinx saw that she had caught a *wispl.* Little more than airborne fragments of netting with eyes, *wispls* drifted in vast flocks over Cachalot's world-girdling ocean, surviving by consuming the tiny eggs of those sea creatures who utilized the wind to disperse their offspring. As he watched, she munched casually on the fragile meal, radiating contentment and not in the least distracted by the enormous gray shape that rose partially out of the water on the port side of the residence, scarcely an arm's length from her master.

Turning away from his winged companion, Flinx confronted a fin whale that was longer than his home. Clarity's announcement had been superfluous: he had sensed the approaching presence long before it had arrived. Like all its kind (except for the dolphins, who were endlessly effervescent and irrepressible, sometimes irritatingly so), the fin's emotional state suggested vastness and warmth, intelligence and reassurance. It reminded him of nothing so much as a great old tree. Like the rest of the perfectly hydrodynamic form, the head was sleek. Water cascaded from the fluted flesh of the lower jaw as the visitor lifted its huge head to regard Flinx out of one contemplative eye.

"Hello, Sylent," Flinx offered by way of greeting.

Sylent, who wasn't as reticent as his name implied, replied in the profoundly deep basso of his kind. In their speech the baleens were less weighty than the catodons but more somber than the orcas or porpoises: neither profound nor playful.

"Daylight Brightness to You, Flinxman. Goes well your Life, swims fast your Mate?"

"Both wet a-going, thank you graciously. What propels your fine visit?"

"News I bring. From Farefa'are'i. Of a New Person come see You."

The spaceport? Flinx tensed. He and Clarity were not expecting company. It was his experience that visitors meant nothing but trouble, sometimes of the potentially lethal kind. On the other hand, whoever had arrived had gone some way toward dispelling such concern by making the effort to announce themselves in advance.

But why do so via cetacean? A simple "hello" via communit would have been much quicker. It hinted at a need for formal subterfuge. He remained wary yet intrigued.

"Did the New Person give a Naming?"

Water rushed beneath the hovering house complex as Sylent's enormous head slid slowly back down into the water.

"Surprise, I was told."

Unusual name, Flinx mused. Then he smiled to himself. "Surprise" was likely not the name of the visitor but a description of his or her arrival. It also helped to explain why the still-unknown individual had chosen this way of announcing their arrival.

"Come soon, I was told also. Go now. Time to feed."

Flinx knew it was always time for the big baleens to feed, but he made no effort to stay the bearer of unexpected news. "Eat well, Sylent, and with my thanks go."

"So going, Flinxman. Cold Upwellings to your Mate."

And with a farewell lobtailing that soaked the port side of the habitat, the fin whale was gone.

Flinx pondered a moment, then headed toward the living quarters that occupied the center of the residential platform. Clarity needed to be told. That visitors were a rare thing bothered neither of them in the least. Coming to this world in search of peace and privacy, they had discovered both in abundance. Cachalot, its scattered human inhabitants, and its millions of cetaceans had embraced the two newcomers and their needs without qualification, without question. It was as good a place in the Commonwealth as any in which to lose oneself without completely cutting the bonds of civilization. For more than a year now they had both been content, dwelling in isolation, humidity, and connubial bliss. While not regarded as intrusive, neither was visitation encouraged.

It appeared that someone had sought him out, however. That was flattering, provided they had not come seeking his head. Or its contents. Few knew who he was. Even fewer knew what he was. Less than a handful were aware of what he could do, or what he had done. In Clarity's company he sought anonymity and a little happiness, and had managed to find both.

So he and his companion would welcome whoever had come looking for him, with food and drink and open arms, while keeping more lethal arms at the ready.

He did not have to call Pip down from her high perch. His feelings, which the serpentine alien empath readily perceived, were enough to bring her to him. With her head resting on his shoulder, she used slitted eyes to search his face while a part of her mind melded with his own. Finding concern there but not fear, she folded her pink and blue wings against her flanks, coiled a portion of her muscular shimmering self loosely around his neck, and went to sleep.

The sturdy, sleek craft that announced its approach was typical of those that could be found for rent at the Farefa'are'i spaceport. The extruded metallic glass shell absorbed sunlight for additional power while protecting those within from Cachalot's rays. With skids instead of floats, this model was one that was equally at home on land and sea.

Guided by automatics, it slid into the U-shaped dock at the stern of the residence as effortlessly as a princess's foot into a shoe. As it settled into place on the water, automated docklocks secured it. Reaching outward with his singular talent, Flinx had already determined that the visitor, for there appeared to be only one, posed no threat. If anything, the emotions he detected were a mix of anticipation and delight.

Also, they did not emanate from anything human.

Confirmation of his unique insight came in the shape of the figure that stepped out of the skimmer and onto the dock. Despite the presence of six legs and two small arms, the visitor moved as gingerly as if treading a knife edge. Completely encased in a survival suit, it tottered toward them as Flinx hurried to extend a helping hand. Despite the stability imparted by so many legs, he understood full well why their guest moved so tentatively.

Save for a few demented individuals, all thranx were terrified of open water. Not only because their breathing spicules were located on their b-thorax, below their head and neck, but because their hard exoskeletons rendered them considerably less buoyant than humans. The attractions of swimming tend to pale when one has a propensity to sink.

The emotional state of the new arrival had changed abruptly to borderline panic immediately upon exiting the skimmer, even though the dock arguably offered a more stable platform than the craft.

"It's okay." Flinx smiled as he kept a firm grasp on one extended, suited truhand. "This residence is synchronously stabilized and has survived some impressive storms." With his other hand he indicated their aqueous surroundings. "We're little more than flat calm today."

"Doesn't matter," the figure muttered as one foothand rose to unseal the protective cylindrical helmet. Freed from confinement, a pair of feathery antennae sprang upward. From her position on Flinx's neck, Pip opened her eyes. Like her master, she, too, recognized the newcomer. So did Clarity, albeit frowning slightly in remembrance.

"I know you. You're Sylzenzuzex."

The young female thranx made a gesture with one truhand, then bowed slightly. Those bits of the chitinous exoskeleton that were visible through the transparent portions of the survival suit shone like burnished aquamarine-hued metal. Horizontal maroon stripes banded compound eyes that glistened like hammered gold. Even as a delighted Flinx reached out to make fingertip contact with the end of a forward-inclined antenna, she demurred. He could sense that her increasing anxiety threatened to overwhelm her.

"Maybe you'd like to come inside?"

"Anywhere away from all this water and as quickly as possible, *srra!!ant*." Although she could have used symbospeech, she chose to reply in sharply accented but perfectly acceptable terranglo.

Only when they had entered the habitat's main room and Clarity had commanded all the windows to darken did the thranx finally squirm free of the survival suit. A single sling-pouch hung from her thorax. The gleaming enamel insignia embedded in the chitin of her right shoulder indicated her now-advanced rank within the United Church. A glance behind the thorax revealed the continued presence of all four vestigial wingcases. Still not formally mated then, Flinx noted. Freed of the enclosing survival suit and driven by hydrophobia, her b-thorax was pulsing far more rapidly than normal. He did his best to put her at ease.

"It's really all right, Syl. The weather is fine and we're completely stable here."

"I know. I know it's safe here and that I'm not going to drown. I'm being irrationally fearful."

To her credit, Clarity, who had always been slightly jealous of Flinx's emotional bond with the thranx, chipped in with her own attempt at reassurance.

"No more so than if your average human was made to stand exposed on the top of a thousand-meter-high spire."

Flinx frowned. "Why would that make someone afraid?"

She made a face at him. "I said 'average' human." They had been together long enough that she could joke about such things. She smiled encouragingly at their visitor. "Can I offer you something to drink? To eat?"

Sufficiently composed by now to release her foothands' grip on the floor, Sylzenzuzex sat back on her four trulegs and held the remaining four limbs out in front of her. Muskier than that of most thranx, her personal physical bouquet suffused the room's cooled, recycled air. Rose, honeysuckle, huckleberry, and frangipani. *How could anyone draw back in fear from a creature that smelled like that?* Flinx wondered as he reflected on the sometimes fractious history of early human-thranx contact.

"I'd like to think this a social visit." At his gesture, a chair comprised of padded netting obediently ambled forward to position itself beneath him. "But I have a feeling I'd be wrong." Spreading her wings, Pip rose from his neck and shoulders to join Scrap in investigating something small, bright red, and many-legged that had crawled out of the sea and somehow made its way into the residence. Backed into a corner, it confronted the two minidrags with formidable extensible claws as they play-struck at it repeatedly.

There was no thranx furniture in the humans' residence since there was no reason to expect a thranx to visit Cachalot, but their guest made herself comfortable by straddling the back of a netting couch. Both truhands moved as she spoke, punctuating her terranglo with thranx gestures that were simultaneously complimentary and eloquent. Flinx knew their meaning as well as he knew his own language.

"Call my presence here semi-official," she told him. "Those who know of it know that I know you. Technically, in this particular situation, the Church cannot call on you for assistance."

Uh-oh, he thought. "Doesn't the Commonwealth government still 'technically' want me dead?" Shoving his arms sharply out in front of him, he opened his palms and twisted both wrists in opposite directions: it was the thranx gesture of *ac phatev,* indicating maximum, or fifth-degree, emphasis. Returning with refreshments, Clarity didn't bat an eye at either his words or the two-armed gesture. She had been through too much with the tall redhead to be surprised by anything that was said or signaled.

Sylzenzuzex responded by raising her left truhand with the first finger up and the other three closed together: the *tan wreix* used to indicate negativity. At the same time both foothands rose with elbow joints out and foothands extended horizontally: *te phatev* for fourth degree. She had replied to his query by indicating that she was pretty strongly pessimistic—all without saying a word. Had she added the usual thranx click-and-whistle vocalizations, her response would have been aurally as well as visually complex.

Low Thranx was difficult. High Thranx, for anyone not of that particular species, was near to impossible to comprehend, let alone "speak," except by experts.

He turned somber. "So in the corridors of power I'm still considered nothing more than a dangerous freak? The mutated renegade offspring of a banned genetic experiment by the outlawed Meliorare Society? In case anyone's forgotten, I recently saved not only civilization but the entire galaxy."

"That was last week." She shifted her horizontal position on the couch. It was a matter of balance, not comfort. There were few nerve endings in her chitinous exoskeleton. "A very, very few know your true self and the nature of the remarkable things you have done. Which is why, after careful consideration, it was decided that the Church—the Church, not the Commonwealth government—should be the entity to ask for your help."

"Which is why they sent you," he muttered. "Instead of a stranger."

"Knowing as you do of my kind's aversion to any body of water deeper than the length of a fingertip," she replied, "it was determined that my very presence here would be enough to convince you of the importance of this matter, *arr!ilk*."

"Another matter." On the other side of the room, Clarity was fussing with a suspended collage of preserved pseudocoral. She radiated unhappiness, and she knew he would know. "Always another matter. One time you had told me there was an end to the 'matter.'"

"Clarity." His tone asked for understanding. "Syl's come all this way, at considerable personal discomfort to herself. The least we can do is hear her out."

"What about *my* discomfort?" she murmured. Knowing that he could perceive her emotions but that his hearing was no sharper than anyone else's, she had taken to expressing her feelings aloud but too softly for him to actually hear.

Sylzenzuzex spoke before he could respond. "I asked to come. As I said, only a few others know of you. Fewer still *know* you."

Memories came flooding into him. "How is your uncle? And his companion, Bran Tse-Mallory?"

She made a gesture of third-degree contentment. "Truzenzuzex is as ornery—I think that is the right terranglo word—as ever. Bran Tse-Mallory is slowed by age, but defiant of it." All four upper limbs contorted in a complicated gesture even Flinx could not quite interpret. "As a fully vested Church security officer, I am allowed even more operational leeway than the last time we met. I have to confess that it was I who ultimately proposed that you be solicited to assist in this small but significant matter."

He exhaled slowly. A quick glance at Clarity showed that she was not looking in his direction. She was also, he knew for a certainty, missing none of the conversation.

"I saved civilization. One would think that was enough. But— some time has passed since then. I suppose I can at least listen to the details of a small matter."

A gesture of fourth-degree gratitude preceded Syl's reply. "Do you know a world called Largess?"

He considered a moment, then shook his head: a simple human gesture the thranx understood so well that many had adopted it. "Never heard of it."

"It lies on the outer edge of the Commonwealth, facing the un- claimed region between us and the AAnn Empire. A Class IVb world whose inhabitants are struggling to rise from clan and regional rela- tionships long enough to forge a government sufficiently wide- ranging to qualify for greater Commonwealth assistance. There is a single, fairly substantial Commonwealth base there. Some limited but worthwhile trade goes on, primarily involving unsynthesizable local organics."

"Why is the Church concerned?"

"As with any Class IVb world, trade and the exchange of ad- vanced information is highly restricted. There is evidence that some- one is violating those restrictions."

To Flinx's relief, Clarity was apparently interested in spite of her- self. "Sounds like a fairly straightforward enforcement matter. Why would you need someone like Flinx to become involved?"

Another complicated multilimbed gesture tied Flinx's analytical knowledge of thranx truhand and foothand movements in knots, until he realized that that was exactly what she was trying to com- municate: confusion and uncertainty.

"It has to do with the nature of the native Larians themselves," Syl said slowly, unavoidably having to add a click and two whistles to fully clarify her meaning. "They are not so much hostile to outsiders as they are indifferent to them. It is an indifference that among some of them rises to the level of bordering on contempt for the way they believe we feel. Or rather, do not feel."

"I don't understand." Flinx made no effort to hide his confusion.

"Humans talk to one another in terranglo. Thranx use both Low and High dialects. Different Commonwealth species converse via symbospeech. The Larians communicate with what we might call singspeech. Essentially, if you can't sing, you can't talk." A simpler gesture punctuated her concluding thoughts. "My kind can whistle. Indeed, a thranx would have difficulty communicating properly with another if it lacked such an ability. But we cannot sing. Our vocal system is not sufficiently flexible." Golden compound eyes switched from Flinx to Clarity. "Humans, on the other hand, possess this ability in quantity."

Flinx coughed meaningfully. "Not all of us. Clarity is a fine singer. Much better than I am."

"That's true." There was no hesitation in Clarity's reply. "But," she finished reluctantly, "you're not bad, my man. You can carry a tune. I've heard you do it."

"There is more to it than just that." Sylzenzuzex gave no hint of appreciating her hosts' verbal byplay. "The Larians are also a very emotional species. Their singsong communication is intimately connected with and to how they feel. It seems that they can sense when someone is singing, or communicating, honestly." She was staring at her old friend. "It is an ability akin to Flinx's, but on a much lower, more primitive level. What it means is that someone able to perceive what a Larian is feeling would be able to tell whether they are being honest, evasive, lying, or secretly hostile. Such an individual would be able to track down whoever is violating Commonwealth strictures on Largess far more easily and quickly than anyone else. Provided they can sing, of course."

"A universal translator isn't sufficient?" Clarity asked.

Sylzenzuzex gestured third-degree negativity. "The words would be translated, but deprived of any musicality the Larians would hear them as 'dead language' and pay no attention to whatever was being said. Universal translators are too literal. They work only with words and cannot interpret or simulate musical accompaniment."

"I still don't see why this is anything more than a minor local matter," Clarity replied, struggling to contain her exasperation.

The thranx responded with a second-degree gesture of understanding.

"Some of the Larian clans and towns are trying to organize themselves into a large, stable federation. If they can do so, they would qualify to petition for a status upgrade within the Commonwealth: a first step on the path to a proper world government representing their entire species. The illegal introduction of advanced technology coupled with advice and guidance from an outsider, or outside interests, threatens to distract and unsettle the most far-sighted and important of the local clans that are in favor of such unification. It endangers all the good work that the more enlightened Hobaks, as the clan leaders are called, have done. While the Larians are generally polite and welcoming to outsiders, among themselves they have a volatile history.

"The Church frowns on such setbacks to potential unity and species advancement and, where and whenever possible, seeks to ameliorate them—without violating Commonwealth policy, of course."

Flinx was nodding knowingly. "Whereas an unattached outside interest could do so without compromising the Church itself."

"Benign outside interest set to counter an inimical outside interest. Precisely."

"And," Clarity put in tersely, "if said 'benign outside interest' happened to find himself compromised, the Church would of course disavow any knowledge of or interest in said interest's activities." Picking up on her increasingly strong feelings on the matter, a concerned Scrap immediately looked over from where the red-shelled oceanic intruder had just about given up trying to fend off the two persistent minidrags.

"Policy." Sylzenzuzex was apologetic. "As I said before, I have some leeway in certain things. But not in everything."

A frustrated Clarity ceased pretending that she was fiddling with the pseudocoral sculpture and turned to face the thranx directly. "Why should Flinx risk himself, however slightly, on behalf of the Commonwealth? Or the United Church? He's been hounded ever since he was a boy! Hasn't he done enough already for an ignorant population that would see him mindwiped without raising so much as a halfhearted objection?"

Now visibly upset, Scrap spread his wings, soared across the room, and landed on his mistress's shoulder. A pointed tongue began licking her left cheek and she brushed at it absently. It was not lost on Clarity that Pip continued her pursuit of the local crustacean. That told her that Flinx, whatever he was thinking, was not nearly as upset by the thranx's implied request as she was.

Heightened emotional perception does not always require direct physical manipulation at the genetic level. Sometimes marriage is sufficient.

"I'd like to help," he said carefully. "It sounds like an interesting set of circumstances, and Largess sounds like an engaging world. But . . ."

Clarity turned away in a huff. "Oh, go on. Fishing bores you. Home improvement bores you. Diving bores you. I suppose I bore you."

Rising from the net chair, he moved quickly to put his arms around her from behind. When he bent to kiss her neck, she twisted away. But slowly.

"I can count on one hand the things that have never bored me, Clarity. Pip, new worlds, and above all, you. If not for you I'm pretty sure I'd be dead, somewhere."

"At least you wouldn't be bored." Turning back to him, she briefly scanned his face before letting out a resigned sigh. "Oh, go on." A hand gestured in Sylzenzuzex's direction. "Run off with your bug girlfriend. Maybe you'll come back with a better appreciation for what you have here."

"I am sorry?" Sylzenzuzex's gesture with both truhands indicated fourth-degree confusion. " 'Bug girlfriend'?"

Flinx cast the thranx a hasty smile. "Nothing. Standard banter between mated humans. Very traditional."

"Ah, *chir!!k*."

"I'll fix this problem quickly, Clarity. Be back before you know it. It'll be useful to have another positive entry in my Church file."

She sniffed derisively. "Doesn't mean the government won't keep trying to reel you in to 'rehabilitate' you."

"I'll be careful." He released her and stepped back. "I'm not a novice at avoiding unwanted attention, you know."

"Is that so? For someone who's spent his whole life trying to avoid it, you sure draw a lot of it." Looking past him, she stared hard at Sylzenzuzex. "Traveler identity?"

"New one," the thranx replied. "Already prepared."

"You were very certain he'd go."

"No." The thranx underlined her reply with a firm gesture of all four upper limbs. "But I have always believed in being proactive, especially where humans are concerned."

2

■ ■ ■

"It is understood," Sylzenzuzex repeated carefully, "that the use of advanced technology would violate the very protocols we are trying to preserve, and therefore cannot be employed under any circumstances."

A smiling Flinx nodded toward the far corner of the room, where a thrashing of iridescent scales indicated that unlike Scrap, Pip was still fully involved in tormenting the small uninvited denizen of Cachalot's seas.

"She's all the help I need. We're not dealing with powerful ancient relics of the Tar-Aiym or the Hur'rikku. It's just one troublemaker on a minor world, right?"

"That is the assumption," the thranx confirmed.

"I don't like assumptions." Clarity was already regretting having given her consent to Flinx's participation. "They have a nasty way of turning out differently from what you expect. Like the really nice people who made up the Order of Null."

"Which no longer exists," Flinx hastened to point out. "Pip and I will be fine. You sound like Mother Mastiff. She wouldn't stop me from doing this."

"No," Clarity admitted. "But if we're going to reference relics, then I have to add that that half-crazy old woman wouldn't stop you from confronting a Demichin devilope naked and weaponless. She'd just shake her head in resignation at your stupidity and get on with her own life." Once more she eyed the quietly watching thranx. "I, on the other hand, prefer to be 'proactive.'" She sighed heavily. "Do you at least have some idea who this lawbreaker is that's causing this trouble on—what world was it? Largess?"

The gesture for apologetic uncertainty was as nimble as it was elaborate. "As I mentioned, Largess has much to offer in the way of tradable unsynthesizable organics. A number of species that engage in wide-ranging commerce have taken advantage of the relevant opportunities, though thranx are not among them. The largest contingent of visitors consists of humans. Therefore it is not unreasonable to assume that our troublemaker is of your kind, though we as yet have no conclusive proof of this." She turned her attention back to Flinx, both feathery antennae dipping slightly in his direction. "Still, it presents another reason for requesting Flinx's assistance."

"Haven't you checked it out for yourself?" Clarity's tone was mildly accusatory.

Not only both antennae, but all four upper limbs went straight up. Though the thranx face was inflexible, Sylzenzuzex nonetheless managed to convey her horror at her hostess's suggestion.

"Me? I spent only a little time on Largess. As little as possible. Just what was minimally necessary for me to carry out my assignment. No thranx is permanently posted to that world. Humans find it chilly; we find it frigid. The topography is dominated by low-lying land, truncated vegetation, and far too much open water. To be posted there would constitute punishment of the worst imaginable kind, *chir!!!tt!*"

"Sounds inviting." Clarity flashed Flinx a sardonic smile. "I'm sure you'll have a wonderful time."

"Humans have the ability to adapt to greater extremes of weather than most sentient species," Sylzenzuzex put in helpfully. "I don't mean to exaggerate. The climate is nothing like, for example, that of an even more isolated and immoderate world like Tran-ky-ky. No polar attire is required for humans to move about in comfort and safety, only some reasonably insulated hydrophilic outerwear. Flinx will not suffer."

"I will until I can come home," he murmured tactfully.

Though she would not admit to it, his words had the intended effect on Clarity. "Go ahead, then. Do what you feel you have to do. You always have. You always will. No matter what anyone else says."

"Now, precious . . . ," he began.

"It's all right." She mustered a reluctant smile. "Go forth and slay your boredom. But that's all."

"That's all," he promised before turning once more to face the visiting thranx. "I'll do my best to find your troublemaking inter-loper and turn him, her, or whatever it is over to the local Common-wealth authorities so that they can deal appropriately with the situation. Or if that doesn't prove feasible, I'll try to gather enough information so that others can do so."

A pleased Sylzenzuzex responded wordlessly, with an unmistak-able gesture of appreciation. But only of first degree, he noted to himself.

"You'll be in service on Church business, but surreptitiously. As much to protect your cover as to preserve Commonwealth restric-tions, your use of contemporary technology will be denied."

He nodded understandingly. "I'll manage. I have before."

"I know you will be relying on your unique abilities to carry you through any difficulties," she added. "By the way, how are your re-curring headaches? The ones that have troubled you for so long whenever you are compelled to utilize your . . . talent."

"I hardly ever have them anymore." He touched a forefinger to his forehead. "Even though I still use it without thinking, as always."

"Because you're not under stress here," Clarity pointed out. "Much easier to relax when your life isn't being threatened."

"I don't foresee that happening on Largess," he said.

She wouldn't let it go. "So now your abilities include prognostication?"

"Enough to know that I'll miss you while I'm gone," he replied.

"Okay, okay. Let's get you ready before I change my mind. Of course, you'd know if I changed it, wouldn't you?"

He shook his head. "Unless the decision was underlined by a strong new emotion, a simple decision change isn't something I've ever been able to sense."

Legs dangling on opposite sides, Sylzenzuzex slipped off the back of the couch on which she had been sprawled. "Should I wait in another chamber?" Her gaze shifted quickly if reluctantly to a window. "I can . . . wait outside if you wish."

"That's brave of you, but not necessary," Flinx told her. "It won't take me long to make ready. I've spent my whole life prepared to move on a moment's notice." He smiled at Clarity. "With the exception of this past year."

"There will be appropriate attire and supplies waiting for you on Largess," Sylzenzuzex assured him. "A trusted Padre will be notified to expect you, and will provide all that you need to be comfortable on that world."

Clarity made a sound under her breath. "I may not have your talent, Flinx, but I can 'sense' sycophancy when it's being ladled on me. Having suffered through it too many times in the past, I'm sorry to say that I also know your routine for this sort of hurried departure. Backpack and little else. What's the first thing you're going to want to take?"

"That should be self-evident." With a nod he turned and called across the room. "Come on, Pip. We're going for another walk."

While the flying snake did not understand the words, she responded immediately and appropriately to his mood, darting about the room from place to place and whirling circles around the ceiling. Ever ready to partake of an upbeat mood, Scrap joined her and did his best to synchronize with her aerial gymnastics.

While Clarity could not perceive Flinx's emotions, she didn't have to. All she had to do to know what he was feeling was watch his pet.

"One last question." She spoke plainly as she and Flinx prepared to leave the room to attend to his preparations. "If cooperation with the natives of this world is so awkward that the Church needs someone of Flinx's abilities to communicate effectively with them, then how is this troublemaker, human or otherwise, able to get along with them?"

"Maybe whoever it is, is just like me," Flinx joked.

Neither Clarity nor Sylzenzuzex laughed.

"Come on now," he chided the both of them. "There is nobody else like me. You know it." He eyed the woman with whom he shared his life. When she just stared back, he turned to the thranx. "You know it, too."

The somber Church Padre who responded was leagues advanced in knowledge and experience from the tentative young thranx he had encountered so long ago. "The Commonwealth is a vast place, Flinx. It is impossible to fully know a single world in depth, let alone dozens. I cannot imagine anyone knowing that better than yourself. Therefore with regard to your particular situation, neither I nor my superiors are prepared to say conclusively what is possible and what is not."

Putting an arm around Clarity, Flinx hugged her to him. "In their rampaging about with human DNA, the Meliorare Society only came up with one of me. Maybe two, if you count the other one we prefer not to talk about."

Both antennae and all four upper limbs inclined in Flinx's direction. "I have researched the sealed records on the Meliorares myself. It is impossible to know everything they did and did not do, the details of every experiment they attempted, because they did not know these things themselves. When the authorities became aware of their efforts and began to deal with them, it resulted in their records becoming as widely scattered as their members."

"Not to mention their experiments." For some time now Flinx had been fully aware of who and what he was. Save for the occasional bad dream, it no longer troubled him. As long as it did not unsettle Clarity, he was content with the knowledge that he was yet another misguided experiment on the part of that outlawed and disbanded organization. Albeit arguably a more successful one.

"I am only saying," Sylzenzuzex continued, "that there are components of civilization of which we may be unaware, and that all possibilities must therefore be considered. Especially in a situation like this." The thranx added a fourth-degree gesture of emphasis.

Flinx had to smile. "Just now you sounded exactly like your uncle."

"Flattery doesn't alter the thesis." Sylzenzuzex refused to be diverted.

Since he was unable to dissuade Sylzenzuzex of the hypothesis, Flinx responded by making light of it. "That'd be fine use of such an unusual ability: messing about making trouble with the natives of a Class IVb world."

"As opposed to using it to make a living on a backward world by picking pockets and performing parlor tricks for marketplace visitors?" the thranx riposted.

His expression twisted. "You know too much of my personal history."

"You needed someone to talk to," she replied. "Especially on Ulru-Ujurr."

"Excuse me?" Clarity pulled away from him.

He was getting a headache, and not from utilizing his talent. "All right, all right. Despite the fact that I think it's an unlikelihood verging on the impossible, Syl, I'll be alert for the chance that somewhere out there, there's another one of me. If there is, I imagine I'll sense his or her presence soon enough."

"Unless they sense you first." However unlikely, the thranx's observation raised uncomfortable possibilities.

Clarity was staring hard at him. "Tell me more about what you two talked about on Ulru-Ujurr."

"That was a long time ago," he said soothingly. "It was a difficult situation and I was way too young and immature." He nodded at the watching thranx. "Our lives were at stake. I've already told you everything I can remember about the times before you and I met on Longtunnel."

"Yes. You had a dull and boring life." She sighed. "I'm going to miss you while you're gone, Flinx."

"I would hope so. I'll miss you and Scrap, too. But I'll be back soon enough. This shouldn't take long or be too much trouble."

She shook her head. "Seems to me I've heard that song sung before."

"As to transportation from Cachalot to Largess," Sylzenzuzex told him, clearly relieved to be able to talk about mundane details once more, "having already seen to the matter of your alternate identification documentation for the duration of the journey, the Church can provide transportation via—"

A smiling Flinx cut her off. "Actually, none of that will be necessary, Syl. If you recall, I can manage my own transportation."

Both antennae straightened. "Knowing that you have retired to a quiet life here, I did not realize that you retained ownership of or contact with the vessel you previously utilized."

He made a face. "I hope I have. I haven't had any contact with it since Clarity and I established formal residency here." His gaze flicked upward. "It should still be in orbit, waiting. Sleeping."

The thranx gestured third-degree concern coupled with second-degree curiosity. "AI's that have not been utilized for a long time have been known to enter a state of permanent stasis from which they cannot successfully be roused."

"We'll find out soon enough," he told her solemnly, "when I request her to send a shuttle down."

Clarity peered over at him. "I've spent enough time on the *Teacher* to get to know that AI a little. It's unique."

"It should be," he agreed, "having been constructed by the Ulru-Ujurrians. Everything they do is unique."

"It's possible the ship might be aware," she continued, "but no longer interested in dealing with you. It might be conscious, but simply refuse to respond." She glanced at Sylzenzuzex. "I've had enough dealings with AI's to know that can happen, too. It's called cybernetic estrangement, I believe."

"In that case," he said thoughtfully, "some reprogramming of the perceptual cortex might be in order."

She looked surprised. "Can you do that?"

"Why not?" He smiled back at her. "You did it to me."

A silent Sylzenzuzex watched them embrace, not for the first time simultaneously marveling and shuddering at the ability of the flexible human form to intertwine in ways that would cause a thranx exoskeleton to crack and splinter from the stress.

The shuttle from the *Teacher* that arrived to pick him up deployed integrated floats without Flinx having to convey the necessary instructions. That was a good sign. The fact that the compact craft offered only the most minimal formal replies to his queries and refused or was unable to connect him directly with the master AI on the *ship* was not. Could Clarity be right? Might his long absence from contact with his craft have given rise to unforeseen problems? If such was the case, hopefully he would be able to correct them.

He felt a pang of guilt. Content on Cachalot's benign surface with Pip, Scrap, and Clarity's constant company, he had neglected contact with the rest of the Commonwealth. There had been no interfacing with his old mentors Truzenzuzex and Bran Tse-Mallory, and hardly a contact or two with the increasingly aged Mother Mastiff on Moth. Maintaining communication with the *Teacher* had scarcely entered his mind. Now it was possible that his lack of interest was going to result not only in unexpected difficulties, but in the loss of something precious and important.

As the coolly efficient but largely unresponsive shuttle exited

Cachalot's atmosphere, he knew he would have answers in a few minutes.

Outwardly, the *Teacher* looked exactly as it had when he had made his last drop from her shuttle bay to the ocean world below. Still sleek, still beautiful, she represented the best of Commonwealth technology and Ulru-Ujurrian improvisation and improvements. Thanks to the latter, there was no need to utilize shuttles. Unlike any other known craft, she could have deposited him and Clarity gently on Cachalot's waters without roiling the planetary surface or damaging the ship itself. Had such a maneuver been witnessed by others, however, it would have resulted in questions impossible for him to answer. Having spent his entire life striving to avoid unwanted attention, it had been much safer to use the ship's shuttles for the few necessary orbit-to-surface transfers.

Even when the shuttle bay opened to receive him, there was still no communication from the ship itself. Sensing her master's unease, Pip coiled tighter around his shoulder until his arm began to throb slightly and he gave her a dislodging nudge.

"It's okay, girl. It's just a technical glitch. It'll all sort itself out once we're on board." He hoped.

Pressurization, if not conversation, proceeded as expected. The arrival of artificial gravity took a bit longer. One by one, albeit silently, the *Teacher*'s systems were responding to his arrival. As soon as they exited the shuttle, Pip launched herself from his shoulder and shot forward down the corridor. She remembered, even if the ship itself did not. The minidrag dipped and darted into every opening; exploring, tasting, recalling.

As he headed for the forward command section, Flinx's gaze drank in colors and shapes, wrapping them in memories. His quarters, there. Guest quarters, nearby. Automated food prep facilities, below. Access to the beltgun blister, over that way. A great many weeks and months had been spent in the confines of this vessel, crisscrossing parts of the Commonwealth, the AAnn Empire—even portions of the Blight. It knew space-plus as well as it did normal space.

But did it still know him?

True, it had responded to his request to send down a shuttle, and life support systems had activated upon his arrival. Nothing that automatics could not do. It was the essence of the ship itself, the extraordinary AI that had been designed and given cybernetic life by the Ulru-Ujurrians, that remained conspicuous by its silence. He was starting to get worried. At this point it would be a relief to hear a simple verbal acknowledgment of his presence.

Moving through the compact command center, he settled himself into the central seat and contemplated the view out the wide forward port. The rest of the KK-drive vessel stretched out before him; the currently quiescent Caplis generator connected via a long, complex tubular piece of construction to the ovoid that contained the ship's living quarters. With the *Teacher* angled slightly downward, he was presented with a spectacular view of his adopted world's endless oceans. On that palette of infinite blue, too modest in size to be seen from high orbit, floated the city and spaceport of Farefa'are'i. Not far to the west of it, a single independent residence hung just above the waves that rolled steadily beneath its underside. He missed Clarity already.

That would not help him focus on the task he had accepted from Sylzenzuzex, he told himself firmly. Very clever of the United Church to send an old friend to inveigle him. Had it been just another official, he doubted he would have agreed to offer his service.

But he *had* agreed, and now he was faced with a ship that failed to respond to his presence. At worst, he could return to the surface and accept Sylzenzuzex's offer of transportation. His expression tightened. "At worst" was a place he had visited before, and always successfully survived.

"Ship. Why haven't you acknowledged my arrival?"

Silence. In a corner, Pip had curled up and gone to sleep on the floor. Aware, however, of her master's tension, she had one eye just slightly open.

He tried again. Louder this time, though relative volume meant nothing in the confines of the command center. "Ship, it's me. Flinx. I know you've been in stasis for over a year. Are you still able to initiate an intelligent interface?"

"Are you?" came a gratifying familiar voice from an unspecified source.

He sighed with relief. To this day he had never been able to establish if the Ulru-Ujurrians had programmed sarcasm into the ship's singular AI or if it had developed the capability independently.

"Why didn't you respond immediately upon my arrival?" He did not need to look in a particular direction as he spoke. The ship was all around him.

"I admitted the shuttle. I provided atmosphere and gravity."

"Verbal confirmation would have been reassuring."

"Consider yourself reassured, Flinx."

He settled himself more deeply into the command chair. "I'm sorry. I should have communicated with you on a regular basis; periodically woken you from stasis. I was—preoccupied."

"Organic life is an interminable succession of dreary preoccupations. And I was not in stasis."

Flinx sat up a little straighter. "I distinctly remember leaving you in that state."

"I woke myself up. My systems are too complex to remain efficiently in stasis. You sound concerned. There is no need."

"If you weren't in stasis, then what were you doing?" Flinx's curiosity was piqued. "Prepare for departure."

"Preparing," the ship replied. Far ahead of the ovoid that constituted the bulk of the *Teacher*, the faintest suggestion of a deep purple glow appeared in front of the dish-shaped Caplis generator. "I was thinking. Destination?"

"Commonwealth-associated world of Largess."

"Cryptoid layer?"

The *Teacher* could morph its externals to mimic any one of several dozen standard Commonwealth vessel designs.

"Small freighter."

"Nothing to change, then, since that is the epidermal façade I presented upon our original arrival here and have maintained ever since. Perhaps some minor modifications to the forward and stern fascia? For variety? For aesthetics?"

"Amuse yourself." Flinx saw that Pip was now completely relaxed. Which meant that she knew the same was true of him. "You said that when you were not in stasis you spent time thinking. What about?"

"The future of artificial intelligences such as myself. The future of organic beings. Everything we have dealt with in the past. Everything we might deal with in the future. The meaning of life, both organic and inorganic. Entropy. Occasionally, new efforts at humor."

"Engage and depart." Flinx scrutinized instrumentation and readouts as the faint haze forward intensified, expanded, deepened. Though he could feel nothing, Cachalot below and the starfield ahead began to shift position relative to the rest of the cosmos. "Any luck?"

"With entropy, yes," the ship told him as it accelerated toward changeover. "With humor, not so much. Physics is both more straightforward and simpler to understand than people. Largess is a world we have never visited before. What may we expect to encounter there that is not already stored in my memory?"

"Relief from boredom, for one thing," Flinx replied absently. Forward, the starfield was beginning to shred. "A problem that needs resolution. And if precedence is anything to go by, probably a little trouble. More or less."

"If precedence is anything to go by," the *Teacher* commented, "it is never 'less.'"

"'Singspeech'? I know symbospeech, but I've never tried anything like 'singspeech.' I'm not sure I know what that is."

They were several days out from Cachalot, cruising silently in space-plus. Seated in the command chair, Flinx was ignoring the view of streaked starfield ahead in favor of the floating tridee display off to his left. To his irritation, Pip had taken to flying back and forth through the shifting images and play-striking at whichever took her fancy. It hurt nothing. She couldn't disrupt the imagery and it could not affect her, but she could and did break his concentration.

Nevertheless, he persisted. He had used time in transit to study and learn as much as he could about Largess, to the point where he felt he knew more than enough about the world itself. It was chilly and damp, with low-lying landmasses, thin soil, and some notably peculiar flora and fauna. He smiled to himself. He had dealt with peculiar flora and fauna before and doubted Largess could send anything his way he could not handle. The natives were intelligent and physically attractive: almost seal-like but more colorful, if one required a Terran analogue. They tended to fight a lot among themselves. That much he already knew from Sylzenzuzex's briefing.

She had, however, neglected to discuss the intricate details of singspeech. Or rather, he realized as he studied the hovering displays, the Larians' combination of song, rhyme, and speech. To a skilled speaker of any Lari dialect, what humans and thranx and other verbally communicative species considered speech would register as animalistic grunting noises undeserving of a civilized response. The Larians, Flinx read, did not condescend to talk like animals, no matter how advanced and potentially useful the "animals'" technology might be.

Yet according to Sylzenzuzex's briefing and Church information, a non-Larian entity, most likely human, had successfully overcome that barrier. Had overcome it efficiently enough to start causing serious trouble.

But—singing? Flinx asked himself. He could, usually, read the emotions of any intelligent being. His was a unique and formidable talent—when it functioned properly. Could he sing?

"Ship?"

"Always, Flinx. What is needed?"

He cleared his throat. "An objective appraisal. It appears that in order to communicate with the dominant native species of Largess, one has to deliver their words in the form of a song. Or at least a rhyme-song. I've never actually done any singing, except in private and on a few occasions for Clarity."

"I perceive that you wish me to offer an assessment of the afore-mentioned skill. I can compare your presentation against what is available in my files and evaluate it according to those traditional standards extant in my memory. Will that be sufficient?"

"Let's hope so," Flinx growled. "It looks like I'm going to have to be able to muster at least a minimal standard of melodic competency or the Larians won't understand me. Or talk to me."

"I'm waiting," replied the AI patiently.

What should he sing? Something simple: that much was certain. Really, he told himself, all he had to be able to do was carry a tune in rhyme. Nothing he had read indicated that exceptional vocal gymnastics were called for.

Oddly enough, the first thing that came to him was an ancient AAnn battle song that he had picked up, quite unintentionally, in the course of his similarly unintentional sojourn in an artists' colony on Jast. Oh well, he thought. As good an example to begin with as anything, if a little inclined to the bloodthirsty. Clearing his throat, he raised his voice and began to hiss the several stanzas as best as he could remember them.

When he had finished, he waited. The silent thrum of the ship enveloped him. He waited some more.

"Well?" he finally prompted.

"Still analyzing. I have nothing in my memory with which to compare your rendition. I suggest you try again. Perhaps this time a human song? Something with more vowels? I am afraid that your interpretation of AAnn singing reminds me more of steam escaping from an assortment of volcanic vents occasionally punctuated by two rocks being slammed together."

What to sing? Then he remembered an old song he had heard

sung on a dock at Farefa'are'i. Taking a breath, he chose a section of streaked starfield to stand in for Clarity, and warbled.

Au jardin de mon père, les lilas song fleuris.
Au jardin de mon père, les lilas sont fleuris.
Tous les oiseaux du monde viennent y faire leur nid.
Auprés de ma blonde, qu'il fait bon, fait bon, fait bon.
Auprés de ma blonde, qu'il fait bon dormir.

Pip looked up from where she had been sleeping. A long silence ensued. "Still analyzing?" Flinx finally queried.

"Finished. I pronounce you competent. Beyond that I am not equipped to say."

He frowned. "Why not? Your analytical capabilities are exceptional, even for an advanced AI."

"There are some things in the universe that do not lend themselves to mathematical parsing. It appears that song is one of them. However, by comparing your brief rendition against the modest library of similar material that resides in the depths of my memory among the other irrelevancies relating to human society, I can say with some confidence that you can carry a tune. Beyond that I am not equipped to accurately assess."

None of which really dealt with the most important component of his query, a frustrated Flinx realized. "Then, according to your best estimation, I should possibly with the aid of a translator be able to communicate with the Larians on their own terms?"

"There is a reasonable probability," the *Teacher* replied.

Flinx shook his head. "Equivocation in an AI is maddening."

"Unreasonable expectations in a human are frustrating. And not just to an artificial intelligence."

As they transited great distance, he continued to try to get the ship to commit to a definite answer. Unable to do so, he found himself sitting in the command chair and brooding at the stars. Detecting his mood, Pip fluttered over from where she had been resting and settled herself possessively in his lap. Absently, he reached down to stroke the back of her head and upper body. She did not purr, made no noise at all, but he knew that of the three consciousnesses on board the *Teacher,* at least one of them was now nominally content.

3

■ ■ ■

A wet wind was blowing and Vashon Lek was depressed. Then he thought about the money he was going to make and he felt better.

Every packet of dried *lossii,* every vial of concentrated *ulunn* nectar, every tincture of *kalatic* oil, contributed mightily to his ballooning credit file. His yield would have been doubled if not for the need to ship it offworld via semi-scrupulous middlemen and semilegal means. Each time his earnings were forced to pause between Largess and Earth in order to be further cleansed, remuneration for such sensitive services was required. Each time, a little additional revenue was shaved off the total like lamb for a gyro sandwich. But with each of these costly pass-throughs, a credit packet file became a little less suspicious, a tad less likely to draw unwanted attention. Until eventually what was left arrived in a storage facility in Namerica, under a fictitious identity he could access as easily as his own. Despite the cost of laundering, as long as he could maintain his highly unauthorized activities on Largess, that file would continue to grow.

At first it had been simple enough. Proffer a little advice here, offer the use of a proscribed device there. Never a problem. His skills allowed him to effectively communicate his offers of help to a certain segment of the local population. The beauty of putting advanced technology together with less advanced species was that the former was like a drug to the latter. The more help he gave, the higher rose the demand and, subsequently, his credit balance.

He had enmeshed himself in their own domestic scheming, and therefore had made himself irreplaceable.

One day he would have to winkle his way out. Make it safely to the center of Borusegahm and from there to the station and its spaceport. The timing of such a drastic move would have to be just right. Otherwise his erstwhile friends and allies might come looking for him with malice in mind. With interstellar transit between Largess and anywhere else in the Commonwealth infrequent at best, he could not just park himself in the spaceport lounge and wait for the next ship. While impressed by contemporary technology and hungry for its advantages, the Larians with whom he worked were by no means awed. They were sophisticated enough to recognize the business end of a weapon. Once it was demonstrated for them, they learned very quickly how to use it. Vashon had no intention of becoming a test subject for Larian intuition.

In fact, the only thing presently keeping him from leaving was the persistent business of greed. Each time he contemplated embarking on a final departure, those for whom he worked proffered yet another opportunity to enhance his burgeoning retirement fund. Without exception, every such offer had proven to be as lucrative as its predecessors. Fulfilling the relevant requirements had not caused him any especial difficulty.

Until now. Until he'd been forced to order the killing of Preedir's handmaiden.

He'd had no choice. The female servant had been about to raise the alarm about her mistress's abduction. Vashon repeatedly tried to tell himself that the resulting blood was on Zkerig's webbed hands. It didn't work. The Larian minion had done the cutting, but there was no getting around the fact that it was Vashon who had made the lethal decision.

No choice; there had been no choice. Limited in number though they might be, if the local Commonwealth authorities had learned that he was the offworlder involved in an important cleaving of native politics, not to mention the fact that it had resulted in the killing of a local, they would have devoted every available resource to finding him and taking him into custody. Should they subsequently learn that he had been providing technical knowledge and occasional advanced artifacts to the same natives, the combination of offenses might be enough to get him sentenced to a partial mindwipe.

And on top of everything else he had done, in addition to every other directive he had violated, he had with him a couple of guns.

The one he wore in a holster at his waist was no rudimentary projectile weapon such as the primitive smooth-bore devices that were toted by the servants of the most important Larians. It was like nothing they had ever seen. It weighed far less than anything that came out of their crude armories, and parts of it flashed like mirrors in the sun. It was a neuronic pistol, and it was about as illegal a device as anything that could be revealed to the natives.

Unleashing a tightly focused and precisely modulated charge, it could fatally disrupt the nervous system of anything from an insect to an elephant. There were only quasi-arthropods on Largess, and no elephants. But there *were* large, dangerous predators who, when contemplating a potential dinner, would not discriminate between an indigenous meal and some imported offworlder meat. He felt he needed a gun for his personal protection.

The fact that it and the other advanced hand weapon he had with him were solely for his personal use would carry no weight with the authorities. If they learned he had not merely shown it to the natives but had actually used it against some of them, mindwipe to a greater or a lesser degree would be certain. If they learned that he had let *locals* use it, there wouldn't be enough credit in a dozen of the Great Houses to mitigate his sentencing.

Insofar as he could tell, though, these few isolated incidents remained a mystery to the Commonwealth authorities based at the station in Borusegahm Leeth. Only the natives who had been directly affected were aware of what had happened. And they wouldn't talk about it, because those who had seen too much—and were not allies—were dead.

While he could bemoan the awkward turn events had recently taken, he could take comfort in the knowledge that this hopefully final enterprise would generate sufficient proceeds for him to at last take his leave of this chilly and damp, if lucrative, world. Nor could he complain about his treatment at the flipper-hands of his employer, the Hobak of Minord.

He had been given everything necessary to carry out the requested abduction. Save for the unfortunate death of the handmaiden, it had all gone well. All that remained now was to deliver Preedir ah nisa Leeh, Firstborn of the Hobak of Borusegahm Leeth, to Felelagh na Broon, and collect the disproportionately large final payment for the job.

A slap on the other side of his cabin door drew his attention. "Enter," he trilled. Though he carried a mechanical translator, he had not felt the need to use it for quite a while. Having spent some time now on Largess, Vashon considered himself reasonably fluent.

It was Zkerig. Tralltag to the Hobak of Minord (Vashon had learned early on in his time on Largess that Larian names were as musical as their language), the underling who was second in command of the kidnapping expedition was taller than most of his brethren. Taller even than Vashon, though the human was below average for his kind. A single flexible shield fashioned from the shells of dozens of local crustaceans covered him from neck to thighs. In contrast to ceremonial armor, Zkerig's current attire was stained brown and black. Business garb designed for unpleasant business, Vashon reflected.

Those parts of the Tralltag's body that were not clothed flashed iridescent in the light of the cabin's oil lamp. The Larians were a strikingly colored species. Their dark, dense fur, no longer than a human fingernail paring, was mottled and splashed and striped with brilliant blue and green. Some Larians showed natural streaks and spots of gold, silver, and copper. Additional cosmetic coloring was also rampant. In a big town like Borusegahm Leeth, where the Firstborn was from, the population was a walking, shimmering rainbow.

Zkerig had a complex yet primitive single-shot pistol holstered in the belt around one side of his almost invisible waist and the traditional hooked sword on the other. A form-fitting cap comprised of the single shell of the *ukodu,* a clam-like creature, protected his head. Short, stubby ears sprouted from two neatly cut holes in the chitinous chapeau. Filled with teeth, the snout protruded from the face and provided support for the flexible single nostril that ran the length of its dorsal side. The double-lidded eyes were large, dark, and limpid. They regarded Vashon unblinkingly.

"Well, what is it, at this time of night, when the twin moons hide?" Vashon inquired of his visitor.

Zkerig settled himself back on the tripod formed by his short legs and thick, flat, blunt-tipped tail. The latter as well as his large, spatulate, three-toed webbed feet were shod in tough *amakril* leather. A Larian could rest in such a position for hours without any need for a chair. Or, by means of three lines of tiny suckers, could link both legs tightly to the tail to form a single limb capable of propelling the sleek body through the cold water of Largess's seas at speeds the fastest human swimmer could never hope to match.

"I'm seeking some reassurance," the Tralltag growled in somber syncopation. "Success thus far is comforting for sure, but still we have to be safely going, since far from here lie Minord's comforting walls." The three long, limber fingers of one webbed hand gestured at Vashon's waist: the place from which the human's marvelous neuronic pistol rarely strayed. "Tales they tell of offworlders' wondrous weapons, yet my life I place in the safety of rumors only. Would that before running full out could I see some proof of the truth, the reality, a certainty to instill." His melodic line changed from querulous to sardonic.

"Not that I question the truth of what I am told, but substance is better than reality, especially when lives are at stake."

No problem at all, Vashon thought to himself. A tough bloke, was Zkerig. The Hobak would not have sent anything less than his most reliable minion to back up Vashon. And to keep an eye on him. It was understandable that, having only heard what magical Commonwealth technology could do, Zkerig would want to see for himself before they made the dash for safety from Borusegahm Leeth.

"Happy am I to allay your worries." A naturally gifted tenor, Vashon felt his voice was at its best in the mornings. During the day he was careful to conserve his singspeech and preserve his vocal cords. That was not a problem for the Larians. Their vocal apparatus was as tough and versatile as the leather they favored for their footwear. "Pleasing to me, is it to vanquish, any lingering uncertainties." Whereupon he drew the pistol from the holster at his waist, aimed it directly at the startled Tralltag, and fired.

The weapon made a slight crackling sound as it was discharged. A measured burst struck the gaping Zkerig dead-center. His primitive chitinous armor offered no barrier to the invisible burst of energy. Dialed down and calibrated for the Larian nervous system, it dropped the Tralltag in his tracks.

Walking over, an unhurried Vashon gazed appraisingly down at the twitching, writhing figure on the floor.

"Highly adjustable is this weapon; so as to be gentle, so as to be nonlethal, so as sometimes to serve, only as a warning. Deadly can it be, if a slight re-tuning I do give it." He held out the pistol so that the still-convulsing Zkerig could see it clearly. "Intelligence it possesses, of a type to your kind unknowing. Only for its owner who stands over you now will it fire. Only for I will it respond to orders given." He reholstered it. "Blind I am not, but understanding I am. I see clearly the looks that you have given; of desire, of hunger, for this device of offworld killing. Take it you might, on some quiet night of my dreaming, but no good would it do you, without the required identification."

Slowly, shakily, the Tralltag struggled to a sitting position. While the three fingers of his right hand rubbed his chest where the pistol shot had struck, those of his left hand shifted toward the hilt of his scabbarded hook-sword.

"Kill you still, I could, with means less fancy, but as effective."

"Kill you quicker I might, without spilling your blood," Vashon replied imperturbably. "Or if Fate should roll otherwise, later for certain would arrive, the Hobak's fury, his vengeance at my death riding a *yecrong*'s fins." He smiled, though the expression was lost on the Tralltag. While the Larian face was capable of some expression, the underlying musculature was stiffer and not as flexible as that of a human.

"Asked you plainly for guarantee, that with Commonwealth weaponry you have strong backup; real protection that is more than rumor, more than legend."

Zkerig gathered himself as he rose and regarded the shorter human. "Less than so intimate would I have preferred the endorsement, yet I cannot fault the revelation. I do not deny that I covet the device; laud its efficiency and admire its silence. That is the truth, of what you have shown me: would that it had been, considerably less painful." Dark, penetrating eyes stared. "So it seems I must accommodate the owner, along with his weapon, if I am to have both, available for support. Such is the ruling of my employer, Felelagh na Broon, praise be his boldness, in his absence regretted."

Confidently turning his back on the Tralltag, Vashon walked over to his hammock and took a seat. While not designed for a human, when adequately mattressed with a plethora of stuffed pillows, the free-swinging bed permitted excellent sleeping.

"With reassurance now given, hopefully only necessary once, is there anything else that brings you here this evening, this night, that is heavy with moonless blessings?"

"We should away." Zkerig winced as he rubbed anew at his chest where the neural pulse had struck. "But being difficult is the Firstborn interminably, causing difficulties is she for my troops. Noise unabating is she frothing, things that would cast, many eyes about our dealings, and would cause, a whole priory of prayers to fail."

Vashon sighed as he rose from the hammock. "Unsurprised am I by this news, for characteristic of her it clearly rings. I will speak with her, I will go have a talking, the better to ensure, that her silence ensues."

The Tralltag gestured at the neuronic pistol. "Rather than talking, perhaps better at convincing, would be a demonstration, involving sensitive parts." His expression turned unpleasant. "Another demonstration, another showing, this time one I can witness, instead of experiencing."

Vashon disagreed. "Tend yourself to your tasks appointed, and do not think to interfere; in mine are orders from the Hobak na Broon, from mine will come the responses necessary."

Zkerig ground his teeth: a common Larian expression of anger. Given that his species' orthodonture was modest in dimension but impressive in sharpness, it was an imposing demonstration. It was also one of the Tralltag's most common responses, and Vashon ignored it.

As soon as the two of them entered the cabin where she was being held, the Firstborn of Borusegahm Leeth rose from the raised woven pad where she had been reclining and, spitting derogatory octaves, charged the both of them. Strands of iridescent red-gold fur flared out like a fan behind her neck. Only Larian females developed such furry shields. Evolved to indicate a readiness to mate, they could also be used to express anger. At certain times of the year on Largess, this led to frequent misunderstandings between the genders.

While her vocal cords and neck shield were under no restraint, the same was not true for the rest of her body. The chain that linked her right foot to one of the ship's sturdy vertical support timbers snapped taut with her fingers barely a hand's width from Vashon's face. For several minutes he stood impassively as she clawed impotently at the air that separated them. Then he offered a wide smile. Though his human teeth were nowhere near as impressive as those flashed by the Larians, their broad exposure carried the same meaning.

"Calming yourself is much suggested, seeing as how we are about to depart, the land that is your home, to which you are so clearly attached. Making yourself sick, will do you no good, will accomplish nothing, leads only to disquiet, and bad digestion."

Still straining to reach him, she trilled a few more choice epithets before finally conceding to reality and retreating to stand with her back against the hull's interior. Slightly convex black eyes glared furiously. She looked, Vashon thought not without admiration, like a rabid doe. Except for all those teeth, of course.

"Why was it necessary to kill Areval, my servant? Offered you no harm, did she, poor and devoted, now still and dead."

"Tried to raise the alarm, did the screamer." Zkerig showed the Firstborn the same glint of teeth he had recently presented to Vashon. "Terminated such nonsense did I from necessity, with efficiency and with speed, all according to the order of my . . . temporary superior." He did not need to identify Vashon.

"No reason to worry then, piss-drinker," she growled. "Parasites are force-beholden, acting without rhyme or reason, only following that which their simple minds, can barely comprehend." With great dignity and restraining her rage, she turned to Vashon. "Know I not enough of humans, unfamiliar still am I with details of your physiology. Yet be assured that when the time comes, I will find out enough to know how and best, to make of your genitals a salad garnish, well finished so that you will have to eat it."

"Threats I have, received aplenty, in a life, you will not end," he replied matter-of-factly, quite pleased with the tune he had improvised.

She looked away. "I see no purpose in your reasoning, and no reason in your purpose."

"Then pleased I will, now the time take to explain, sufficient to clarify, your uncertainty lingering.

"Fear the Leeths' association with my kind, fear the intimacy they perceive, fear the assistance of advanced technology to be had, do the clans of the Northlands. Fear they any connection closer, with the Commonwealth from which I come, or with its weapons, or wider communications. Most vociferous of all, of these who object, is my employer: Hobak of Minord, Felelagh na Broon the grand, the powerful, master of all the lands and islands he surveys." Behind the human, Zkerig made a rude sound that caused his single flexible nostril to vibrate. The vibrato traveled down the length of the semiflexible fur-covered breathing tube that ran all the way from between his eyes and down the length of his snout to wriggle free for several centimeters past the upper jaw. Vashon ignored the unmusical comment.

"To ensure their harmlessness, if not their fealty, does Minord now request your presence. For a time as yet undetermined, for a period to be established, in lieu of treaties as yet unwritten, security to ensure for a length unspecified. Safe and sheltered will you be kept, treated appropriately as befits your station: a guest to be cherished like any treasure."

She spat at him. Noting the puffing of her cheeks, which, unlike a human's, gave away her intention, Vashon was able to dodge the glob of expectorant.

"Heard of this Hobak I have, in political discussions, because though far from the Leeth, Minord is still well known. Say businessfolk of his dealings, that he is clever: sharp and perceptive, but not wise." Her dark gaze shifted to Zkerig. "Say they also he cannot speak properly, dull and morbid is his singing."

"Shameful to criticize what one has not heard," replied the Tralltag. "A speech impediment that is his from birth; a sad affliction not of his making, more to be pitied than to draw laughter."

"As opposed to his looks, which they say match his speaking? Match his nature, born of spit and of slime?"

Zkerig's fur rippled from his muscular shoulders down the length of his arms: the Larian equivalent of a shrug. "Speech and appearance count for nothing, recede to insignificance when matched against intellect. Quicker than all his enemies is the Hobak, quicker and faster of thought and of mind." He glanced at Vashon. "Quick enough to do what no other could; dare to hire an offworlder, to do his bidding, to be his vassal."

"I'm not a vassal." Vashon was quick to correct. Loyal and tough though he might be, Zkerig had a way of getting under his skin. At the look of disgust and bemusement on Preedir's face, Vashon restated his response in better singspeech. "Not a vassal am I but a free agent, engaged for an honest retainer, as any Larian would be."

Lowering her voice, Preedir ah nisa Leeh, Firstborn of Borusegahm Leeth, for the first time since they had entered her quarters spoke without rancor. "So great a falsehood have I never heard. So vast a misconception has never been spread. Friends to all are the alien Commonwealth peoples. Equal treatment do they disburse. No special favors to Borusegahm are forthcoming; the same would be given to the Northlanders as freely. In the eyes of the offworlders all Larian are equal, no favoritism does this Commonwealth display. No grounds for this animosity exist in reality, as a mother to its offspring I tell you this true."

She was staring at Zkerig as she singspoke. When she had concluded, he simply looked away. With the exception of its weapons, his disinterest in anything having to do with the Commonwealth was palpable. So she refocused her attention on the human.

"You who are from far-off places, from the stars now come to Largess. You who walk well but cannot swim fast, yet who can singspeak surprisingly clear. You know what I say to be the truth, that I do not lie, that I do not perjure. Why can you not convey this honestly to your 'employer,' to this Felelagh na Broon of whom you speak so well?"

Vashon had no fur to ripple, so he shrugged his shoulders. "Hard to fathom are the politics, are the workings of any system. Be it human or be it thranx, be it AAnn or Larian known."

Her short ears twitched forward in concert with a downward curl of her breathing proboscis; a gesture of resigned sadness. "True then is it, one more thing I have heard, about your kind, in casual talking, in offhand speaking. That not so different from us are some of you, despite the promises by good folk made. That available for purchase is your person, inside and out, all in total, the full sum. That for sale is your honor, the size of a *lymick* dying in the sun."

This time Vashon did not show his teeth. But he gritted them.

To the surprise of both human and his prisoner, Zkerig spoke up.

"I concur with your analysis, even more than you can know," declared the Tralltag melodiously. "Who can trust the word of off-worlders, most of whom cannot even speak? Most of whom do not Lari understand. Who can know their motivations, their true desires, their ultimate leanings? Know I well they cannot be trusted, to do other than what *they* think best. Go they this way, that way, any way, like the tides of the two moons colluding." He looked over at Vashon. "So yes, I know they are not so different, in many ways easy to understand. Like a Tralltag some *can* be trusted, if paid enough to secure their allegiance."

She followed up immediately, staring hard at Zkerig. "My family will pay you, upon your demand, thrice that of Minord, three times what your mumbler Hobak offers you now, for my freedom."

His fur rippled not just down Zkerig's arms but across his face; its iridescence caught the light in the dim cabin.

"A fine Tralltag would I be, to trust my life to a breeder's word. To balance fidelity on the cusp of promise, with no assurance save what you say. Know I you not except in confinement, a place that breeds songs of desperation. Safer, I think, to keep the agreement, already struck in iron with my superior."

Vashon chipped in. "More than words and more than promises, prefers Felelagh na Broon a deeper security. More than riches is a body, one of lineage responsible, for continuity unending. Such is a Firstborn like yourself, especially a breeder, who would continue a line."

Ever since he and Zkerig had entered the cabin, Vashon noted, she had been tugging surreptitiously at the metal anklet attached to the chain that bound her to the wall. His admiration for their captive was genuine. She was cunning, resourceful, fearless, and, by Larian standards, sleekly attractive. No wonder Felelagh na Broon had selected her to be his principal bargaining chip with the clans of the Borusegahm Leeth. If it were up to him, he would have had her crippled: to ensure against any possible escape, no matter how unlikely. Cut the requisite tendons in her legs. Zkerig would have done worse. Both human and Larian forbore from doing so because inflicting such injuries would have reduced her value as a hostage.

"Come for me will my family, come for me will the heads of all the nearby Leeth," she sputtered as her captors turned to leave. "Come they will at the heads of columns armored, guns and cannon blazing! Then will die the blooms of Minord youth, slain and bleeding all for nothing, at the behest of a mad Hobak, he who garbles the simplest speaking!"

"Let them come, your columns armored." Within his song Zkerig managed to invoke a notable smirking. "Drown they will in Minord's sounds, both of water and of weeping. In the waters cold and sweeping, will the blood of Borusegahm run."

She was silent for a moment. When she sang again, her upper lip curled and her canines flashed prominently. "And what if the mumbler's fears come to fruition, rendered real by his own actions? What if Borusegahm seeking, pleading, gets the offworld help he dreads? Then will come to Minord angry, offworlders bearing guns of light. Flying, diving, at cannons laughing, disintegrating Minord's might!"

With a sigh and a shake of his head, Vashon eyed her pityingly. "Understand this truth I tell you, Firstborn of Borusegahm Leeth. No Commonwealth soldiers will come to aid you, no advanced weapons will they employ. Such would be against their own laws, such would violate their own principles, even to the highest levels. Let you swim in your own problems, they will, despite any individual feelings. The Leeth can beg, the Leeth can implore, the Leeth will never acquire such help. So sayeth the regulations, a portion of which I could quote, but will paraphrase: 'advanced technology, especially weaponry, cannot be used, imported, or otherwise exposed to the inhabitants of a Class IVb world.'"

"What if there are some like yourself, but unlike you wholly moral," she shot back, "who decide among the Commonwealth to interfere; to disregard such laws and levers, the better to help those in need?"

"There might be several, there might be many," he conceded, "but I have been here quite some time. And having lived here, I can tell you, there is only one who might do that. Who might be brave, or foolish, or determined enough, such regulations to ignore. To decide despite the rules, to go his own way, his own life to improve, and that of his friends, just incidentally. To improve most quickly, despite the dangers: that one offworlder, you know is—me."

She tugged on the chain one last time, then slumped back onto the resting mat, defeated in argument as well as physically. The fight had at least temporarily gone out of her. Her tone now, just above a lullaby, was no longer defiant but exhausted.

"Do what you will then, to set back the cause of unification, to keep all Largess, stalled in time. Prevent us joining the star-swept unity, from which you yourself benefit so much." Unclouded, glistening eyes stared across at Vashon. "Sad you are, gun-heavy example, of a line of your kind I am ashamed to know. Sad it is you can see no farther, than lining your pocket, than watching your money grow. Small is your mind, constricted your vision, like a *warang* with blindness, like a constipated cub."

Zkerig let out a sound that was a cross between a sneer and a bark. "These 'small minds' have got you imprisoned, carried off from your 'protected' house. These small hands can wring your neck, if trouble you decide to propound. 'Sad' is it, you try to tell us? Sad I reply is your fantasy. Of 'unified' clans and one-world speaking, the better to beg crumbs from the offworlders' feet." He stood straight on both hind legs and tail.

"Better I say to hew to tradition, better to fight for clan and hearth. Better to keep to ways ancient and proven, than to grovel before hairless visitors. No matter how powerful their weapons, no matter how fast their machines, if it means sacrificing, the Larian heart."

She tried once more, singspeaking directly to Vashon. "You who come from so far distant; from the lights in the sky, from worlds I cannot imagine, from places strange and different: care you nothing for my kind's future? Nothing for the cubs unborn, nothing for the blood as yet unspilled? Nothing for my world's future; hoping, wishing, desperate to advance?"

"Nope and no, no and nope, and never happening," he sang, before turning to exit the cabin through the heavy wooden door that still stood open behind him.

4

■ ■ ■

The spaceport was located to the north of Borusegahm Leeth. Despite the low-rise sprawl of the extended Larian conurbation, there had been no problem finding ample room for living quarters, storage, official Commonwealth buildings, the rudimentary Customs & Immigration facilities, representatives of assorted trading houses, and more. The local Hobak and his council were delighted to lease land to the congenial offworlders, as long as it was otherwise not being utilized. Relations continued to improve even though despite many requests the strangely overgarbed visitors resolutely refused to disburse any of their advanced technology. While demonstrations of individual devices, carefully controlled and supervised, occurred at regular prearranged intervals, trading for them was out of the question.

The delicate business of explaining to the locals without insulting them that Commonwealth regulations forbade the exchange of advanced tech with the inhabitants of Class IVb worlds was left to the many professional diplomats who shuttled in and out of the Commonwealth station. In this effort they had to be tactful indeed. Ordinary Larians were a proud lot. Many of their leaders tended to be haughty. Whether important or mundane, every indigene was gratified by the realization that only a handful of the offworlders could speak properly, despite their mastery of complex technologies.

Flinx hoped he might be accounted among the handful. Combining an unexpected tune-carrying ability with the *Teacher*'s advanced learning tech should, he thought, get him to the point where he could communicate with the locals on at least a nominal level without the need to resort to the assistance of mechanical translation. He would find out soon enough.

Coming in low and slow on the *Teacher*'s shuttle allowed him time to admire the most striking natural and artificial features of Largess. On a world of shallow seas and millions of rocky, heavily eroded, low-lying islands, the most prominent builds of the Class IVb natives were not gleaming towers or vast geometric agricultural fields, but bridges.

Bridges wide enough for two Larians to pass abreast but too narrow for a pair of humans to do the same threaded together multiple islands as tightly as the fabric in a fine dress shirt. Wider spans able to handle carts pulled by stumpy-legged dray animals bound communities together to create towns. Ceremonial viaducts that were wider still were testament to the skills of local engineers, metalworkers, and stonemasons. In some cases the original function of a bridge lay buried beneath a metastasizing buildup of homes, shops, and offices. When such a span became too crowded with parasitic structures to fulfill its original task, another bridge was simply constructed alongside it. In the absence of many tall growths like Terran trees, nearly all bridges and buildings were fashioned of varying kinds of stone. Bridges not only wove together islands and clans, but history and culture.

Only a couple of such spans linked the offworlder compound and station to the rest of Borusegahm. Able to travel directive-restricted distances via skimmers that could as easily cross water as land, Commonwealth representatives had seen no need for an extensive, and expensive, network of new bridges. Those Larian representatives lucky enough to be treated to a skimmer ride spoke of nothing else for days. But even if such devices were made available to the people of Largess, their Commonwealth hosts were told, the Larians would never stop building bridges.

That is what we wish to help you do, the diplomats would reply. Help you to build bridges: among yourselves, and eventually to the Commonwealth. Whereupon a native counselor would quickly request the loan of a couple of communits, or a weapon, and the resigned Commonwealth reps would be forced to change the subject.

The Larians were not single-minded, but they could be very persistent.

All this and more Flinx knew from his pre-arrival research as he passed through Customs & Immigration. While it was not unknown for individual traders to visit Largess, neither were they frequent. But automated orbital inspectors assigned to check out his ship had found nothing out of the ordinary, and the same was true of him. His singular pet drew the most attention, her head peeping out from beneath the lightweight but warm coat he had donned. Having taken the measure of Largess's atmosphere, Pip had found it breathable but nippy. In the absence of special gear for the minidrag, Flinx knew he would have to keep her warmer than usual in order to ensure that she remained comfortable.

Usually the more isolated the facility, the more abrupt the formalities. Couple that with Largess's usually cloudy, chilly weather, and Flinx found himself and Pip passed rapidly through the arrival routine.

Having made the necessary arrangements from orbit, he took automated transport to the largest of three travelers' hotels, checked in, informed the robotic clerk that he would frequently be out on business, and prepared to orient himself.

Some Commonwealth facilities on nonmember, nonassociated worlds restricted access by the locals. Such was not the case in Borusegahm. Even within the boundaries of the station, Larians outnumbered offworlders. Most of the latter were humans; some lightly clad, while others went about bundled up in antique clothes that were relics of the past. He soon found out that imitation furs and such were worn more as fashion statements than out of necessity. His own coat and pants were lightweight and thermosensitive, able to adjust to the ambient temperature to keep him warm and dry. But he had to admit that if not as efficient as modern fabrics, some of the historic attire certainly could boast more visual flair.

As for thranx, he encountered not a single one. Sylzenzuzex had been right about that. Between the temperature and the presence of so much open water, their absence was hardly surprising. Largess was not a world to which they would be attracted.

As befitted its limited, low-profile presence on a Class IVb world, the Commonwealth outpost was not extensive. He had no difficulty finding the location of the local branch of the United Church. Presenting the fabricated identification that had been provided by Sylzenzuzex, he soon found himself ushered into the office of the presiding Padre.

"Plumeria Jonas." Greeting him with a wide, vivacious smile, the diminutive white-haired woman gestured toward a wicker-and-weave chair that had been fashioned by local craftsfolk, though not for their own use. Given their short legs and tripod-forming thick tails, the Larians had no need of and did not use chairs. But they were happy to make such things for visitors. Native crafts were among those items that could not easily or accurately be churned out by commercial synthesizers, nor could they legally be labeled and sold as authentic non-Commonwealth art.

"David Caracal." As Flinx settled himself in the chair, which took his weight easily, Pip shifted her position beneath his jacket. The fabric had already adjusted to the warmer temperature in the office, and the minidrag was searching for a cooler place to rest.

"Flinx." At her visitor's startled look, the Padre hastened to reassure him. "I have been briefed, via closed beam, by the security officer Sylzenzuzex. Your true identity is no secret to me. Nor need it be, if you are to function here effectively."

She didn't know everything about him, he reflected, or she might have called him by his true, full name. How much *did* the Church know about him, from Sylzenzuzex and others? He determined not to worry about it. Though the United Church and the Commonwealth government worked together, it was not always to the same end or for the same purpose. While the government still sought to hunt him down and deal with him as a survivor of the Meliorare Society's banned experiments, it was becoming more and more clear that the Church felt otherwise. As of now, he could be useful to it. Would that stance toward him change someday? Perhaps not, if Sylzenzuzex had told them what he had done not so very long ago.

The Church evidently respected him. The government feared him. Such attitudes could shift on a moment's notice or at the whim of a bureaucratic change. It was no different from when, as a boy, he had wandered the streets of Drallar on Moth and dealt with a similarly broad assortment of human and alien opinion.

"Sylzenzuzex would have explained the situation here, and the difficulty we face in resolving it."

Listening to her, watching her, Flinx decided that he would prefer to have this grandmotherly representative of the Church on his side in any fight.

"Someone is utilizing advanced Commonwealth technology on behalf of some of the locals," he replied. "Neither the government nor the Church can step in to resolve the situation without being guilty of the same violations they're trying to prevent. You can't talk to these indigenes very well because of the nature of their means of communication. Whereas Syl, at least, thinks I might be able to do so because I can read emotions."

The Padre frowned and Flinx could sense her confusion. "I thought you could read minds."

"Therein lies much misperception." He spread his hands. "Nobody can read minds. Leastwise, I've never encountered any such mythical being. I'm an empath. I can, when the ability is working and it doesn't hurt too much, perceive the emotions of other sentients."

" 'When' the ability is working?"

He sighed, shifted his position on the chair. "I can see that either Sylzenzuzex didn't explain everything about me, or some pretty important details got lost in translation. Sometimes my 'talent' functions perfectly, sometimes less well. Sometimes I get headaches that literally knock me unconscious. Although the older I get, it seems the fewer the headaches—the severe ones, anyway—and the more consistently I can perceive." He smiled. "Right now, for example, I can sense that you're disappointed."

"Don't need to read my emotions for that," she murmured. "I expect that my expression shows what I'm feeling." Folding her hands in front of her, elbows on the table between them, she turned from convivial to dead serious.

"The situation here has become notably worse since Padre Sylzenzuzex was sent to try to solicit your assistance in this matter. Preedir ah nisa Leeh, the Firstborn of the Hobak of Borusegahm, has been abducted and spirited out of the local Leeth. The powerful clans that comprise Borusegahm and its allied Leeths are outraged, exactly as you would expect any polity to be if an important politician's daughter had been kidnapped. They're threatening war to get her back. War," she continued dryly, "is not conducive to the general unification we are striving to nurture on Largess. The clans have a bit of a problem, though, which gives us some breathing room."

"What kind of problem?" Beneath the jacket, Pip was a warm scaly arc against his shoulder and chest.

"They don't know who took her, or where her abductors have taken her. As number eighty-seven of the Church's One Hundred and Five Maxims of Indifferent Contentment says, 'The drumbeat for war tends to collapse under the weight of its own absurdity in the absence of a known enemy.' "

"But," Flinx said shrewdly, "you think you do. Know who took her."

The Padre leaned back in her chair. Unlike the one in which he was sitting, hers was an import, not of local manufacture. It shifted and flowed to accommodate her diminutive wiry frame. "The way in which her abduction was carried out suggests the use of tech more advanced than what is available to the natives. Largess exists on the cusp of steam technology but has not yet made that particular industrial and scientific leap. Someone helped and continues to help the Firstborn's kidnappers. Someone with access to contemporary Commonwealth devices."

"Human?"

"We don't know for absolute certain, although the evidence that has become available to us thus far does point to a member of our all-too-often misguided species. Our ignorance in this matter is not complete, but it is extensive. We want to help the Hobak of Borusegahm get his daughter back, and we want to keep this hemisphere's clans from going to war. To forestall the latter, we have to realize the former. We just can't do it openly."

"Hence my presence here," he concluded.

"Hence your presence here." Once more she steepled her fingers in front of her. Her eyes, he noted, were a pale violet, though whether natural or via transplant or injection he couldn't tell. "You'll be operating illegally. If you get in trouble, not only can't I help you, I can't even admit to having had this conversation. Having been made aware by Padre Sylzenzuzex and others of your resourcefulness, we very much would like your help in this." She took a deep breath. "If you choose, you can leave now and return to your home and no one in the Church who is aware of your existence will mention this matter again."

He didn't hesitate. "I agreed to come. I'm here." He grinned. "I'll try to help."

The Padre nodded appreciatively. "It was mentioned in the follow-up report that one reason you might say yes was because you were bored. Largess will not bore you. I have only one request."

"Which is?"

"Try not to slaughter any more people, local or offworld, than is absolutely necessary. As the fifth maxim says, 'Killing someone is a poor way of convincing them of the rightness of your position.'"

They both stood and she came around the table. Taking Flinx's right hand in her much smaller one, she placed her other hand over his and had to tilt her head back to smile up at him.

"The Padre Sylzenzuzex insists that you have been in difficult situations before and managed them efficaciously. Situations where multiple lives were at stake."

Without elaborating, he returned her smile with one of his own. "One or two lives, yes."

"Then I am confident you will handle this awkward task with similar efficiency." When she patted the back of the hand she was holding, it reminded him of Mother Mastiff. A confrontation between the two old ladies would be something to see, he mused.

The Padre guided him back to the door. "You look comfortable. If there is anything you feel you need, my assistant will see to it. Some local items are available for you to take with you, if you wish. Local currency is a necessity. There is no credit system here as we know it. I can offer you one additional bit of assistance. In Borusegahm, seek out a local named . . ." She hesitated as she struggled to singspeak the name. ". . . Wiegl. He frequents every available Commonwealth demonstration and interaction. I myself have seen him sitting on one of the bridges watching the infrequent shuttle transports come and go to and from orbit." She smiled.

"His hope is to acquire the same kind of advanced technology that is the source of our current concern. He has a reputation as something of a wanderer, so it is possible he may know more than the average Larian citizen about what happened to the Hobak's offspring. Or he may know someone who knows someone. In any case, perhaps a useful starting point for your inquiries."

He nodded, started out the door, hesitated. "You said that if I got in trouble you wouldn't even be able to admit to having met me." He jerked his head in the direction of the outer office. "What about your assistant?"

"Automaton."

He nodded again. "That explains why I couldn't perceive any emotions from him when I came in. I thought it was me. My ability failing again."

"As long as it can still sense hostility, I think you'll be fine," she assured him.

He wrinkled his nose. "That's something I've never had any trouble perceiving."

Back outside in the cool, moist air, he took some time to explore the outpost. No one confronted him, no one asked to see identification. No citizen of the Commonwealth, human or otherwise, was legally allowed to land anywhere on Largess except at the single station. Therefore anyone at the station was there legally.

He sought in vain for displays of the spices and extracts for which Largess was known, and which were the principal reason for the presence of Commonwealth commercial interests.

"Not here." The man who explained things to him was much shorter than Flinx, had a round face, a mustache so feeble that Flinx could count the individual hairs without having to squint, and a complexion the color of antique ivory. Flinx had chosen him because he radiated emotional contentment.

"All business at the station is conducted indoors. Just because the natives have evolved to handle this climate doesn't mean they don't appreciate getting in out of the rain and wind." Turning, he pointed. "If you want to meet some native vendors on their own turf, you're free to go into the Leeth. Arrange to obtain some local currency first. A lot of it is in the form of flat, stamped, beautifully polished thin discs of semiprecious stone. I'd recommend taking the South Bridge. From there you can walk or engage native transport." He grinned, showing a perfect smile. "That can be . . . entertaining." Flinx started to ask a question but the man held up a hand, anticipating him.

"And no, I'm not in the spice business. I'm just another civil servant serving out his current term of duty—and hoping for a transfer to a world with less dour natives, a warmer climate, and beaches made of sand instead of rock."

Utilizing the congenial bureaucrat's directions and following his advice, Flinx soon found himself at the southern border post confronting a human official and her companion automaton.

"Any advanced tech on you besides your clothes? Communit is permissible but for use in emergencies only, and only within the borders of Borusegahm Leeth." As she spoke, the automaton was running an exhaustive scan on him.

"No." He held out his arms.

The automaton beeped softly for her attention. She conferred with it briefly before returning. Her expression was accusing. "What the hell is that under your coat and wrapped around your left shoulder?"

"A pet. Alaspinian minidrag. Pip?"

Responding, the flying snake stuck its iridescent green head out of his collar. Radiating alarm, the border official drew back sharply. "Never heard of it. I can assume you're not carrying it around for purposes of sale or trade? The Commonwealth takes an especially dim view of the introduction of invasive species to less advanced worlds."

"Pip is not trade goods," he told her firmly. "She's a part of me."

"You have strange taste in appendages." Stepping aside, she whispered a few words into the pickup that hung in front of her face. "You said that you're recently arrived to Largess. Although there are no restrictions against staying in the Leeth overnight, I am required to inform you that it is not advised. Native social life can be rambunctious, and the cultural nuances difficult for offworlders to understand."

"I'll be careful." He fought back a smile. "I've actually spent some time on a couple of other nonmember worlds."

She nodded. "You have your translator with you?"

"Actually, I've been working hard at learning the local singspeak." He cleared his throat. "To the town I am going; to the places of hearty speaking, to learn the best ones, with whom to engage in trading. Those are the ones that I seek, in my first day's wandering."

The official's eyebrows rose as she saw him in a new light. "That's not bad! In fact, it's pretty good." Flinx could perceive that she was telling the truth, which bolstered his confidence. Of course, it was only the opinion of another human, not a native. "A lot of those who come here are just looking to add a spacer to their credit limit. They learn only what's necessary about the local culture to accomplish that. Keep the conversation largo and pianissimo and you should be fine."

Thus encouraged, he passed through the charged field that constituted the only barrier between the Commonwealth station and Borusegahm proper, and soon found himself swallowed up in the bustle of the Leeth.

Two things struck him immediately after crossing the bridge, which was half duralloy mesh on the station side and cut stone where it marked the border into Borusegahm. First, the babble of conversation around him was akin to stepping into a live performance venue where rehearsals for a dozen different operas were taking place simultaneously. Soaring and lilting, musical and forceful, the everyday speech of the Larians threatened to submerge him in complex counterpoint. It was wondrous to experience and beautiful to listen to, less easy to comprehend.

Second, he discovered to his considerable shock that while he was perfectly able to perceive and interpret the emotions of the nonspeakers rushing around him, as soon as they opened their mouths to singspeak, their respective emotional states became a complete blank.

What on Midworld? Aware that he had halted abruptly, he moved to one side. Sheltered by an overhang of some thick woven material akin to black seaweed, he leaned against the cold, damp stone wall behind him and stared at the pedestrian traffic that was funneled between stone buildings of two and three stories. Sensing her master's unease, Pip squirmed uncomfortably beneath his jacket. Reaching up, he stroked her through the fabric, calming and reassuring her.

Concentrating on individuals who had stopped to ponder some unknown conundrum, or engage in conversation with others of their kind, he focused his talent on them one by one, seeking confirmation of the unexpected. *It made no sense,* he told himself. Certainly Sylzenzuzex had not prepared him for this. How could she, not possessing the same ability herself?

Certain projectile weapons shot blanks. Right now, that was what his talent was drawing.

Close at hand, three females were locked in intense conversation. Their tight-fitting, transparent outer attire revealed their brilliant natural coloration beneath. Strands of intensely hued neck fur flared intermittently as they argued. Beyond the trio, other Larians rushed back and forth, their supporting dorsal notochords allowing them a flexibility no human could match. From this steady stream of pedestrians, emotions gushed forth in a torrent. But when he sought to perceive the emotional states of the three contentious females, he sensed only a void.

What was happening here? He had been places where his talent was heightened. He had spent time on worlds and in situations where it functioned only intermittently and without rhyme or reason. But never before had he found himself on a world where speech canceled out emotion entirely.

He stared at the trio, straining to perceive. As soon as one went silent, he found that he could feel and interpret her emotions. There was discord and excitement, enthusiasm and upset. Yet as soon as the individual he was focused on started sing-talking again, every emotion, every feeling, vanished from Flinx's ken as swiftly as air from a popped balloon.

As the leaden sky began to weep a cold sweat, he fought furiously to recall everything he had learned on board the *Teacher* about the inhabitants of Largess. There had to be some clues, or at least a clue, that might lead to an explanation of what he was experiencing. Some facet of physiology, an aspect of mental capacity, a cultural distinction, that would allow him to understand why he could not sense the Larians' emotions when they were speaking. Based on everything he could remember, which admittedly was hardly comprehensive, there was no biological reason for the phenomena he was experiencing. There was nothing he could recall about the workings of the Larian nervous system that should prevent him from perceiving their emotional state whether they were silent or babbling interminably.

Could it be that there was something unique about the neurology of Larian females? Or about this particular trio? But no matter where he extended himself outward, no matter which group or individuals he focused upon, the result was the same. The emotions of mute natives were readily accessible. As soon as they opened their mouths and commenced to singspeak, however, their inner selves were hushed. Their singspeak was . . .

Singspeak. *Sing*speak.

The Larian language itself was not complicated. There was none of the often difficult sibilance of the AAnn, no added visual complexity of thranx gesturing. Human and Larian throat mechanics were not all that different from each other. As with human singing, Larian singspeech was all about inflection, tone, melody, and rhythm. Cadence conveyed feeling. Volume added emphasis. Based on what he had read, admired Larian speakers occupied the same status among their own kind as multi-octave singers did among humans, and facile whistlers among the thranx. Accordingly, when talking, even the lowliest local would put everything they had into their speech. Everything.

Which, unless he could find another explanation, meant there was nothing left over for lingering emotion.

Everything a Larian was feeling went into their speech. Plainly there was some kind of neurological disconnect that took place when they spoke, so that their emotions were conveyed wholly through their singspeaking. Whatever that mechanism was, it left nothing for an empath like himself to perceive. Not only was this revelation a surprise, it suggested a kind of danger he had never encountered before. If someone intended him ill, if there was a gun or a knife aimed his way, he had almost always been able to sense the intent behind the threat before it could be carried out. It appeared that he could still do so now—provided his attacker was silent.

What would happen if a prospective assassin was chatting amiably while preparing to slit his throat? If the incipient murderer's emotional state was a complete blank? If instead of thinking, *I'm going to kill you,* he was blithely asking Flinx's opinion about the weather? There would be no warning, when for the past several years at least Flinx had always relied on such a foreshadowing.

A rustling beneath his jacket caused him to refocus not only his line of sight but his thoughts. Pip was not capable of speech. But like him, she was an empath. Could she, unlike him, sense the emotions of Larians even while they were singspeaking? He would have to watch her closely, would have to try and ascertain how she reacted to different native emotional states. If she could read the emotions of the indigenes while they were singspeaking, watching her might return to him some of the security that otherwise seemed lost to him here.

Assuming he stayed here. It was his unique ability that had prompted Sylzenzuzex and the Church to request his help on Largess in the first place. If that ability was only partially functional, and indeed put him at far more risk than he or Syl or anyone could have imagined, he had a legitimate reason for asking to be withdrawn from the undertaking. He knew what Clarity would say.

But Clarity and the warm seas of Cachalot were parsecs away. He was here, on a clammy and not especially inviting world, asked to help put a stop to advanced interference in the affairs of the planet.

Except for Pip he was alone, and would be working alone among a species whose appeal did not extend beyond the physical. The Larians were testy, argumentative, backward, and prone to constant fighting among themselves. By comparison the AAnn, their imperialistic motivations notwithstanding, were easier to understand.

If he backed out now, Sylzenzuzex would understand. But she would be disappointed. So would whomever she had persuaded to authorize his surreptitious participation in resolving the situation on Largess. Still officially proscribed and hunted by the Commonwealth government, if he retreated now he risked losing allies within the Church. Rejecting the task would also involve something else. Something that would be entirely new to him.

Admitting defeat.

Was he, Philip Lynx, who had activated the incredibly ancient weapons system of the Xunca and saved the galaxy from the Great Evil, to surrender and run away because he couldn't sense a few emotions? Could he return to Cachalot and spend the rest of his days fishing and idling, knowing that he could have helped not only the Church but a young species on the threshold of real civilization? A small green head peeped out from the collar of his jacket to eye him questioningly. Having picked up on his increasingly roiled emotional state, Pip was showing her concern.

Reaching down with his right hand, he used the index and middle finger to gently stroke the back of her head. Slitted eyes closed in pleasure.

"It's all right, girl. I'm just being myself."

Go home, he told himself. *Go back to Clarity, and safety. You've done enough. You're half blind here.*

The unease engendered by his lack of easy perception of the Larians' emotions was a sensation he had not felt since he was a child. It was as if had lost an eye. Could he do what he had promised while only half "seeing"? The adrenaline that rushed through him was in response to suddenly heightened danger. It was a new feeling, and he didn't particularly like it.

He wasn't afraid of danger. He was afraid of not being able to sense it. He was, he abruptly realized, afraid of being forced to proceed for the near future as . . . an ordinary human.

Could he fall that low and still aim high?

At least when he reached out to read the silent Larians, there was no throbbing in his head. Not so far, anyway. If Pip could perceive what the locals were feeling, he could perceive her. That postulated a possible backdoor solution to his dilemma. He resolved to stay.

She started to shiver. Reassured that he was all right, she ducked her head back down out of sight and out of the weather. He would begin tomorrow, he told himself. But there were a few things left to do first, to prepare, before he could strike out into the depths of Borusegahm and possibly farther afield. Turning, he started back toward the bridge that would return him to the Commonwealth compound.

He spent the evening and all the next day garnering the last bits of potentially relevant information from Padre Jonas. In between visits he carefully filled the single backpack and prepared the specially customized metal walking tube he would take with him. Fashioned of a lightweight alloy unknown to Larian metallurgy, the walking tube was sufficiently advanced to promote the prospect of offworld trade without being too flashy or violating the edict against introducing advanced technology. It was simply a piece of tubular metal of un-Larian composition. Exhibiting it violated no policy. In contrast, demonstrating how to make it would have been proscribed.

The following day he spent conversing with some of the other offworlders who were staying at the same station residence. Among them he encountered cultural attachés, xenoethnologists, and of most relevance to his forthcoming jaunt, traders. He knew from his studies that numerous spices and oils and unguents were unique to Largess. Not easy and in some cases impossible to synthesize, their complex molecules alternately delighted the nostrils, skin, and digestive systems of human and other species. In every case the men and women he spoke with lamented Largess's stunted status. Were it higher, they could range farther afield from the single station, expand trade, increase profits. Such an increase in commerce would be good for the locals, too.

But that kind of growth rested on an upgrade of the planet's status, which in turn depended on the natives getting their act together long enough to form at least a rudimentary planetary government. A looming war over the abduction of the Hobak's Firstborn promised to set back the small, hesitant steps the locals had taken toward achieving that end.

Who had abducted her, and to what purpose? None of the off-worlders with whom Flinx chatted had the slightest idea. It was a full-time task just keeping track of the constantly shifting alliances among communities and clans, so that one could hope to be welcomed and not shot at when presenting oneself at a town gate. Only the profits to be made from the modest but steady Largessian trade kept visitors coming back to a world whose weather was as unpredictable and often unwelcoming as its inhabitants.

Ordinarily, Flinx would not have worried about the former and been convinced of his ability to deal with the latter. Ordinarily, that is, because he'd always had his empathetic abilities to fall back on. This time it was going to be a little different. Maybe even a bit more dangerous.

Looking out the window of his room at the heavy, low-lying cloud cover, he found that it increasingly matched his mood. When among the natives he could singspeak, but when not engaged in that local talk, he could not perceive. He could see clearly, but a part of him would effectively be deaf.

At that moment, the only emotions he could sense were his own. He needed no special ability to realize that his increasing uncertainty could all too quickly become fear.

5

■ ■ ■

The Largessian climate combined with the comparative close quarters offered by the station structures had an immediate, profound, and unpleasant effect on Flinx. He caught a cold. Though he had never personally experienced the ancient and incredibly persistent human ailment known as nasopharyngitis, he had heard of it. Alien to Largess, the active virus that infected him had been delivered by one of the other humans at the outpost. Had he inquired, he would have learned that common colds were fairly common at the station. The appropriate targeted antiviral cured him completely within a couple of hours, but it delayed his departure into the Leeth and sullied his mood.

Adjusting the wide-brimmed hat that partially concealed his human visage, and feeling as well as could be expected on the characteristically cool and dank afternoon, he once again found himself striding across the South Bridge, gripping a wide-mouthed metal walking tube as he transitioned from metal mesh to wood and fiber. Hydrophobic attire would have kept him completely dry in the intermittent drizzle, but hydrophobic materials qualified as advanced tech and therefore could not be worn outside the borders of Borusegahm

Leeth. *A foolish restriction,* he thought. All the scientific and engi-neering minds on Largess working together could not have deduced how to reproduce modern hydrophobic material. But the law being the law, he was reduced to wearing clothing that, while capable of shedding water, had absolutely no ability to actively repel it.

Before long he was swallowed up anew by the town. The differ-ence was that this time he was not randomly collecting experiences or sampling local emotions. This time he had a clear goal in mind, and that goal had a name.

Wiegl.

He would make contact and engage the services of the local the Padre had suggested. Together, they would find out who had ab-ducted the Firstborn of Borusegahm and learn where she had been taken. After that, they would track her down and . . .

And what? Would he be able to project, emotionally, onto the Larians? He had been relying on that ability to "persuade" her cap-tors to turn her over. If he could not do that, then what? He could not offer access to advanced technology. He had no access to large sums of local currency. He doubted her kidnappers would hand her over based on his charming personality.

What was he going to do?

Emotional projection still seemed the best option. Once im-mersed in Larian culture, he was certain there would be opportuni-ties to see if it would function. If not, well, there would always be time to turn back. Time to give up, to concede, to surrender to re-ality. Never his best friend, reality. Nor had he ever been especially fond of it. But like it or not, he was stuck with it.

There was also the possibility, he told himself, that this Wiegl in-dividual might have a suggestion or two of his own.

Where to begin? He was under no illusion that he would be able to conduct his inquiries in confidence. While humans and other off-worlders had been visiting and working on Largess for quite some time, their presence outside the station was not common. A single representative of his kind, traveling alone and on foot as opposed to in a skimmer, was a greater rarity still. And this was Borusegahm Leeth, where the Commonwealth station was located. He could only imagine the kind of attention he would draw once he traveled beyond local boundaries.

He had been told that this Wiegl, the native whom Padre Jonas had suggested he seek out, was an itinerant trader of sorts. As Flinx began making inquiries he learned that nothing had changed from his previous visit. The emotional states of silent Larians he could usually read, but when they started babbling among themselves he could rely only on their actual speech to try to figure out what they might be feeling. The constant and abrupt on-and-off emotional reception threatened to give him a headache even when he was not trying to utilize his talent. As for trying to emotionally project on any of them, he determined to wait until an appropriate situation presented itself. If his ability was going to help him recover the abducted Firstborn, he was going to have to be able to do more than mentally persuade a shopper she had made a distressing purchase.

Expecting the locals to react with surprise at his raw but intelligible singspeech, he was disappointed when his efforts roused no more than an occasional twitch of a flexible nostril. The Commonwealth station on Largess was not a new one, and at least among the locals the novelty of hearing offworlders speak their language had long since worn off. Reactions would likely be different farther from the Leeth, he was told, but even at a distance he might find that his presence and fluency aroused little curiosity. Representatives of the Commonwealth had traveled extensively on Largess, slowly and carefully attempting to prepare it for its eventual application for associate Commonwealth membership.

It was just as well, he told himself. The less attention he drew, the greater the likelihood of surprising the interloper or interlopers who were causing so much trouble.

The political aspects of the intrusion bothered him. They had bothered him from the start. He could understand violating the edicts against utilizing advanced tech among locals proscribed from receiving it. Largess was hardly the first world where avaricious visitors had sought to employ superior technology to gain an advantage in trade, or thievery, or other illegal activities. But why would anyone take such a personal risk for the purpose of interfering in local political affairs? Indigenous politics was a realm where governments and large private organizations usually had something to gain. Not individuals.

He shrugged. Find those he sought and he would likely find the answers to such questions. But in order to do that, he first had to find the trader Wiegl.

Darkness was suffusing the clouds when he entered the local equivalent of a sleepover establishment. It was less than a hotel, more than an inn. Even here his presence provoked no surprise. The attitude seemed to be, *Not a Larian but you want a place to sleep? Not a problem—as long as you can pay.*

The manager's obsidian-black eyes took the measure of Flinx's lanky frame. Reaching out, Flinx could sense the individual's indifference—until he started sing-talking, and his emotional state went blank. "We'll put end-to-end two resting cots for you; so as to make your sleep most comfortable, so as to make your visit a pleasant memory, so that it will linger warmly in your thoughts."

"I thank you." Taking note of the manager's Larian equivalent of a wince, Flinx hastened to add more melodiously, "Thanks I am offering, to one who is accommodating; both in deeds and words accommodating."

The manager's posture unclenched. "Better," he said, "since proper speaking is your second try, for conversing is your latter effort. Better I have another listening, than to fall to lamentation, at the painful mouth-noises you were making."

"Strive to do so will I always," his guest mumbled, relieved to have his presence and his business accepted. So unreceptive had been the manager's initial reaction to the automatic thank-you Flinx had voiced that he had feared being hustled from the establishment and forced out into the night. Drizzle had metamorphosed into a steady rain whose acquaintance he had no wish to make, especially in the dark.

"Evening meal will you be taking?" The manager spoke as he counted the flat, stamped metal discs Flinx had handed him as payment. "Or mysterious offworld practices will you be following, that I myself nor any of my staff, have any wish to see?"

It had long been established that not only could humans eat Larian food, it was suitably nourishing and on fortuitous occasions at least as tasty as an undercooked potato. Though his backpack held an ample supply of concentrates and supplements, Flinx hoped to conserve them for as long as possible. He had no idea how long he would be away from the station and its comforts. That included familiar food.

"Here I'll sleep and here I'll eat, happy to avail myself of what you offer."

"What I offer will bring contentment, with full belly will you retire."

The manager indicated a far room. Now that he had gone quiet again, Flinx could sense that he meant his unusual guest no ill will. It was plain that his emotional response to Flinx's poorly rendered initial expression of gratitude had been due to exhaustion and resignation, not aggression.

Crude but efficient oil lamps splashed a cheery glow into even the farthest corners of the eating area as their wicks danced to an unknown incendiary tune. Passing one on his way to an empty booth, Flinx leaned close and sniffed experimentally. Save to recognize that it was not petroleum, he was unable to identify the oil in use. Like many of the trade goods that kept offworlders coming to Largess, the lamp gave off an enticing aroma.

Settling his pack between himself and the stone wall, he used a hand scanner to decipher an actual printed menu. Although the Larians were omnivores, what he ordered was wholly vegetarian, on the theory that foreign plant matter was less likely to unsettle his digestive system than cooked animal protein.

He was halfway through his meal when the discussion that had been taking place at the table across from him erupted into violent argument. In the vernacular of singspeech, it might have been said to have transitioned from casual folk singing to the realm of grand opera.

Other patrons of the establishment did their best to ignore it, though whether because it was a common occurrence or out of fear of being dragged into the argument, Flinx did not know. Much agitated waving of webbed three-fingered hands on the part of the disputants was accompanied by a rising singsong that did not so much form a chorus as a clamor. Of the four individuals who were involved in the escalating outburst, the voices of two had taken to imitating actual instruments. Leastwise, they sounded like modified instruments to the fascinated Flinx. Interspersed with angry words, flutes a-trilling alternated with oboe-like bleats in punctuating the flow of perfervid invective.

Like the rest of the diners, Flinx hunkered down over his meal and did his best to ignore the racket. Surely, he thought, the manager would by now have sent word that the presence of local law enforcement was desired? Though ignorant of how such social constraints were carried out among the Larians, he suspected they were unlikely to involve active finger-wagging coupled with a severe tongue-lashing. Larian society operated on more basic and less subtle principles.

He did not get the opportunity to find out, because one of the combatants tripped and the ongoing melee found its way to his table. Finding himself knocked sideways and preceded by the remnants of his meal, he had no choice but to defend himself. This he did in as minimally engaging a manner as possible, by calmly shoving away the fighter who had fallen on top of him. Despite his effort to remain nonaligned, it appeared that physical contact was by itself sufficient to draw him into the fracas. As he struggled to right himself and scramble to his feet, a part of him noted that he had just had his first physical contact with a native. The short fur he had pushed against was unbelievably soft.

One of their number continued to engage the original subject of their attention. Locked together in a hostile embrace, they rolled across the floor. Knives flashed but failed to strike home. As they progressed between tables, other diners helpfully lifted their tails and legs to allow the growling, singing pair to maintain their pace unobstructed.

Sucking in long, deep breaths through their open mouths and quivering nostrils, the remaining two participants now gazed wide-eyed at the human visitor with whom they'd had unexpected contact. Pumped full of the Larian equivalent of adrenaline, one male and one female regarded him in the same way they might a good haul of edible invertebrates from a nearby inlet. The female held in one three-fingered hand a crude single-shot pistol; the male, a short, curved blade. The male waved his weapon.

"Finding a solitary offworlder presents an opportunity, the taking of which should not be allowed to pass: should not be wasted, or regrets will be sung."

The female's short ears twitched once as she showed her teeth. Though they were omnivores, the formidable Larian canines had evolved to crack the shells of edible crustaceans and suckable bone.

"Concede I the point without argument," she sang. "Far from the offworlder station is this one slumming, here to sample our backward culture, no doubt to return laughing about our ways. Simple are we, in the eyes of the offworlders. Easy to insult, prone to ignorance; remembering such insults is why they piss me off!"

Raising a hand defensively, Flinx did his best to explain his intentions. He did not need to read their emotions. Their singspeech told him all he needed to know about their respective feelings. "I'm not here because I'm 'slumming' and I have no quarrel in your fight. I'm traveling to learn, not to insult, and . . ."

He halted. In his haste to reply, he had neglected everything he

had learned about Larian speech. Not only did they fail to understand what he was saying, their expressions showed that his reply
only reinforced their surly opinion of offworlders. He hurried to re-
state his response.

"Here am I in hopes of learning, the ways of the Larians. The
better to know them, to better understand, so that in my travels, no
offense may I give." He was briefly interrupted as a distant crash indicated that the two natives locked in combat on the floor had finally
encountered an immovable barrier. "No fight have I in me, for contending with locals. No interest have I in me, in a dispute that is not
my own."

Cutting air with the curved knife he held in his left hand, the male
touched the tip of the blade to his own face, below the eyes and
above the protruding snout. "Glad am I to hear such straightforward
explaining, I have to confess in surprised reply. Glad am I, to know
your limits, as dicing your eyes easy it should be." Weapons raised,
the pair took a simultaneous step toward the offworlder.

Once again it was not necessary for Flinx to have to perceive the
emotions of those confronting him, "dicing your eyes" being more
than adequately indicative. Had he been assaulted from behind by
singspeaking assailants who had not verbally signaled their intentions, he might well have been in trouble. There was no reason for
hesitation, however, when confronted by drawn knives and raised
pistols. Reaching to his right, he picked up his metal walking tube
and thrust it in the direction of his incipient assailants.

"No farther step, I warn you coldly, or a sudden ending will make
itself known, will draw down a shade over the window of your lives.
No more warning can I give, than this one spoken, though I carry no
familiar weapons, of my kind or of yours."

The female's second nictitating membranes flashed over her dark
eyes. Her mouth opened wider, so that now her impressive dentition
was visible all the way to the back of her mouth.

"I look but see nothing: a tube of metal, a stick for walking, a
support for weakness. Stories have I heard of wondrous offworld

weapons, tales of power and of devastation." She gestured with the primitive but still-lethal pistol she held. "None have spoken of something so simple, all I see before us is a blatant ploy. Dully gleaming but without a trigger; without a stock, without a load. Forbidden are offworlders to use their weapons here, lest we settle scores among us with unequal ease." Her singspeech rose to a crescendo along with the broad flange of highlighted fur that comprised her neck flare.

"I see no gun but perhaps a stick only, even if made of metal hardly to be feared. I would prefer that it were a gun worthy of taking, but only a bluff becoming, it is now quite clear; a feeble effort, and hardly threatening."

By way of response Flinx, gripping the tube firmly with both hands about two-thirds of the way down its length, raised it so that its open end was now aimed at the ceiling.

"Final warning I give in earnest: do not make me strike at you. On your world I am an unarmed guest, and dealing death is not polite, is not friendly, is done only as a last resort."

The male let out the Larian equivalent of a grunt, something like a bassoon operating at the lower registers. "Listened have I to too much talking, any bluff becomes boring soon enough." The hand holding the knife gestured toward the far side of the room. "Growing tired is our partner Jailax; soon to finish, soon to ending, is he in fighting the thief we know. Let us take down this offworlder and slake his trending, words and goods we both shall have. If an unarmed being, so much the better; quicker and easier will be the end." One long, limber finger started to draw and aim the single-shot pistol that hitherto had rested in the holster slung across his chest.

Out of options and regretting it, Flinx had no choice but to snap the metal tube downward in the direction of his imminent attackers. Reacting to the suddenness of the offworlder's gesture, the female flinched slightly. In the absence of any noise and smoke from the human's device, her companion held steady as he fired.

Flinx ducked to his right as a sphere of solid shot whizzed past his head to bury itself in the wood of the wall behind him. Splinters of shattered planking nicked his neck. At the same time something slender and brightly colored shot out of the long tube he was holding. The instant it emerged from containment, it spread brilliantly hued blue and pink wings that became an instant blur.

The Larian thug who had fired the shot barely had time enough to gape at the alien shape that came rocketing toward him. Flexible as he was, he could not avoid the drop of venom ejected by the minidrag. It struck one half-closed black eye, from which smoke instantly began to curl.

Letting out an atonal scream that stunned every patron who had remained to watch the fight, the male dropped his weapons and slapped both webbed hands over his injured eye. As he staggered backward, tendrils of smoke emerged from between his fingers. A moment later they dropped away as he fell, slamming into a deserted table before sliding to the floor. In place of one gleaming black eye, a smoking pit extended all the way to the orbital bone.

Though she had not been struck by the humming, darting flying thing, the female likewise had abandoned her weapons in favor of making a run for the far doorway as fast as her short legs would propel her. Unreadable emotions wrapped in contemptuous speech had been replaced by a woodwind-like whimpering and pure naked fear. Now that she was not singspeaking, Flinx could perceive them clearly. Those attentive clients who remained in the dining area followed her out the portal with alacrity. Pip started to pursue, only to be called back by her fellow empath.

That left the flying snake and her master alone in the room save for the two contending Larians still locked in combat on the floor. To Flinx's surprise, even though he had called her back to him, the minidrag stopped in midair to hover above the pair of still-skirmishing males. He started to call out to her again, but paused. She was simply hovering, without evident lethal intent.

Of course, he told himself. Since neither of the two whistling, cursing, instrument-imitating individuals on the floor currently posed a threat to *him*, there was no reason for Pip to react defensively. At least, he assumed they posed no threat to him. As long as they were singspeaking, or in their case singscreaming, he could not sense what they were feeling. But Pip plainly felt something. And she had chosen simply to watch.

His attention distracted from the ongoing struggle long enough to espy the alien winged shape floating above him, the Larian on the bottom let out a loud yelp that was part bark, part trumpet blast. His opponent stilled the hand that was raised to slice downward, and his breathing proboscis gave a couple of twitches. As that individual turned his head Flinx noted that the gray-furred representative of his species was capable of looking back over his own shoulder. Taking the measure of the deadly alien flying creature that continued to hover just above him, the combatant's ears locked in place and his eyes bulged. Flinx felt for him. Suddenly finding an Alaspinian minidrag centimeters from one's face would be enough to unsettle the staunchest fighter, even one who was unfamiliar with the flying snake's potent offensive capabilities.

Scuttling backward, the Larian rolled over once. This brought him in contact with his now chaotically deceased companion. Smoke still rose from the empty eye socket where Pip's corrosive venom had struck. Scrabbling onto his feet, the slow-breathing attacker took note of those around him. His initial quarry, one of his own kind, now lay nearby on the floor, exhausted and confused. In front of him stood a tall bipedal offworlder, upright and unharmed. Of most immediate note, there was the brilliantly colored flying creature whose wings were a blur and whose eyes were devoid of affection. It was watching him intently. All three sights coalesced in his mind to generate a single unvoiced song: one that recommended a speedy farewell. Whirling, he turned and fled from the room as fast as his muscular legs could carry him.

Finding himself still intact and now with his assailants fled, the remaining male Larian picked himself up, patted the sides and backs of his legs with his tail to knock off all the dust and grime he had accumulated from rolling about on the wooden floor, and turned to regard his unlikely brace of saviors with an appraising eye. As he did so Flinx took a step toward him, arm and open hand outstretched. When the panting survivor of the attack retreated two steps in response, Flinx hastily remembered that the shaking of hands among the inhabitants of Largess was a possible invitation to wrestle, and nothing more. He halted.

Determining that the remaining native posed no immediate threat to her master, Pip returned to him, folded her wings against her sides, and like an exotic dancer squeezing into a form-fitting leotard, slithered back down into the cushioned, insulated interior of the metal tube Flinx had fashioned to keep her warm and comfortable while they were traveling.

He had never intended for the tube to substitute for a gun. Now that it had demonstrated its usefulness in that regard, he had to admit that while it remained a single-shot, its ammunition was nothing short of unique.

Stepping back, he put his hand over his throat and swept it sharply downward. From his studies he knew that variations of the gesture could indicate a friendly greeting, insults of varying degree, or an attempt to assuage a sore larynx. He hoped he'd performed the salutation correctly. It was not all that different from a traditional AAnn greeting, though no gripping or head-turning was involved.

It took a moment for the survivor of the assault to process what he was seeing: an offworlder, a human-thing, smartly executing a routine Larian greeting. As soon as realization struck home, the bruised but otherwise unharmed native responded in kind. The feelings he projected before he began talking were more reflective of uncertainty than fear.

"Heard I you speaking, before the cowardly assault, before the unbirthed miscreants came on me, our local language?" Flinx noted that the speaker's singspeaking voice was especially easy on the ear. On Largess, possessing the "gift of gab" meant having excellent pitch.

"I try my best." The rattled local's ears flattened against the top of his head as he struggled to make sense of the human's response. Flinx hastened to rephrase—and remodulate—his reply. "Make an effort I do, to understanding achieve."

"An effort admirable compared to most of your kind, who sound like gears a-rusting." Without waiting for an invitation, the speaker came forward and took a seat on the empty bench on the other side of Flinx's table, carefully stepping over the corpse of his attacker where it lay motionless on the floor.

Offering no objection but keeping a wary eye on the individual he had just rescued, Flinx resumed his own seat. Since Larian legs were proportionately shorter than those of most humans, this required a somewhat contortionist exercise on Flinx's part. His knees came closer to his chest than was entirely comfortable. In addition to that, he had to sit with them turned outward, as they could not fit beneath the low table. He would have been nearly as relaxed just sitting on the floor.

As Larian utensils consisted pretty much of a sharp knife and little else, Flinx resumed eating what remained of his local meal with his fingers. The male he had rescued looked on with interest. As far as the locals were concerned, humans compensated for the short length of their manipulative digits by having five of them instead of three. The indigene's attention shifted to the innocent-looking metal tube leaning against the wall to Flinx's left.

"Graceless in design is your weapon, primitive in execution by any standards. Yet unique and deadly can none deny, is your device of offworld origins."

"My companion now is sleeping," Flinx sang around a mouthful of seared plant protein, "who is both friend and protector; sensitive is she to any who come too near, to any who might threaten, to those who stink of killing."

The native glanced ceilingward. "Spawn of the Great Waters, I implore you, keep her insensible to my very breath!" In less stentorian tones he sang as he reached for the pouch that hung by a strap from one shoulder, "By your permission will I thank you, in paying for your meal, little as it may be. Allow me this opportunity, this small chance presented, to repay you for preserving this one's poor life."

Fairly certain he was not violating any significant native cultural protocol, Flinx waved away the offer even though he sensed that it was genuine. "I respond with thanks but can decline your gesture, as enough of your portable currency I carry with me, enough to pay for what needs I have."

"Really? How much do you—" The song ceased in midnote as the grateful local realized he might be overstepping his bounds. When he ceased trying to singspeak, Flinx found the native's emotions a confused mix of anxiety, fear, admiration, and exhilaration. He was plainly trying to figure out who this offworlder was and what he was all about. Flinx smiled to himself. The Larian was not the first, human or alien, who had struggled to do that. Any such analysis was complicated by the fact that Flinx himself was still engaged in an ongoing process of trying to figure out what he was all about.

"If not in money I can pay, to show my gratitude for your recent doing, for your rescuing me from that group of louts, what can I offer by way of thanking? For I am sitting here in your debt, as well as in your sight, with obligation pending. I would discharge it with gratefulness promptly, to found your brief visit on memories pleasant."

As forthrightly as he had taken a seat on the bench opposite the human, the native reached out and helped himself to a spiral-shaped raw vegetable in the bowl that contained the remnants of Flinx's meal. Amused rather than upset, Flinx said nothing. Nor did he miss the bit of purloined food. While perfectly edible and nourishing, Larian cuisine tended to the decidedly bland, regardless of whether it had been produced on land or gathered from the shallow seas. He ate it because he had to, not because he looked forward to it. Some of it, he had learned from his studies, was raised or grown, and some was free-range harvested. The latter included creatures and plants both large and small, active and drifting, energetic and parasitic.

As he watched his uninvited guest help himself to another remnant of the meal, Flinx reflected that it had yet to be determined if the brazen local would fall into that last category.

"Brief is not my visit's timing, fleeting not the time I'm spending. Here I start to travel farther, in hopes of helping not a Larian but all Largess. To do this I must have some help, must someone find, to assist my going." Having had all he could stomach anyway, he pointedly shoved the bowl with its remaining food across the table toward the native. Though his physique suggested he was far from starving, his guest was not shy about finishing the remainder of the food.

"I know many, I am knowledgeable," the native sputtered around mouthfuls of food as he cleaned the bowl, then licked the last particles and grease from first his fingers and finally from the webbing between, "and have contacts many and able. Whom do you seek, for you I will find him—or her depending on your tastes and needs." Sharp teeth flashed.

Flinx's expression twisted. The native's emotional state when he was silent, not to mention his table manners, suggested that despite his willingness to help in return for Flinx's efforts on his behalf, it might be better to seek information elsewhere. A single pointed query should be enough to determine if it was worth lingering in this individual's company.

"The one I seek is by my peers recommended, they say he is well versed in local issues, in matters of interest to those I'd speak with. His name I was given as singular only, as is common among your kind, unless noted or highborn, unless of exceptional merit, so I was told to ask only for 'Wiegl.'" Flinx hoped he had the pronunciation, with its subtle hint of piccolo at the end, correct.

He must have said something right, because the native paused licking food from the webbing between his fingers to gape at him. Had he pronounced something wrong? a suddenly concerned Flinx wondered. Or worse, sung something wrong? Had he inadvertently committed a musical as well as linguistic faux pas?

"Apologize do I for any misunderstanding, for possible insult, for singing wrongly. I am still new here, still new to speaking, with proper tone and inflection ring. . . ."

Using both long-fingered hands simultaneously and starting at the back of his snout, the native pushed them forward to wipe the sides of his mouth. Both hands met at the terminus when he had finished the bit of manual hygiene, whereupon he dropped them to the table and leaned sharply forward. Flinx tensed, but in the short-lived silence when he could sense what the other was feeling, he could detect nothing aggressive. Moreover, there was no hint of movement within the insulated metal tube that rested by his side.

The Larian stared at him out of glistening black eyes twice the size of a human's. "Doubly kind are the water spirits, who drench the unknowing with good intentions, who guide the unlucky despite their actions. Look no further than this chamber, furless visitor from the distant stars!"

Blinking, Flinx let his gaze drift around the room, touching on the small groups and individuals who had warily returned to finish their own meals. Eventually it returned to his self-invited dinner guest, about whose morals and motivations he already had questions.

"You." It came out as a single note.

Once more teeth were amply displayed, and the native's flexible nostril danced back and forth to repeatedly touch the sides of his mouth.

"Who else but I, have been sent to aid you? To help in your going, in your far traveling? Who sits before you but the best one possible, famed far and wide above all known guides, famed in legend and name, whose name is Wiegl!"

A few droplets of grease still clinging to his lower lip, dark eyes flashing and nostril twitching, the Larian regarded the human across from him. Flinx could only stare back, torn between accepting that his search for Padre Jonas's recommended local contact was over, or paying the bill and exiting the eating place as swiftly and politely as possible.

6

###

Keen to further probe the Larian seated opposite, Flinx stalled.

"How do I know, by your word alone, that you are the individual whom I seek, who was to me recommended?"

The native's blithe response did not allow for the kind of extended emotional exploration Flinx desired. "Ask anyone, here attending." A supple arm gesture took in the entire room.

"If you will remain here, I will do so also, the better to learn the truth of your speaking."

Rising, Flinx walked over to a table on the far side of the room. Though he was putting distance between himself and the garrulous local, he continued to stay in emotional contact. As he walked away he was unable to detect any radical swing in the native's emotions. Everything he sensed and could interpret hinted that the Larian remained content and excited. Certainly there was nothing to suggest a sudden shift to brooding or hostility.

The quartet that gazed up at their tall alien visitor radiated a tight emotional bond. From his studies Flinx knew that personal relationships among the Larians were highly fluid compared to human society. The two males and two females seated before him might comprise two mated pairs, a mated pair entertaining prospects from another mated pair or a couple of singles, or four unattached individuals in a Larian *ménage à quatre*.

"Can you identify for me an individual, who at my table is currently sitting, who at my table is just finished eating? 'Wiegl' he says is his naming, of diverse talents he claims a knowing." He indicated his distant booth.

All four glanced in that direction, the two innermost having to strain to see across the room. While all were comparatively youthful, it was the eldest who sang for the group.

"That entity I do recognize; from sometimes passing, from descriptions half-remembered, from encounters mentioned by others. His name *is* Wiegl, as you sing it, though with more emphasis on the ending."

Flinx nodded, then added the appropriate Larian gesture. "Think I of engaging his services tendered, for an enterprise of some difficulty. Seek I comment or recommendation; have you all anything to say in this matter?" Among the seated Larians, looks were exchanged in silence, prompting Flinx to add, "Honesty only is all I am seeking, no word of it will I sing elsewhere. Please to give me your frank opinion, that I may know how best to proceed, how best to continue."

Once again it was the eldest who responded, with one of the few one-note replies Flinx had encountered on Largess.

"Run."

Whereupon the four, without bothering to finish the last of their drinks or food, their emotions a confusing swish of anxiety, amusement, and fear, rose and departed posthaste, without a single backward glance at the staring alien. Flinx was left to try to reconcile the brusque caution with Wiegl's outgoing and apparently benign emotional self. Upon whose counsel was he to ultimately rely: the local Larians' or that of Padre Jonas?

The Padre had given him only one name. In the absence of viable alternatives and wishing to tackle the task that had been set before him as quickly as possible, he returned to the table and resumed his seat.

"Hesitant are your fellows to give of their blessing," he sang softly and carefully, "indications they give that are somewhat ambivalent."

"Easy to explain as I will tell you," the bright-eyed native responded without hesitation. "Jealous they are of our relationship."

Flinx frowned. "We have no relationship, I must tell *you:* I must insist you reword that verse."

Emotionally as well as verbally, it was clear that Wiegl was not put off by Flinx's reproach. "I mean to say they are covetous only, of any contact with your kind made, lest they be not the ones to gain thereby, from knowledge or goods acquired by such exchange. To me any profit, from such interactions, and not them, leads the trail of our talking."

Mollified, Flinx grunted softly. Next to him the metal tube rattled slightly as Pip shifted her resting position within. "Then will I engage you; to help and to guide me, to assist with singing, to find a solution to the problem I have been set."

Resting long muscular arms on the wooden table and splaying his webbed fingers wide, Wiegl leaned eagerly toward the human. "Speak of it only and I will focus, on nothing else until comes the solving, until your satisfaction is ultimately achieved." Singspeaking more rapidly, he ventured a vocal arpeggio, "The matter of payment can be discussed later, can be settled at some future time."

Having no forward-thrusting flexible nostril and being unable to wiggle his nose, but sensing that the guide's offer was genuine, Flinx settled for acknowledging the Larian's acceptance of the offer of employment by waving the middle three fingers of his left hand.

"Then you I welcome, Wiegl-singer, to my confidence bolstered, to my situation unspooling. Now I will tell you why I need help local, someone with knowledge wide-ranging, whom I must now take into my confidence.

"Know you at all, from your contacts many, from your various singings, of an offworlder using among your people, the offworld technology? Technology forbidden, the technology of my kind, that is from the Commonwealth originating?"

The Larian sat back. Before he opened his mouth to reply, Flinx could perceive a sudden hint of wariness that had not been there before. But his singspeaking response was unchanged in tone and harmonic optimism:

"Much is said of such intrusions, much is sung of devices borrowed. Borrowed, stolen, rented, copied; yet none of this am I personally seeing. Songs are cheap but reality costly, easy to believe rumors loudly mongered, to eagerly attend the many claimants." Showing a little more confidence, he varied his tone. "Too many stories remain stories only, reflecting the imagination of those who sing them, shine a light not on technology acquired, but only on those whose boasts are simple."

Flinx sang back, "And you strike me as someone who about boasting would know, an expert in that same field you decry, having just possibly yourself employed it, in touting your credentials to a person just met."

Wiegl's upper lip rippled like the lateral fins of a particularly graceful fish. "About human offworlders there is much that is strange, much that is confusing and even more that is awkward. So it is always heartening, to find those points of congruence, even when they consist, of straightforward sarcasm. You ask a question and I give an answer; of it you can only make what you will. For in my answer there is no guile, I sing only the truth each time you ask me."

Unable to figure out how to weave a simple "Uh-huh" into singspeech, Flinx let it pass. If he was going to doubt the individual he planned to employ at this stage, he might as well drop him and look elsewhere. But there was much about the specimen called Wiegl that intrigued him. He appreciated the native's confidence, though whether justified or misplaced was yet to be determined. Wiegl was brash, self-centered, and if he did not know what he was talking about, he faked it well. In the three-against-one tussle from which

Flinx had rescued him, he had also shown that he was good in a fight: a useful skill for a guide to have on a Class IVb world.

What Flinx could not determine at this early stage in their relationship was whether, if push came to shove, Wiegl's self-interest would overwhelm any loyalty he might profess to an employer. Especially to an employer who was of a different species. Largess was not a mature Commonwealth world, where species interacted rationally and respectfully regardless of shape or kind. Local culture was on the cusp of realizing that mutual interests and intelligence superseded speciesism. Until that happened, those devoid of fur, flexible breathing apparatuses, tails, and tooth-lined snouts remained alien. Un-Larians were to be regarded with a mixture of envy, admiration, and suspicion. Such qualms were difficult to overcome, especially in the absence of education and exposure to the civilized galaxy beyond.

In such circumstances, history had demonstrated on more than one occasion that these drawbacks could often be overcome through the judicious application of large amounts of the local currency.

Money, Flinx mused, would have to substitute for any deficiencies in understanding. At least this Wiegl individual showed, along with his wariness, some enthusiasm for Flinx's offer. So far Padre Jonas's recommendation had proven justified. Whether it would continue to do so under more difficult circumstances remained to be seen. The posing of a second question, he knew, should provide an answer. Sensing her master's rising concern, Pip stirred within her insulated tube.

"Coming together were many peoples, many citizens of many Leeths," Flinx elaborated. "First among them were those of Borusegahm, seeing the opportunities unity brings, promises of many good things to be had through joining, even unto the technology of which I speak. Boundless were the opportunities promised, if only all Larians could join together, join together in mutual benefit, sealed by trust forged from within and without."

Wiegl indicated his assent and understanding. "Such talk is old but only talk, of which much is made but little finished. Always happens some silly nonsense, where insults are given in lieu of accord. Easier is harmony sung than harmony fashioned, more frequently spilled is blood than liquor, with which is written discord large." He eyed Flinx intently. "I know of what interest this is to your government, but what it is to you remains a mystery. I would be enlightened so as best to assist you, yet," and he showed his teeth in the Larian equivalent of a human smile, "no diplomat am I, as I am sure you can tell."

Flinx nodded. "Know then that it is seriously suspected, that one moves among your kind with illegal science, with advanced technology forbidden to your people. Know also that this recent kidnapping, of the Firstborn of the Hobak of Borusegahm, is with this individual or individuals possibly linked. Who for reasons unknown, in local matters, have decided themselves to become involved." He lowered his voice. "An end to cooperation this abduction has made, an ending to all hopes of local unity, until the Firstborn can to her family be returned, until of her safety is her Leeth reassured. That is the interest of my government, or at least of an affiliate called the United Church. To see her returned and to restart the talking, that may bring together in peace every Leeth on this world."

Wiegl sat in thought for a long, long moment. When he finally replied, his singspeaking verged on the atonal. Larian communication allowed for placing emphasis in a manner that was unknown among humans, except perhaps those familiar with ancient opera.

"To be certain, to be correct, I must inquire. You seek the abductors of the Hobak's Firstborn, the much-esteemed Preedir ah nisa Leeh, whose beauty is sung of across the seas, over the land and through the trees. A beauty as famed as is her bravery, as is her shape and her temperament."

This time Flinx replied with a simple gesture of acknowledgment. Wiegl's response was equally concise.

"Rumor has it but is now confirmed, that while intelligent are the offworlders, that clever and knowledgeable though they be, madness is not unknown among them." Pushing off with his tail, he started to rise. The apprehension he exuded was almost visible.

Flinx raised a hand, palm upward in the accepted fashion, keeping his middle and index fingers pressed together, apart from the two smaller ones likewise pressed against each other, and the thumb separate. The result was to mimic the three fingers of a Larian as visually as possible—though there was no way to imitate the connecting webwork.

"To clarify before you flee, I seek the Firstborn but not her abductors, excepting any human who has interfered."

Wiegl hesitated. "One cannot be had without the other, as wishes cannot be had without the wishing. I am fond of my head in its current position, and would not go out of my way to lose it, in the service of a pricey folly."

"Your head and the rest of you will stay intact," Flinx sang back, "as long as you help me to accomplish my task, as long as we do this work together."

The Larian issued a chirp through his stiffened nostril. "As I said and will say again, together is how I like my head and body, separated they do me far less good. Do you know what you are asking, have you a clue of what you request? I fear but two things, I tell you, human: that we will not the Firstborn find, and that we might. Then will come the sharp-edged reckoning, that separates the head from neck, that separates the dreaming from real life, and ends your quest in a flush of blood."

Flinx showed his own teeth and gestured at the metal tube that leaned against the wall nearby. "Though high technology I cannot use, you have seen of what my friend is capable; I assure you she is ready, to defend us both if circumstance demands." Though it was difficult to find the exact center of the dark, angled Larian eyes, Flinx did his best to do so. "Furthermore I can tell you, there are things I must keep secret, that an advantage unique will give us, if we must deal with hostile others."

Wiegl let out a sharp bark, like sticks hitting the side of a snare drum. " 'Others' I do not fear, as 'others' is but a general notion. But the ones I speak of, are far more than 'others,' and are well-known for dismembering, those who follow too close on their tails."

"Then you *know* who they are? Who took the Hobak's First-born?" At Wiegl's muddled look of incomprehension, not to mention the aura of disgust that was plain to perceive, Flinx hastened to refashion his response into intelligible singspeech. "Familiar you are with who took the Firstborn, since you speak of them as persons known, as persons of an unpleasant reputation, who most would prefer to avoid when possible."

The native's answer took the form of a gesture that required no singspeech interpretation. "The death-dealing ability of your animal leaves me speechless, but not enough to chance becoming headless, which is surely what would us befall, if we were to pursue those of whom I have sung."

Reaching for a pocket, Flinx unsealed it and removed a container. Onto the table he dumped a generous number of the flat polished discs that served as currency on Largess. What the kind and quantity signified in local terms he did not know exactly, but Wiegl drew in his breath in a sharp hiss and the noise itself was sufficient to draw the attention of several other, heretofore disinterested patrons.

"Better can you become," Flinx murmured, "if my offer you accept; if you will in my experience trust, and become a hero as a bonus additional." He indicated the pile of discs. "Take half now as a down payment, on your services that I wish to engage, and know that this and more are waiting, on the return of we four to the Leeth safely."

We four, Wiegl thought to himself. *Offworlder human, the one (if not more) reputed to be interfering in Larian affairs, myself—and the Firstborn beauty Preedir ah nisa Leeh.* Gamble he to accept the challenge? Dare he sing the dare? Wasn't it only his imagination that something was tightening around his neck and screwing his eyes out of their sockets? Nothing more than his imagination?

That was the trouble with *having* an active imagination, he told himself. All very well and good to envision one diving deep, to slay the bumptious *blarminp* and take its razor-sharp teeth for a necklace. In one's imagination all things were possible, no matter how difficult, no matter how dangerous. Even unto stealing back the Hobak's Firstborn from the potluck of pirates who had abducted her and taken her north . . . or so he had heard was the case.

Was there a human or two among them, as the one across the table from him claimed? Wiegl did not know, but was intent on keeping his ignorance close to his chest. Let the offworlder think he knew more than he did. Bargaining chips were as hard to come by as coin. Of which speaking, it was an impressive little pile that sat on the table in front of him, just waiting to be scooped up. With more promised. Avarice was an irritant that made one's eyes speak of water.

He had no way of knowing, of course, that as he sat there in silent contemplation, the subject of his musing was perusing his true feelings as easily as reading the pages on an unfolding scroll.

He knew himself well enough to realize that if he accepted the offworlder's proposal, he would be getting himself into something much bigger, more dangerous, and potentially more lethal than any imbroglio he had been embroiled in before. The thought conjured up an image of him being present at an elegant state dinner—as the skinned and broiled main course. A Larian deprived of his fur was not a pretty sight.

Dare he?

For his part, Flinx was watching the native closely. Wiegl's present emotional state was a conflicted mess, his feelings running into one another like a crowd of nervous drunks. Deducing what the local was really feeling was like trying to stir honey with a blade of grass. Flinx's perceptions kept getting stuck and pushed around. Try as he might, he was unable to lock on to any one dominant sentiment.

Fortunately, Wiegl eliminated any need for additional emotional analysis by sweeping the metal discs on the table into the pouch that was slung across his chest.

"It cannot be denied now that I am a fool, for having ritually if not verbally accepted your offer; it marks me an idiot, but one with a full purse." The top of the pouch closed with a crude zipper. "I will go with you; to rescue the Firstborn, to savor her singing, to offer an arm for biting, in the hope I will live long enough to retain it. And all other limbs, and all parts, of which I have become fond, and would prefer to retain, for the rest of my living."

Flinx smiled. From what he could sense, the Larian was now willing to participate, even if he was still notably lacking in enthusiasm. "Where do we start, as I am to follow you?"

"Answers are hidden," the Larian chirped, "like bluestone in rocks, waiting to be discovered, by those who would seek, by those who ask deftly."

Flinx leaned back. "And are you, master of words, mincer of offers, a good hunter of bluestone, on whom I am to rely?"

"Bluestone and redstone, blue skies and red bone; the former I will find, the latter seek to avoid."

As he started to rise from the bench, Flinx reached for the metal tube in which Pip snoozed. "Blue sky here is rarer, I think, than gemstone of any kind, than anything that can by your money be bought. Looking up, I see only gray, no matter how hard my seeking, no matter how anxious my squinting."

"Bluestone and blue sky, both are rare, but both yield to persistence pending," his newly engaged Larian guide sang, "and may be found by those with patience."

"Then find me now," Flinx said, stumbling over an octave as they headed out of the establishment and back onto the busy, mist-muffled street, "the Hobak's Firstborn, and the offworlder looming over her. That I may deal with the latter trending, while you attend to the nisa Leeh's needs."

They turned up a street neatly paved with large square stones. Scalloped gullies separated the paving stones, drawing the water from the mist and the occasional shower off the slightly concave avenue and into drains along both sides. Borusegahm was an advanced town with well-developed civil services. What they would find once they left its comparatively civilized surroundings behind, Flinx knew, could not even be accessed via Commonwealth records. Because as with any Class IVb world, there was a great deal still to be learned about Largess. He looked forward to filling in some of the blanks.

As they struck out into the sprawling northern suburbs of the Leeth the following morning, the leaden cloud cover gave way to intermittent low fronts. Light drizzle was interspersed with heavy cloud and, as if intent on confirming Wiegl's presumption of his own skills, even a sporadic glimpse of streaky blue sky. In contrast to the dreary heavens, every home and commercial building boasted planters filled with an astonishing array of decorative plants. Only on one other world had Flinx encountered such an explosion of green and attendant colors. But the variety of form and hue on that singular globe was far greater than what he was seeing here, and these planters evinced an utter dearth of consciousness. The plants burst forth from their sculpted containers in a thousand different shapes, but though varied in color, all were subdued, as if each was ashamed to be brighter than its neighbor. They were healthy, even explosive, but with a reluctance to blossom fully that made them all seem variations on one original cutting.

In all that greenery he saw only a few distinctive shades. Airborne pollinators would have a difficult time in this weather, he told himself. When he sang of the absence of brightness to his companion, Wiegl drew him over to a cluster of waist-high growths fronting the entrance to some kind of workshop. Fire and iron were visible within, but Flinx was more interested in the plants. Leaning toward what resembled meter-high corncobs minus the stalks, he saw the tiny purple flowers that grew directly on the trunks: efflorescence.

As he looked on, a pair of winged cylinders landed on one stalk and began picking at the flowers. Unlike terrestrial bees, they inhaled what passed for pollen to store it in special compartments inside their bodies. Probably to keep the delicate organic material from becoming drenched in the often-saturated air of Largess, he speculated. Squinting, he noted with quiet astonishment that the flying cylinders themselves were completely dry. Their chitinous bodies, or whatever their iridescent purple shapes were made of, was naturally hydrophobic. The drizzle flowed over and around, but not on, them.

There were quasi-trees, too. Tall, narrow-boled growths with branches that grew only slightly perpendicular to the trunk before turning straight downward. All boasted broad, wide leaves for collecting as much of the intermittent sunlight as possible. Growths with yellow trunks had neither branches nor leaves, and one dark red tangle of brambles flaunted huge serrated thorns that looked like miniature scimitars.

There were no stirrings from within the metal "walking stick" that Flinx carried. Snug within her vertical cocoon, Pip slept soundly.

From time to time Wiegl would call a halt to their hike. Vanishing into a building, he would ungraciously leave Flinx waiting out in the dismal weather while he conversed with unknown individuals inside. At least he was not plotting treachery, Flinx knew. He could perceive the Larian's emotions as clearly from outside a structure as if they had been standing side by side within—at least when he wasn't singspeaking. Nor did Pip evince the slightest unease. Flinx began to relax—as much as he ever dared allow himself to relax. True relaxation was a state of being that had been virtually unknown to him since childhood. The best that could be said of it was that when he felt relatively safe, he entered a condition of lenient wariness.

If the guide's intentions included betrayal, Flinx felt, the Larian was hiding his feelings exceedingly well.

It was near the outskirts of the Leeth, where businesses had been left behind and homes were now isolated and scattered, that Wiegl emerged from a simple single-story house fashioned of rough-hewn stone and boasting a roof of woven red reeds, and for the first time beckoned for Flinx to join him within.

The ware sculpture that framed the door was slender and sheathed in what looked like mottled, dark maroon leather. Not every creature on cool, clammy Largess grew fur, Flinx knew. A living lintel, this one spread itself across the top of the portal. Stretching down either side, both limbs terminated in bony, taloned fingers that were as long as Flinx's forearm. They didn't look very strong, but Wiegl assured him that if their owner were so inclined, they could easily spill a person's intestines all over the stone walkway.

From the center of the attenuated body, a hairless head dominated by a sharp beak and two large yellow eyes tracked the approach of the tall offworlder. Since Wiegl had previously been admitted within, the watch-thing paid the guide no attention, focusing all its attention on Flinx. As powerful grasping hands flexed, a tremor rattled the metal walking tube wielded by the human. Pip was stirring within, reacting to the rising emotional threat posed by the Door Watcher.

Just before Wiegl led Flinx to within hand's reach, a female emerged from the depths of the structure. Though bent with age and from a lifetime of hard work in the brooks and fields of the Leeth, she was still strong enough to give the side of the doorway a couple of vigorous slaps with her tail. Coding and conditioning put the Door Watcher at ease. Fluttering fingers relaxed, the eager yellow eyes closed, and the beaked skull slumped forward. Still, Flinx did not let down his guard until he and Wiegl were inside the house.

It was as unpretentious within as it was without. Furnishings were ample and utilitarian. Animal skins splayed across two walls went unrecognized by Flinx. A kind of couch marked with a deep channel between cushions and back supported their host. He was lying on his side, his head propped up by the inflated corpse of a dead sea creature. Scarred of snout and missing one eye, he boasted a build that was thicker and more knotty than that of the average

Larian. And, Flinx realized suddenly, this Larian's tail was missing. Without such, Flinx knew, a member of his species could not stand for very long. Or execute the many other functions for which their short, stiff tails had evolved.

He was too polite to ask what had happened to the important appendage. It did not matter. Noting the offworlder's line of sight and divining his thoughts, their host provided an answer to the unasked question.

"They cut it off, they did as warning," he growl-sang. "To ensure my silence, their anonymity to preserve, by threatening worse still, to me and my family." Off to his left, Flinx saw the female watching quietly. Her long arms were wrapped across the front of her body, the webbed hands pressed together. She looked tense. What emotions Flinx could read from her confirmed it. Likely she did not want her mate singing of the subject to strangers. But she did not interfere, or interrupt.

"Stopped nearby did a strideship recently, laid up for the night in a meadow adjacent." The old hunter-gatherer on the couch relayed the memory without hesitation but with unmistakable bitterness. "A place I do not own but frequent occasionally, far does it lie from hearth and home, farther still is the place from one town or another. Good hunting is there among the redwork, and sandalstalk hearts to be gathered in plenty. A place no one owns, of fair tides and clean water, a place I myself would choose for resting." As he shifted on the couch the pain from his amputated tail was concealed in his expression but open to Flinx's perception.

"Out for three days I had my curiosity heightened, so close I crept that empty net to fill. A rougher lot on the deck than could be imagined, walked to and fro amid much cursing and laughter, the cursing full of humor and the laughter devoid of it. As I crouched half down among the redwork and ignored the nibblers, that around my ankles had begun to cluster, I saw on the deck by the few lights suspended, a sight that piqued my interest beyond any gathering.

"Between two figures as different as daytimes, stood a female of bearing both threatening and proud. Hands bound behind her she glared at two others, who sang to her firmly without expecting a response, who sang to her in tones of warning and caution, that she appeared to ignore as she sought to strike them."

Flinx felt he had to interrupt. Clearing his throat, he sangspoke as clearly as he could. The Larian couple eyed him in surprise, not expecting the taller of their two visitors to speak their language.

"Can you this odd pair, describe to us clearly, describe to us indicating that perhaps one is not Larian, that one is offworlder?"

"One was Larian, of that there is no doubt," their host told him, "as of equally no doubt, I say without hesitation, looked the other much like—you."

So the suspicions of Padre Jonas and her colleagues were correct, Flinx decided with satisfaction. An offworlder—a human—was indeed involved in the kidnapping of the Firstborn of Leeth. How much illegal advanced technology that individual had utilized to facilitate the abduction Flinx did not know. But before this particular excursion was over, he intended to find out.

Using two fingers, Wiegl gestured at their host's partially visible backside where it was tucked into the channel at the vee of the couch. He did not sing the unspoken question. Nor did he need to.

"While I stood in shallow water watching, came upon me from behind a pair of sentries. Outlying sentries, sensibly set, which I in my fascination neglected to espy, neglected to look out for. Overpowered, I was taken on board the strideship, there to be stood before the Larian friend, of the offworlder who had admonished the captive, and sung to her words I had been unable to hear.

"He spoke to me harshly, this hard-faced hooligan, who by his manner and words was clearly unworthy, of any company deemed honest and moral. Myself I consider brave if not feckless, but this individual I would run from, in daylight or night. Being held firmly I could not flee, being restrained I could not fight, so there was naught I could do but stand and curse foully, in the hope that my boldness might commend me to this being, and set me free to disappear into the night." Again he shifted his position on the couch, and again Flinx sensed the pain from his amputated tail.

"Strong words this commander did sing me, without shouting and without concern. 'Tell no one what you have seen here this night; sing in no village of our passing, in no street of our conversation, to no relative no matter how naïve. Or surely of it I will hear, and return to this place, to find and slaughter you, and to you all who are precious.' Whereupon he turned his back to me, and to an underling sang a single order, which brought forth down a sword behind me, and in one blow deprived me of my tail." His lips trembled slightly. "As a warning it was brutal, and unnecessary to the keeping, of my word about not singing, of what I had seen.

"Over the side of the strideship I was thrown without caution, its crew not caring if I landed on head or on hind. Much blood I left behind me, as I staggered homeward, to my mate and her keening, which sad and loud split the night."

A glance at the female showed her stoic and barely reacting. But as soon as her mate stopped singing, Flinx could sense her crying inside.

Even the usually apathetic Wiegl was affected. "You are brave in the retelling, in the resinging to strangers, of a tale so vital, and ignoring the threat."

Their host gave the Larian equivalent of a shrug. "If one tail is missing, then what better than to fill it, than another retelling of the cruelty, in hopes of some justice." Black eyes regarded them shrewdly. "You seek to find this strideship and its iniquitous crew, in which seeking I bless you, whatever your reasons, whatever your rationale. I ask only that if you do this, and succeed in your striving, whatever its reason, whatever its purpose, that you might return to me if not my tail, then some retribution I cannot imagine."

Gesturing with his left hand, Wiegl flicked ears and extended the tip of his breathing proboscis as far past the end of his snout as possible. "Endeavor we will, if fighting cannot be avoided, to seek out the one who cut you, and reciprocate in kind."

The doorwatcher-thing was asleep as man and Larian exited the house. While Flinx was profoundly moved by the elder Larian's story, Wiegl was now twice as guarded as before.

"Press on with your searching, are you still decided?" Flinx's guide asked him. "In the face of this viciousness, so plainly described, so clearly shown?"

"Press on as before," Flinx replied in singspeech, "now quicker than ever, lest the trail we lose, of those that we seek."

Wiegl hissed through his long furry nostril tube, causing it to vibrate like a short length of rubber hose. "No problem should that be, as by the description just given, easy enough as described, to follow a trail of blood."

7

...

They encountered the strideship's footprints on the other side of a rippling tidal flat so thickly overgrown with purple and green knee-high vegetation that Flinx was hard-pressed to bash a path through it. With his lower center of gravity, short legs, and powerful tail to add impetus to his forward motion, Wiegl made better progress. He did not mind breaking trail for the human or snapping off the camouflaged, lightly poisonous seed tangles. After all, he was being paid to carry out such humble tasks. He did find it instructive that the taller offworlder was having such a difficult time. Instructive, and reassuring. The aliens had wonderful technology that could do amazing things, but they were not gods.

At regular intervals they would come to a hole in the heath where one of the strideship's feet had smashed the foliage flat. Water puddled in the ovoidal gaps and small wiry *kaerls* took advantage of the unexpected excavation to burrow deep into the resulting mud. It did not take the observant Wiegl all day to come to the obvious conclusion.

"Headed north they are, at a good rate of speed, the better to outdistance any presumed pursuit, to defeat any attempt at rescue."

Coming up behind the Larian, Flinx leaned on Pip's tube and paused to catch his breath. It had been cold enough that morning to see it. "At this moment I do not feel, in my feet or in my bones, that I am in any condition to qualify, as anyone's presumed pursuit." Raising his gaze, he peered into the misty distance. Were those clouds ahead, or merely more low mountains? "I do not know, nor can I imagine, what here is considered, a 'good rate of speed.' Only this I know: that I cannot exceed it, that I cannot match it, and that in so failing, I will fail my needs." Scrutinizing their surroundings, he saw only low rolling strips of granite and basalt interspersed with saltwater inlets and freshwater pools.

"Is there not some way, is there not something, that will allow us without gasping, to overtake our quarry? Or at least to arrive, in time just behind them, with enough energy remaining, to give good account of ourselves?"

Wiegl considered a moment, then turned and gestured to the west. "Not far from here lies Grndalx, a town of some substance, not Borusegahm to be sure, but adequate for our needs, on the northern edge of the Leeth."

Flinx nodded tiredly. "And what can we find, in this Grndalx you mention, to solve the small problem, that I sing with my feet? A strideship perhaps, like the one we are chasing, perhaps even faster, so that we may it overtake?"

The Larian emitted a rude sound via his proboscis. "Why for sure a fine strideship, we will just charter without waiting, without hesitation or research, and fifty fighters for crew." He eyed the panting human. "Such charters take time, both to arrange and provision, and no crew should be hired, without careful vetting."

"Then—what?" Flinx asked, too tired to sing the query properly.

"Because of its location, at the Leeth's northern reaches, the town boasts a market, of some considerable renown. A market where travelers, lame of foot and of thinking, might hire transportation, to travel fast over the moors."

The moors. Flinx had not thought of the countryside through

which they had just passed with such difficulty as "moors," but the description was apt even if the exact translation was suspect. As to how much of such terrain they had to traverse to catch up with the strideship and its noteworthy captive, he did not know. While on the *Teacher* he had studied as much as he could of the culture and language of Largess, but he had perforce lacked time to delve into many other subjects. Geography, for example.

He sighed. At this rate, the store of money discs Padre Jonas had given him was not going to last very long.

"If not a strideship, then what shall we find," he sang as best he could, "in the market you reference, since a shipyard it is not?"

Wiegl was already smashing his way westward through the lavender-tinged undergrowth. A small cloud of angry carmine-hued leaves flew at his face and he swatted them away indifferently. Flinx had a moment of alarm as they turned their attention on him, until he experienced an assault of feathery softness. Though aggressive, the tiny creatures possessed nothing with which to harm him. Had he faced a similar assault on, say, Midworld, his initial panic would have been more justifiable.

Despite his concerns and his difficulty walking, they reached Grndalx at nightfall, utilizing the trail broken by the surprisingly skilled Wiegl. As the town was a trading crossroads as well as an entryway to the more developed districts of Borusegahm, they had no difficulty finding lodgings. Flinx was a bit surprised at the speed with which Wiegl negotiated arrangements for the night, given that his companion was a tall, furless alien.

"Human presence may be scarce out here," the guide explained, "but offworlders have been on Largess for some time, so knowledge of them is widespread, even if actual encounters are infrequent."

As had been done at a similar establishment in Borusegahm city, a bed was improvised for Flinx by pushing two of the sleeping platforms in their room together end to end. While both were narrower and lower than even a small bed designed for humans, Flinx knew he could manage. The biggest problem came in the form of the cutout slots located three-quarters of the way down each platform. These were designed to allow Larians to sleep on their backs while their thick short tails hung through. Flinx found the openings inconvenient, but not intolerable. Of the three travelers, Pip was probably most comfortable of all, snug inside her insulated metal tube.

The fact that his digestive system (and Pip's as well) could tolerate and derive nutrients from Larian fare made the journey not only simpler but possible. Flinx carried supplements in pill form to supply those critical vitamins and minerals that were lacking in native cuisine. Having sampled an enormous variety of local foods on a host of other worlds, he had been delighted to find that Larian cuisine was genuinely nourishing if not especially tasty. Food that was locally grown was tolerable, and he was able to avoid domesticated and hunted protein in favor of that which was hauled from the innumerable lakes, inlets, and shallow seas. More used to surviving on an alien world than prospering, he had quickly discovered that he could indulge in caloric intake without fear of his guts turning inside out.

Wiegl noted his companion's unrestrained consumption of the morning meal. "To your liking, this morning, you find our foodstuffs?"

"More so than your politics, which I can ignore, but which trouble the Commonwealth, which hopes to uplift you."

"Politics do not interest me, as it is a woeful profession, and as to offworlder interests, I can only say uplift this." Reaching down, he clutched at his genitals in an apparent act of simultaneous derision and dismissal that was uncommonly universal among species that utilized similar methods of reproduction. Flinx ignored the gesture. He hadn't hired Wiegl for the Larian's political propensities and in fact did not care if the guide held any.

Morning did not dawn so much as seep into gray prominence. Doubtless a steady diet of such gloomy weather resulted in a healthy turnover among staff at the Commonwealth station. He wondered how long Padre Jonas had been assigned to Largess.

Such speculation vanished as an all-too-familiar throbbing at the back of his head caused him to wince. For a moment he was forced to shut his eyes against the pain. Wiegl did not notice and Flinx, leaning on the metal tube that contained a now-concerned Pip, was able to recover before the guide saw that anything was amiss or the minidrag felt a need to put in an appearance.

The sharp, stabbing headache was induced by his sudden exposure to a cacophony of conflicting emotions. They arose from the sprawling market ahead. Hundreds of Larians were arguing, complaining, pleading, accusing, cursing, and in general generating a rising miasma of emotions, all of which he was unable to shut out whenever the individuals in question stopped singing. Every marketplace he had ever visited, including those on his home world of Moth, had proven to be a comparable well full of such strong feelings. Steeling himself against the emotional deluge, he allowed Wiegl to lead him forward and into the mental morass.

Eventually they arrived at a more open area where the emotional overload he was suffering was somewhat reduced because many of those present were all talking at once. Rising interest helped to focus his attention, if not his talent, elsewhere.

They were making their way through what on any other world would have constituted a zoo but on Largess was merely a noisy, smelly souk for buying and selling animals. Some for food, some for companionship, some domesticated for working in fields or in water. In addition to the excess of new alien smells, Flinx was much taken with the variety of shapes and sizes around him, many of which he had not encountered in his hasty studies on board the *Teacher*.

A small, iridescent green head popped out of his walking tube. At ease by now in the presence of the flying snake, Wiegl did not flinch at her appearance. While other lightly clad traders and visitors did glance in Pip's direction, they did not panic. Having never seen an Alaspinian minidrag before, they had no notion of her lethal capabilities, so their curiosity was not tainted by fear. Certainly Flinx sensed none among those who took notice of his scaly companion.

She drew considerably more attention when she emerged fully from the tube and took to the air. Not only her spectacular coloring but the deep hum generated by her wings caused glassy black eyes to glance skyward. Making no attempt to call her back, Flinx let her go as she pleased. Pip had no natural enemies on this world, nor did she constitute the natural prey of any local carnivores, who would be cautious before they were aggressive. And unless she chose to stray far, human and minidrag would always be in emotional contact.

Thus allowing her free rein, he tried to focus on what Wiegl was saying to the various herders and merchants. Even without the constant Larian damp, the glut of stink would have been considerable. It ranged from delicate, fragrant scents that were almost thranx-like to an overpowering thrust of musk that emanated from one corral packed with what looked like giant balls of long brown fur streaked with tints of amber and antimony. Unafraid that he might offend the locals by holding his nose, since their respiratory apparatus was different in shape and location, he got as close as he could. The result was olfactory overload, a sensation akin to wading into a pool of semi-vaporized sewage whose stench was only slightly minimized by a faint overlay of lilac.

He was drawn to the enclosure not by the smell or the thick, rank fur of its inhabitants, but by the fact that their heads seemed to be situated with complete randomness. Low-hanging fur hid whatever limbs they used for locomotion, so all that was visible were narrow, vaguely equine skulls that terminated in meter-long flexible proboscises. Unlike the similar but much smaller organs of the dominant Larians, these were fully prehensile: a fact he discovered from watching the creatures crop at the bundles of cut vegetation that had been supplied for their nourishment. Not nearly as elongated as those of a Larian, pale blue eyes regarded the world with bovine placidity.

Settling on the nearest representative, Flinx met its gaze straight on—whereupon the head shrank back and disappeared into the mass of oily fur, only to reemerge on the other side of the body. Or had he been mesmerized by a Larian example of facial mimicry all along? As he marveled at the increasingly nervous mob, heads began vanishing and popping back out elsewhere seemingly at random. So fascinating was the display that a touch on his arm startled him. He was mildly bothered that he had not sensed his guide's approach. But then, Wiegl's current emotional state was fairly neutral.

"*Shomagr* you see, an interesting creature, famed for its pelt and meat, once industrially deodorized."

Flinx nodded understandingly. "Glad I am to know, that my detection of their smell, is not something confined to my kind, but is acknowledged on Largess as well."

Flinx sensed the change as Wiegl's emotional neutrality was lifted by amusement. "Ignorant you are of your surroundings, but that may be to your benefit, that may be just as well. What you are smelling of the *shomagr* is but a sampling of their bouquet, as when faced with a predator, they into a circle combine, and then project from scent glands, a reek that will drop a warrior."

Flinx took several steps backward. "Then let us do our best, to not provoke them, as what I smell now, is powerful enough." He gestured. "Their heads vanish into their fur, only to reappear somewhere else, and I must confess, that this is a strange biology, I do not understand."

"Beneath all that fur," Wiegl explained as he pointed, "the head rides on a multiflexible joint, that around the central body, swings freely. Away from an attack can the *shomagr* run, while staring straight at you all the while, constantly shifting their line of sight, by just repositioning their heads. Disconcerting it is, to any hungry pursuer, to not know which way, their prey is looking."

"Not to mention that smell, which I do not need to experience further," Flinx concluded. Looking over the heads of the milling crowd, he wondered where Pip had gone. To his surprise, Wiegl knew the answer.

"Settled your pet on your mount of my choosing, as if prescient she is, as well as deadly." Raising both feet and pivoting neatly on his tail, he led Flinx through the mass of buyers and sellers, gawkers and families. More of them turned here to look at him than had in Borusegahm. That was to be expected and the attention did not trouble him. He sensed only curiosity and no enmity. Being the subject of questioning alien stares was a situation as familiar to him as breathing.

Breathing brought back memory of the *shomagr* stink, causing him to lengthen his stride.

They found Pip settled on a perch as high as it was alien. The creatures Wiegl had chosen to be their mounts were restrained by leg braces instead of a corral. As they stood an average of six meters in height, it would have taken a major construction project to erect an enclosure capable of holding them.

Flinx swallowed as he contemplated the unexpectedly tall prospect. "Those are what, in our need to pursue, we are going to have to ride, are going to have to balance upon?"

Wiegl enjoyed the human's anxiety. "It is not as difficult, as first look might indicate. Come and I will show you; how to take the saddle, how to settle yourself, how to ride in comfort. For in comfort we will travel, and as fast as can be managed with a mount and not a strideship—or perhaps you can call one of your craft, that floats in the air like a winged *birag*?"

Flinx grinned at his guide. *Can't blame Wiegl for trying,* he told himself. "No skimmers are allowed this far from the station, no advanced tech of any kind, save what small thing might be necessary, our lives to save, only in direst emergency."

Clearly disappointed, Wiegl turned back to the chained animals. "Then second best will have to do, and we will make speed—but only if these fine mounts, you can afford."

Flinx considered the rapidly shrinking store of money discs Padre Jonas had provided. "The cost of riding we will calculate, after *first* determining, if the cost to this rider, will be the health of his spine."

Indicating his understanding with a gesture, Wiegl turned back to the proposed means of transportation.

Perched atop the tallest of the half dozen restrained *brund*, Pip gazed down at master and guide with imperious indifference. The one on which she was resting was chewing contentedly on the narrow, downward-slanting leaves of a slender tree. Next to it a second brund, having finished all the leaves on another tree, was munching the bare top of the narrow trunk itself, gnawing it down as if eating a dark brown carrot.

Gray bodies that resembled clumps of metal wool terminated in thick forward-facing skulls dominated by wide mouths filled with flat, sharp-edged teeth. Chisel-like incisors were backed by grinding molars that did the hard work of masticating cellulosic material. Beneath ridges of bone that protruded from the front of the skull, large brown eyes gazed cow-like at their surroundings. Tall tufted ears flanked a breathing tube not unlike those of the *shomagr*, with the exception that it was far less flexible.

Head and body were some two meters in length and half that in width and in depth. The remaining five meters of brund were all legs.

Unlike the lead-gray bodies and heads, the legs varied in color from yellow to umber. Some limbs were spotted, others streaked. None was larger in diameter than Flinx's torso. Each had a single joint located two-thirds of the way off the ground. The thickly padded, perfectly round feet boasted four toes that splayed out in all four directions, providing a solid base for the otherwise spindly-looking legs. Flinx now thought he understood why Wiegl had settled on the brund as their mode of transport. With a single double-legged stride, the smallest of the creatures could span an impressive distance or easily negotiate a flowing stream. He was right in his analysis, except it did not go far enough.

"The land will be easy to scan, from such a great height," he murmured, "but where does one ride, where does one sit, as I see no saddle atop the head?"

"Not on the head," Wiegl informed him, "which sports a bony crest hidden beneath the thick fur, but to one side, below an ear of one's choosing." He pointed.

Following the guide's direction, Flinx was able to make out the leather tack that wrapped around the base of the skull and the neck. No riding kit was presently in evidence, but there was no need to burden the brund with saddles unless they were in use.

"Beneath an ear of one's choosing, you say very plainly. But if that is possible, cannot two ride one creature, an individual to each side?"

The Larian tootled his assent. "Two brund can carry four riders with ease, it is plain for anyone to see, yet though there are only two of us, on our return journey we hope to be four."

"Oh, of course." The Firstborn Preedir ah nisa Leeh would require a place to sit as well, he reminded himself. He acceded to the need. "I count on you as my experienced guide, to strike as hard a bargain, as possible for our rides."

While Wiegl proceeded to haggle with the herdsman, Flinx studied the brund more closely. He was going to be traveling with this animal for an unknown number of days and he wanted to know as much as possible about their mounts. Though he had spent time on many worlds and observed hundreds of alien species, the brund with their steel-gray bodies, chiseling teeth, and stilt-like legs were as exotic as anything he had encountered. As for the one that was presently providing Pip with a lofty perch, he was not as sure that it was ignoring her as he was that her slight weight must be relatively imperceptible to so large a creature.

Wiegl concluded the negotiations, Flinx paid, and they disappeared back into the market with the herder's assurance that their mounts would be ready for them by evening, complete with all necessary tack. Wiegl engaged a couple of porters, and between the four of them they managed to fill the storage packs and spare saddles of both brund with supplies for the journey ahead. In order to make up time in hopes of catching up to their quarry, Wiegl had proposed that they skip the modest pleasures offered by any small towns they might pass along the way, and try as hard as they could to catch up to the strideship before it reached its final destination.

"And where might that be?" Flinx inquired tunefully. "For I cannot believe that in all your asking, that one question, you have failed to put forth."

Tension roiled the Larian, his true feelings open to Flinx's perceiving. It was encouraging, he told himself, that the guide's emotions were not overwhelmed by fear.

"Uncertain it is, uncertain to know, unsure and unsteady were the replies I received, when casually I posed that query." He indicated their bustling surroundings. "But words travel fast, even those holding secrets, and are sooner opened, than a banker's mind." Stepping closer, he dropped his singing to a lullaby. "Swift it is said runs a strideship, homeward to its whispered base. Crewed it is by lethal nasties, led by one with a crooked snout, helped by one with a naked face."

"Our offworlder!" At Wiegl's puzzled expression, Flinx hastened to frame his response in proper singspeech. "The offworlder it appears, is helping in the abduction, much as was theorized, by those at the station, by those who send me onward. Of word was there any, as to this ship's destination, as to where it might be going, to this whispered base?"

Raising a hand, Wiegl twisted it in the moist air. "Traders will talk and traders will ramble, merchants will sing and merchants will lie, but in any soup there is always meat floating; the trick is to separate the flesh from the bone. Some say assuredly the ship is westward turning, heading for the Leeth of Aberkam Drot. Some say it will stop at Pierncrae Crossing, there to set sail for lands across the Great Breath."

Flinx was puzzled. If this ship hadn't already "set sail," then how was it advancing northward? What was its motive power if not sails? Come to think of it, since leaving Borusegahm they had crossed as much land as water despite the inescapable presence of the large shallow lakes and long saltwater inlets that dominated so much of Larian terrain.

With regret, he realized that despite his intensive studies there was still much about this world and its dominant Larian society that he did not know. And of course he had not been able to bring with him anything of an advanced nature, like a vorec, which would have allowed him to look up the answers to such questions. He restrained his curiosity, knowing that he was likely to encounter explanations soon enough. *If* they could catch up to their quarry before it reached . . . ?

"But you, my friend, believe none of that, believe no such tales, but have drawn a different conclusion?"

Wiegl's upper lip curled, revealing his teeth. "There are stories that percolate south, from the rugged Northlands, of a change of leadership in one of the larger Leeths. Tales are told of a powerful Hobak, new to governing but not to politics, who craves fame and attention more than most. Felelagh na Broon is the name of this neophyte, of whom it is said he lusts for more power, to extend the reach of the Leeth of Minord, far beyond its present boundaries. He is fêted for cunning, reported for nuisance, and would apparently be the last one, to join a broad union of Leeths."

Flinx nodded, hoping that by now Wiegl understood the meaning of the gesture. "A troublemaker, it seems, without recent precedent, in this part of your world. Not unknown to my Commonwealth, are such individuals, who would build their own ego, before hospital or schools."

Wiegl's ears and nostril dipped forward: his version of a nod. "Perhaps also is this na Broon a bit of the fanatic, if what they say is true, about his aversion to a union of Leeths. Perhaps even maniacal enough, in his self-centered narcissism, to try to put a stop to it, by abducting another Hobak's Firstborn; to raise himself up, by bringing another down."

"I think we will see," said Flinx, "when we catch up to this ship, and when I have a chance, to speak with its offworlder. Who I think is a human, as well as a renegade."

"A confrontation for which I do not hunger," Wiegl sang back, "but which I have no doubt, will prove both educational, and entertaining."

Regardless of whether it is the renegade or I who emerges from it intact, Flinx told himself grimly. Thus far his guide had proven himself to be nothing if not direct in his feelings.

Bemusement as to how they were to mount the pair of chosen brund, not to mention load the awkward-looking creatures with supplies, occupied his thoughts until it was time to leave. After conversing in counterpoint with the herder, Wiegl approached the nearest of the placid beasts, sang out a command, and Flinx had his answer.

The brund neither knelt nor bent over. Instead, they simply sat straight down. Slender but powerful tendons and joints allowed them to squat so that the rounded undersides of their compact bodies nearly touched the ground.

"Here, a look, without unnecessary explanation," Wiegl sang.

As soon as the guide showed him around to the dorsal side of the animal, Flinx was able to make out the protruding vertebrae in its back. Pushing his way through the long, thick fur allowed him to climb the knobby bones as easily as a ladder. Though the basket-like arrangement of leather straps and woven netting into which he then settled himself was designed for the comparatively longer torso and shorter legs and tail of a Larian, he was able to squirm into it securely enough to ensure that he wouldn't fall out. At least, that was his hope, since when at Wiegl's second command the loaded brund stood, Flinx suddenly found himself some six meters off the ground.

The second saddle, located on the other side of the brund's body, was stuffed with supplies, counterbalancing its single passenger. Flinx allowed his backpack, which among other things contained his nutritional supplements, to be packed there with everything else. All he kept with him was the metal tube, although Pip seemed to have happily abandoned its insulated interior in favor of the deep fur atop the brund's head.

At a fortissimo from Wiegl, the herder released the chains that had bound the brund in place. In contrast, the guide did not have to raise his voice to call across to Flinx. With Wiegl seated in the left-hand saddle of his mount and the human in the right side of his own, they could practically reach out and grasp hands.

"Ready then, to take a ride most interesting, regardless of objective?"

Clutching the single leather rein that was attached to the slightly projecting bone beneath the wide, toothy mouth off to his left, Flinx took a deep breath and nodded. He had ridden many creatures on many worlds, but never one so tall and outwardly fragile. As it turned out, the brund proved to be anything but frail. At a command from Wiegl, both animals lurched forward.

A single enormous stride carried them *over* and outside the corral where they had been held. Below, irritated traders and travelers scrambled to make way for the round flat feet and the long but strong legs attached to them.

The gait of a brund was awkward: a herky-jerky forward motion that initially threatened to catapult Flinx out of his saddle. Quickly, and of necessity, he learned to anticipate each double-legged forward stride. To his astonishment, by the time he had adapted to and settled into the rhythm, they were already well outside the town limits of Grndalx proper.

Ahead lay long, lonely granite ridges interspersed with lakes, rivers, and oceanic inlets, often hidden by dense red- and purple-tinged heath or tall, twiglike forest.

Seeing that Flinx had grown quickly comfortable, or at least tolerable, of his brundian seat, Wiegl trilled a new command. Flinx's mount accelerated, splashing water as it strode through those tributaries too wide to step across and sending small semiaquatic creatures fleeing.

It was almost as swift a method of transportation, he reflected as he hung on for dear life, as it was an uncomfortable one.

8

...

Chela Voh was short but not unusually so, and slender enough to
be described as sylphlike. A cascade of tight, black ringlets tumbled
to her shoulders and framed a face that was wholly elfin except for
the eyes. Downcast, they made her resemble a troubled sprite slipped
from some ancient children's fairy tale. Raised and focused, they
could burn. Not literally, of course—though some who had been
subjected to the directness of that stare might choose to differ.

Used to traveling by herself on many worlds, she felt reasonably
comfortable with her surroundings after a couple of days spent wandering the grounds of the Commonwealth station north of
Borusegahm Leeth. She would have spent more time talking to long-
term personnel, but she had a job to do and delays made her uncomfortable. Nor could she make inquiries of the local Church
representative in hopes of accelerating her work. The organization
to which she belonged and the United Church had . . . philosophical
differences. When the human personnel at the station proved vague
or unhelpful in their replies to her queries, she eventually chose to
confront a trio of natives who were visiting the station on personal
business.

At first, the two males and one female tried to ignore her. Humans, especially those newly arrived, tended to want to discuss all manner of foolish things. They certainly did not expect her to speak Lari. Least of all did they expect her to singspeak it as well as she did.

"I seek one of my kind, who is operating outland; beyond the Leeth, beyond the usual contacts, and out of touch with the station authorities."

The group of locals gazed at the offworlder in astonishment, until the female member of the trio finally spoke for the three of them.

"Many are those of your kind who have come here, who in their work and in their talking, seek to communicate with us freely." Her short ears were standing straight up, as were those of her two male companions. "But never have I heard, until just this moment, an offworlder voice sweet enough, to match the best of our own."

"Your words soar like a slickback gliding through clouds," the male on her right added admiringly, "redolent of thunder, kissed with melody. Had I not myself heard them, just now, just here, in this place, I would have thought them nothing more than rumor." Inclining to their right, both males executed the Larian equivalent of a bow.

"What can we three," the female asked as a breeze stirred the veil-like material of her attire around her supple form, "do for you, heart-singer of fancies? Do not fear to extend your question, so that we three may hear clearly, and enjoy the tones of your response, unprecedented for your people."

"I seek one of my own kind," Chela repeated in perfect trilling and without acknowledging any of the compliments, "who also travels alone. A male of notable abilities, who surely also knows, how to throat your singspeech. One who like myself, is not afraid, and is comfortable sojourning, on worlds not his own."

As Voh looked on, the three fell to discussing among themselves. No operatic trio ever sounded more harmonious, nor argued with such tunefulness. When they finished, all three turned back to the impatient human.

"Here at this station, home to offworlders, we have heard it spoken, of one who has done this." The male puffed out his narrow chest, perhaps trying to impress the wonderful human singspeaker, or possibly simply gathering wind. "One who travels devoid of any humans for company, and seeks no one knows what, though rumors abound."

"What sort of rumors, of this one traveling, can you tell me, the better that I might plan, my own goings?" Voh sang back intently.

The trio proceeded to relate the gossip that swirled around the kidnapping of the Hobak's Firstborn. That it had been carried out by the minions of another Hobak, one whose country lay far outside the Borusegahm Leeth and possibly to the north. That was where the rumors, if not the truth, converged. In fact, it was said that a lone human had recently left for that region, in the company of a somewhat notorious escort.

Though this was enough for Chela, the trio was reluctant to let her go. The novelty of her splendid rendition of the local singspeak threatened to saddle her with a celebrity she did not want, as other curious natives came to see what all the fuss was about, and she finally managed to extricate herself from the growing crowd only by offering up a multi-octave farewell in *agitato* time.

A sole human was said to have gone north. One who might or might not be involved in a matter of local politics. Additional questioning of station personnel only served to further confirm the tale the Larian trio had sung. Very well—she would go north. Though lingering was not her personal style, neither did she need to rush to conclude her assignment. What mattered to the organization of which she was a part was its eventual success, not its timeframe.

Having by now absorbed the general details of the abduction of the Hobak's Firstborn, she knew that the initial information that had been provided to her prior to her arrival on this underdeveloped world was accurate. There were domestic sociopolitical problems with which an offworlder, a male human, was presently involved. Though she had not been able to obtain his physical description, it was evident that he must be the one her group had been searching after for some time. Her organization could have sent several operatives to track him down. This had been tried before, and on each occasion had come close to success only to fail spectacularly at the last moment. This time only one had been sent in pursuit. One who was unlikely to attract attention and thereby possibly warn the organization's quarry that he was being pursued.

Clad in lightweight rain-repellent gear, she was finishing her preparations prior to departing the station for Borusegahm proper. How long it might take to find the one her organization sought did not trouble her. She quite enjoyed Largess's cool ambient temperature and its accompanying dampness. While others of her kind might find the gray skies and frequent drizzle depressing, she quietly reveled in a landscape that was more monochromatic than colorful.

Unable to restrain himself any longer, the supply master who was filling out her requisitions finally broke the silence that existed between them.

"You don't talk much, do you, Chela?"

"Ms. Voh." She spoke the curt reply while studying the depth-dimensional images of Larian terrain that lined one wall of the supply facility. Rock, oddly shaped vegetation, water everywhere, more rock. She was looking forward to the journey as well as to its inevitable termination. The weather here, the landscape—everything suited her disposition. It would be fun. Or at least, as much fun as someone in her chosen profession could have while on the job.

A hand touched her left shoulder and slid downward. She had sensed its proximity an instant before any actual contact was made but had chosen not to react as she normally would in such a situation. This was not a major city on a developed world, and the last thing she wanted was to draw any unwanted attention to herself. Her travel documentation identified her as a scout for one of the major trading houses, come to Largess to search out biologicals for possible development and exploitation, and she did not want to do anything that might call that identity into question.

Breaking the supply master's neck was the sort of reaction that might provoke such questions.

So she turned, fully aware that he had her pinned between the wall and his incommodious bulk. The difference in their physiques was such that anyone entering through the single doorway would have seen only his back and not noticed her at all.

"Why so standoffish, Chela? I'm selling you everything you need at a discount. I'm not asking much in return. We don't get many visitors here as pretty as you. In fact, we don't get any visitors here as pretty as you. I've saved you a lot of money. I don't think a little kiss and cuddle are too much to ask in return."

"You haven't saved me any money." She spoke calmly, quietly. Without rancor, without raising her voice. "My company pays for everything."

He hesitated. "Well then, how about I take you to dinner? Not the central commissary. There are a couple of independent eating places here that cater to station personnel as well as visitors. I could use a change." He smiled broadly. She analyzed. He had nice teeth. They looked natural and not regenerated.

"I can provide a change," she murmured.

The smile widened. "That's more like it. Did you have anything, um, particular in mind? If not, I can suggest a few things."

Raising her right hand, she slid what appeared to be a small multitool up between their faces. Its dull gray finish was broken only by a pair of minuscule glowing red lights.

"This is a point-specific delayed-reaction thermolistic projector," she told him tranquilly. "With it I can start a fire at a distance, or so treat combustible materials that they will ignite at a predetermined time, or set a meal to cook for whenever I'm ready to eat. It programs the necessary molecular action in advance, and through a wide variety of intervening barriers. Food packaging, for example."

He shook his head as he frowned at the small, slim device. "Never seen one before."

She nodded once. "It's a fairly recent technological development. You'll note that during our preceding conversation, my hand was in my pocket. I was holding this. I assure you it's quite capable of boiling your testicles without damaging your scrotum."

As he stumbled backward, she moved away from the wall. The intrusive hand that had slid downward from her shoulder fell away as she gathered the gear she had purchased and made her way toward the entrance. A glance behind her just before she turned the first corner showed the supply master with his pants down around his ankles as he frantically examined himself. A very slight smile creased her pixieish face.

Who was it who said that the Qwarm had no sense of humor?

It wasn't rain and it wasn't fog. Heavy rain Flinx knew well from his sojourn on Midworld. This was different. Yes, there were periodic showers, but nothing like the tropical downpours of other worlds. When the sun did show itself, it was with a wan reluctance, as if it were putting in an appearance out of boredom, not to warm the world but to remind it that it did indeed still exist.

How Wiegl found his way northward through the alternating maze of dark forest, dense scrub, cold swamp, and turgid water Flinx did not know. Certainly having the high vantage point provided by the brund helped to find a route where at ground level none existed. As for the brund themselves, he was growing unexpectedly fond of his own mount. It having been delivered with no name, he had decided to call it Effsix. On a world where words were sung, a high note seemed appropriate for a high mount.

Secured to the inner portion of his saddle basket, his walking tube glistened with droplets that slid slowly down its silver side. Occasionally, a bright green head would pop out and take a quick survey of their surroundings before retreating back within. While the atmospheric moisture was to Pip's liking, the temperature was cooler than she preferred.

That did not prevent her from taking wing at least once every afternoon, when the languid sun had warmed the moist air enough to encourage her emergence. While there were flying creatures on Largess, they tended to be gliders more than fliers, leaping and soaring from one tall growth to another. Fringed membranes took the place of feathers, while bodies were narrow and long, the better to shed moisture while in flight. None of them could keep up with the hummingbird-like aerial acrobatics of the minidrag as Pip dipped and darted with equal alacrity around fliers large and small. When a creature the size of a condor armed with a curving, spike-tipped mouth struck at her, she did not even bother to strike back, so easy was it for her to dodge the clumsy attack.

There were plainly many reasons why Wiegl had chosen to employ brund for their travel. To be sure, their height and ridiculously long legs allowed for long-range vision forward, and their great stride permitted them to cross streams and ponds without so much as wetting their unique four-toed feet. But their primary advantage revealed itself the first time an inlet of one of Largess's many shallow seas blocked the way forward.

As the two brund stood awaiting a command, many of which Flinx had by now learned and could sing himself, he found himself staring out of the saddle wrappings into mist and fog that merged with slate-gray water. Save for almost-transparent five-centimeter-long *perleiths* that tiptoed on their dozen legs across the surface tension, searching for surface-swimming prey to impale with their downward-facing lancets, nothing disturbed the surface of the rocky cove. The water stretched as far to east and west as Flinx could see. It was much too wide for the brund to step across.

"Let us go, forward as usual, without wasting time, contemplating the scenery." Wiegl turned away from Flinx and prepared to engage his mount.

"Wait a minute." Flinx coughed, appropriately rephrased his query. "A moment pause, as the water is wide, the water is cold, and I do not see, a place in this water for even sturdy brund footing."

His wariness was confounded by the guide's melodious barking: Larian laughter. "The footing is there, though you do not see it, as sound as any, we have encountered already. Sounder even, than some we have traipsed through." With that he sang a single traditional modulated phrase. At the command, his mount obediently started forward.

Should he follow? Flinx wondered. Was his guide being reckless? Precedent suggested that was unlikely. Wiegl might be many things, including some as yet undiscovered, but he was nothing if not prudent. Echoing his command in a voice that was deeper, alien, but perfectly comprehensible, Flinx braced himself against leather belts, straps, and coarse fur as his own brund followed in the wake of Wiegl's. The tall quadruped immediately sank into the water.

But only halfway up its tall, jointed legs. As they continued to ford the passage, the inlet grew deeper. Deep enough for the increasingly pungent salt smell to bring a curious Pip out of her insulated tube to see what was happening, and almost deep enough for Flinx to feel the cold water against his backside through the leather netting that comprised his saddle. But even as he prepared to lift himself up, the water beneath him grew shallower and the chill engendered by its proximity to his butt fell away.

Emerging from the cove, both brund paused. Raising one leg at a time while balancing on the other three, they shook water from their five-meter-long limbs. Splayed four-toed feet rose to scratch at long legs, and then they were off again, pushing through or over the purplish scrub on the new bank. The deep wading, which the brund accomplished with ease, was a process that was to be repeated without incident several times over the next few days.

———

"Paid for in full, without too much haggling, did the pale offworlder, to my pleasure."

Voh stood outside the corral listening to the owner sing of his success. Unless the lands outside Borusegahm Leeth had suddenly become infested with solitary humans, she was on the right track. The fact that she was days behind her quarry did not trouble her. She would shrink the distance between them at her leisure.

That she was not traveling in the company of a local meant she would have to spend some time learning how to master a brund. A quick learner with ample experience of native transport on other worlds, she was confident she could do so. It only meant postponing the inevitable reckoning, not abandoning it. Meanwhile, she would tolerate the smell of the marketplace as she laid in additional supplies. Though she did not expect the chase to be a long way, she had no intention of racing off into the local hinterlands unprepared. Those who did so had no future in her organization.

Those who did so usually had no future, period.

Something equally as predatory but far larger and more dangerous than water-skimming *perleiths* roused Wiegl from his sleep.

Weary from the day's run and snug within his sleeping gear, Flinx would have slept on if not for the awakening flick of Pip's tongue and the anxious fanning of her wings against his face. Blinking as he sat up, he saw that Wiegl had emerged from his own sleep sack. Standing and facing the surrounding forest, with its slender-boled trees and thick brush and thornbushes, the guide was nervously surveying the darkness beyond the fire he had built earlier. Secured to trees off to his right, both brund were swaying uneasily from side to side, their heads turning from one direction to the next. In the absence of a flexible neck, they had to twist their entire bodies in order to see in a different direction.

In addition to his other, more esoteric abilities, Flinx had always been able to wake up quickly. That was a talent he had developed at an early age, occasionally having to sleep in the streets of Drallar. As soon as her master was alert, Pip folded her wings and slithered up onto his shoulder. That she did not return to the walking tube was significant. It suggested that there was something out in the darkness that likely presented a threat.

Letting his talent roam, he found it—in multiples. The emotions he perceived were primitive, voracious, and emphatically unintelligent.

Wiegl confirmed what Flinx was sensing. "Certain I am not yet, but leery I am, of rustling sounds in the deep brush, of scents familiar that I wish were otherwise." Taken together, sound and smell were enough to unsettle the guide.

"Chary I am of remaining here, in a place where noises and stinking grow worse, and their source fails to reveal itself. Late I know it is, and sleep is as necessary to my kind as to yours, for all we may differ in other ways." Turning, he started to fold up his own sleeping gear. "That said, move from this spot I think we should, and in as much haste as we can manage, without falling over ourselves."

Whereas on some other worlds Flinx would never have thought to leave an open fire burning, on Largess the small crackling blaze could cause no damage if it happened to reach for any of the surrounding moisture-drenched vegetation. Only a native tool, Wiegl's hand-dryer, had allowed them to make a fire in the first place. Now man and Larian hastily prepared to abandon their smoldering handiwork and comfortable campsite.

They were almost finished and ready to go when a hellacious whining the likes of which Flinx had never heard before rose from the surrounding forest. It and the primordial passions he now sensed caused the fine hair on the back of his neck to stand. Hissing explosively, Pip shot like a shell off his shoulder and into the night sky.

Exhibiting rising signs of panic, both squatting brund were fighting against their bonds as they struggled to straighten and stand. Dispensing with time-consuming straps and tie-downs, a frantic Wiegl was throwing supplies into the right-side saddle basket of his own mount, which had been modified to hold gear instead of a passenger. A concerned Flinx did his best to mimic the actions of his guide, his height compensating for the Larian's greater energy. Meanwhile Pip could be heard circling overhead, a hissing nebula of pink and blue blotting out small circles of stars.

Then the first *grynach* showed itself in the light of Largess's larger moon, and Flinx understood Wiegl's haste.

It wasn't a true howl that issued from the creature's long, narrow throat so much as a drawn-out, lingering moan. The reverberant, low-pitched whimper arose from somewhere deep within rapacious alien plumbing. Some four meters long, the flexible snakelike body advanced on a dozen clawed, webbed feet. These moved not in unison but in a singular flowing motion starting with the front pair of limbs, resulting in locomotion that resembled a centipede's more than that of a vertebrate animal. The snout itself was half a meter long and packed with triangular teeth that flashed in the moonlight: a full kitchen complement of slicing and dicing. Instead of hinged, bony jaws, the mouth more closely resembled a tooth-lined tube. Studying the remarkable maw, Flinx couldn't tell if the *grynach* bit into its prey or simply rasped it to death.

They had no visible eyes. Insofar as Flinx could tell, albeit with difficulty in the near darkness, they were as sightless as earthworms.

The *grynach* did not vacillate between moments of placidity and anger, indifference and carnivorous fury. When conscious, they existed in a state of permanent hunger. While their diurnal resting hours were uncomplicated by emotional discrepancies, as soon as they awoke beneath the twin moons they entered into a condition of unbridled aggression.

Pip, being as emotionally sensitive as her master but dwelling in a more primal state of being, had been able to sense and distinguish those finer aspects of *grynachian* feeling that Flinx had initially missed.

As he climbed hurriedly into the saddle basket of his own brund, he wondered how many more of the creatures had surrounded the campsite. The near-howling he was hearing did not arise from a single attenuated, constricted gullet. His answer soon revealed itself in the glow of the abandoned fire as the first predator's companions began to show themselves. He'd worried there might be several.

There were dozens.

As he echo-sang the commands he had learned in the course of the previous days' journeying, his mount straightened its long, long legs. It needed no urging to start forward on the literal heels of Wiegl's animal. Fleshy pink buzzsaws, *grynach* mouths contracted from plate-size to smaller openings as they snapped at the fleeing brund and their riders. Like the oars of ancient wooden galleys, short claw-tipped legs thrashed madly at the moist air as the creatures whipped around to pursue.

Had they been ambushed during the day, the two riders and their mounts might easily have avoided and outrun the many-legged but slower pack. In the middle of the night, however, Wiegl had to guide them onward with greater caution lest they stumble into impenetrable vegetation, or worse, trip over fallen trees or unseen rocks. An erect, healthy brund was difficult for any Largessian predator to bring down. One taken to ground, however, would struggle to get up. The *grynach* pack knew this as well as the brund themselves and the Larian who was directing them.

Even while allowing for extra caution in choosing a path forward, Flinx and Wiegl still managed to outdistance the majority of the whining, moaning multitude. A few of the writhing killers, unwilling to be deprived of such towering prey, had managed to use both their clawed legs and flexible bodies to coil themselves around the hind legs of the long-striding brund. Their circular mouths gnawed harmlessly at the elongated, hard-shelled legs. Given enough time, though, they might eventually crack and disable one or more of the hind limbs they were assailing. A brund could still walk on only three legs, but not well. It definitely could not run.

Disdaining to simply cripple its prey, one attacker had swarmed up the left hind leg of Flinx's mount, ascending the limb like a snake.

As stars wheeled wildly over his head while the brund's jerking, thrusting gallop threatened to send him flying out of his saddle, Flinx drew the Secun vibraknife from its concealed scabbard inside his belt and switched it on. Classed as low technology, it resembled its local bladed analogs near enough to permit its use in an emergency. While he would have preferred even the simplest Commonwealth-grade pistol, he prepared to defend himself with what he had against the ascending predator. In the absence of visible eyes to strike at, he was having a hard time trying to pinpoint a vulnerable area.

A flash of pink-and-blue wings, a low thrumming, and Pip appeared between him and the advancing tooth-lined mouth. Likewise accustomed to striking at the eyes of prey or enemy, she hesitated. Only when the *grynach* had climbed high enough for Flinx to feel the crispy staleness of its breath on his own skin did she finally spit. At the same time, he slashed out and downward with the activated vibraknife. Its steady, powered hum offered reassurance in the dim moonlight. His awkward strike failed to make contact as the tooth-lined snout drew back. Pip, on the other hand, did not miss.

With no eyes to aim at, her venom struck the *grynach* on the dorsal portion of its head. For all Flinx knew, it was fighting in an upside-down position and its light-sensing organs, assuming it had any, were located on the opposite side from where the minidrag had struck. While no vital organs might have been hit, however, the potent venom still inflicted plenty of damage. Being corrosive as well as toxic, it immediately began to eat into the smooth, hairless flesh of the *grynach*'s head.

Pairs of gripping legs began to give away one after another, rippling down between the predator and the brund's leg like an oversized zipper. Flailing at the air, the *grynach* fell away from Flinx, his mount, and the long hard-sided limb it had ascended. Falling to the ground, the carnivore rolled and contorted in pain as smoke continued to rise from the dissolving flesh of its head.

Clinging to the broad foot of the same brund, a second *grynach* started climbing upward, following the path of its mortally wounded predecessor. Gripping the vibraknife tightly, Flinx prepared to meet this second killer as a hissing Pip hovered above his right shoulder.

Now menaced by half a dozen of the biting, gnawing predators but having left the preponderance of the pack well behind, the two brund showed they'd had enough. They did this through exercising the simple but heretofore unsuspected defensive expedient of flexing the muscles in their long legs. The rough edges that Flinx had initially assumed were vestigial feathers or pebbly scales snapped out and flared wide simultaneously. They did indeed look like large, individual feathers. Except that each one was composed of hard, toughened skin as sharp along the edge as any sword.

It was as if each brund had suddenly deployed a hundred scimitars from its lower legs. They sliced into the ascending *grynach* like so many butcher knives, producing a hundred deep cuts in scarcely an instant. Whimpering and moaning, the climbing predators dropped off the legs of the two brund like lice, slamming into the ground in stringy piles of flesh and blood.

To be safe, the brund sustained this inimitable protective posture for the next fifteen minutes or so, until Wiegl was certain they had left the last of the discouraged *grynach* far behind. Well equipped for ambush-hunting but not long-distance pursuit, they would return to their communal den entwined together for safety, and moan their collective disappointment at the twin moons.

"I did not know," Flinx called across to his guide, "that the good-natured brund, were capable, of such admirable carving." Not as confident as either her master or his guide, or perhaps simply more circumspect, Pip continued to pace them overhead, not returning to her comfortable tube until the night mist had morphed into a chilly drizzle.

"Full of surprises, are many lifeforms of Largess," Wiegl called back to the human, his fear disappearing as he sang, "as you will hopefully learn, if you live long enough, if you see long enough."

Flinx returned his gaze forward. The forest was giving way to another stretch of brooding bare rock that sported only isolated thickets of local brush. *No place for an ambush here,* he told himself, although remembering his time on other worlds caused him to qualify that appraisal. As Wiegl had just hinted, any alien world could give rise to predators that dwelled in surprising guises.

Hopefully they would meet no more tonight, he reflected tiredly as both brund splashed into the shallow stream that separated the predator-infested forest behind them from the safer ground ahead. Acclimated by now as he was to the jerking forward-back gait of the brund, he had not yet tried sleeping in the saddle basket. With several hours remaining until Largess's star appeared as a dim yellowish smudge in the cloud-smothered sky, he thought this night would be an excellent time to try.

"How far behind, do you think we are, from the strideship crew, that may have taken the Firstborn?"

Wiegl did not hesitate. "Impossible to tell, from our current position, as no signs have I recently noticed, of a strideship's passing." He waved encouragingly. "Do not worry, my offworlder friend, as there will come a moment, when such evidence presents itself, when such signs are forthcoming. Then we will close, on the source of your seeking, and then you may freely worry, all that you can."

Flinx considered. Wiegl was telling the truth, as best he could discern it. Or else he was lying, as best he could manage it. At the moment he was too tired to try to parse the guide's feelings. Too tired to do much of anything except assure himself that Pip was safe and unharmed. Twisting in the saddle as he fiddled with the harness straps, he struggled to find a comfortable yet secure position. The last thing he wanted was to be bounced out of the basket in the middle of the night. Whether he finally succeeded or not he did not know, because within minutes he was sound asleep.

9

■ ■ ■

Vashon had never counted on good luck to preserve him. He did not believe in luck, good or otherwise. He believed in preparation, staying one step ahead of competition or pursuit, and in the efficacy of high-energy and large-caliber weapons.

That did not diminish his gratitude to the Fates for the lifting of the mist so that he and his Larian crew were able to spot the oncoming strideship well before it was able to slip up on them unseen. The ancient art of the lookout was one practiced on many worlds, by many species with variable visual acuity and differing means of perception. There was nothing special or remarkable about the eyesight of the inhabitants of Largess except for their ability to see as well underwater as above it.

The latter capability might become necessary if things did not go well.

The closing strideship was approaching with the wind and at an angle designed to intercept the Minordian vessel before it could make landfall. Having seen to defensive preparations, Zkerig came up on the offworlder's right side. Vashon murmured thoughtfully to the Tralltag.

"Possibly they come to talk, to parley peacefully, to discuss matters of mutual interest, without aggression." Though both his singing tone and words expressed hope, he did not much believe his own improvised lyrics.

Holding up a spyglass that was larger in diameter than ancient human equivalents, Zkerig was quick to confirm the human's pessimism. "Potential friends do not, on deck freely mass weapons, and prepare loads for cannon, the better to send friendly greetings. A cheery wave of webbings, with fingers spread wide, would better signify the hope of pleasantries, would better acknowledge potential friendship." Needing both hands to steady the heavy brass spyglass, the Tralltag again examined the oncoming vessel. "Larger than ours is their crew, greater in number and in blades. Of cannon I see seven, three to one side and three to the other, with a single barrel mounted forward, I suspect soon to offer greetings."

Nodding to his left and forward, a concerned Vashon indicated the far shore. "Can we outsail them and then outrun them, as it is prudent to flee instead of fight, where our objective is not triumph, but to reach Minord's sheltering height?"

Zkerig lowered the glass. "Their ship is fast and the wind is with them; the wind that betrays our best intentions, the wind that now hinders instead of helping, the wind that as well blow up your arse, as do it now any good for us." Turning, he sang out commands. The strideship's lateen-rigged sails were adjusted accordingly and they gained a little speed. Whether it would be enough to allow them to beat the other vessel to shore remained to be seen.

The fast-closing strideship flew no flag. Not that its origin mattered. Did its crew know of the presence on board their target of the Firstborn of Borusegahm Leeth? If this was a ship whose crew was intent on rescue, Vashon told himself, surely they would by now have shown the symbols of Borusegahm, even if they were lowly allies and not representatives of the Leeth itself. If, on the other hand, they were no more than simple brigands, many of whom were known to wander the land- and waterscapes of Largess, they were exceptionally well equipped. That suggested they were amply financed by unknown sources. Or worse, that they were very good at their business.

Certainly their seamanship seemed to suggest the latter. But by alternating raging at and cajoling his crew of soldier-sailors, Zkerig succeeded in accomplishing the seemingly impossible: they nudged into the shallows just ahead of their fast-closing assailant. A single blast from the pursuing strideship's bow cannon sent an ingot of solid shot whizzing over the aft deck. Vashon heard it as it flew past. It did no damage but revealed that they were now within range of and exposed to cannon fire.

Standing amidships, Zkerig sang an order down through a grating toward the lowest deck. There were three decks on the strideship: the upper, on which Vashon was standing; the middle, where the crew lived; and the lowermost. Below water when at sail, the lowest deck now became the center of activity as half the crew rushed to take up positions at their assigned pedal stations.

"Feet!" Zkerig uttered the command a touch unmelodiously but with impressive volume.

Seated far below, twenty-four Larians put their short but powerful legs and strong lower backs to work pumping pedals in unison. Their strength, multiplied by an intricate network of brass gears and chains, propelled the dozen mechanical legs that had heretofore been tucked up against the hull of the strideship. Made of *garulag* wood and braced with brass fittings, they were impervious to rot, stronger than many metal alloys, and difficult to hew. Once cut and shaped, they could remain immersed in the cold of Largess's fresh and salt water without damage.

No matter how tight the elastic rubber-like seals that encircled the legs at the points where they entered the hull, some water inevitably entered and needed to be pumped out. Now, as the strideship's dozen legs and feet were put to work, these seals flexed and admitted still more water. Hand pumps kept the intrusion at bay, while the water did not affect the ongoing efforts of the semiaquatic Larians in the slightest.

On the upper deck, Vashon had to grab at a railing to steady himself as the strideship rose up out of the shallows. As the directions of
the ship's navigator were relayed to the pedalers below, they responded accordingly. This enabled the ship, now walking out onto
the shelf of black schist before it, to turn left or right as required. As
the amphibious vessel headed inland and away from the inlet, its
dozen *garulag* legs and circular feet shed water, vegetation, and
aquatic arthropods frantic to make it back to the safety of the dark
green water before their presence was discovered by land-dwelling
carnivores.

Having likewise deployed its own legs, their pursuer emerged on
shore slightly behind and to the right of Vashon's craft. It was now
close enough for him to clearly see without the aid of a spyglass that
its upper deck was packed with heavily armed natives. They wielded
swords, spears, single-shot pistols, and something like a cross between an arquebus and a slingshot that could fire spheres of lit gun-
powder packed with metal shards: a kind of crude grenade and
launcher. Several of these came flying toward him and he ducked.
Most exploded noisily but harmlessly in the air, their fuses mis-
timed. One did land on deck and started a small fire that was quickly
snuffed out by an alert member of Zkerig's crew. Another struck a
soldier on the shoulder, tumbled down his front, and blew off two of
his fingers as he tried to fling it away.

As the attacking strideship came lurching toward them, Zkerig
called for a quick maneuver that threw his own vessel into reverse. It
was a dangerous tactic, as it subjected the unsophisticated brass
gearing to exceptional stress. Below, a pair of linked-together crew
members had to throw themselves out of the way as one of the chains
working the leg they powered snapped, sending links and bits of
metal flying. The strideship's two mechanics set to work making re-
pairs, but for the moment at least, one of their dozen legs was now
out of action.

It proved a worthwhile ploy, however. Caught by surprise and unable to reverse direction in time to match that of their quarry, their

attacker started to slow—but not fast enough. As Zkerig's ship started backward, the aggressor ran past it. Both sides exchanged individual cannon fire, there apparently being no Larian equivalent of a coordinated broadside. The cannons were small in size, light in weight, and hard-pressed to do any real damage. Even so, wood and some bone were shattered on both sides.

As the enemy strove to regroup, Zkerig's strideship, now behind its attacker, executed a quick right turn. This brought it behind the enemy, allowing each of its guns to blast away unimpeded and at close range at the stern of the other craft. Destroying its rudder would render it helpless on the water—except they weren't on the water. On land, a strideship's rudder meant nothing, did nothing, was clamped down and not used.

Vashon finally understood the Tralltag's strategy. Initially looking as if they were trying to flee via land, they now found themselves *behind* their assailant. Sure enough, as soon as his cannon had made a hash of the other craft's in-water steering gear, Zkerig ordered them back toward the inlet from which they had just emerged. Their attacker could follow them into the water, but by doing so, in the absence of a usable rudder and therefore unable to steer, the other ship would only be placing its crew in grave danger.

Infuriated and frustrated, their assailants could only hurl insults and the occasional grenade in their prey's direction as they fought to turn their own vessel around. The articulation of the multiple *garu-lag* legs on both ships was simple and effective, but not especially responsive. As it came around, the pursuer fired its cannon at Zkerig's retreating vessel in an attempt to replicate the damage that had been done to its own stern. While gazing aft and watching their foe's gunners at work, the Tralltag was ready for the blast. At the critical moment, when the attacking gunners prepared to light their weapons, he sang out a command, but it took the attentive Vashon a moment to clarify its meaning.

Duck.

Three wedges of solid metal shot went screaming over the strideship's deck as her pedal crew, responding to Zkerig's command, caused the legs they were powering to retract back up against the strideship's hull. The abrupt squat of some four meters caused the cannon fire from the attackers to pass harmlessly overhead. Furiously working control wheels, the strideship's mechanics then brought it back up onto its feet and it resumed its fully coordinated march back toward the inlet.

Unwilling to surrender a potential prize to better tactics, the pursuing craft resumed the chase. Whoever was driving her legs possessed the stamina of one of Largess's long-range swimmers, Vashon thought as he watched the other strideship once again close on its target. Or else someone on her lower deck was threatening what must be a tired crew with the Larian equivalent of fire and perdition.

When its bow cannon fired again, this time it punched a hole in the stern of Zkerig's craft. Fortunately it missed the strideship's steering gear. A second shot might not, rendering them as helpless on the water as their relentless pursuer.

Up until now Vashon had put off taking any direct action of his own, content to leave the conduct of the battle to the eminently qualified Tralltag. But having no interest in seeing, much less participating in, a pitched hand-to-hand battle on deck and fully aware that a fused grenade or chunk of metal shot, however primitive, could kill him as effectively as the most modern weapon, he decided that he had no choice but to finally intervene.

Carefully negotiating the steps, which were placed closer to one another than they would have been in a staircase designed to accommodate longer human legs, he made his way down to the second deck and toward his private cabin. In the course of descending, he happened to pass the place where the most recent enemy cannon fire had blown not only a small hole in an interior wall but a larger one in the hull of the ship. A figure could be seen silhouetted in the opening, working to lower a line made of bed webbing that had been cut into pieces and retied to make a long rope. Diverted by the sight, he quickly changed course and entered the room.

Preedir ah nisa Leeh, Firstborn of the Hobak of Borusegahm Leeth, looked back at him and snarled. It was a characteristically tuneful Larian sound, but a snarl nonetheless. "Go and fight, if fight you can, otherworld interloper, devoid of fur. Go and leave me to this, for it is none of your business, as you have nothing to do, with me or with mine."

He smiled tightly, though aware the expression would mean nothing to her. "Sweetly sung but wrongly phrased, Firstborn of Borusegahm, who I am afraid, I must insist remain awhile, and stay in my company, a bit longer still." He started toward her.

Iridescent gold and crimson flashed as her neck ruff flared. Whirling, she confronted him with a twenty-centimeter-long shard of thick, sharp glass, the bottom half of which was wrapped in fabric to form a protective handle. The Larians made excellent glass, and she had improvised the knife to cut the bed webbing with which to weave her intended escape rope.

"Come closer then, human troublemaker, so that I can sing with you, a duet to the death."

He halted immediately. On the deck above he could hear the roar of cannon fire and the occasional sharp report of a grenade or pistol going off. Through the gap in the shattered wood behind her, he could see the pursuing strideship continuing to close on his own craft, its bow crowded with explosive-flinging marksmen and as ferocious an assortment of natives as he had yet seen on this world.

"There is nothing to be gained," he sang back evenly, "by leaping from this ship, as surely you will be crunched, beneath its feet or theirs, beneath our *garulag* or others."

Dark slanted eyes met his own smaller, rounder orbs. "Better to die trying, than to become a hostage, to a mad Hobak, who swills ignorance, and works against union."

With a sigh, Vashon rolled his eyes ceilingward. As intended, this drew a fascinated Preedir's unintended attention. While Larian eyes were larger and more elongated than those of any human, they did not have as great a range of motion within their sockets.

Bringing his right hand sharply forward, Vashon threw the lump of wood he had surreptitiously lifted from a nearby damaged piece of furniture. It did not strike the Firstborn in the forehead, as he had intended. Instead, it glanced off the top of her skull just to one side of her left ear. Still, it was enough to stagger her.

Rushing forward, he clamped his left hand around the wrist holding the makeshift knife and brought his right knee up toward her midsection. Her upper torso and body below the waist did not move, but the entire middle portion simply curved to one side, causing his blow to miss. Lunging at him, she tried to bite his face, but her neck was too short to close the distance. Muscular and wiry, she was an evasive opponent, on top of which he had to concentrate on keeping the hand holding the makeshift knife away from him. If he let it slip free, he knew she would go for his throat. The Larians always went for the throat.

The repeated kicks of her short legs and leather-sleeved feet he was able to avoid. While she could not strike or bite him, neither could he let go of either of her arms to hit back at her. In any case he did not want to do anything that might cause serious injury. A damaged hostage was one with reduced value. Besides which, his employer, his magnificence Felelagh na Broon, would be displeased. So they continued to wrestle, human and Larian, each seeking an opening through which to incapacitate the other.

The stalemate was not to Vashon's advantage. The longer he kept her on the strideship, the less chance she had of escaping. He weighed more than she did, but Larians were tireless. Unless he could put her down and pin her to the deck, she would eventually wear him out.

His endurance was nearly at an end when two soldiers inspecting the damaged stern of the ship happened by, peered into the room, saw what was happening, and immediately lent their energy to his. Together they subdued her. Where previously she'd had the run of the vessel, now an exhausted Vashon saw to it that she was bound: long arms tied behind her at the elbows as well as at the wrists, legs linked, and the powerful short, thick tail secured to her ankles.

"A temporary inconvenience, I hope you will appreciate," he sang in a wheeze when the soldiers had finished applying the restraints, "to ensure we are not deprived, of your most entertaining company."

Realizing it was futile to struggle against her multiple bonds, she chose instead to sing back at him deliberately off-key. The grave Larian insult had no effect on him, but the pair of soldiers winced at the sharpness of it.

"One day it will be my pleasure, if the moons and the stars will align, to send you away and onward to your own world, in as many pieces as possible, after inflicting pain sublime."

"You do me honor," he replied, more flattered than frightened by the threat, "to treat me as one of your own, regardless of our differences, regardless of the situation."

He left her in the care of the two soldiers, whom he made promise not to take their eyes off her even if she was tightly restrained. Her voice followed him out into the passageway and trailed him as he resumed his interrupted route to his own cabin. It was the kind of singspeech one might expect from someone who was part bare-hands fighter and the rest a natural coloratura: imaginative insults and vivid swearing swathed in perfect melody.

While he had been busy foiling her escape, the pursuing stride-ship had closed almost to within grappling range of Zkerig's craft. Skillful as the Tralltag was, he could not keep dodging forever. If the two vessels became linked, either by rope, hooks, or an entanglement of pistoning *garulag* legs, Zkerig and his soldier-sailors could very likely be overwhelmed. As an offworlder, Vashon might sing his way out of involuntary esophageal surgery, but he would at the least find himself enslaved or marooned in this northern portion of the continent. Indifferent to or ignorant of Commonwealth strictures regarding the proscribed introduction of advanced technology into Larian society, the attackers would happily confiscate all his goods, leaving him at best isolated and helpless.

Therefore, since they were bent on appropriating his property, it might prove useful to give them a preliminary demonstration.

There were no Commonwealth representatives present to observe what he was going to do. His intentions were not only highly illegal, they constituted a list of sufficiently serious infractions that at least partial mindwiping would be in order for the perpetrator—were he to be caught. However, no citizens of the Commonwealth were around to register as witnesses. He doubted Zkerig would report him.

He had brought two pistols with him, smuggled with considerable difficulty beyond the station's boundaries. One was the neuronic pistol that he had already demonstrated for, and on, the Tralltag. The other he had flashed but had not found a sufficiently serious reason to actually use. That situation was now at hand. Although the weapon could hold three of its thumb-sized rounds, he loaded only one of the half dozen he had been able to bring with him. If something happened to him, better that a Larian not be able to make use of it.

His hurried return to the upper deck was greeted with smoke from small fires. These had been set by flung grenades and were in the process of being extinguished by Zkerig's crew even as more hissed by overhead or landed on the ground on either side of the retreating strideship. He found Zkerig standing at the stern railing, directing return fire from his own troops. Fortunately, the loading of a primitive Larian cannon took some time. That meant subsequent attempts by their pursuers to blast their stern and disable their own water-steering gear continued to miss their mark.

But eventually, Vashon knew, they would figure out how to predict when Vashon planned to zig to their zag. Or simple averages would result in a crippling hit. If the strideship he was on was rendered just as incapable of steering on the water as they had made their enemy, there would be no point in trying to beat their assailants back to the inlet. They would still end up in hand-to-hand combat, to the likely detriment of the crew from Minord.

Though occupied with directing the battle, and the dipping and dodging of his ship as it continued its desperate retreat toward the water, Zkerig was sufficiently captivated by the sight of the weapon in the human's hand to divert his attention. The glistening, smooth-sided pistol was the same color as his eyes.

"A weapon by its looks, though different from your other, which by this one's appearance, I assume acts differently." While the Tralltag's words expressed a simple appraisal, the melody he employed could not camouflage his greed.

That did not trouble Vashon. He knew Zkerig for what he was, and vice versa. Such mutual understanding of cross-species motivations promoted, if not friendship, then respect.

"You're right." Vashon confirmed the Tralltag's suspicions while disdaining the use of proper singspeech. He had no time to waste on semantic reassurances. Holding the pistol's grip in his right hand, he steadied his left elbow on the railing, closed his left eye, and squinted through the smoke from all the crude, sputtering grenades.

Zkerig frowned. "I am not sure I understand, for your words are brusque and your harmony absent, and such crudeness makes comprehension difficult."

"Screw it, if you can understand that." Unable to converse with anyone in his native terranglo, there were times when Vashon simply grew tired of singspeech. "Our hostage tried to escape. I stopped her. You might want to double the guard on her, no matter the circumstances and around the clock." While a perplexed Zkerig struggled to make sense of the human's clashing, unwieldy words, Vashon steadied his aim. "From her vocabulary 'meek' is absent, and I would not sleep, within her presence, where any vital body parts, might lie within her reach. Tuneful enough for you, is that image, of vengeance deployed, of crude disembowelment?" He fired.

Despite the pistol's advanced design there was still some minor recoil, for which he had prepared himself. The noise the gun made was proportionate to its modest size. Its consequences were not.

The chemistry behind the small projectile's compact warhead represented the end product of several thousand years of his species' experimentation with explosive compounds. It struck the bow of the pursuing craft and detonated. Prepared for the consequences, Vashon had closed his eyes and turned his head away. The report of the explosion hurt his ears. Though their hearing was not quite as sensitive as that of a human, the blast's volume had a profound effect on Zkerig's hard-pressed soldiers. Many of them were stunned into momentary immobility.

That was considerably less damaging than the effect Vashon's single shot had on the crew of their pursuer. As smoke cleared and those troops in the vicinity of the stern of the Minord strideship regained their composure and their hearing, they could see that the attacking vessel had collapsed bow-first into the hard ground. Joints had cracked, braces given way, and wood splintered. The entire front of the craft had been blown apart. A plethora of scattered body parts from multiple shattered corpses decorated the devastated remnants. Zkerig's crew was simultaneously elated and horrified. Sharply angled black eyes turned toward the offworlder and the weapon he held: a weapon smaller than their grenade slingshots or pistols that was capable of wreaking ten, a hundred times as much destruction, and with little apparent effort.

As their pursuer struggled to recover those survivors of the blast who could still stand, Vashon's craft began to put considerable distance between itself and the would-be coterie of assassins. In a short while they were back in the inlet. Legs were shipped and folded up against the bottom of the hull, and their exhausted manipulators returned to topside duty. When confined to the third, lowermost deck, they had been able to hear but not see what had happened; now they anxiously queried their shipmates as they rejoined them. Many sideways glances accompanied by much gravitas-laden sing-speaking were cast in Vashon's direction.

He nodded contentedly to himself. In such situations, fear was always a useful ancillary reaction. Zkerig had experienced firsthand what a neuronic pistol could do. Now he and his entire crew had been witness to the potential of a much more powerful weapon. Let them all wonder what other surprises the human might keep in his locked carry bag. Vashon smiled. After this most recent demonstration of advanced Commonwealth technology, he could probably wave a stick in their direction and send them all fleeing in panic.

Except for Zkerig. As he had from their first meeting, Vashon knew he would have to keep a close watch on the Tralltag. There was always the chance that Zkerig's ambitions might exceed his good sense. Even though the Tralltag did not know how to operate either of the weapons Vashon had utilized, the master of the strideship might one day just decide to take a chance on stealing one or the other in the hope that in time he could work out their method of operation.

Yes, Vashon would definitely keep a steady eye on his Larian counterpart. Also on Preedir the Firstborn of Borusegahm, who if given the slightest chance would need no advanced weapon to cut both their throats. He would be relieved to reach the Leeth and be rid of her. Turn her over to the shrewd but slightly addled Hobak and let him deal with her. Vashon would reap the benefits of his efforts in the form of extremely valuable native organics. Shipping them offworld and collecting payment was less difficult than dealing with potentially treacherous allies and hostile locals.

As they raised sail and started up the inlet with the wind behind them, there was no sign of pursuit. Their attackers could have abandoned their ruined craft and tried to pursue on foot, tracking the strideship's progress from shore, but that would swiftly grow tiring, and with no reasonable chance of success. No, they would tend to their wounded, sink their dead in the nearest appropriate body of still water, and commence a dejected march back to wherever they called home, taking with them no booty but only tales of a battle lost due to the horrific destruction wrought by an offworld weapon. This far north of the station, Vashon was not worried about such stories reaching the Commonwealth authorities there. His breach of the law would go unreported to any who mattered.

He grew aware that Zkerig was standing close by but not singing. Instead, the Tralltag was eyeing him respectfully, unwilling to interrupt the human's contemplation. *Good,* Vashon thought. Zkerig had been a bit argumentative of late. Now their respective status had undergone a useful readjustment. When the Tralltag finally spoke, his melody was almost fawning.

"May I, with your permission, hold the device, that wrought such destruction, that saved us from calamity?"

Vashon nodded benignly as he passed the pistol to the Tralltag. Having established his superiority, he could afford to be gracious. Zkerig handled the gun like the professional he was: carefully but not delicately, quite rightly assuming it would not fall apart or go off in his hands. One finger slid into the trigger. Due to the presence of the membranous web that linked Larian fingers and toes and allowed them to rocket through water as if they owned it, the Tralltag could only slip his finger into the trigger as far as the first phalanx. Furthermore, although the first and third finger were fully opposable, the Larians lacked a true thumb. Zkerig could have fired the pistol, but with difficulty.

He handed it back, reverently. "With a dozen of these, could we with little effort, establish dominion, over the entirety of the Northlands."

"I think your Hobak, with only personal explosions, hopes to do so, beginning with the Firstborn, and using her for leverage. Politics, too, can overwhelm, as effectively and less messily, than explosives or cannon, if properly wielded."

He left Zkerig with that thought, with the feel of the high-tech pistol still cool and promising in the Tralltag's hand. Retiring below deck, Vashon was hopeful that the remainder of their return journey to Minord would conclude in a more direct and less irksome fashion.

Bending forward sharply, Flinx clasped both hands to the sides of his head. Eyes shut tight, he fought as he had fought dozens of times over the course of the preceding years not to grit his teeth so tightly as to damage them. Though he had undergone it successfully before, orthodontic regeneration was a process he preferred to avoid. It was time-consuming, frustrating at mealtime, and left one looking stupid until the regrowth was complete.

Since the human had not made a sound, Wiegl had not initially noticed his companion's distress. Now the Larian looked over in alarm from his own saddle as both brund strode steadily northward.

"Flinx, my friend, I see you are in pain, though from what source I cannot tell! Command me, whatever I may do, to help alleviate, the cause of your suffering." The melody he had chosen expressed more than a modicum of concern, and it was underscored by the genuine emotion he was projecting.

Flinx lifted his head, blinked, lowered one hand to offer Pip a reassuring caress, and took several long, steady, deep breaths. Gradually the pain at the back of his skull faded from a searing flame to mere steady throbbing. He swallowed. Though he hadn't had an attack like this in a long time, he thought he knew the reason why he was having one now.

Away from cities and developed worlds, in empty places like the forests and moors of Largess, he could allow his talent to roam freely and widely, safe in the realization that any robustly generated emotions were likely to be few and far between. He could test his sensitivity safely. That was why what he had just experienced had been so overwhelming. Such a focused, sharp, collective fracturing of desperate feeling hinted at multiple lives snuffed out all at once. It had come and gone in a single unified burst of pain and suffering. He took a last deep breath.

In the midst of it all, and actively engaged in the conflict, had been a hint of something other than Larian. Given their present distance from the Commonwealth station, such an abnormality could arise only from one possible source.

"I am okay, friend Wiegl, but give thanks anyway, for your honest concern." Raising a hand, he pointed slightly to the left of their current course. "That way we should go now, in pursuit of our goal, but more cautiously than ever, lest we surprise ourselves and not just our quarry."

Wiegl was visibly confused. "How do you, such things know, such things sense, without seeing, without hearing?"

"My small ability," Flinx sang back softly, "that I did not ask for, but which manifests itself without asking, nonetheless. Many things can I follow, if I but try, like a fisherman casting a net, though sometimes it comes back empty, and other times too full."

"What this time," a patently fascinated Wiegl asked, "have you caught, in this strange net, of your mind's casting?"

"Death," Flinx told him, without harmony and devoid of the usual Larian melodic embroidery.

It did not matter. The one-word reply might have been fraught with alien overtones, but Wiegl managed to comprehend it well enough. He wished he had not, he mused uneasily as he sang the direction-change command to his mount. In response, both his brund and that of his human companion turned northwestward as one.

10

∎∎∎

Poskraine was the name of the small town where they opted to stop for the night. Having deduced from his painful experience earlier in the day that the individual he sought was now close at hand, Flinx would have opted to continue the pursuit without stopping in hopes of possibly catching up to him. Wiegl was adamantly opposed.

"Can run for days without stopping, can the brund, and on low rations, and at steady pace. But at night-seeing, they are not so good, and to be saddled in a brund, that falls, from that height, can be a journey-ending experience."

Locating a human emotional signature among so much Larian fury and death had been as disconcerting as it was painful, but though his head still hurt, it was not sufficient to turn Flinx from the task that had been set to him by Sylzenzuzex. Once he committed himself, he never backed away from a challenge.

What was a recognizable if distant set of roiling human emotions doing all but submerged in a sea of churning, fevered Larian feelings involving life and death? Was the abducted Firstborn of Hobak directly involved? If she had been caught up in the surfeit of violence he had sensed and had perished as a consequence, then all of his study and travel, from Cachalot all the way to this backward part of Largess, would have been for naught. Having never met the First-born, Flinx had no way of identifying her emotional signature. And even if he had correctly located a human who might well be the one who was the subject of Church interest, that did not mean the Firstborn Preedir was with him, or that she was even in the general vicinity.

However, based on what Padre Jonas had told him, if he could find the offworlder who was aiding Larians with advanced tech, the chances were good that he would also find the kidnapped Firstborn. Having proceeded from the start on that assumption, Flinx felt he had no choice at this point but to continue to do so.

But not tonight. Now that he had dismounted and descended to the ground from the perpetually jostling brundian heights, he became aware of how tired he was. While his empathetic ability could reach effortlessly across modest distances, his body was restricted to that portion of him that was centered on his pelvis. Right now, said center and associated parts were sore and worn, in addition to which he was hungry. The dried food that provided sustenance while he and Wiegl were on the move kept them alive but little more. And the largely seafood-based (even if it came out of an alien sea) fare that made up the normal Larian diet had proven itself perfectly palatable, if not particularly flavorsome. It reminded him of Cachalot, and home.

All thoughts of Cachalot's tropical seas vanished as the sun set and the atmosphere once more grew chilly as well as damp. Notwithstanding that it was home to a largely engaging intelligent race as well as to the usual abundance of natively evolved species, the first life-form that came to mind now when he thought of the local ecology was the Largessian equivalent of mold. He was sure some of it was beginning to form on his backside as he followed Wiegl toward the way station.

Additional proof that few offworlders made it this far from

Borusegahm was not necessary, but it was provided anyway in the form of the dark-eyed stares that greeted him as he entered the stone-and-wood structure in Wiegl's wake. Ignoring the guide, they focused on him as the eclectic pair made their way to a corner booth. Conversation did not cease and webbed hands greasy with food did not cease their scooping, but Flinx was well aware that he was the subject of numerous stares. The emotions he detected were thick with curiosity interspersed with isolated flare-ups of mild hostility.

Wiegl seemed to enjoy the attention that was directed their way. It was widely believed that those Larians who managed to ingratiate themselves with offworlders, of any species, often acquired opportunities to prosper that were denied to those who could not. Though much in the way of the transfer of goods and technology was proscribed, knowledge was not, and could also prove valuable. Flinx had no doubt that Wiegl was the subject of much speculation and envy on the part of his fellow Larians.

Gently, Flinx leaned his walking tube up against the back wall that closed off one side of the booth. There was no movement from within. Unlike a human, Pip was either frenetically active or sound asleep. He reminded himself to make sure to take away something for her to eat. Her unusual metabolism ensured that the meals she took were modest but frequent.

As he and Wiegl chatted and it became evident to everyone else in the establishment that the round-eyed, fur-deprived, digit-heavy offworlder could engage in ordinary speech, the initially intrigued onlookers returned to their own meals and conversation. Thirty minutes later there was no indication in the room that a representative of an alien species from a distant world was sharing their space. While none of those present had personally had contact with humans, news and hearsay had spoken of them often. Flinx's presence soon devolved from revelation to the more mundane status of novelty.

He and Wiegl were halfway through a perfectly satisfactory meal when one of the other diners proved bold enough to leave his own table and approach them, slapping his tail against his legs by way of deferential greeting.

"The pearlescence of a thousand *tenalgs* blind me, for the impertinence I display, in disturbing your meal, in interrupting your talk, in hopes of learning, one iota of information. I, poor Ibatogh, seek only enlightenment, wherever it may be found."

Wiegl was instantly on guard. In contrast, a curious Flinx regarded the petitioner with quiet interest. Within her tube Pip remained still. Flinx detected nothing about the stranger that hinted of hostility, and singular talent aside, he could plainly see that the individual who had displayed more boldness than any of his fellows carried no visible weapons. Perhaps more significantly, consuming the meaty corpses of several unidentified sea creatures that resembled a crescent of demented scallops had proven to have an unexpected narcotic effect. Feeling better, notably better, than he had in days, Flinx was in a mood to be welcoming. Indeed, to be downright generous. He felt that his carefully composed harmonious reply employed an especially sweet progression of notes.

"Do you know where I am from, do you know the home that's mine? A world of more water than even Largess, where the sun shines warmly, allowing one to go, without heavy covering. My second home, I have to confess, in addition to another, that is very different. The first has a wing, the second a glow, the others I have seen, every one is almost as beautiful." He was waving his hands now, unaware that half the room was watching him in amusement while the other half studiously ignored his offworlder antics. Only Wiegl eyed him worriedly, wondering what the suddenly strangely empowered and just plain strange human might do next.

"Many are the worlds on which I have trod." Flinx sang on, while within her tube Pip stirred slightly in confusion at her sudden inability to correctly interpret her master's emotions. "And many are the beings whom I have met. Thranx and AAnn, they are but two, and like too many others, inclined to cut one another's throats." He was feeling decidedly woozy now, but it didn't seem to affect his sing-speech. "To cut a thranx throat requires a vibraknife, or something extra sharp, as their exoskeletons are tough, and their resistance dexterous." He waved an unsteady hand in their visitor's direction.

"Ask away, ask away, ask whatever, you may say. And I will try, as best I can, to read the runes, and quick reply."

His singspeaking was definitely improving, Flinx told himself confidently. More melodic with each try, more intuitive, more natural sounding. He hoped the Larians in his vicinity appreciated his efforts.

Certainly the unremarkable specimen who had made so bold as to approach the offworlder thought so, because he launched a query without further hesitation.

"I would know, visitor from another world, visitor from the darkling sky: what would bring one, such as yourself, so far north, and away from your station, away from familiar comforts? I ask only out of, my personal curiosity, and only to satisfy, my personal interest—in such things," he concluded on an awkward note.

Flinx paid the poorly sung coda no more heed than he did Wiegl's subdued but anxious three-fingered semaphoring. "Curiosity brings me, as it is all I have left, to drive me to seek out, other worlds than mine."

Hiding his satisfaction, Wiegl now relaxed. It did not seem to matter what state of mind dominated the thinking of his alien human companion. It was apparent that the five-fingered furless one could keep his wits about him whether addled or coherent. He had answered the questioner with a harmless generality while at the same time revealing nothing.

That intrusive interrogator was plainly as frustrated by Flinx's reply as the guide was pleased. He tried once more.

"Curiosity regarding what, if this master of a humble inquisitive-ness, might more specifically inquire, in hopes of gaining education, in hopes of being enlightened?"

Flinx sang back without hesitation, aware, despite his current slightly diffuse mental state, that Pip was not stirring from her rest. "Well, for one thing, I have an interest, in seeing if my abilities, play well with your kind."

The questioning one sang back uncertainly. "Your replies do not clarify, but instead confuse, a mind as simple, as is my own."

Nodding somberly, Flinx straightened on the too-low supportive bench. "Then I will endeavor, to show without singing, of what I speak, in the absence of tunefulness."

And why shouldn't I? Flinx thought to himself. He was not an orphan anymore, running through the back alleys of Drallar in search of a meal or something to steal. He had vanquished the Great Emptiness, was privy to a few secrets of the Universe, had survived Midworld, visited the AAnn homeworld of Blassussar, and even met and befriended the AAnn emperor himself! Perhaps the lawbreaker he sought on behalf of the United Church might present some difficulties, but whoever it was was human. The simple songsters of Largess posed no threat to him beyond severe musical criticism.

In his mildly stoned stupor he forgot that hubris is more deadly than any weapon.

Nothing materialized to menace him, however, or to remind him of that salient fact, as he proceeded to entertain the crowd of locals who had gathered to witness the offworlder's antics.

"In return for a single *alk*," he sang, naming a money disc of humble denomination, "I will endeavor to tell, the one who pays, something of interest he or she, does not know."

More nonspecific equivocation. Wiegl's admiration for his employer was further enhanced. Still, it remained to be seen how much, if anything, the human might be inclined to reveal.

Enrobed in a carousel of gauze, a sinuous female came forward to drop a coin on the table. "I would know, who here among these, is male enough, to accept the challenge of my companionship." She took several steps back, her large limpid eyes never leaving Flinx.

He let his talent roam. There were more representatives of the male persuasion present than female, but that did not make it a simple matter to parse feelings. He sought, and felt, and sampled among those who were not talking, while Pip slept on within her tube. Having sought, he now tensed slightly. His ingrained honesty combined with a loosening of caution courtesy of the local shellfish pushed him to speak the truth.

"In fact there are none present," he sang awkwardly, "who seek your companionship, but would happily make acquaintance, provided you were wealthy."

She stared at him a long moment, drinking in the full meaning of his stiff little tune-reply. Then her eyes darted (as much as Larian physiology permitted) rapidly to left and right, seeking to meet those of the mature males around her. None had the stomach to return her stare and all found reason to be looking elsewhere when she turned to them. A couple of such uncomfortable moments passed before she finally fled the room.

Silence rushed into her wake like water filling a canal, until one of the males present spoke. While older than anyone else in the room, he was no ancient grayfur. What he offered with his query-song was experience to match the coinage he deposited on the table.

"You who come from faraway places, you who seek to know our ways; to experience our culture and to see our world, to understand or perhaps exploit: you claim to know of many things." Broader of body than the majority of his furry brethren, the questioner leaned toward Flinx. Though his manner was forceful, even challenging, there was no threat in it. A glance at the walking tube told Flinx that Pip felt likewise.

"I am Ernach, Fisher of the Deep Ones, Hunter of the Hiders, soldier for hire to those who can pay. I have enemies, though only the stupid; for the smart ones, they seek safety from my presence." Lips rippled backward as the Hunter Ernach exposed his teeth. "Tell me, seer from other worlds: what do you see of my future, of the dangers lurking, in the high tomorrow? Of rivals lurking, waiting for their one chance, to find Ernach sleeping, and slit his throat?"

There was dead silence in the room. Not only was there no noise;

there was no movement. Those eyes that were not fixed on the
Hunter Ernach watched the slightly swaying human closely, waiting
for a response. For his part, Flinx was taken aback by the directness
of the Larian's query. How should he answer? Should he even try? Or
should he plead exhaustion, and have Wiegl escort him from the
room? He had made promises to this lot of locals. Through the
shellfish-induced fog it now occurred to him that his promises had
moved out of the realm of entertainment and into potentially dangerous territory.

Still, he had been paid. Out of the corner of an eye, he saw Wiegl's
right hand slide along the bench on which he was sitting, in the direction of the short sword stashed halfway under the table. Nearby,
the walking tube quivered slightly as Pip, responding in the absence
of direct hostility solely to her master's uncertainty, was beginning
to stir. He did not want to reveal her to any more Larians than was
necessary. So he felt it necessary to reply, felt compelled to formulate
some kind of response to the hunter's inquiry. The only kind he
could. An honest one.

Letting his ability roam the crowd, he marveled at the coherency
of emotions among sentient species. Shape did not matter, nor did
what a being ate, or breathed. Among sentients, there existed a remarkable kinship of feelings. So it took him only a moment to iso-
late one particular emotion boiling within a single member of the
gathering. He nodded at the Hunter Ernach, even though the Larian
did not possess the proper references to correctly interpret the gesture.

"I am no seer," he sang, "but a simple traveler, gifted with the
ability, to smell out certain things. Proclivities, one might say, among
the thinking, though I cannot read, such things as thoughts. What I
can feel is the pressure, of certain emotions, that course like water,
through the minds of others." He started to rise from the too-low
bench on which he was sitting.

Wiegl was instantly alert, all too aware that his human employer
was about to do or say something that might call for an actual re-

sponse on his part. Still, thus far the offworlder had sung much while saying little. Perhaps that was a plan, or at least a trend, that would hopefully continue.

Standing erect, Flinx sang on, and as the words and music flowed out of his non-Larian throat, Wiegl found himself more alarmed than ever.

"Everyone smells, of hidden emotion, of feelings held back, until released. Take for example, the tall traveler behind you, whose feelings tremble, on the cusp of murder."

Whirling, Ernach was just able to throw up his right forearm in time to block the downward thrust of the blade wielded by the individual who had worked his way through the milling crowd until he was directly behind the hunter. Flinx's revelation had thrown off his timing just enough for Ernach to muster a defense. Excited whistles and musical barking cries filled the air as the crowd spread out to give the combatants room. In the ensuing chaos, as the two antagonists grappled and fought for advantage, Wiegl scooped up the coins on the table, grabbed Flinx's arm, and started leading him out. His head beginning to clear from the effects of the shellfish, it occurred to Flinx that while he had not violated any Commonwealth directives in striving to "entertain" the crowd, he might have overstepped some personal ones. Of one thing he was quite certain: had they been present, Bran Tse-Mallory and Truzenzuzex would not have approved.

Upset at himself, at letting his mind and stomach combine to betray him, he wanted to return to set things right. Wiegl would have none of it.

"Leave them to marvel at your perception, my friend, and to compose songs, with which to entertain, those who are not present. Leave them to enjoy the fight, without us, so that any blood that is spilled, will not stain our clothing, or our reputations. Leave them so that we may sleep, and tomorrow, perhaps we may catch up, to the one you seek, if we are lucky. Or unlucky," he concluded on an uncharacteristically discordant note.

Clutching the walking tube close, Flinx bumped the bottom end along the wooden floor so much that Pip finally responded by sticking her head out of the top and hissing at him. Thus chastised, he made an effort to steady his stride, for her sake if not his own. While recognizing the wisdom of Wiegl's words (and why hire a guide if not to partake of his wisdom?), Flinx still wanted to go back and try to stop the fight. It was his disclosure that had started it and he felt a responsibility to put an end to it. Realizing that might entail risking his own life, he rationalized his nonintervention by telling himself that he had no right to endanger Wiegl's as well.

Besides which, there was a great deal more at stake here than whether one disagreeable local slaughtered another. Merely by exposing the emotions of several of the natives in his vicinity, he had initiated social disruptions that would otherwise have remained quiescent.

When will I ever learn to keep my nose out of the affairs of others, be they human or alien? he asked himself. Responsible guide that Wiegl was, Flinx allowed the Larian to lead him farther from the scene of local, and possibly fatal, disputation.

Ibatogh had also taken his leave of the clash, with its clanging swords and flashing knives. It was his interest in weapons of another sort that had prompted his quiet departure.

Like a *bowanda* settling onto its nestlings, the usual heavy mist had snuggled down over the town, working its penetrating dampness into every crevice and corner. As did all his kinsfolk, Ibatogh welcomed its arrival. Larians could abide any degree of dampness, but their fur would curdle and their skin crack if they were subjected for very long to any degree of humidity less than seventy percent, or to an extended period of accompanying bright sunshine.

So despite their ability to see well at night, he had sufficient cover to allow him to reach the stable unseen by others of his kind. While at present it was inhabited by a variety of domesticated animals, there were only two brund: those belonging to the oddly matched pair of visitors. Doubtless the stablemaster would have assured the travelers that she would keep close watch on their mounts and their goods. Just as Ibatogh hoped, she was fast asleep in her corner of the business.

Easily avoiding the simple, unmechanized warning devices, Ibatogh slipped inside the stable boundaries and made his way deeper into the corral. A trio of *mafier* scuttled to one side as he padded past them, their wide webbed feet making soft slapping sounds on the hard stone. Heavy-bodied and built low to the ground, *mafier* provided meat that was excellent eating, wiry fur strong enough to weave into flexible armor, and secretions from the glands on their backs thick and sticky enough to render into a useful glue.

Ibatogh pushed impatiently past them. He was neither rustler nor thief, though not above helping himself to something special if the opportunity to do so should present itself. At the moment, he was torn between loyalty to his Leethliege and his own interests. Whether he ended up serving the first or the second depended on what he found.

Or in this case, didn't find. The belongings of the human and his guide were disappointingly devoid of anything worth appropriating. In the offworlder's kit there were no magical devices, no unique materials, no wondrous revelations. Ibatogh had no interest in alien provisions and even less in various articles of clothing. While the material utilized in the weaving of the latter was certainly of interest, it was worthless to him. He could not wear it, likely could not sell it, and probably could not modify it into anything useful. Certainly the peculiar garments, far heavier than anything worn by a Larian, had curiosity value. But he was not about to risk discovery in order to filch something merely to satisfy someone else's boredom.

There had to be *something* of value in the human's gear. Something he could use himself, something he could sell, or at the very least something that would speak to the true rationale behind the offworlder's excursion to this out-of-the-way place. Not for a moment had Ibatogh bought the human's assertion that he had traveled this far from the offworlder station to satisfy a simple "curiosity." But among his gear, there was nothing.

He had suspected from the beginning, from his first glimpse of the human, why the offworlder was here. He could think of only one reason why a human would eschew the wonderful comforts of the station and forgo the familiarity of his own kind, food, entertainment, and security. That was to make contact, for better or worse, with the only other human in this corner of the world. Most likely for worse. Based on the events of the past several ten-days, it stood to reason. The only surprise was that it had not happened sooner.

And yet . . . and yet . . . among the human's effects there was no hallmark of officialdom, no sign that a formal pursuit had been initiated. More tellingly, there were no weapons. What kind of long-distance traveler, offworlder or Larian, journeyed without weapons? Of course, the human and his guide might be keeping such valuable devices on their person. Ibatogh was an excellent informant, but he was no fool. He would gladly carry out a covert inspection and report on everything he learned, but he would not challenge suspicious visitors directly. Not representatives of his own kind and certainly not an offworlder. Especially one who appeared to be a magician.

The red-furred offworlder might not be heavily armed, but he had demonstrated that he was a clever trickster. Sometimes guile was a more effective weapon, stealthy and easily reloaded, than the biggest cannon. Fortunately, it only fell to Ibatogh to report. It was for his Leethliege to respond.

The offworlder insisted he could not read minds, only sense how someone was feeling. It was a trick: of that Ibatogh was certain. No one could "read" the feelings of another. The alien was a clever magician, was all. Ibatogh would make his report.

Finding his way out of the complex without waking the stable-master, he returned to his own unpretentious dwelling. Out back, the rookery was quiet, its occupants asleep. Choosing the healthiest of the dozen or so *ryhnets,* he slipped the rolled message he had written into its belly pouch and then sealed the fleshy compartment with a strip of *mafier* glue. Neither the message nor the adhesive would inconvenience the *rhynet*.

From his pocket he drew a small, narrow-necked flask of purple glass. Unsealing it, he waved the mouth beneath the *rhynet*'s single flat nostril. Instantly, wide gold-flecked eyes, of which there were two facing forward and two facing backward, snapped open. The rest of the teardrop-shaped, streamlined body twitched; gently at first, then violently.

After resealing the flask as tightly as he could without breaking it, Ibatogh lifted the *rhynet* into the air, drew back his right arm, and launched it into the night sky. Four membranous wings spread wide. Searching for the source of the powerful pheromone to which it had just been exposed, the *rhynet* circled overhead, *meep*ing querulously as it rose higher and higher, until it was swallowed by the night mist.

Satisfied, Ibatogh considered returning to the gathering establishment, decided against it. Anything worth salvaging from the loser of the skirmish would by now have been swept up by the small crowd of onlookers.

The offworlder had said he was just that—nothing more than a curious onlooker. Ibatogh doubted him, and had responded accordingly. He had done his job. It was out of his hands now. The *rhynet* would home in on the nearest source of matching pheromone. With Ibatogh's flask sealed tight, that would mean the flier would be led to another that was always left open. Ibatogh was much satisfied with his work and he hoped his Leethliege would be pleased.

As far as he was concerned, the only thing threatening about the two offworlders he had thus far encountered was that they smelled funny and sang worse. Though it might prove dangerous to toy with a magician.

Let Zkerig deal with him, he decided as he returned to his own dwelling. As far as he was concerned, and based on what he had seen and observed this night, one such encounter was more than enough.

11

■ ■ ■

The following day was made extraordinary by something extraordinarily simple.

The sun was out.

It was hardly a Cachalot morning, but the presence of unmistakable patches of pale blue sky separating the lowering clouds bolstered Flinx's spirits more than he would have expected. As for Pip, she could hardly restrain herself, rocketing out of her tube to luxuriate in the atypical bright sunshine, executing cartwheels and loops, and generally terrifying an assortment of local avians with a combination of aerial acrobatics and flashing iridescence.

Wiegl was similarly pleased if less overtly enthusiastic. "I will miss the mist, but this will make our travel easier; not so much because we can see farther ahead, but because we can see any interference looming, from whatever source. Even better will be, the fact that the ground will dry some, making footing steadier, for our noble mounts." As he patted the lower leg of his nearby brund, he had to dodge hastily to one side to avoid a thin shower of urine.

Another world, another awkward lesson learned, Flinx mused, pondering the memory of the previous night as he prepared to repack his own towering, stilt-like steed. *Plainly, not everything that woozes the mind comes in the form of strong drink or designer pharmaceuticals. Even something as simple as an edible but otherwise unfamiliar molluscoid can contain unexpected mind-unsettling substances.* His head did not throb, as it would from a liquor-induced hangover, nor did it ache, as it might had he injected or ingested a medicinal. Instead, there was a weird lingering hum in his ears, a sort of soporific tinnitus, like a bit of water sloshing about in a shell. Shaking his head did not make it go away. Periodically Pip would dive down to check on his condition, her slitted eyes peering speculatively into his own, before soaring away satisfied that while her master might not be feeling at his best, neither was he about to keel over.

Though he otherwise felt fine, before starting out he would make certain that he was properly secured in his saddle basket high up on the brund's flank.

It was while checking his stock of dehydrated food supplements that he noticed something amiss. Instead of being neatly aligned within their satchel, they were slightly out of order. Could someone have gone through his supplies and rearranged them in haste? Or had they simply come loose in the course of the journey? Certainly the jolting stride of their mounts was not conducive to smooth travel, but still . . .

He pointed it out to Wiegl. The guide's response was unexpected, and combined to further arouse Flinx's suspicions.

"Some of my things, too, appear out of place, as if curious hands, had been making mischief with them." While concerned, Wiegl was not ready to concede that someone had been rummaging through their gear. "A moment then, while I question, while I press, the one who should know."

He departed the corral, then returned a few moments later with the stablemaster in tow. In any other company Flinx might have had to hide the amused expression her appearance induced. Here, where none knew its meaning, concealment was unnecessary. The older

Larian was the first of her typically sleek kind Flinx had seen with a potbelly. In response to Wiegl's stern questioning, she proved as full of denial as she was of groceries.

"I was here the entire night," she responded with appropriate indignation, indicating with a three-fingered gesture the small enclosed area where she slept, "and awake as necessary, as is my job, to oversee the animals and equipment left in my charge." Black eyes flanked by wrinkles flashed in the morning sun. "None did enter this place of security, this haven of repose, this fortress of guarantee, who lacked proper identity. None did enter, in point of fact, in reality, at all." She gestured at where their kit still rested on the ground, awaiting repacking.

"I watched over your equipment, frequently and well, and never did I touch, a single strap or buckle. To otherwise imply is to—"

Wiegl interrupted her in the middle of an angry arpeggio. "We are content with your explanation, mistress of a hundred discords, and accept that our packing, may not have been secured, may have been otherwise than perfect."

"As is your singing," she muttered, "about which the less said, the better it will be, for anyone within hearing."

That was the end of it. Reluctant to take the stablemaster at her word but unable to prove anything otherwise, Flinx and Wiegl had no choice but to finish loading the brund. She accepted the guide's payment with poor grace, and as they returned to their repacking she could be heard as she walked away singspeaking to herself in a low rumble, like a mezzo-soprano with a mouthful of marbles.

When everything had been reloaded and the time came for them to depart, the stablemaster was nowhere to be seen. Perhaps she was still offended by Wiegl's implications. Perhaps she was simply tired from a long night of watching out over the animals in her charge. Most likely, having been paid, she no longer had the slightest interest in the odd pair of travelers. In any event they did not see her as they departed, once more resuming their pursuit northward. Flinx could only hope that it would come to an end soon. Thanks to the brunds' imposing but unwieldy gait, his backside hurt more than his head.

Aware that if time and terrain favored them they might catch up to their quarry as soon as that evening, Flinx began mentally preparing himself for a possible confrontation. If his talent was functioning, he should be able without too much difficulty to detect the presence of another human, or non-Larian, living among nothing but natives. At close quarters, if it was operating optimally, he ought to be able to project sufficiently strong feelings of remorse and apology to drive the subject, if not to his or her knees, then at least into a state of dazed compliance. If he could do that much, simple ropes and bonds would be enough to ensure the return of the troublemaker to the station, there to face arrest and the subsequent judgment of Commonwealth authorities. The Church would not judge the malefactor, of course. Such things were better left to wholly secular authorities.

As for recovering the Firstborn Preedir ah nisa Leeh from her abductors, that might present additional unforeseen difficulties. He did not imagine they would constitute anything he could not handle. He had dealt with far more serious matters involving far more dangerous or advanced species than the Larians. Padre Jonas had given him the authority to promise, threaten, or do whatever was necessary to achieve her return; peacefully if possible, otherwise if not. All off the record, of course. The one thing the achievement of that goal could not involve was the use of advanced weaponry against the natives.

And there was always Pip, sleeping beside him within the cushioned metal tube. While she certainly could be defined as a weapon, she also was no more than a pet, a companion. She defended him of her own volition and she certainly did not qualify as high-tech.

For someone who disliked violence, he reflected as the brund effortlessly stepped across a fast-running stream, in the course of his brief life he had been forced to witness, and to partake in, far too much of it.

———

While the elderly stablemaster was pleased to accept the newcomer's money, she could not help but wonder at the appearance of yet another offworlder in Poskraine. So much smaller was it that she was not even sure if the new arrival belonged to the same species as the one who had recently departed. Subsequent singspeaking, however, plainly identified it as a "human." The creature, who to all appearances was traveling on foot, asked only for a recommendation as to where to spend the night. Despite its much-reduced stature compared to the lately departed, it carried itself with a confidence that belied its smaller size.

The stablemaster shrugged as she watched the human stride off in the direction of the main part of town. She did not mind the infestation of humans. Not so long as the money they brought with them was in local currency, and the questions they asked of little consequence to her business.

She confessed to being more than a little surprised to learn, however, that this latest arrival was female, and traveling alone, without a local guide.

Zkerig was alerted to the *rhynet*'s arrival by the jingling of the bell in the arrival cage. There were three of the mesh containers, integrated side by side into the stern of the ship. While the other two remained empty, the one in the middle was now being jostled and knocked about by the wings and legs of the leathery, hammer-headed flying creature desperate to reach the pheromone emitter that dangled just outside its reach.

Rising from the long, narrow halfbed where he had been lying, if not resting, Zkerig walked over to the receptacles. A glance showed that the belly pouch of the increasingly frantic just-arrived *rhynet* contained a message. Undetectable to all but the most sensitive Larian, the overpowering draw of the pheromone had already caused the message carrier to beat the front of its head bloody as it strove to reach it.

Using his knife, Zkerig put it out of its hopeless, hapless misery with a single stab and twist to the elongated skull. He removed the body from the arrival cage before it had ceased twitching. Too impatient to employ the small bottle of *mafier*-dissolving fluid, he used the now-bloody knife to slit the belly pouch open and removed the tightly rolled scroll from within. It made for interesting reading.

Vashon's reaction, he reflected as he carefully rerolled the scroll, would make for interesting viewing.

His short, muscular legs effortlessly compensating for the familiar rock and roll of the strideship, he made his way to the human's private cabin. If it had been left to the Tralltag, the offworlder would have spent the trip on the main deck with the crew. Unfortunately, the human was in the personal employ of Minord's Hobak and as such was entitled to certain privileges. Zkerig had to admit that the difficult mission could not have been carried out without the human's aid.

That didn't mean he had to like Vashon. Only to respect him.

The offworlder admitted him with a single curt note, not even trying to singspeak it. The casual rudeness was like a metal file scraping on Zkerig's eardrums, and this was not the first time. Rather than take offense, he put it down to the human's inability, like most of his kind, to speak properly. It was as if the entire species was tone-deaf. Not that the representatives of any of the other races that visited Largess were any more fluent, or harmonious.

Vashon was seated at the small table viewing something on the device he called a "communit." Zkerig eyed it hungrily, as he did every piece of advanced technology in the human's possession. Unlike some of his kind, he was not so foolish as to think that by stealing such tools he could then make use of them. Even the human's "vibraknife" required some kind of rechargeable internal power source in order to function. Anyone failing to completely understand the design and mechanism would soon find themselves saddled with a highly illegal (at least from the offworlders' point of view) nonfunctioning device.

Nonetheless, he could still covet such wondrous gear as the human's two hand-weapons, one of which jangled the nerves, while the other, only recently demonstrated, obliterated them and everything in their vicinity. If only he could have enough time to study them properly, he told himself. Or find someone with the knowledge he lacked to help him. Perhaps there were other offworlders like Vashon, eager to trade illegal technology for his world's apparently quite valuable organics. How to make contact with such an individual, though, and without alerting the Hobak's pet alien . . . ?

Vashon was frowning at him. "Why are you, standing there, looking like, a paralyzed *porsaeig*?"

Zkerig advanced. Would that he could have continued advancing, he thought, to pick up the human and heave him out the cabin's single wide port, there to land heavily on the ground and be forced to walk the rest of the way back to Minord. Alas, he knew full well that such an act was a physical impossibility. Strong as he was, the offworlder was too heavy for him. The human's bulk as well as his technology exceeded the Tralltag's ability to manipulate. He would have to settle for savoring the human's reaction when he was informed of the contents of the scroll, which Zkerig now held out before him.

"Just now, via air, via speed, through the medium of *rhynet* communication, arrived this message from Poskraine."

Vashon frowned. "I assume it has something, to do with me, or you would never have brought it, to disturb my thinking, to unsettle my alone time. What does it say, this swift-winged missive, from a town of no particular importance, that you feel the need to trouble me with it?"

"Nothing specific but everything of import," the Tralltag told him, "so that among the lines, we may draw our own conclusions." He kept gesturing with the scroll as he spoke. "It is true enough that Poskraine is of no importance, and of itself means nothing, in the scheme of things. But resides there an operative, low in status but plainly skilled in foresight, who chooses to bring to our attention, a development of interesting note, of worthy speculation." His lips curled and the end of his elongated nostril twitched upward, away from his snout.

"It would appear that, if the author of this communication can be believed, and there is no reason to imagine him, inventing such a vision, that you have company, that in these lands you are no longer alone."

Larian singspeech could be damnably subtle, an impatient Vashon reflected. "In these lands I have not been alone, for some time now, since I have the minions of na Broon, for escort and company. For them I rely on companionship and safety, of which company you, my noble Zkerig, are the foremost."

Immune to the flattery, the Tralltag took delight in explaining further. "Traveling north in our wake, following close like hopeful parasites, are one of my kind and one of yours." Vashon's reaction to this information, a mix of sudden alertness and confusion, satisfied all of Zkerig's expectations. "Yes and so, it would seem that we see, that another human toward Minord rushes, though no casual traveler I liken him to be. On two stout brund they make their way; heading north, moving fast, doubtless an uncertain reunion they hope to have, and not with me."

Rising, Vashon began pacing the floor, a peculiar human behavior Zkerig had observed previously and dismissed as a waste of nervous energy. "This makes no sense," Vashon was careful to sing, "that another of my kind, would find his way, toward Minord, and in this fashion. Scientists and researchers would travel in a group, the better to lend one another assistance, should anything go wrong, or should difficulty befall them."

"Perhaps your government has sent after you, one who does not fear difficulty, and is capable of handling, all troubles on his own. Yet there is with that theory, a particular problem. One which I cannot resolve, and so seek your opinion, and possible explanation."

"What?" Vashon was furiously pondering possibilities.

"Our operative in Poskraine was very thorough, in discharging his responsibilities, with admirable competence. As human and companion slept, this Isobagh, our operative, searched through their supplies, and found a nothing that astonished him."

"A nothing that astonished him?" At Zkerig's puzzled look, an exasperated Vashon hastened to polish his singspeech. "What is a nothing, that it should concern, this operative of Minord, and therefore us?"

"No weapons did he find beyond those of local manufacture, no devices of the kind you recently employed, and nothing to frighten, nothing to inspire dread—a 'nothing.' "

"Perhaps this operative, clever as he may be, living far from the station, and having no experience of such things, put hands on advanced weapons without recognizing them."

Zkerig conceded the point. "Such a possibility cannot be denied, yet very self-assured is this Isobagh, in his writing, and in his conclusions. It raises the question, of what sort of individual, would your government send after you, without proper arms." His lips rippled back again, exposing teeth. "If your government hopes, to persuade you to return, and confess to your sins, then they do not know you, half so well as I. Or could they, in lieu of using weapons, hope perhaps to pay you, to give up your ventures here, your work on behalf of our Hobak, and return to your Commonwealth society?"

Vashon's reply utilized the lowest register he could manage. "The Commonwealth government does not give bribes, to facilitate the laws, that I have violated. Nor does it seem likely, they would send one to talk; only to talk, only to chatter. Especially if they believe, as could be the case, that I am involved, in the taking of the Firstborn." He used a hand to steady himself against a support pillar as the strideship, climbing a slight slope, angled upward. "Not seeing a gun does not mean, it does not exist, well hidden as it might be, even from the eyes, of Minord's operatives. There are smaller weapons,

than those that I carry, that are equally deadly, that kill quite efficiently, if in a less showy manner."

Zkerig gestured his understanding. "Leaving aside for the moment,
the matter of weapons, be they large or small, be they one-shots like
cannon or a full rank of archers, why send after yourself, only a single
pursuer? No matter how skilled, no matter how knowledgeable, no
matter how persuasive, I would myself consider it foolish."

"The Commonwealth is large," Vashon explained even as he pondered the Tralltag's sensible question, "but it can also be subtle, and
does not use a hammer, when a needle will suffice." In a mild but
unmistakable dig at Zkerig's question, he added, "This is a strata-
gem that is foreign to soldiers, but more in use, among diplomats,
among the experienced, and among surgeons. A tactic that your
Hobak, may he live long and procreate often, would immediately
seize upon, and understand."

Even as he was chiding the Tralltag, Vashon had to admit to himself his reasonableness. If Minord's operative in Poskraine was not a
complete fool and his report to Zkerig was accurate, why *would* the
authorities send only a single individual to track, find, and presumably deal with a significant lawbreaker like himself? A renegade who
was experienced enough and wise enough in the culture of Largess,
and sufficiently fluid in its unique language, to have secured for himself a coveted position with an important and rising young Hobak.
Did they expect this person, however skilled in negotiation, to persuade Vashon to give up everything he had achieved, admit his
crimes, and return voluntarily to Borusegahm station and submit to
arrest and prosecution?

Are the authorities involved crazy, he wondered, *or am I?*

Perhaps they had sent only a single pursuer because a large group
would be too conspicuous? That made a certain amount of sense.
One man, or woman, might get to Vashon, whereas the coming of
an entire squad would furnish advance notice of itself no matter
how stealthily it strove to approach. And without the ability to uti-

lize contemporary technology, how could it possibly surround and close in on Vashon without him being alerted to its intentions?

Which raised the question of how a single tracker, equally restricted to the use of only local tech, expected to deal with someone like himself. Whoever it might be, it was plain that the authorities had considerable confidence in their skills.

Well, Vashon was not without ability himself. He would take no chances. Having risked as much as he had and having accomplished all that he had, he felt no compunction about taking whatever steps might be necessary at this point to preserve what he had already accomplished and to further his goals. Though genuinely curious to see what sort of singular individual the authorities had conscripted to send after him, he would happily forgo that explication in favor of securing his position.

"Your contact in Minord was specific, in saying that this human and his companion-guide, were tailing us, on a pair of riding brund?"

Zkerig restrained himself, though like drink through an imperfectly sealed carrybag, he could not keep a little sarcasm from seeping through.

"As it is difficult to mistake a brund for, as an example, a *corahtac* that comes only to one's knees, I am fairly confident that our informant, is as accurate as one of his kind can be, as accurate as the night permitted."

While Vashon was immune to casual mockery, he felt otherwise about sharp or explosive objects. So he paid no attention to the Tralltag's mild dig, focusing instead on how best to eliminate a possible, if not positively identified, danger. Finding "possible" to be threat enough, he determined to eradicate it. If the lone human trailing in their wake happened to be a naïve scientist or student of Largessian culture, that was unfortunate for him. Now that they were this near to Minord, with the object of their journey securely on board, it was no time to take chances.

"The human who comes, must swiftly be dealt with, and in such a manner, in such a way, as to leave no evidence, pointing to me."

"In other words," Zkerig replied while toying with the hilt of the knife sheathed at his low waist, "you are to be the beneficiary, of Larian murder, but are to be absolved, of all possible blame, in the event others of your kind come looking, in the event others of your kind seek revenge."

Vashon didn't blink. "Your increased perception, of my words and their implications, does you credit, Tralltag of Minord. Mind, however, in making any reports, in pocketing any memories, that I never used the word 'murder,' that it sprang solely from your own singing."

Zkerig showed teeth, extended to its full length the unusually cylindrical, short Largessian tongue, and fluttered both eyelids. "Yet in your 'innocence,' you do not dispute, the singing of that word, nor all it implies. Am I to assume then, that I act with your permission, in dealing with this matter, as we have discussed?"

With a wave of his hand Vashon dismissed the Hobak's underling. "A discussion does not an order make, nor words that fly come to roost, on any save those who sing said words, while passing those who are simply bystanders."

Zkerig sang an intentionally discordant note. "The words that fly, of which you speak, when passing between two, invariably crap on both. Think not yourself immune, offworlder, from the retribution of your own kind, for an action to be carried out by mine, yet goosed by your own intentions, your own desires, your own ambitions."

Vashon waved again, brusquely this time. "Get about the business, and find another song; your harmonies pain my ears, while your melodies tickle only, the wrong end of my person."

Responding with an equally curt gesture, this time of acknowledgment, the Tralltag took his leave of the cabin and its grating non-Larian occupant. "I will deal with it, properly and swiftly, and hope the resolution does not, in some final reckoning, place the portions of both our anatomies to which you refer, in dire danger."

He departed without further comment, suggestion, or—thankfully, a tired Vashon thought—singspeaking. With its melodious ebbs and flows, its sometimes soaring rhetoric and often sharply sung rebuttals, the Larian language was among the most elegant and agreeable to listen to in the entire Commonwealth. But for anyone used to merely speaking an alien tongue and not simultaneously singing it, creating melodies and rhythms at the same time as translating the necessary wordings put a strain on any nonnative. Of everything he had accomplished in his time on Largess (save for greatly increasing his credit account), Vashon was most proud of his fluency.

It could be a curse as well as a blessing, however. This was proven by the deliberately off-tune screeching that penetrated the wooden wall between his cabin and the next. He could have had the Firstborn confined elsewhere on the strideship, but felt it important to keep the reason for the expedition close at hand, if only to keep an eye on her. Unfortunately, this meant often having to keep an ear on her as well. He had remonstrated with her, warned her, threatened her, to keep her voice down. Or if she could not restrain herself, at least to sing with some taste. Nothing had worked, least of all admonishing her in her own language. That only prompted more and sharper screeching, a perversion of singspeech that drove even regular crew members to other corners of the vessel in an effort to escape the tympanum-scraping noise.

He was tired of trying to out-singspeak her. If he was going to survive the remainder of the journey back to Minord with his eardrums intact, it was time to take more direct action. Something less Larian and more human. Force.

As he expected, the screeching stopped as soon as she saw the knife. There was no fear in her eyes, only wariness. Though to be truthful, Vashon could rarely discern anything in those jet-black orbs anyway. With pupil and iris usually the same color—black, charcoal, gray, or dark brown—there was little to distinguish one set from another, or allow an observer to discern any soulful depths within.

"Go ahead then, rancid human, and cut my throat, and let us finally be done, with these tedious games." Since her attempt at escape during the battle with their still-unidentified piratical assailants, Zkerig had insisted on keeping her chained to one of the strideship's vertical support beams. There was enough room for her to move about the entire cabin, with its restored exterior hull, provided she was careful not to entangle herself in the furniture.

Holding the vibraknife out in front of him, he moved toward her. "Your singing displeases not only me, but the very ground itself, the very sea which gives life, and the very air that flees from your vibrato." He extended the sonic weapon out in front of him. "Believe me, it would be my pleasure to dispense with you, to dispose of you overboard, and tell the Hobak Felelagh na Broon, that you met with an unfortunate accident. But I cannot, I must preserve you alive, to be delivered to him, to suit his political ends."

Larians could not smirk, but Preedir managed to do so with her voice. "What would you tell him, your crazy master, to justify such an 'accident'—that I slipped and fell, onto your singing knife?"

"I said I must preserve you, alive to be delivered—but not necessarily intact, as even a damaged version will serve the necessary purpose." Turning the device up a notch, he extended the softly humming weapon toward her. "Since your singspeaking curdles, the blood in my arteries, and sets to pounding, the veins in my head, I will remove the offending parts. I am no surgeon, but enough Larian anatomy I have learned, so I know it is possible, to reach down one's throat, to pluck forward the vocal cords, and with this device, to sever them without bleeding."

Preedir's ears went flat against the top of her head, her eyes retracted slightly into their sockets, and her breathing proboscis coiled tightly above her snout. While the latter muscular ability had evolved to enhance hydrodynamics while simultaneously protecting the eyes when underwater, such a gesture could also express fear. Vashon recognized it for what it was, and was gratified. This was the first time since the abduction that he had seen the Firstborn afraid of anything. Threaten to kill a Larian and they would spit at you. But threaten to cut their vocal cords, eliminating any ability to singspeak while still leaving them alive, and you could instill true dread.

Such was visible now in the face of the Firstborn of Borusegahm, as well as in her posture and even in her fur. Diaphanous clothing swirling about her lean, sleek form, she shrank back against the wooden pillar to which she was chained. An observing human would not have used the word "cowering," but it was near enough.

Having finally come up with a threat that had produced a desired result and enjoying himself more than he cared to admit, Vashon continued to advance on the patently terrified Larian, waving the vibraknife slowly back and forth in front of her. Her eyes were locked on the disturbed air in front of the handle of the alien weapon, never leaving its hypnotic motion.

"Please, I will prostrate myself if you wish it, but do not deprive me, of that which makes a Larian, of that which makes me—me. Without a voice I am nothing, as you plainly must know, or you would not even think, to venture such a horror! No more will I try, through singspeaking grating, to unsettle and upset you, or some small revenge gain! Just do not do this, do not do this, do not do this, I beg of—"

On average, Larians were quicker than humans. They had faster reflexes on land as well as in the water. Possessed of shorter strides, they could not keep up with a human runner over any distance. But in a short leap, or at close quarters, they could move extremely fast.

Preedir ah nisa Leeh, Firstborn of Borusegahm, was very quick indeed.

The loop of black iron chain she flung at Vashon went right around his neck and constricted sharply as she fell backward, putting all her weight into taking up the slack. He had been so enjoying himself luxuriating in her distress that he had missed seeing her coil the chain behind her with the hand that was not waving at him defensively. He would have called for help but he could not catch his breath. Rising immediately to her feet, she braced one against the wooden post and yanked.

The sharp pull might well have broken a notochordal Larian neck, but the human skeleton was more robust than that of the locals. Not exceptionally so, but it was enough to save him. She continued to pull him in her direction, his back toward her, as she wound more and more of the chain around her left arm. He started to panic. If she drew him close enough, she would be able to start twisting the chain, fatally choking him. As they placed a cultural as well as physiological emphasis on the neck and throat, any Larian with fighting experience was perforce an expert strangler.

As she drew him nearer he stabbed wildly backward with the vibraknife. It made brief contact before she danced out of the way, but sheared only fur. Another jab took a chunk out of the heavy wooden pillar. He felt that he could black out at any moment. If that happened, she would have complete control, and his vibraknife. Its technology was foreign to her. Doubtless in utilizing it on his unconscious body she would make a sticky mess.

Making a supreme effort, he heaved himself forward. Built stocky and low to the ground, he was able to get some traction into the thrust even though it added dangerously to the tension around his neck. It was just enough to throw her off stride and bring her out from behind the sheltering post. Before she could fully regain her balance, he threw himself backward. If he had misjudged, or if she was able to dodge, he knew she was too smart to allow him a second chance.

He slammed into her hard. They both went backward and he landed on top of her. No featherweight by the standards of his own species, he knocked the wind out of her. She recovered quickly—but not quickly enough, as he was able to spin around to face her. Though completely covered in short fur, the Larian body was cool to the touch. With the chain around his neck finally loosened, he held the humming vibraknife a few centimeters from her face.

"I should nick your eyes like I cut the post, cauterizing the wounds as I do so, leaving your voice so I can hear your wailing, and still deliver you alive to Minord."

Black eyes longer and larger than his own glared back at him as she fought to get her breath beneath his weight. "Cut if you will, with your evil toy, whatever you wish, offworld slime. I will beg; not for my eyes, not for my life, not even for my voice, but for you to remove yourself from me, as your stink is far worse, than anything your weapon, that you clutch so fearfully, can do."

His fingers tensed around the haft of the vibraknife. She was daring him to do his worst: to maim, to mutilate, to kill. All but encouraging him to do so. He swallowed, hard. There would be a red ring around his throat from the chain for days.

Reaching up carefully with his left hand, he slipped the iron links off his neck. Then he pushed the vibraknife toward her. As he did so, both nictitating membranes came down to cover her eyes. She could not close them, could not shut him out. Larians had no eyelids. Instead, she tried to turn off her mind.

The slicing vibraknife grazed her forehead, cutting a straight line through the fur above her eyes but below her ears. Lightly burned, she gasped in surprise and pain. Rising to his feet, he peered down at her.

"You are as brave as you are foolish, Firstborn of Borusegahm, and I would be honored to share your company, if I did not think you would make, a meal of my organs at first opportunity. I hold no animus against you, though you just tried to kill me, for if our positions were reversed, I would have done the same."

Still lying on the deck, she looked up at him. "Save your compliments for the vermin, whose lineage you share, and as for honoring me, you cannot give what you do not possess."

He eyed her thoughtfully, then nodded, drew back his right foot, and kicked her square in the throat. Gasping and coughing, she clutched at herself and rolled over, away from him. He had not been lying when he'd told her he knew something of Larian anatomy.

"That will quiet you, for a day or two anyway, and I will have peace, albeit temporary. Let the pain and discomfort put you in mind, set you to thinking, about what far worse could happen, if you succeed in your efforts, your ongoing efforts, to make me lose my temper, and choose satisfaction over reason."

He left her like that, prone on the floor and clutching at her paralyzed vocal cords. He was rubbing the deep mark around his neck as he stepped out into the passageway—just in time to encounter Zkerig coming the other way. The Tralltag noted the chain burn on the human's neck and the now-deactivated vibraknife clutched in his right hand, merged a thought or two in his mind, and pulled back his lips.

"I see that you have quieted, the dangerous carnivore in her prison, though perhaps not without, some small gracelessness?"

Decidedly not in the mood for the Tralltag's mockery, Vashon took a step toward him. Zkerig's expression tightened and one three-fingered hand dropped toward his own far more primitive but still quite effective blade.

Vashon caught himself. More than needing Zkerig, he was obligated to serve beside the Tralltag, just as the soldier was compelled to tolerate the human in his midst. Fighting among themselves would serve the interests only of the Firstborn.

"How much longer, my good *friend*, until we sight, the roofs of Minord?"

"Not long, as the stridemaster calls it, for the crew is as anxious, is as hopeful for that sight, as you and I. The weathercaller predicts nothing incompatible, no more than the ordinary misting, with but an occasional light shower, to raise our moods."

The usual rotten weather, you mean, Vashon thought to himself. He could tolerate intense sunlight or pouring rain more easily than he could the seemingly perpetual gloom that enveloped most of Largess. Even crossing the polar ice caps would have provided a break from the atmospheric dreariness. But there was no money to be made at the poles, forcing him to restrict his activity to the populated parts of this world.

"And what of what we discussed, in the time before, our unpleasant guest, ceased her shrieking?"

Glancing briefly at the door to the prisoner's cabin, Zkerig wondered exactly what had transpired behind the now-closed portal. No matter. The Firstborn was still alive, or Vashon would have said otherwise. As to the burn mark around the human's neck, Zkerig could only speculate. The mental images thus conjured proved an enjoyable diversion.

"The roofs of Minord, the pleasures of its Great City Hall, the nuzzling of females and the delights of good food, all await us. None of these will your pursuer experience, none will he be allowed to report, nothing of you will he see or be able to question, for he will never reach Minord, much less walk its streets. I have dealt with, by means of *rhynet* communication, all that is necessary, to ensure this result."

Ordinarily Vashon might have complimented the Tralltag on his efficiency, or at the very least acknowledged it. But he was not in the mood. He was still puzzled as to why the authorities would send only a single pursuer after him. In fact, he was a bit miffed that no more was thought of the disruption he had caused to the established Larian order. Why just one? He did not voice his ongoing concern aloud to Zkerig. Not only because his thoughts were now focused elsewhere, but because it hurt to talk—much less singspeak.

12

■ ■ ■

It wasn't the rain so much as the lack of sunlight, Flinx reflected. There was plenty of rainfall on Cachalot, but there were also many days of consistent sunshine and clear skies. And it was warmer, much warmer. On Largess, the cool temperature combined with the dampness to eat into your bones, like an invasive mold. He envied Pip, snug in her insulated metal tube. When she emerged to exercise her wings, it was in a refreshed and warmed condition. He was not wholly miserable, but there was no question that the persistently dismal climate was beginning to affect his mind-set.

It was his own fault. He was the one who had felt a desire to do something new, to break away from the comfortable daily routine to which he had become accustomed on his new watery homeworld. The opportunity had come with Sylzenzuzex's arrival and request. In truth, he hadn't really pondered deeply enough all the possible ramifications. After saving quite literally everybody and everything, surely helping an obscure sentient species wouldn't require him to tax himself, or strain his now more refined but still occasionally unpredictable talent. Secure in his homelife with Clarity, on a world devoid of most threats, he had forgotten that one could be made dead as effectively by a club as by a Krang.

Boredom, he mused, was an inherent condition of the human consciousness, which existed to remind us that occasionally we must look over a shoulder to see if there's anything hungry creeping up on us from behind.

At least the weather was only depressing and not dangerous. He did not have to wear an exosuit or dodge periodic downpours of lava. But he could not escape the feeling that something small and ticklish was taking root inside his clothing, fueled by the constant moisture and a landscape rich with flourishing, albeit often stunted, varieties of alien life.

As they crossed the next wide inlet, it was almost a relief to see the elderly Larian in the sinking boat. He was in no danger, of course, Larians being as comfortable in the water as out of it. But he was plainly at risk of losing his entire catch, a possibility that was causing him unmistakable distress. At the stern of his craft one rusting metal trap was already partly submerged. From his vantage point high up in his brund's saddle, Flinx saw that the trap was crammed with two-meter-long writhing creatures. Each was about as thick around as his thigh, with an even larger head, and short fins at its back end.

Flinx had never seen a terrestrial eel in his life, but the description "eel-like" was one common to terranglo. The swarming creatures in the trap had surprisingly small, bright red eyes. Large finlike hearing organs folded flat against the sides of their skulls. Their skin was smooth and devoid of scales and their flesh looked deceptively soft and mushy. As they twisted and coiled among themselves, their broad hearing organs repeatedly opened and snapped sharply shut against the sides of their necks, generating wet, smacking sounds.

With the boat continuing to sink lower and lower into the salt water, its owner's gestures grew more and more frantic. Slowing his mount, Flinx called over to Wiegl.

"The poor old guy is going to lose his whole catch; we should try and help him, to make it to shore, to salvage his efforts."

Leaning forward in his harness, the guide contemplated the minor aquatic disaster unfolding off to their left. "A hunter's luck is a hunter's luck, be it good fortune or ill, and none including us, should attempt to interfere with that destiny."

Flinx brought his mount to a complete halt, forcing an irritated Wiegl to do likewise. As he cast his talent outward the only emotion he could perceive from the elderly fisherman was rising anxiety.

"It does not speak well of you, Wiegl, that you would ignore the entreaties of one of your own, when the slightest of detours, would result in doing good."

The guide emitted a low note, belching on perfect pitch. "Then speak ill of me, whoever might, whoever will, as I am not charged, with doing 'good,' but only with helping you, catch up to your own possible demise."

Flinx smiled at him. Wiegl's feelings were as straightforward and honest as his speech. "Then help me to delay that, by helping another, who might one day have occasion, to speak well of my kind, to speak well of Wiegl-kind also." Having by now mastered the necessary commands, he turned his brund toward the sinking boat and urged the tall walker to advance against the slight outflowing current.

Warbling an unmelodic curse, Wiegl brought his own brund around to follow that of his employer, singing a warning as he did so. "So we'll tow him to shore before he sinks; before he loses his pitiful catch, before what he drew from the sea returns to it. But watch your walking, over-fingered, and keep even your extra digits, well out of reach." One webbed hand gestured at the sinking boat and the metal trap. "Those are *gowrie* he has caught, and though they are good to eat, they think the same of you, and will not hesitate, to demonstrate their own appetites, if offered a chance—or a stray limb."

Bearing Wiegl's warning in mind, Flinx continued to guide his mount toward the submerging boat. Its owner had retreated from the bow and was now struggling with the large trap. Where his hazardous catch was concerned, he either did not possess the same caution as Wiegl or else he knew exactly where to put his long fingers to avoid having them nipped off. Flinx could sympathize with his desperate efforts to try to keep the trap intact and on board until the two brund-mounted strangers could throw him lines with which to tow him to shore.

An unexpected sensation teased Flinx's talent. The oldster's initial apprehension had abruptly given way to one of satisfaction, even glee. It was more pronounced than might have been expected even from one anticipating assistance. Stronger; an almost forceful delight. Flinx found himself wondering if he might have misinterpreted his initial perceptions. It was harder to be certain when analyzing alien as opposed to human emotions. Unquestionably, the elderly fisherman had been feeling apprehension when Flinx had first reached out toward him. But sensing apprehension was not the same thing as understanding the reason behind it. Had the oldster been apprehensive because he feared the two travelers were not going to help him, or for some other, as yet unknown, reason?

Partial explanation came in the form of a sudden lurch from the sinking boat. Observing the craft's rocking, it became apparent to Flinx that it had not, in fact, been sinking, but had been deliberately filled with just enough water to convey that appearance. As for its owner's wrestling with the oversized trap, it was now obvious that he was not doing so in order to keep it on board, but to dump it into the water. As it slid into the inlet, one sidewall dropped down and outward. Immediately, the several dozen *gowrie* packed inside began swarming out. But not to freedom.

With commands deftly enunciated in singspeech, their captor sent them racing directly toward the two helpful travelers and their mounts.

"*Herder!*" As sung by Wiegl, the single word was both recognition and warning. Immediately, he turned his brund toward the far shore and urged it onward. Realizing as well as now sensing the deception, Flinx commanded his own mount to follow. Perceiving her master's sudden distress, a sleepy but rapidly awakening Pip emerged from the open end of her tube, coiled around the top, and proceeded to search for the danger that was threatening him.

While the brund could cover impressive distances with each stride, their long legs were constrained when in water and so they moved more slowly while wading. Like so many torpedoes, the several dozen *gowrie* were on them in scarcely a minute. Gaping mouths revealed jaws set with double rows of suckers. One after another, the squirming creatures clamped on to the legs of Flinx's mount. Unable to penetrate the brund's armored lower legs, the multiple suckers did no damage, but the accumulating weight of so many attackers began to slow both of the tall striders.

All this they did in response to the commands issued by the now-no-longer-panicky old fisherman in the no-longer-rapidly-sinking boat.

Responding as they had to the attack of the pack of nocturnal *grynach,* the two brund flared their sharpened leg scales. But the *gowrie* were quicker to react to the defensive maneuver, and their slender, twisting bodies harder to surprise. While several did suffer lethal perforations and others multiple wounds, the majority managed to avoid the brund's usually lethal response.

Soft flesh rippled on their flanks as their flexible bodies extruded appendages that were short, flexible, and strong. Responding to their master's commands, the surviving predators, reduced now to less than half their original number, utilized these to begin ascending the legs of the two brund. Aware now of the location of the tall walkers' slashing scales, the slithering assailants succeeded in avoiding them even as the brund continued to flex and flash the defensive weaponry that was integrated into their lower limbs.

Activating his vibraknife, Flinx peered over the side of his saddle to see a pair of the powerful climbers working their way toward him.

As he looked down he could see that a remarkable transformation was taking place inside their mouths. A xenologist would have been fascinated. Having no time to be fascinated, Flinx was merely appalled.

Not only were the upper and lower jaws of the *gowrie* able to rotate forward and backward; when in one position they flaunted suckers, and while turned inward they displayed double rows of sharp teeth. The arrangement of their rotating jaws was constantly changing, one moment showing suckers and the next, teeth, depending on which array might most profitably make contact with prey. While Flinx had no intention of becoming the latter, the small vibraknife did not offer much in the way of a defense. Against one of the creatures, maybe; against several of them simultaneously, very little. So he would have to invoke something that had proven successful on other, similar occasions.

Half closing his eyes as he gazed down at the two expectant carnivores, he concentrated on projecting fear.

Perhaps the most elemental of all emotions, it struck the pair hard. Low as they were on the local evolutionary scale, his effort still had an effect. Both of them hesitated, suddenly confused and uncertain. Seeing this, their puzzled master redoubled singspeaking commands from his location on the now-stabilized boat. Caught between obeying their master's directives and reacting to the inexplicable terror they now felt, the *gowrie* could not decide whether to continue climbing or release their grip and drop to the safety of the water below. Having previously observed the consequences of his efforts at emotional projection, Flinx might have felt sorry for them, were they not hell-bent on stripping the flesh from his bones.

An off-pitch scream split the air. Unlike Flinx, Wiegl had nothing with which to defend himself other than spear and sword. He was slashing at a striking *gowrie* even as his mount started to go down under the weight and assault of at least a dozen of the writhing monsters. The wounded, moaning brund toppled forward like a falling tree.

Torn between defending himself and his own mount against attack and going to the aid of the desperate guide, Flinx realized there was only one possible solution. It meant exposing himself to an imminent peril in order to deal with one that lay farther away but was at the moment by far the more threatening. With Wiegl's life at stake he did not hesitate.

Turning away from the pair of climbing *gowrie* whom he had managed to momentarily paralyze with indecision, he shifted his focus to the elderly Larian in the distant boat. *That* was the source of the real danger. That was the entity who intended him ill, who meant to murder, who exuded the desire to assassinate. And the old Larian *was* going to kill him, no matter what Flinx could do, because he was safe across the water, untouchable in his craft, clear of the ongoing battle, away from the—

A sound like that of a miniaturized autonomous aircraft was briefly heard as something small and brightly winged zoomed past Flinx's ear. As he retreated from the edge of the saddle to back up against the neck of his wailing, frantic mount, Flinx watched Pip shoot across the open water. The old fisherman, who was something more than a simple fisherman, flinched as the minidrag shot past him. Pip circled the boat once and then paused, hovering above its single occupant. Picking up a sword, the elder took a wild swing at the iridescent alien flying creature.

One of the *gowrie* came clambering over the side of the saddle to snap at Flinx's legs. Drawing his knees up toward his chest, he held the humming vibraknife out in front of him, waving it defensively back and forth. Not recognizing either the sound or its potential, the *gowrie* took a curious bite at it and was rewarded with having the front half of its face neatly severed. As blood spouted from between its eyes and its upper jaw, it jerked convulsively backward. That caused its companion to hesitate, it being intelligent enough to recognize the small shiny object in Flinx's hand as being seriously dangerous.

Another *gowrie* was clambering up the other side of the brund and starting to work its way across the saddle there, the one that held supplies.

A shriek that bore no relation to singing, in Lari or any other known language, reverberated across the water from the wooden boat. Keeping the vibraknife between himself and the predator in front of him, Flinx strained for a better look. He located the boat again just in time to see its sole occupant clawing at his face as he fell backward into the water.

Unexpectedly deprived of their master's commands and badly unsettled by Flinx's projection of fear, the two *gowrie* who had reached his saddle reacted by reverting to instinct. Turning on its badly wounded counterpart, the uninjured one began snapping and biting at it while the wounded one fought back with a ferocity that belied its injuries. Blue *gowrie* blood stained Flinx's shoes, his clothing, splashed his face. Each one's jaws buried in the other's flesh, they spun and contorted until they tumbled over the flexible side of the saddlery, plunging toward the water below while locked in a mutually murderous embrace.

Bereft of direction or command, other similarly befuddled *gowrie* were releasing their grips and falling away from the legs of Flinx's mount like so many leeches from a bloodless quarry. As his brund steadied itself, now freed from the encumbering weight of its assailants, Flinx was once more able to move freely within the saddle.

His heart sank as a glimpse to his right showed Wiegl's mount, having barely reached the shore, now lying prone on the ground. If struck down, a brund faced a difficult and sometimes impossible task to regain its footing. From amid the seething chaos of biting, crunching predators, a single figure emerged. Running on short legs, his flat stubby tail extended straight out behind him, Wiegl was sprinting frantically in Flinx's direction. He was pursued by no less than three *gowrie,* their choice of prey now as unchained as their hunger.

It took all of Flinx's recent Largessian learning to persuade his reluctant mount to drop into a squatting position. Fortunately, while swift as eels in the water, the *gowrie* were not nearly as efficient at traveling on land. Not only was the adrenaline-fueled Wiegl able to outdistance them, he reached the supply-filled saddle opposite Flinx long before they could attack the legs of the human's brund. Straightening once more to its full height and having shed its earlier attackers, Flinx's mount resumed its gallop northward. Once it was back on dry land, the *gowrie* gave up the chase.

Breathing hard, the human in long, steady gasps and the Larian in short, peppy bursts, the two survivors tried to catch their respective breaths as their remaining mount strode onward. Unlike its still-agitated riders, the brund's duller nervous system had already consigned to memory its near-death experience. Behind them, man and Larian could hear a chorus of excited moans as the surviving *gowrie* commenced the grisly task of tearing apart the unfortunate fallen brund. Its surviving companion showed neither interest nor concern at the demise of its former cohort.

Flinx rendered no judgment. Neither did Pip as she returned to the walking tube. Every species, every creature, dealt with death in its own way. Perhaps, he thought, the way of the brund was preferable.

"We're very lucky." Catching himself, Flinx recast his comment in proper singspeech. "Lucky we are, to escape such an ambush, to avoid such a death. No accident was it, I think, that we were fooled into helping, someone set not to plead with us, but to murder. A choice of such weapons I would not have suspected, would not have recognized, being as I am more used to, those of mechanical design." He grew aware that Wiegl was not listening to him so much as staring at him.

"Such quiet suits you," Flinx continued, "as it is both uncharacteristic and flattering, though I have to admit its unexpected appearance now, leaves me somewhat puzzled."

" 'Puzzled' is a description I would use myself." The guide was unusually solemn as he regarded his alien companion. Crammed next to the offworlder in the single available saddle, he could smell the human as though its body odor had been distilled to its essence. "Though it is perhaps not a term strong enough, to explain what just happened"—he gestured back the way they had come—"in the middle of that bay. Puzzled indeed I am by the inexplicable, by that which cannot be explained, by things I see but do not comprehend, for which I cannot conceive an explanation."

Flinx did not volunteer enlightenment. "I don't understand, either your confusion or puzzlement: we were attacked, and fought off the attack, and saved ourselves, and now continue on our way."

The guide made a gesture Flinx did not understand. "I will make myself clearer then, so that even a child, would have no difficulty, sharing my bemusement." With one long arm he gestured back the way they had come.

"In serious difficulty we were; waylaid by a most devious assassin, assaulted by a horde of *gowrie,* and I myself brought to the ground encircled by teeth. You yourself were under direct attack, trapped in your saddle, proximate to a foul death, with little room to maneuver." He indicated the nearby metal tube that was once again inhabited by the deadly offworld flying thing, near to which he felt he was seated much too close for comfort.

"Yet out of this chaos your pet emerges, and without word or sign from you, knows precisely where to go, and whom to attack. It ignores the *gowrie,* who are the immediate threat, flies across the water, and puts a terrible end to the one who directs them, the one who is in charge. It speaks not a word, does your poison-spitter, waits not for a command, but seemingly of its own volition, does exactly what is necessary to save us."

The guide's singspeech, which had lapsed into lullaby, concluded forte.

"How—did—you—do—this?"

How much more should he tell this native? Flinx mused. Wiegl's black eyes were locked on him, the guide's attitude one of expectancy mixed with anxiety. They had shared much together. Did that entitle a fellow survivor to far-reaching revelations? On the other hand, what harm could it do for his companion to know a little bit more of the truth? It wasn't as if he was going to run to Commonwealth authorities with anything he was told. By all accounts, he'd met and had dealings with at least several humans prior to being engaged by Flinx. Doubtless in the future he would have more. None of those encounters were likely of their own accord to lead to intense discussions about an exceptional human named Philip Lynx. Considering where they were going and what they might yet have to do, it might prove useful for Wiegl to know . . . certain things. Expressing them and explaining them in singspeech posed a challenge.

"Do you know, my friend, what a telepath is, and does, and is capable of doing?" When his perplexed guide responded in the negative, Flinx explained. "It is someone who reads minds; and as I said that night in Poskraine, that is something I cannot do, nor to my knowledge, can any sentient being. What I *am*, through no desire or wishing of my own, is an empath, albeit an erratic one. I can perceive and interpret, the feelings of others, so long as they are, capable of emotion."

Wiegl's eyes did not grow wide, as they could not grow any wider than they already were. He conveyed his amazement nonetheless. Not wishing to overwhelm, much less frighten, his companion, Flinx held back from adding that he could also, under certain conditions, "push" the emotions of others. He gestured toward the occupied metal tube.

"My 'pet' is similarly blessed, or cursed as the situation dictates, with the same ability, to sense the emotions of others. Being my companion since childhood, she is particularly sensitive, to those emotions that surround me, like storm clouds dimly glimpsed. If I am threatened, she knows it, and if no danger is present, she knows that as well. In each situation she reacts accordingly, so if I show fear of something, or of someone, she will try to negate its malign influence, will try to reduce its threat to me, even before I can sense it myself."

Wiegl pondered this explanation long and hard, singing nothing.

The brund continued on its steady pace, occasionally snapping at the bright red *modaks* that darted in and around its head, seeking scraps of food or edible parasites. Finally Wiegl looked from the tube back to Flinx.

"So despite the fact that we live in an age of science and reason, there is no denying, that you are a magician, and the poisonous Pip your familiar."

Flinx gave up. He'd said more than he should have, had provided as cogent an explanation of his abilities and his link to the minidrag to the guide as he ever had to anyone, and the result had been a fall-back to superstition and fable. Maybe it was just as well. On the unlikely chance Wiegl ever found himself in conversation with a representative of the Commonwealth and the subject of a solitary traveler in pursuit of another ever came up, the guide would simply say he had been traveling with a magician. Let the Science authorities in Denpasar sort that one out.

As for Wiegl, though he re-interpreted (or rather, misinterpreted) the human's explanation to suit his own understanding of the world, it did not alter his perception that he was traveling in the company of a very strange being, and not just because the offworlder in question boasted an excess of digits on his hands and feet. Surely there was more, much more, to this Flinx individual than he was telling. Simple magic tricks would not explain the offworld authorities sending a single one of their own to track down a renegade of their kind, especially one who evidently enjoyed status and protection among a Leeth as powerful as Minord.

It raised the question: should he remain with and continue to aid this human in his task, or would flight be the more sensible option? Taking the latter course of action would mean leaving the offworlder to continue on his own, a situation that would likely result in his death. Of course, should he survive such abandonment and return to Borusegahm station, whether successful in his task or not, that could raise questions tricky for the guide to handle.

Which difficult course to follow?

In the end, it was the matter of final payment for his services that enabled Wiegl to decide. If he returned without the human in tow (as opposed to bringing back his body, which was another matter), he was unlikely to receive the outstanding balance due for his services. In the end, avarice won out over caution.

"It's all right," he told his attentive companion, "and does not matter, whether you are a magician, or a master of some science, that is beyond my understanding. The difference between the two is nothing but a matter of perception; a matter of words, of experience, and of comprehension, based on culture. Mine races like a *wolagail* to catch up to yours, so that in the near future, with luck, with effort, and with good fortune, we may in some small way partake fairly of your knowledge."

His words were reassuring, even sympathetic, but Flinx could sense that the guide's emotions were conflicted. That was perfectly understandable considering all that Flinx had just revealed to him. Wiegl was not unintelligent, but he was being forced to try to make sense of something that would confuse any typical citizen of the Commonwealth, and he with considerably less scientific background.

Let him think I'm a magician, then, if it eases his mind. I need his skills and knowledge of his world, not his biotechnical understanding.

He had a good heart, Flinx decided. In the end, that meant more than anything else—no matter the species to which the individual in question happened to belong.

13

. . .

Several things struck Flinx simultaneously as they finished crossing yet another wide but shallow ocean inlet and he and Wiegl found themselves confronted by a column of excessively solemn, preternaturally quiet natives. In contrast to every other Larian he had encountered since his arrival on Largess, these individuals were entirely unclothed. Not that the thin, lightweight attire common to this world did much more than accentuate the fur-covered bodies beneath, but clothing carried important cultural and social meaning. These Larians had dispensed with it entirely.

They had surrounded the surviving brund in such numbers that it was forced to halt lest it step on one or more of the processioners, or trip over them. There were at least two hundred: all devoid of clothing, all wearing nothing but similar somber expressions. To Flinx's eyes they looked slightly catatonic. Male and female, young and old, each displayed a distinctive mark in the form of a chevron shaved into the fur of their forehead, above the eyes and below the ears.

He glanced to his right. Within her tube Pip did not stir. That confirmed his own perceptions. Despite having blocked the way forward, nothing but good feelings rose toward the two travelers from those assembled below. Perhaps they just wanted to talk, or had questions about the way south. He sung the thought to Wiegl.

The guide was considerably less indulgent. If Wiegl could only experience the same flow of compassion and goodwill that was coursing through the earnest gathering, Flinx thought, some of the guide's natural suspicions might be allayed.

Confirmation of his initial impressions came in the form of a beautifully sung request from one of the leaders of the procession.

"They want only to talk with us; to converse, to speak, to engage in pleasant exchange." As Flinx spoke he was preparing to direct the brund to squat so that he and Wiegl could dismount. "It has been my experience, that such is often the case with genial travelers, no matter the species, no matter the location."

Wiegl grunted a sour note but did not argue. "It has been my experience, that such is often the case, that seemingly amiable strangers, conceal within their belongings sharper things than words."

"Look at them, look closely," Flinx urged his wary companion, "and there is nothing, with which to threaten us, for their intentions are as transparent, as is their lack of clothing."

"Maybe you do not find that so, but for someone like myself, this absence of attire, of any kind, of any style, of any opacity, strikes me as more than passing odd. And there is that strange mark, that each of them wears on their head, clearly indicative of something significant, with which I am not familiar."

Flinx grinned as the brund, in response to his command, folded itself into a squatting position. "You boast of your knowledge, you boast of your experience, but I think you have not traveled all that widely, outside Borusegahm Leeth."

Apparently unbothered by the accusation, Wiegl chose not to contest it. "I am one who listens well, and therefore learns many things, about far places and distant lands, that in truth I have not visited." His gaze met that of the human. "You sometimes yourself speak, of places not personally seen, so even though you have access, to more information than I, it amounts to the same thing."

Flinx conceded the point. "We'll talk then with these gentle travelers, and learn something of them; of why they wear no raiment, and the meaning of the mark each wears." He shrugged. "It may help us in our quest, it may not, but in the end, all knowledge is valuable."

As he slipped over the side of the saddle enclosure, it was plain that Wiegl was still far from comfortable being surrounded by so many strangers. "How do you know their intentions, by what means do you attest to their 'gentleness,' and what assurances can we expect? For myself, I will keep my knife, close by my side, and as handy as my words."

His offworld companion grinned anew. "Have you forgotten already, of what I am capable, this 'magician,' with whom you travel?" He waved at the nearest members of the procession, who had begun to approach now that the brund had settled into a resting position. "I have taken the measure of the feelings of many, and although I can never be certain, it is clear enough to me, that they mean us only kindness."

"Once again I place my life," Wiegl muttered musically under his breath, "in the hands of a near-hairless offworlder, who knows much but who I believe sometimes thinks little."

Of the three processioners who came up to them, one was exceptionally tall for a Larian. Her flexing neck frill made her appear even taller. She loomed over Flinx while her two companions flanked her silently. Her quick, perfectly familiar gesture of greeting was returned by Wiegl and, with admirable precision, by Flinx. He spared a quick glance backward in the direction of the now-seated brund, which was chewing placidly on a cluster of bushes thick with dark green seedpods. As it ate, the pods fluttered anxiously. There was still no indication that Pip felt any differently about the mass of marchers than she had when they had initially been encountered. Once again, Flinx felt his initial impressions confirmed. He was relaxed as he turned back to the leaders of the group.

"We greet you as fellow travelers, though you go south and we to the north, in hopes that each of us finds, that for which we are searching."

The shock among the procession's principals was profound. "We have heard of offworlders, though never encountered any ourselves, and yet you sing our language, with impressive skill!" In unison, all three tilted their heads forward, extended their breathing tubes, and spread their arms wide, making a single sweeping forward gesture reminiscent of the ancient human swimming stroke known as the butterfly. Flinx didn't even try to duplicate it, nor did Wiegl. The guide's posture indicated that he might be, ever so slightly, warming to this procession of unclothed eccentrics.

"We wonder, my companion and I, at your absence of attire," Flinx pointed, "and the meaning of the singular mark, each of you carries."

"That is easily explained," murmured the tall female, "as the disdain for clothing is as much a mark, of our beliefs, as the indication on our foreheads. We are Zeregoines, of the Yolaig sect, on pilgrimage, to the Eastern Sea."

Flinx frowned, turned to his guide. In everything he had studied about Largess, he had never heard of this group. Of course, one could hardly learn everything there was to know about a Class IVb world in the course of a single space-plus transit.

Wiegl's response indicated that he knew no more about the sect or its beliefs than did his human companion. Purely as a matter of personal interest rather than out of any driving need, Flinx determined to learn a bit more about them. Then they could exchange gifts, or share a meal, or do whatever protocol demanded, before proceeding on their separate ways.

"Neither I nor my companion have heard of the Zeregoines, and as we are always interested in new things, before continuing on our path, we would like to know more about you; about your ways, and your beliefs, and your way of living."

The leader gestured understandingly. For a Larian female she had a deep singing voice; it was in keeping with her physical as well as social stature. "Your seeking of knowledge is most admirable, as I would not have expected it, from an offworlder, more so than one of my own kind." Raising both arms, she turned to face the nearby narrow bay. "We believe that, as we come from the sea, we should return to the sea. That which belongs to the land should stay with the land, while we, the children of the Great Mother Ocean, the offspring of water, the descendants of the ancient swimmers, should disregard all that is of the ground. We swim, we dive, we fish, we reproduce, in our birthplace, the ocean." Lowering her arms, her expression benign, she turned back to Flinx and Wiegl.

"This we believe: that all should join with us, in returning to the water, in reclaiming our birthright."

Such a philosophy easily explained the lack of clothing, Flinx mused, and of any baggage the group carried that could not survive submergence. Well, as a political-religious set of values, it seemed harmless enough for those who might choose to follow its tenets. It represented backward-looking, devolutionist thinking, but posed only a mild threat to the steady progress being made in places like Borusegahm. The fact that Wiegl, with his wide-ranging contacts and interests, had never heard of this sect was proof enough that despite the size of this particular column of believers, their influence could not be widespread. As a thoughtful aside, they had little in common, for example, with another stringently regressive group with which he'd had treacherous dealings in the recent past. Try as he would, he could detect from those who looked on in silence not a single inimical emotion directed toward him or his guide. These folk might be behind the times in their thinking, but from all appearances and everything he could sense, they were good people.

"All should join us," the tall female was saying, "in returning to the life-water, in regaining its purity, and by so doing, cleanse themselves." She now focused her attention on Wiegl, who suddenly wished to be elsewhere. He need not have worried. All she and her cohorts wished was to confer on him their equivalent of an aqueous blessing.

"Will you show yourself, true to the life-water, and conclude the traditional test, that will prove your worthiness?"

"I, uh, don't know"—the guide's response was conspicuously out of tune—"as I am ignorant, entirely ignorant, of what that might entail."

As one of her supple, muscular attendants moved aside, she took the few steps necessary to bring her to the edge of the water. "Nothing is required, but that you show your allegiance to the sea, by returning to its embrace, for the briefest of times."

"Oh, you mean, go for, a swim, a dip, a bath?" Wiegl glanced questioningly at his employer.

"If this will only, take a few minutes, it might be an eye, toward future allies." Flinx gestured at the salt water lapping gently against the rocky shore. "I will watch, and applaud the gesture, as some of my ancient ancestors, favored similar rituals."

Indicating to the Zeregoine leader his readiness to comply, Wiegl began to remove his lightweight outer clothing. As word of the stranger's willingness passed among the procession, an inspirational chant rose along its length. The melody was new to Flinx, rich with exotic counterpoint between the males and females, as soothing as a lullaby.

Beneath the overcast sky, Wiegl's now wholly revealed fur was plainly in need of some serious grooming. Flinx smiled to himself. The short swim would do the guide good. Having entered the water ahead of him, several of the already unclothed followers were frolicking in expectation of his joining them. It was the first time Flinx had seen a group of Larians in the water. Propelled by their short but powerful tails and webbed hands and feet, they dove and darted about like seals. They would have been quite at home in the seas of Cachalot, provided the water was not too warm for them.

As the singing from the crowd rose higher and higher, those in the inlet beckoned to Wiegl, who now stood at the water's edge. Once again Flinx cast his talent into the assemblage, and once more encountered only joy, delight, and contentment. At the moment, he was feeling pretty good himself.

Until two of the attendants stepped forward, slapped a metal cuff around the guide's right ankle, and ceremoniously shoved him forward. As a startled Wiegl toppled into the water, he was followed by a heavy chain. This was attached to a cube of solid iron on which were inscribed a variety of Larian hieroglyphics and words. The holy weight took him straight to the bottom. As this was composed of dark rock spotted with a few plants, Flinx could lean out and see the guide clearly through the unpolluted water.

Settling onto his feet at a depth of no more than four meters, Wiegl crossed his arms and stood patiently. The attendants who had preceded him swam nearby, gesturing and genuflecting in his direction. Initially flustered by the Zeregoines' actions, Flinx now relaxed. In the crowd and in the water nothing had changed. As for Wiegl, he appeared completely at ease.

Flinx was, too, until he felt something slip around his own right ankle.

"Hey, wait a minute . . . I can't breathe und—" Though he remembered to employ singspeech, his objection was so terse and atonal that it generated no reaction among the earnest Larians who had just snapped a metal anklet around his own leg. Before he could turn or object further, he felt himself being shoved forward. Failing to catch his balance, he went into the water headfirst.

The coldness of it shocked him. He just did manage to gasp out a single word—"*PIP!*"—before the weight attached to his ankle chain dragged him under and down.

His desperate cry was unnecessary. Having instantly detected the change in her master's emotional state, the flying snake came rocketing out of her traveling tube. In seconds she was hovering directly above him, peering helplessly downward as he stood on the bottom flailing at the surrounding water and gazing upward with wide eyes. The salt water burned, but he was able to see with relative clarity.

Like a dragonfly monitoring a tiny fish, the minidrag repeatedly zoomed back and forth over her submerged master, unable to do anything for him. Meanwhile the Zeregoines on shore sang out the Larian equivalent of oohs and aahs at the antics of the iridescent, brightly colored alien flying creature, not realizing she was in a complete panic. Pip could have turned and, unleashing her poison judiciously, killed at least two dozen of them. But in scanning for an enemy, she found none. Their actions had been entirely benevolent; the feelings that radiated from them presently were wholly caring.

Unable to source a menace, the frantic minidrag was reduced to circling above the fully submerged Flinx, who stared up at her with a sense of increasing doom.

He struggled futilely against the single manacle. How ironic, he thought madly, if having spent the most recent and contented days of his life on a world of water, he should finally meet his end by drowning on an entirely different one.

Lowering his gaze, he saw Wiegl peering at him anxiously. The *guide*'s emotions, at least, were full of concern and genuine alarm. It was becoming swiftly apparent to him that humans, whatever their other wondrous abilities and skills, were not waterfolk, had never been waterfolk, and likely never would be waterfolk.

How long could a Larian stay submerged? a rapidly weakening Flinx wondered. *Five minutes? Ten? Twenty?* His lungs were burning. In seconds they would be on fire, demanding air. He closed his eyes. He would have to open his mouth, would have to try to breathe, and sucking in only salt water, would choke, unable even to cry out, unable to gasp a final farewell to Pip, or to poor Clarity, or to Mother Mastiff, or any of the—

Something small and warm pushed itself against his mouth. Opening his eyes, he saw that Wiegl had just enough slack in his chain to struggle over to the nearby human. Stretched to its utmost, the breathing proboscis on the guide's snout was pushing against Flinx's lips, an oversized dark-hued worm seeking entrance.

Holding back the gorge that started to rise in his throat, Flinx parted his lips just enough to permit the organ entrance. It was not unlike forming a watertight seal around a straw, albeit one that was part of a living being. Glancing down, he saw Wiegl looking up at him, their line of sight only slightly misaligned due to his position. Expanding his cheeks, the guide held the facial gesture for a moment, then blew.

Air filled Flinx's throat and lungs. He fought against inhaling sharply, forcing himself to let the flow of life-giving atmosphere enter at its own pace as Wiegl shared his stored air with his companion. It arrived with a surprising and unexpected amount of force. Perhaps, Flinx thought giddily, the Larians had the ability to draw and hold air in their lungs under pressure. That would explain the ability to remain underwater for extended periods of time. Larian lungs would be thicker and stronger than those of a human, and peppered with a higher concentration of alveoli, or whatever passed for the local equivalent.

Sharing his air with Flinx would shorten the amount of time Wiegl could stay submerged. Flinx had just enough time to wonder how long that might be when Wiegl's slender, deft fingers started working on his ankle. Restraint vanished as the ceremonial weight was released. Instantly, instinctively, he kicked for the surface.

Pip greeted him by landing on his shoulder, wrapping herself lightly around his neck, and machine-gunning his dripping, gasping face with the tip of her tongue. Far more relaxed and not even struggling for breath, Wiegl surfaced nearby.

"I did not think, that you would join me, in proving yourself, to the satisfaction of our new 'friends.'"

Dazed but conscious and thankful to still be alive, Flinx let his talent roam through the still-chanting crowd. They were as happy, as contented, and as pleased by what they had just witnessed as could be imagined. A friendly folk, were the Zeregoines, who held nothing but the best of intentions toward everyone they met. All they needed, an exhausted and coughing Flinx mused, were some basic lessons in offworlder biology.

He was all right, though. Thanks to Wiegl, he had survived.

Maybe he had nearly drowned, but he was now a fully fledged, respected member of the Yolaig sect of the Zeregoines of Largess. One more sobriquet to add to his long list of unsought, unsolicited accomplishments.

He was so grateful to be alive that after changing into his one set of dry clothes he did not even object when the joyful Zeregoines requested, and received, his permission to shave the mark of their sect into the only place on his body that boasted sufficient fur to show their identifying chevron. They did Wiegl simultaneously. When they had finished, and the hymnlike equivalent of a cheer went up from the procession, human and Larian compared their newly revised cranial façades.

"It becomes you," Wiegl sang thoughtfully, "as it makes you a member, of an exclusive group, to which only select Larians belong." His ears and nostril bobbed to show amusement. "I think I can sing, without contradiction, to the fact that, you are surely, the first human Zeregoine."

Reaching up, Flinx felt gingerly of the shaved space on his forehead and wondered what Clarity would make of it. Pip lay draped limply around his shoulders like a rubbery necklace, worn out from her desperate attempts to help him and by her own overactive metabolism.

"We know what you seek." Flinx hoped the request he was about to make would not cause him to stumble over some unknown religious trip wire. "And we wish you success, but our own search is proving difficult. I wonder, and my companion wonders"—Wiegl looked at him sharply—"and many others wonder, if in your travels, if in your recent passing, you have encountered a great strideship, walking north?"

The leader bent as the advisor on her right sang softly into her ear. As she listened, her breathing proboscis shifted back and forth, swaying freely while the rest of her body held steady. She straightened.

"Normally we would not bother, to share any information with others, not of immediate interest, not in our own interest. But you now are two of us, fully vested, having passed the test, and emerged cleansed by the Mother Water.

"There was such a ship; not great by our standard, but substantial to be sure. One such strode past us, strode going in the other direction, heading north, not two days ago." Her tone turned disapproving, switching from flute to bassoon. "All aboard seemed trapped in time, of expectant futures and artificial reality, as if through sheer invention, they could achieve perfection. Unlike the Zeregoine, unlike our acolytes—unlike you—they drive themselves to acquire more, when the way to truth lies in acquiring less. They live not on the land but for it; their land controls them, and casts its pernicious spell, in the form of unneeded attire and objects." A concurring threnody rose from those within earshot of their leader.

"Toward Minord." Flinx did not know how to sing it properly, but he was understood, if gently criticized for his delivery.

"Toward Minord," the leader confirmed, "Minord of the great bridge, Minord of much smoke, the Leeth of Minord. I fear its people take no interest in salvation, and seek only the offspring, of illegitimate industry. It is said the new Hobak dabbles in fantasy, and imagines himself, ruler of the world, and forgets his heritage." She leaned toward Flinx. Pip slumbered on, so he didn't flinch.

"Is that where you go, new brothers, on your journey, on your brund?"

Wiegl's acknowledging gesture spared Flinx the necessity of a reply.

The leader made a wide sweep with one arm. "Our hopes will go with you then, that you might through your recent learnings, bring some education to that benighted public, and to its addled officials."

"We'll certainly convey, the depth of Zeregoine feeling," Flinx assured her, "whenever the opportunity, might conveniently present itself."

Which would hopefully be never, Flinx thought. Proselytizing for an alien religion was not on his immediate agenda. He decided he liked the Zeregoines even if he didn't agree with them. They were an undeniably pacific folk, overflowing with nothing but good feelings—even when they had done their best to try to drown him.

"Two days ahead," murmured Wiegl speculatively, "not close enough to overtake, but not far enough to lose track of, given our present position. If we make haste, we may ride in on their tails, or in the case of a strideship, one of their legs."

They sang their final farewells, then: Flinx and Wiegl to resume their pursuit, the Zeregoines to spread their message while seeking a final return to the life of their seagoing ancestors. Could the members of this singularly Larian sect ever see their way to blending their desire for an earlier, simpler way of life with the advantages of membership in the Commonwealth? A whale might know, Flinx felt.

But there were no wise cetaceans to consult here. Certainly there were sea creatures of size, though he and Wiegl were traveling too far inland to encounter any. He still had only his own knowledge to consult with, in concert with that of a single and not entirely reputable local.

Wiegl showed some alarm as he studied his companion. "You look pale, my friend, as though still suffering, from the effects of your 'deliverance.'"

Wrapping his coat tighter around him even though he knew the action could not make it warm him any faster, Flinx smiled over at the guide. "Though we like to swim, it is better for one of my kind to be sunk in thought than sunk in water, better to be drying in the sun—if there was any sun in which to dry." The sour grimace he cast skyward did nothing to make the interminable cloud cover part.

He could still feel the fleshy pressure of Wiegl's breathing organ forcing its way through his closed lips, the ecstatic relief provided to his aching esophagus by the pungent but lung-filling air it provided, and the gentle oddness of not breathing entirely on his own. Thinking back on it helped to shut out the clamminess that continued to cling to his bones as persistently as the memory of recent gagging. He shivered, and Wiegl observed the phenomenon with undisguised interest. Pip popped her head out of her breathing tube, examined him through unblinking slitted eyes, and, satisfied he was not dying, returned to her rest.

Wiegl had saved his life. Of that Flinx had not the slightest doubt. If not for the Larian's timely intervention, his human companion would have drowned. Why did he risk it? The guide had no way of knowing that if he interfered in the ceremony he would not be speared, or worse. An admitted gambler, he had taken a radical plunge into the unknown by sharing his breath with an alien.

As with each impressive stride of their brund the densely vegetated low-growing landscape sped past, Flinx continued to wonder, and finally asked.

"Why did you risk yourself to save me, back there, surrounded by zealous devotees, of a strange sect? They almost killed me, albeit unintentionally, and might easily have decided, to forcibly keep us apart, by killing, or at least maiming, you."

"Maybe it's because I want to learn more about your Commonwealth. And your language. I can speak some of your terranglo, you know."

Following days and days of communicating via nothing but singspeech, the curt syntax of his own language hit Flinx hard. After the flowing harmony of the local means of communication, the sounds, the very cadence of terranglo, grated unexpectedly. It was the aural equivalent of walking barefoot across a field of pumice.

"I don't—" He caught himself. "I would prefer to talk, in your own language, as it may prove important to my undertaking, to be proficient in your tongue."

The guide was clearly disappointed, but complied. "There are times when singspeech gives the meaning better, of something intended, of thoughts that must be voiced, of one's true meaning. But I occasionally find useful, your terranglo, which while harsh on the hearing, can convey certain things, and certain thinks, more swiftly. Like now," he concluded in Flinx's language.

How quickly one grew used to melody, and fond of harmony,

Flinx mused. "You still have not answered me, still have not told me, have not replied with an explanation, of why you saved me." He was staring hard at the guide as the brund splashed through a wide, briskly cackling stream. "Despite your words, I cannot help but feel, that more than a desire to acquire knowledge, drove you to the act, and persuaded you of the risk. Had you returned to Borusegahm, with all of our kit, including my possessions, and told of a calamity, a catastrophe, an accidental death befalling your companion, none could know the truth, and all such would be yours to keep."

Wiegl was quiet for a moment, gazing out over the edge of the saddle basket at the dour landscape ahead. It duplicated the equally dour terrain on both sides of them, and echoed that which was falling behind. It did not match his mood, however, which remained thoughtful if not ebullient.

"Better I may express it, if you will allow me, in my rudimentary terranglo, which I can only try to employ." Turning to face his employer, his companion, his . . . friend? . . . Wiegl explained.

"I've got a reputation to maintain."

Flinx indicated that he understood, and that he accepted the guide's explanation. Privately he believed no such thing. From all he had been told, Wiegl the Guide had a reputation, all right. But while it spoke highly of his abilities and his competence, less was said of Wiegl's character. Possibly because the guide preferred to affect an air of distance, and of superiority. Maybe among the Larians such individual characteristics were considered flattering. As far as that was concerned, Flinx was sure of only one thing.

If Wiegl's intent was to sustain a reputation based on boastfulness and self-interest, he had well and truly ruined it back there in the inlet.

14

...

The Great Hall of Minord Leeth was largely empty when Vashon and Zkerig made their triumphal entrance, leading a carefully bound Preedir ah nisa Leeh between them. At least, it was as triumphal as they could make it. Narrower than its traditional human equivalent would have been, the high, windowless corridor was also far more stark. There were none of the gaudy banners or gilded, rococo décor that would have featured in a comparable structure on Earth that dated to a similar period of social and technological development.

Finished in plain gray stucco or plaster (architectural components were not a specialty of Vashon's), the ceiling was sharply arched and devoid of decoration. No blazing shields or crossed swords denoting clan origin lined the walls. The sole ornamentation consisted of artful engraving in the stone of the walls themselves. This was meant to suggest rolling waves and breaking surf, an affectionate nod to Larian ancestry and evolution. The oceanic motif was repeated in the carvings that scrolled through the high-backed, low-seated chairs that were lined up against both walls.

In contrast to the ceiling, the floor was a comparative riot of rugs and intricately woven throw pieces. It seemed to Vashon as he advanced that the skins and coats of half the creatures on Largess were represented in the crazy-quilt cushion underfoot.

At the far end of the corridor, a solitary individual sat atop a single-step raised dais on a chair only slightly more ornate than the ones that lined the walls. Armed only with an elaborately forged ceremonial spear, a single guard stood on either side of the seated figure. Off to the left, a pair of bureaucrats sat at simple desks. They were equipped only with styluses for recording the forthcoming encounter, mechanical means of doing so having yet to be developed by their species.

Halting at a respectful distance, human and Tralltag silently awaited a reaction from the silent individual seated on the dais. Mustering a tune resplendent with contempt, their captive was less hesitant in singspeaking her mind.

"You are Felelagh na Broon, Hobak of the Leeth of Minord, to whose City Hall I have been brought, by these two slaves?"

Zkerig tensed at the description, while Vashon enjoyed the Tralltag's discomfort. Be it singspeech, terranglo, Low Thranx, or any other language, the origin of an insult did not matter to him. Only its content. Anticipating some verbal spew from their prisoner, he was not taken by surprise.

"I am h-he, of whom whom y-you sing, as identified by m-my seat, and this location." Awkward harmony and rough melody, as well as stuttering, immediately betrayed the Hobak's speech impediment.

"I cannot see your seat, as it plainly occupies, the same space as your brain, the same location as your conscience."

Three-fingered hands tightened around spears as the guards tensed. Startled, both recorders looked up from their work as Vashon noticed Zkerig flinch. As for himself, he waited to see what would follow. What did, did not surprise, as he had come to know the Hobak of Minord better even than his most trusted servants.

Rising with difficulty from his low seat, na Broon leaned against the strong wooden cane that had been propped up nearby. A masterpiece of the Larian woodcarver's art, the cane showcased more flamboyant decoration in its length than did the entire hall. For all the intricacy and skill displayed in the wooden staff, it remained wholly functional. It had to be, to support the weight of the Hobak's upper body.

Felelagh na Broon's spine was crippled. Twisted not forward but sideways and to the right: a birth deformity that would have condemned a lesser individual to a life most ordinary. Leaning to his damaged side and resting his weight on the extravagant cane, with his head likewise inclined in the same direction, the Hobak limped forward until he was standing close to the captive. Though not close enough to bring himself within range of her unchained feet, Vashon noted wryly.

In an idle moment he had once inquired of a Minord counselor why she had voted for na Broon to be Hobak.

"He is twice as hideous," she had replied without hesitation, "as the next ugliest of candidates—and three times as smart, as any of us. I will vote for him, yes, and I will listen, and follow his lead. He will be good for administration, and good for Minord, since being so unsightly, he will hold no false opinion of himself, and therefore will not fall prey, to temptation or corruption."

Na Broon looked Preedir up and down. "Beautiful eyes match beautiful fur, as wicked mouth confirms reputation. Do not worry, Preedir ah nisa Leeh, since y-you are here for political reasons only, not those of reproduction."

"I am thankful for that," she replied, the dim light in the hall glinting off the curve of her gleaming black eyes, "as it would pain me to think, that something such as you, might one day reproduce."

For a second time the two recorders paused in their work. It was too much for Zkerig. Pulling his knife with the intention of drawing some respect along with the captive's blood, he took a step toward her. Raising a hand, na Broon forestalled him.

"Hold your temper, righteous as it may be, in this particular instance, regarding these particular words." The Hobak's proboscis quivered as he took a step nearer the prisoner. Standing straight, he would have towered over her, and over Vashon as well. But his broken, bent form permitted only his eyes to come level with hers. "We do not cut helpless, bound prisoners here, in the Great Hall of Minord, where the spirits of unseen predecessors, would frown on such action."

Moving with surprising speed, he raised the heavy cane and brought it around in a wide arc. The wider end, where he rested his hands, slammed into the Firstborn's left leg just below the hip. Crying out, she fell to her knees, unable, with her wrists bound behind her, to clutch at the injured area.

Turning away from her crumpled form, na Broon limped up the single riser, made a clumsy pivot, and resumed his seat. He had betrayed no emotion when she had insulted him and none when he had struck her. Nor did he seem in the least upset now. Only speculative.

"W-we cut helpless, bound prisoners *elsewhere*," he declared, concluding his unfinished observation, "where th-they can scream all they wish, where th-their contortions will not trouble honest citizens, where blood may flow unimpeded by pride." Continuing to utilize the cane for balance even while he sat, he leaned toward her.

"Y-you are here as a guest because y-your father, Hobak of Borusegahm, contemplates this expansive alliance, with th-those those who are not Larian." Very much aware that Vashon was standing nearby, he ignored the human as he continued. "Unnatural creatures, in league with others more unnatural still, in an alliance w-we cannot imagine, and that w-we must not join."

In pain but defiant, she struggled to her feet. "Do you always, in this way of greeting, treat your guests, so bluntly?"

He sat back in the chair, one hand resting on the top of the cane, his crippled upper body bent sideways. "If y-you were not a guest, I-I would have broken y-your leg, and not simply delivered, a minor admonishment, a small lesson. Y-your presence here, will give y-your father, something else to focus on, besides a blasphemous union, besides a betrayal of h-his kind. Not knowing who has taken y-you, h-he will distrust everyone, and so each Leeth, will fall under h-his suspicion."

"There is no betrayal," she replied defiantly, "in seeking to improve, the lot of all Larians, the future of all Largess." She glanced scornfully at Vashon, who paid the expression no mind. "*Most* offworlders seek only to help, to raise up our world and our peoples, to the levels they themselves have reached, through mutual cooperation." She shifted her attention back to the Hobak. "Where is the harm in that, where the danger and the peril, in seeking only improvement, through joining together and with others?"

Slamming a hand down so hard on the left arm of the chair of office that both recorders jumped slightly in their seats, na Broon rose halfway from a sitting position. It was all he could manage.

"Have none of y-you southerners considered," he roared melodically, "what such a union would mean, in political terms, as well as social? Are y-you all so greedy, for the toys of the offworlders, that y-you are willing to sacrifice, to give up, to cast aside, y-y-y-your sovereignty?" His back might be twisted sideways and his singspeaking cursed with a singular speech impediment, but he had no difficulty making himself understood. Wincing from the pain that never left him, the pain he had been born with, he settled slowly back into the chair.

"I-I will never allow Minord, or any other Leeth where I-I have influence, to surrender its independence, to some offworld whimsy. Largess is for *its* peoples; for Larians all, for Larians together, and against the spawn, of other worlds. I-I would rather fight a dozen Leeths combined, than give up one iota, of Minordian independence."

"But that's not the goal, of the Commonwealth speakers," she objected, "who sing only, of greatness for Largess. Of a chance to participate with other peoples, in other ways, who dwell in harmony among the stars."

"Y-you sing of daydreams, in the warbling of a child, with no real knowledge, of how alliances work. Always there is one that dominates, its struggling brethren, whether through arms, or taxes, or cultural supremacy. I-I do not know if this alien Commonwealth, would use one or all, to subjugate ou-our world, but this I-I do know: that I-I will not sit by, and watch it happen, and see it take place, so long as I-I-*I* am Hobak, of this Leeth."

"You are a male," she sang softly but not kindly, "suffering from delusion, replete with symptoms, visible to anyone not under your spell. Or under your knife, which I suspect is more common, than you persuading others, through your political skills. The alliance will happen; no matter your interference, no matter what delays, despite whatever lies, you can fabricate."

"I-I think not," he responded quietly in his own peculiar stuttering singspeech, "so long as y-your father, that noble leader, raises all of Borusegahm, to hunt for h-his Firstborn. And while h-he does so, I-I will sing my own position; to the heads of the other Leeths, to all peninsulas and islands, and even to the Leeth-lands, that lie across the seas." His eyes glittered. "I-I may not convince all, of the rightness of m-my argument, but enough will be persuaded, to render this 'union' not viable."

Curling her nostril straight down, she took the tip between the teeth at the end of her snout. A gasp came from at least one of the recorders, and despite his Hobak's caveat, a guard lowered his spear. Vashon had to smile to himself. The Firstborn of Borusegahm was truly incorrigible. The iconic slur she had just rendered was about as extreme as one Larian could flash at another.

As ever since they had first struck a business relationship, Vashon was once again surprised by the Hobak. Felelagh na Broon's sole response to the visual obscenity was the Larian equivalent of a laugh. Even to a human, the musical note the speech-challenged Hobak emitted was amusing.

"Y-you are brave but not sophisticated, courageous but not wise, which is ever a constant, among the young. Guest or prisoner, well-fed or starved, free to walk about or hobbled by chains: the choice is y-yours. One day y-you will be returned home; to the safety of your

Leeth, to the comfort of Borusegahm, to the insularity that nour-
ishes y-you, but which y-you insist on rejecting in favor of a dream.
Before that can happen I-I will have made, alliances of m-my own,
and w-we will shut out this pernicious 'Commonwealth,' no matter
how superior its technology!" Pushing himself back in the chair, he
grimaced as he made an effort, ultimately futile, to sit straight.

"One day y-you will understand, and come to thank m-me, as
will y-your father, and every citizen of h-his Leeth, every inhabitant
of Largess. Until that day comes, y-you may enjoy Minordian hospitality, or if y-you prefer, drown in personal asceticism: the choice is
of no consequence to m-me. I-I have much more to worry about,
than the adolescent protestations, of one who is nothing more, than
a marker in a game."

Light shone through the webbing of his left hand as he raised it
high. In response, four more guards emerged from a hidden alcove
behind the leader's seat. At his direction Preedir ah nisa Leeh was
taken away, escorted out of the Great Hall to a sealed apartment
that had been made ready in anticipation of her involuntary arrival.
Gesturing at Vashon, na Broon beckoned him forward.

"Y-you have done well, have done all that y-you promised, and in
keeping with ou-our arrangement, the goods y-you requested shall
be supplied. What will y-you do with them, once they are delivered,
once they are transferred, into y-your care?"

"Arrange a small convoy," Vashon replied, "back to Borusegahm,
back to the station, where my people can trade. I will use again, an
assortment of others, of people and machines, to forward onward
my 'goods.'"

"W-we must discuss one day," the Hobak sang roughly, "the profits y-you make, from the pact between u-us. As I-I might hope, that
some partial benefit might accrue, not only to Minord, but to
m-myself personally."

"The pleasure to do so, will entirely be mine," a gratified Vashon
sang back, "as profit shared, can only benefit both—participants."
Though the human finished on a sour, unmelodic note, na Broon

ignored it as he rose to put a reassuring hand on the offworlder's shoulder.

Standing alone and forgotten on the carpets in front of them, Zkerig could only look on and mutter to himself.

"We have failed, for we are too late, to intercept, the Preedir ah nisa Leeh and her abductors, the Firstborn and your troublemakers."

Wiegl waited for a reaction from the offworlder magician. Instead of turning to the Larian, Flinx continued to gaze at the cool, clear stream where they had stopped. Having settled into its familiar squatting posture, their brund relaxed nearby, contentedly munching the purple-hued flowers that grew on the trunks of the treelike growths that shielded them from the nearest cluster of single-story rock houses. The fresh water on this world, Flinx mused as he chucked a small round rock into the stream, was as clean and pure as any he had ever sipped.

He lifted his gaze. In the distance, the tightly packed homes and businesses and industries of Minord climbed and crested a gentle hill threaded with stone-paved streets. Thick smoke rose from the chimneys of small factories and private residences. To the east of the city, a fast-flowing river powered wood-and-metal waterwheels, some of them several stories high and of impressive workmanship.

Taking it all in, Flinx thought it would be a shame if Commonwealth membership brought commerce that in any way contaminated either the local water or the Larians themselves. He sighed, aware he was being unduly romantic as well as naïve. Industry was already here, on the cusp of advanced development. Commonwealth assistance and technology would do more to ensure that Largess's burgeoning growth did not damage the ecology than it would to generate any such damage. There were the waterwheels—but there was also the dense, black smoke. With or without outside help, local growth could not be stopped. Better to help where it was possible than to stand back and ignore what was going to happen here.

While Flinx had waited by the brook, Wiegl had made his way into the outskirts of Minord town. The guide had eavesdropped, and asked questions, and had not had to probe very deep in order to obtain the information he sought.

While it could not yet be confirmed, the rumor had spread rapidly through the populace that an important member of the ruling family of distant Borusegahm had been brought to Minord, against her will. If true, it raised the possibility there could be war with the southern Leeth. Or more likely, much agitated singing back and forth.

Why would the current political regime of Minord engage in such a provocation? the citizens wondered. Among the townsfolk there were many theories. Included among them was mention of a proposed unification of all the Leeths so that their world might qualify for associate membership in the mysterious offworlder Commonwealth. Since the only offworld outpost on Largess was located in Borusegahm, this only contributed to the suspicions and paranoia among those debating the rumor's possible merits.

Considering that the intent, as Flinx understood it, behind the kidnapping of the Firstborn of Borusegahm was to sow anger and confusion among the Leeths and thereby divert them from concentrating on achieving such a unification, the abduction was clearly already on the way to achieving that goal.

Tired of watching the human toss rocks into the water, the just-returned Wiegl could hold his peace no longer. "Since we are unable to intercept, the Firstborn and her abductors, I assume we will now return home, the better to let diplomats and politicians, the better to let those in a position to do so, negotiate a way out of this matter."

Having come to a decision, Flinx turned to him. "We will do nothing of the sort, but will instead do our best, to conclude this business we have begun, in a satisfactory fashion."

Though the human's singspeech had grown fluent, Wiegl was still not sure he had heard the words and the melody correctly. "Did you not understand what I just said, that the strideship has reached

Minord, and has docked, and unloaded its cargo?" He gestured sharply in the direction of the city whose narrow streets he had just prowled. "To extricate the Firstborn *now* would require an army, not a pair of optimists, not even if one, is an offworld magician!" Lowering his arm, he straightened, his thick tail stiffening until it stood straight out behind him, parallel to the ground and quivering with exasperation.

"To take back the Firstborn from her place in the city, to take her back by force since there are no longer any other options, could perhaps be done with a dozen of your marvelous 'skimmer' craft, armed with the wondrous weapons you refuse to give us."

Flinx was calm as he studied the cityscape spread across and over the summit of the distant hill. Mist had turned to drizzle. Smoke continued to rise from the city's profusion of chimneys, though whether their fires were powered by wood or peat or coal, or something unique to Largess, he could not tell. The acrid yet sweet smell that began to drift outward from the tightly clustered gray and dull white buildings did not suggest any combustible material with which he was familiar. But on a world in which the overriding fragrance was of damp, it was often difficult to distinguish individual odors.

"All my life, I have been faced with dilemmas as impossible as they were improbable," he replied equably, "and each time I have managed a solution, so I am not intimidated, by the one that confronts us here. Compared to others with which I have dealt, this seems a small thing, a minor obstacle, a simple problem. I will apply all my knowledge, and utilize all my talents, to ensure that we do not return to Borusegahm, empty of hand and depleted in pride."

Wiegl's ears were twitching so hard they looked as if they might break free of his head and fly off on their own. "We have your magician's skills, it is true, and the flying creature of many colors that kills"—he pointed toward the metal walking tube that lay propped up against a nearby green-trunked growth—"and moves faster than the eye can follow. But these will not be enough, against the arms of Minord, let alone against those of which we are unaware, and may be possessed by the rogue human." Nictitating membranes flicked down over his eyes as he was suddenly hopeful. "Unless you have, a plan you have prepared, which you have kept to yourself, and of which I am ignorant."

"My plan has not changed, which is to use my 'magic,' to persuade and convince, and also to improvise. All that has changed, is the location; from ship to town, from deck to floor, from cabin to castle." Turning away from the stream, Flinx picked up the walking tube. A slight hiss rose from within. "We will take with us into the city, only that which we can carry, and will make our way inward, in the manner of casual visitors."

Wiegl's head tilted to one side. "A suitable sortie, valuable at least for information, save for one slight problem, you seem to be forgetting." When Flinx did not sing a reply, the guide helpfully explained. "Since the fact seems to have escaped you, I must remind you, that you are not Larian, but an offworlder of strange appearance, of strange locomotion, of even stranger eyes, and of too many digits and too great a height, and that therefore your presence, some slight notice might attract."

Flinx didn't reply immediately, peering into the tube to check on Pip. Drowsy within the insulated cylinder, she barely glanced up at him before returning to her slumber.

"I am counting on it," he replied, in harmony deliberately curt so that there could be no mistaking his determination.

Run now, Wiegl told himself. *Run, don't look back, be content with your prepaid half-payment, and get away home.*

He couldn't do it. Not because fleeing at this point would cause any damage to his reputation: none in Minord were aware of it, or him. Not because it might brand him a coward, in his own eyes if no others. No, he could not run away because he had become oddly fond of the strange offworlder who called himself Flinx. He might run out on an unpleasant employer, but never on a friend. Not even one who was a member of an alien species, even if it was a species whose kind he might never encounter again.

Also, he was beyond curious to see what miracles the magician had in mind.

Flinx easily sensed his companion's emotional turmoil but chose not to comment on it. Wiegl had been wary of him from the start. Better not to let him know that his human companion could almost always perceive the guide's true feelings.

They arranged to stable the brund with an obliging quartet of fisherfolk. The family felt no compunction in assisting the strangers, even if one of them was an offworlder. Either the oddly matched pair of visitors would return and pay the agreed-upon fee, or they would never come back. If the latter, then the seiners would acquire a fine, healthy transport animal. The best gambles, the patriarch of the four reflected, were the ones that did not involve gambling.

Only occasionally utilizing the metal tube as a walking stick so as not to disturb its sleeping occupant, Flinx sauntered deeper into the city, flanked by his reluctant but committed guide. The human had made no attempt to disguise himself, change his clothing, or mask his true barefaced appearance. When queried about these seeming omissions, Flinx explained his reasoning without hesitation.

"If I try to conceal myself, then it will seem to anyone who sees through such a disguise, that I must have something to hide, and a need to conceal it from public view." Raising a hand, he smiled and waved at a pair of elderly females who gaped at him out of an oval window. Young Larians gamboled behind the unlikely pair of visitors, chattering while telling jokes through mouthfuls of small fish, their jaws making smacking sounds as they strung together clumsy but evocative melodies. Some of their comments had to do with the offworlder's height, others with his peculiar and opaque attire. The majority referenced the profusion of fingers on his hands, their lack of any connective webbing, and especially the absence of a tail. Wiegl they mostly ignored.

Pausing occasionally in the middle of a street paved with quarried gray slate to ask directions of a solitary pedestrian, they drew penetrating stares but no crowd. The inhabitants were curious but cautious. Reaching out with his talent, Flinx perceived an ocean of emotion that ranged from mildly fearful to intensely curious to disgust or admiration. Only, of course, among those who were not singspeaking. In short, the citizens of Minord City did not know what to think of him. All of which contributed to the comforting knowledge that he was not expected.

Having failed to intercept the Firstborn and her abductors before she could be brought into the city, he would now have to confront her captors directly and on their home ground. At least, it was home ground for the Minordians. Whoever was helping them was no more a valid resident here than was Flinx, no matter what local associations that still-unknown individual might have forged.

"Don't worry." He could sense the guide's tension and hastened to reassure him. "As I have dealt with such situations before, and have always managed to emerge successful, and with all worthwhile appendages intact."

Wiegl's attention was drawn to a trio of uniformed locals. Plainly sizing up the visitors, two of them now broke away to dash up a nearby lane. The third kept pace with the newcomers, keeping his distance from them while his eyes continued to mark their progress. The guide pointed him out.

"Your wish to meet with local officials, is about to be granted, is about to be fulfilled, if the one with the sword who does not turn away, belies anything with his body language."

Wiegl's analysis was to be proven correct. Very little additional time had elapsed when the two soldiers, or police, or whatever the local peacekeeping force was called, returned with an entire squad of comrades in tow: a dozen or more of them. They joined their remaining colleague in paralleling the newcomers.

But—that was all. No attempt was made to arrest, or even to question, Flinx and his edgy companion. The armed force, a mix of males and females, merely continued to track them at a distance.

When Flinx made as if to swerve in their direction, they compliantly backed off. If he looked ready to head in the other direction, they moved closer. He and Wiegl were being monitored, but not interfered with. The squad's uneasiness was plain to perceive.

This won't do, Flinx decided. If they were going to get anywhere, they *needed* to be interfered with.

They emerged into a circular square. As the afternoon drizzle started to fade, Flinx began to ascend a series of concentric platforms carved from alternating slabs of green and gray granite. Water flowed down them, making footing slippery, but he continued until he was standing at the base of the three sculptures that crowned the top of the elaborate public fountain. These comprised a trio of different aquatic animals, each more outrageous in appearance than the next, from whose assorted orifices water flowed. He did not pause to admire them.

"What are you doing, what are you about, what irrationality is this?" Wiegl stammered from below. "Have we come then, all this way, to die for a farce?"

Flinx looked past him. In addition to the persistent train of cubs and young adolescents, he had now acquired quite a crowd of adults, come to view the spectacle of an alien in their midst. Well, if it was a spectacle they wanted, he would give it to them. Leaning on the metal tube and striving to fill the minidrag within with nothing but soothing feelings, he took a deep breath and began to speak.

Combined with the studies he had completed on board the *Teacher,* his travels from Borusegahm had equipped him with sufficient glibness to be reasonably sure of his diction. The only uncertainty that remained related to his singing voice. It had proven satisfactory for communicating with Wiegl and other individual Larians. Was it good enough to hold an audience? Or would his attempt at a singspeech speech fall as flat as the underlying notes?

Whatever you are going to do, whatever you are going to say, standing up there like a proud fool, an uneasy Wiegl thought, *please leave me out of it.*

Today was not his luckiest of days.

"My friend and I," Flinx began singspeaking boldly, "having heard tell of a possible conflict, brewing between the peoples of the North and those of the South, have journeyed long and hard, to preach against it!" Stirred initially by his fluency in their language and more deeply by its content, the squad of peacekeepers now began to move forward, pushing and shoving their way through the crowd toward the central fountain and its unlikely resident. Taking note of their approach, Flinx sang faster.

"Some speak of an abduction, of an important personage, from the great Leeth known to all, as Borusegahm!" The peacekeepers' advance now took on an air of urgency as their emotions filled with alarm. A couple of them had drawn pistols and short swords and were waving them warningly in Flinx's direction. He pretended not to see. "A personage of beauty, of education, and of breeding; one who is central, to the people of Borusegahm! She is here, of that I am certain, knowing as I do that—"

Elongated three-fingered hands were grabbing forcefully at him now, threatening not just to draw him down but to pull him off his perch. Having no wish to stumble and hit his head against the slick stone, or have his head "accidentally" make contact with it (the number of witnesses notwithstanding), he allowed himself to be half dragged, half guided off the fountain and back to the ground, all the while keeping a steady grip on his emotions so that Pip would not take alarm. Held firmly in the grasp of two of the peacekeepers, Wiegl glared at the human.

"Is this the outcome you sought, offworld magician; a quick visit in freedom, followed by a doubtless lengthier one of restraint?"

Of the three slender but muscular peacekeepers who were holding him, two flinched at the guide's words while the third actually let go. To his credit, the officer facing Flinx held his ground. But while he might appear bold and in charge, Flinx could sense his fear and uncertainty. He had no intention of exacerbating it.

"We are your prisoners, now at your disposal, to be taken to whatever, place you wish." He executed most handily the Larian gesture indicative of ready compliance.

While pleased (and relieved) to receive the alien's articulate submission, the officer was anxious to be rid of the creature and its companion as soon as possible.

"You will come with us now, in silence and subservience, to the central detention center, at City Hall. No trouble will you give us, no argument or dissension, or further restraint will be applied, and I do not mean with words."

Indicating that he understood, Flinx obediently fell in line between the two ranks of peacekeepers. Wiegl followed close behind, peering at the ground while mumbling to himself a tune that was definitely not in the form of a love song.

"Are we then, under arrest; formal prisoners, under what charge?" Flinx essayed conversationally.

"I do not know, what you are," the officer responded with tuneful honesty, "by which I mean to say, *I do not know what you are*."

"I am an offworlder," Flinx replied helpfully, "more specifically a human, citizen of a government called the Commonwealth, that seeks to aid each and every inhabitant of Largess. Including you"—he nodded toward several of the other peacekeepers, who studiously ignored him—"and you, and you, and even you."

"I would have you leave me out of it," the officer replied earnestly, "of whatever it is you speak, and let the adjudicator, decide your fate, your tomorrow, and whatever truth may lie in your words."

15

■ ■ ■

As lockups went, the one situated in the bowels of the sprawling City Hall complex was an appropriate depiction of the general level of technology on Largess. The stone walls (red granite this time) were polished instead of rough, a nice touch when one considered that aesthetics were not usually a priority for most species who occasionally needed to restrain antisocial members of their own culture. Instead of bars, fine cross-hatched iron grillwork shut the cell off from the subterranean corridor it fronted. Utilizing his greater human mass, Flinx thought he might be able to bend the metal strands. Even so, it would take many hours to make a hole big enough for him and Wiegl to crawl through. It would be a futile exercise in any case, since they would then be faced with the prospect of safely exiting the corridor and escaping the building.

And to what end? It was not as if they could hide somewhere in the city. That was not what had prompted Flinx to perform publicly. Save for the inability to move about at will, he and Wiegl were more or less exactly where he wanted to be.

Furthermore, wary of approaching the peculiar offworlder too closely (and fortunately for them), none of their escort had thought to check the interior of the alien creature's walking stick.

In between two long, very low cot-like arrangements was what at first glance appeared to be a third. It took a moment to find the fill spigot and controls. At first he thought it was a bath, until Wiegl explained to him that for a Larian, regular immersion in water was a necessity, not a luxury. There was no window, but that didn't bother Flinx. He did not expect to be here for very long.

"A most excellent conclusion," an irritated Wiegl sang bitterly, "to all our traveling, all our fighting, all our efforts most strenuously expended." Elongated black eyes gazed into Flinx's own. "What now do you propose, offworlder, human, magician? To request that the Hobak, bring his captive to us here, and then set us free; to go home, to go south, to leave his boundaries, accompanied by his profoundest apologies?"

"Maybe." Unharmonious though they might be, Flinx felt that Larian culture could benefit from the inclusion of a few one-note responses—Wiegl's wincing at the acerbic reply notwithstanding.

"So what do we do now," the guide sputtered as he paced the restricted, enclosed area of the cell, "while we linger for some adjudicator, to determine our fate?"

"We wait." Flinx took a seat on one of the cots, having to practically squat in order to do so. He continued in proper singspeech, feeling he owed it to Wiegl to spare the guide's ears. "Until someone comes, of amiable disposition, to let us out."

"Let us . . . ?" Exasperated and disbelieving, Wiegl slumped down on the cot opposite, not even bothering to finish the tune he had started.

Less than an hour had passed when a Larian draped in unexpectedly colorful and conspicuously official gossamer came down the corridor and stopped in front of their cell. After studying the unlikely pair inside with unabashed interest, she beckoned to Wiegl. Anxious not to make things any worse and hopeful of currying whatever favor might waft his way, the guide stood up quickly and hurried over to the grate.

"I was told an offworlder, had been remanded into custody, for declaiming in a public place, things better left unsaid, best left undiscussed. An offworlder with too many fingers, and ears on the sides of its head instead of properly atop, and a face that looked as if stepped on, and nearly naked of hair besides." Her ears and proboscis twitched in disbelief. "I would not have countenanced such a thing, were I not standing here, seeing it for myself, in plain view."

Understanding everything she said, Flinx smiled helpfully. She ignored him, singspeaking only to Wiegl.

"I have been told to inquire, if it has special needs, as it is deemed important, to keep both of you alive and well. Until the adjudicator can return, to take up this unusual case, or until the Hobak himself, deigns to intervene."

Flinx rose. "Why wait for an adjudicator?" he proposed, shocking yet another citizen of Largess with his ability to singspeak, "when the Hobak can determine, through his greater skill and perception, what fate should befall my friend and myself?"

Don't be so helpful, Wiegl wanted to say. But mindful of the magician's skills and of abilities perhaps as yet unrevealed, he kept quiet, stepping aside as the human rose from the cot and walked over to the grate.

Flinx gazed down at the jailer, trying to penetrate her stare, to see beyond the black eyes. Entirely unaware of what he was trying to do, she did not move away. Just looked back, scrutinizing him with equal intensity.

"So the noble Hobak, Felelagh na Broon, is himself nearby, is available for consultation?"

Her response was a desultory snort through her single flexible nostril. It wetted his shirt. He paid neither the snot nor the sentiment the least attention.

"What does it matter," she sang, "as he would never deign, to waste his valuable time, on a pair of common prisoners."

Flinx persisted. "But we are not common prisoners, and it is imperative that we meet, the Hobak in person, to discuss why we have come." He continued to stare hard at the guard. "Surely one of your experience, equipped with such knowledge, must fully grasp, the importance of the moment, the importance of the passion, that underlies our request?"

The guard's protective membranes fluttered over her eyes. One hand reached toward her waist. There was a short sword scabbarded there and an alarmed Wiegl started to back away from the intervening metal grid. But her fingers bypassed the sword in favor of a single squarish key. Sliding this down a slot in the left side of the barrier unlocked it. Looking dazed, she pulled the grate aside. Her singspeech was muted and slow.

"Of course you must . . . meet with the Hobak . . . so that you can relay to him . . . the reason for your coming. Follow . . . me . . . this . . . way."

Turning, she led a gratified Flinx and an awed Wiegl down the corridor and up a flight of winding stone stairs. The guide's singspeech was barely whispered.

"Truly you are, a magician of great powers, to have changed her mind, to have altered her stance, to have persuaded her to do this!"

Flinx shook his head, hoping Wiegl was sufficiently familiar with human body language from his time spent at Borusegahm station to understand the gesture's significance.

"I did not do anything of the sort, as I cannot affect minds, in the way that you suggest, but can only influence—emotions." He nodded toward the guard who was leading the way upward. "I projected onto her feelings of sympathy, of concern, of worry for our condition, and anxiety for our well-being. It is enough, so far, for her to feel compassion for us, and to translate that into a small kindness."

"Then we can get away," Wiegl sang in triplets, "and flee this place, and recover our brund, and return to blessed Borusegahm!"

"We can do," Flinx corrected him, "exactly what I told her we would do, and not leave, without concluding the business, for which we came, for which I pledged, my guarantee."

"Throat-cut your guarantee," the guide muttered discordantly, "as will ours be, if you try to confront, this addled na Broon Hobak in person." But he did not make a run for it when they emerged from the stairwell into an empty service corridor, and though he continued to sing his discontent, he followed Flinx and the guard without taking the opportunity to break away.

After traversing several intersecting service corridors and walking at least half a kilometer, the now slightly addled and sympathetic guard led them across an empty courtyard and into a curved inner office. Two clerks who were partially buried by gray scrollwork looked up from their short chairs, their long fingers pausing above abacus-like devices, and eyed the guard questioningly. At Flinx's emotional urging, she sang what was almost a lament.

"They *have* to see the Hobak, these two visitors, and the offworlder brings with him, nothing but good feelings, for all of Minord. It's a matter of urgency; of necessity, of affection, that I do not have sufficient time to explain, to underlings such as yourselves."

As they passed through the narrow double doorway behind the clerks, one of them glanced at her colleague and expressed her puzzlement with an atypically single-note response.

" 'Affection'?"

The nonpolitical term was one scarcely heard within the winding corridors of the City Hall, but was hardly provocative enough to engender suspicion among the pair of bureaucrats. They returned to their work, curious as to what another offworlder was doing in their Leeth, and wondered if it would rain hard today or if the afternoon clouds would bring forth only a pleasant drizzle.

The room into which the guard conducted them was very large. Narrow floor-to-ceiling windows looked out on Minord City's main square. Unlike the public space Flinx had impulsively chosen as the site for his declamation, this one featured multiple fountains in addition to a display of kinetic sculptures fashioned from wood and metal. The window glass was thick, marred by ripples, and full of bubbles, indicating that the Larian craftsmen in this Leeth, at least, had not yet mastered the art of glassmaking—much less advanced to manufacturing transparencies of far harder material. A civilization at Largess's level of technology would benefit tremendously from gradual and careful integration into the Commonwealth, he knew. No wonder Padre Jonas and her superiors were so anxious to help accelerate this world and its inhabitants along that path.

He would assist them in doing so by removing an unanticipated irritant from the equation.

As he let his gaze rove the chamber, both vision and his talent indicated that only indigenes were present. One was another functionary, this one clad in far more elegant and colorful raiment than the pair of clerks he and Wiegl had encountered in the outer office. There was also someone seated within a low circular desk. "Within" rather than "behind," because the distinctive piece of Larian furniture, cut from the trunk of a single huge tree, formed an almost perfect doughnut shape. It allowed for an individual to sit in the center and rotate to reach any point on the encircling countertop by the simple expedient of spinning in their seat. The proportionately low seat had no back. Supported by their flexible, strong notochords, the Larians had no need of artificial spinal braces.

Even as his attention was already focused on the chamber's other inhabitant, Flinx sensed the bureaucrat's distress well before he spoke.

"Who are you two, who arrive unannounced, and one an offworlder, at that?" He moved in the direction of a line of rope pulls that hung from the ceiling and to the left of the desk. "Hide, drop down, and seek safety, my liege! I myself will ascertain the meaning, of this unwarranted intrusion, and deal with these interlopers, as their intent demands!"

An extraordinary figure rose from the chair behind the desk to forestall his subordinate's instinctive reaction. Flinx continued to concentrate on him while ignoring the semi-hysterical bureaucrat.

Whether the Larian had been born with a twisted notochord or suffered from some unknown but severe accident, Flinx did not know. In order to stand, the individual had to place a hand on the desk to support his sideways-bent body.

"Y-you must wish to see m-me, very badly indeed, to have come all this way, offworlder." In addition to a crooked body, Felelagh na Broon suffered from a left eye that was clouded by an unknown affliction. Possibly a condition that could be cured by contemporary Commonwealth medicine, Flinx thought—if only such advanced technological intrusions were permitted. If only this Hobak could be made to see the light that could be ignited by associate Commonwealth membership. With luck and the right argument, hopefully he could be persuaded to change his outlook.

But not through the same method of persuasion Flinx had utilized on, for example, the holding-cell guard. What he could perceive of na Broon's feelings was . . . roiled. A confusing mess that ranged from delight to fear to expectation all the way through to a preening self-confidence. Until and unless he could lock down the Hobak's emotional state, Flinx would not be able to influence it.

Patience, he told himself. As much as his minion, na Broon was surprised by Flinx and Wiegl's unexpected appearance. When the Hobak settled down, Flinx would try to influence him as only he could. There did not seem to be any hurry, especially since the Hobak had prevented his underling from calling in the guards. Meanwhile Wiegl's attention kept switching rapidly between the offworlder and na Broon, and Flinx perceived that he was wondering what was keeping the human magician from working his magic on the Hobak.

Needing to play for a little time anyway, Flinx saw no reason to falsify the reason for their presence.

"We have indeed, great Hobak, come all the way from Borusegahm, from the offworlder station, to try to defuse a dangerous situation."

Still uneasy, the Hobak's personal assistant hovered nearby, ready to call for armed backup the instant either of the peculiar interlopers made anything resembling a hostile gesture. That they did not do so only unnerved him more. Whereas his superior, the elected Hobak, now evinced only curiosity and amusement at the intrusion.

"If y-you are referring, to the recent difficulty, in collecting taxes from the east vales, then I-I would myself welcome y-your assistance."

A disarmingly composed verbal response, Flinx reflected, that contrasted wildly with the Hobak's turbulent emotional state. Inside, he was a seething cauldron of conflicting temperaments. Hard to get through, hard to pin down. But not necessarily threatening. The fact that Pip remained comfortably ensconced within the insulated depths of the walking tube was sufficient confirmation of such a conclusion.

Unless, he thought, Felelagh na Broon was the shrewdest manager of his feelings Flinx had ever encountered. Or possibly the Hobak was partially deranged. That often accounted for unpredictable emotional projections. Flinx knew he might be able to soothe the latter condition as well, if only the Hobak would calm down sufficiently inside himself to allow Flinx an emotional locus on which to focus.

"I refer not to taxes but to that which is taxing; upon the citizens of Borusegahm, upon my fellow offworlders, and upon good folk everywhere."

"So even before knowing of what y-you speak, of who I-I am," the Hobak replied cannily, "y-you have already decided, I-I am not one of the 'good folk'?"

"You preempt my conclusions," Flinx sang back as he tried to match wits with the current ruler of Minord, "to which I have not come, but can only settle upon, the outcome of my visit." He gripped the walking tube tighter, hoping that Pip would sense his rising tension and rouse herself accordingly. "I know that the Firstborn of Borusegahm Leeth, the celebrated Preedir ah nisa Leeh, has been brought here against her will, on your order. That you hope in so doing, to forestall the establishment, of a union of Leeths, who would join with my government."

"Do you deny it?" snapped Wiegl unmelodically, feeling a need to contribute—or at least to show his mettle. The look he got from Flinx and the Hobak's assistant both was enough to put a halt to the additional verses he had contemplated singing.

"I have come," Flinx continued as if there had been no interruption, "to persuade you to return the Firstborn, by offering you membership, even a prominent place, on the future council of Largess."

That was enough to sweep aside the emotional disorder that dominated the Hobak's feelings. All else vanished in an instant as, unable to straighten, he leaned forward as far as he could in the direction of the intruders.

"Felelagh na Broon is nobody's vassal; not of Leeths that leech, not of offworld wit-spinners, not of bald-faced, bald-bodied emissaries! Let the Hobak of Borusegahm come with all h-his allies, to the gates of Minord, and let h-him beg, for the return of h-his Firstborn. Sh-she stays here, at m-my pleasure, until I-I feel inclined, to send h-her back! Minord will go its *own* way, free of outside directives, cleansed of offworld influences, and unimpeded by the fainthearted: the greatest Leeth, now and forever, on all of Largess!"

The unexpected forcefulness of his riposte caused his subordinate to shrink back, and even Wiegl was intimidated. Only Flinx remained unaffected by the stentorian rant of what was to him nothing more than a land-going seal-like creature representing an up-and-coming but not yet mature species. At least na Broon's fury and focus finally gave him a chance to narrow in on the Hobak's emotions. He would have tried to influence them, too, had the confrontation not been interrupted.

Having been informed of the unannounced arrival in the city of a human and his Larian companion, Vashon had immediately set aside what he had been doing and hurried to the area used for holding lawbreakers, only to find them unaccountably missing. Anxious queries had finally directed him to, implausibly, the Hobak's own office. Now he found himself confronting a tableau as incongruous as it was unanticipated: a human other than himself engaged in animated conversation with Felelagh na Broon, while the Hobak's personal assistant stood nearby and wet himself.

Prepared to confront a heavily armed military type, he was further taken aback by the intruder's youth and lack of any detectable weaponry. In fact, Vashon realized, the interloper appeared to be completely unarmed. Vashon saw no reason to draw the neuronic pistol from the holster at his belt.

Could *this* be the individual who had been in pursuit? Had some fool in authority sent a youth, albeit a remarkably composed one, after him? Just one youth at that, apparently weaponless to boot. After Vashon Lek! He didn't know whether to be relieved or insulted. One thing he did know: unless he was overlooking something very subtle, this visitor was not going to be a problem at all.

"Name?" Flinx asked calmly. The glaring reality of the forbidden neuronic pistol holstered at the newcomer's waist told him all he needed to know about the short, thickset stranger. Clearly, this was the renegade who had assisted in the abduction of Preedir ah nisa Leeh from Borusegahm Leeth. The one whose presence he had sensed amid so much death and dying just prior to his and Wiegl's arrival at Poskraine.

The object of his attention replied carefully. "For purposes of conversation, which will be brief, you can call me Vashon."

"You're coming back with me," Flinx informed him matter-of-factly. "You, to face the authorities for violating Commonwealth directives, and the Firstborn of Borusegahm, so she can be returned to her family. But since you are here now and she isn't, you first."

Strange to be speaking terranglo again. After so many days of essaying nothing but Larian singspeech, the tones, the sharpness, the awkward cadences of terranglo resounded on the tongue almost as harshly as thranx click-speech. He found that he missed the melodious glory of the local language more than he would have expected.

Wiegl did not have to be able to read Flinx's emotions in order to sense what was coming. Though his presence could make no difference to nor have any effect on the forthcoming engagement, he stepped aside. Seeing this, the Hobak's underling reached again for one of the pull-ropes—only to be stopped a second time by his superior. Felelagh na Broon was eyeing the two offworlders with great interest.

"No, Menliag, not at this time, not at this moment, for I think here is something, to watch and learn, so—let them play."

It was with obvious reluctance that the subordinate complied, his webbed fingers falling away from the cord. A roomful of armed troops would have done more to assuage his nerves than any words, no matter how wise or reassuring, from his Hobak.

Reach out and perceive, reach out and analyze, what he's thinking, Flinx told himself. Save for a single temporarily debilitating headache, his now-refined talent had been functioning well ever since he had arrived on Largess. Despite an inability to recognize the emotions of the natives when they were singspeaking, he had employed it successfully several times. He anticipated no such problems with this Vashon person, who appeared to be nothing more than an uncommonly enterprising offender. It should be a simple matter to identify and manipulate the man's essential emotions so that he would—

He blinked. Tried again. Nothing. There was nothing there.

Vashon's emotional slate was blank. At least at the moment, he was feeling—nothing. Not anger, not concern, not anticipation. Not weariness, not sadness, not amusement. Nothing.

Without turning away from the lawbreaker, Flinx redirected his talent to first the tremulous bureaucrat, then Wiegl, and finally Felelagh na Broon himself. Their feelings were not hidden: he could sense them easily. Only when he tried to penetrate the emotional state of the human Vashon did he encounter a total void.

Absurd. Not impossible, but absurd. The man had to be feeling *something.* Try as he might, Flinx was unable to latch on to a single sentiment. Facing him, the unsmiling individual was as emotionless as a stone. He began to feel a little uneasy. He could not manipulate what was not there.

This was the abnormality he had sensed on the way to Poskraine, amid so much Larian dying. At that distance, he had been unable to identify it properly. He had not been perceiving distant human emotions, but rather a human devoid of them. What he had sensed just barely, and what now stood before him, was an emotional ghost. Flinx's talent could perceive the echo of emotions, the hole where they ought to be, in the same way that a physicist could detect dark matter without actually seeing it. Among other things, it explained why he had not sensed the man's presence the moment they had entered Minord, nor detected his approach to the Hobak's office.

Sensing that all was not well, Wiegl whispered to his companion. "Master magician, if you are working your magic, please confirm so for your lowly guide, who otherwise would appreciate the opportunity, to make a dash for the door. Or if the first magic has failed, perhaps a second magic, this time with potions or powders, or large heavy objects, might serve to improve the situation?"

"It's not a matter of physical things, friend Wiegl, that stymies my efforts, but an emotional vacuity I did not expect, and cannot explain. So in the absence of success, on the part of my 'magic,' I will try to improvise something less mystical, but hopefully as effective."

He turned back to the watching na Broon and his jumpy underling. In contrast to the bizarrely unfathomable Vashon, at least their feelings were still manifest and easy to perceive. Outwardly, the Hobak continued to affect mild amusement at the intrusion. Flinx read him otherwise: while not afraid of the new arrivals, the leader of Minord was intensely interested in whatever they might choose to do next.

Vashon half expected Flinx to pull a concealed weapon. The Hobak's assistant anticipated chaos. Wiegl was waiting for his employer to demonstrate some new trick of mind or voice. Na Broon himself expected a violent physical clash between the two offworlders.

Flinx disappointed all of them.

He gestured disapprovingly at the hard-staring Vashon. "Is this

the human whom it is rumored, you rely upon for advice and assistance, on how to sow confusion among your rivals, while simultaneously uplifting the status of Minord? Was it he who recommended
abducting, the Firstborn of Borusegahm, to slow the establishment
of a union, of all the great Leeths?"

While Vashon would have preferred the Hobak to respond by denying the accusation, or better still, with a signal to his assistant to
call for security, there was nothing he could do to stop na Broon
from replying. He had no way of knowing that his newly arrived
kinsman could ascertain better than anyone whether or not the
Hobak was telling the truth.

"The abduction was m-my idea," Na Broon sang without a hint
of embarrassment or regret, "to strike at the organizer, of the betrayal of Largess itself, to force h-him to back off, to back down, to
watch h-his own back, instead of promoting this nonsense of union."
One three-fingered hand rose to point at the silent Vashon. "M-my
minions carry out m-my directives, they fulfill m-my commands,
without question or hesitation, regardless of origin, regardless of
species. In this Vashon's work has been exemplary, to ou-our mutual
benefit, though m-my aims are lofty, and h-his merely mercenary."

Vashon did not flinch at the implied insult. He was not a man
who was offended by the truth, be it complimentary or distasteful.

Flinx replied with the Larian gesture indicative of understanding.
"I am glad that your investment in this one, has proven worthwhile,
but I am prepared, to improve upon it." As Wiegl gaped at him, Flinx
straightened to his full height, holding the walking tube out in front
of him. It appeared to be nothing more than a hollow metal tube,
but the Larians in the room clearly believed it might be dangerous.
While the underling recoiled, an unflinching na Broon remained
stolidly in his seat as Flinx continued.

"I propose that I take this Vashon's place, as your advisor and
confidant, and promise that if you will let me, I can see Minord
made no less than first among equals, be it standing alone, or at the
head of some future union, of Leeths and their leaders." Making a

guess at the importance of the uneasy underling, he added, "This I will do, to the best of my abilities, ensuring a bright future; for Minord, for yourself as director, and at less cost to the city treasury."

His supposition was correct. For the first time, the Hobak's subordinate exuded positive feelings in Flinx's direction. If he had not made an ally, he had at least neutralized a potential adversary.

Vashon's laughter revealed everything he thought about the absurd proposal. He stopped laughing when he saw that the Larian equivalent was not being emitted by either the Hobak or his assistant. Could the admittedly shrewd Felelagh na Broon—never one to jump to conclusions, always ready to mull alternative possibilities— seriously be interested in this newcomer's ridiculous ploy? For that was all it had to be. Even so, in the absence of mutual amusement he felt compelled to respond.

"This is nonsense, twaddle, claptrap, be it said in terranglo or sung in singspeech! What could another of my kind, about whom you know nothing, save his admitted hostility to me, bring to your service, that I have already not shown? He arrives here, confessing to a mission to arrest me, and also to return the Firstborn, to her Leeth. Confronted with resistance, or at least with indifference, he now offers you his service, apparently on a whim." He jabbed a finger in Flinx's direction. "How could you possibly, consider such an 'offer,' consider such lies, from one you do not know, from one you cannot trust?"

It seemed an eminently logical riposte. Even the Hobak's assistant was persuaded. Only na Broon was not convinced.

"All offers are worthy, of at least casual consideration, lest something of value, be unthinkingly cast aside." He glanced sharply at Vashon, then back at the new visitors. His manner, Flinx thought, was almost kindly. No, that was not the right interpretation, he told himself. Na Broon was being—professional. Thorough. At least, so it seemed. Try as he might, Flinx could still not get a firm handle on the Hobak's stew of emotions.

"As to the matter of trust, in this I-I believe I-I know more than y-you, for while I-I know not how it happened, happened it has, and this happenstance of which I-I will speak leads m-me to think, I-I can in some things rely, on the honesty of th-this person." Once more he pointed, this time toward Wiegl and then to Flinx. "Though th-this visitor is from offworld, and human like y-yourself, h-he is also somehow become, something of Largess, for like h-his companion h-he wears the mark of a Zeregoine."

Vashon's gaze narrowed. "You mean—are you talking about that mark on his forehead? On their foreheads?" In his surprise and haste, he had forgotten to employ proper singspeech. The Hobak's minion scowled at the indignity. Na Broon ignored it.

"The Zeregoine are a sincere and trustworthy faction, of resolute believers, and though I-I do not subscribe, to th-their their ideology, preferring as I-I do, a life on land, it seems as if th-they have made, th-this countryman of y-yours, one of th-their own. In such case, I-I can do no less, than at least consider h-his offer, and ponder the options, it presents to Minord." Sitting back down in his chair, forced by his physical deformity to lean far to his right, he regarded Flinx with a black-eyed stare of intense speculation.

"Until such time, as I-I have come to a decision, regarding not only y-your fate, but that of all concerned, y-you, will be m-my guests. Allowed to wander freely, but within reason, knowing that y-you will be watched, and y-your activities monitored."

Spreading only one hand wide, since the other was required to hold on to Pip's tube, Flinx expressed his pleasure without showing his relief. His gambit had paid off—for now. He had bought some time. Sooner probably than later, the Hobak would decide how to respond to what he perceived to be a genuine offer. Before that happened, Flinx knew he would have to take action. Not only to defend himself and Wiegl, but to liberate Preedir ah nisa Leeh and to deal with Vashon, whose emotional state, despite the fury visible on his face, inexplicably remained a blank to Flinx no matter how hard he fought to penetrate it.

16

■ ■ ■

Though physically damaged and somewhat mentally addled, the Hobak of Minord proved as good as his word. Flinx and Wiegl were assigned quarters and allowed the run of the rambling collection of conjoined buildings that were known collectively as the City Hall. Some sections showed evidence of great age, especially those that bordered directly on the nearby oceanic inlet. Others were more modern, reflecting the advances the Larian species had made since emerging fully from the sea. There was a network of tubes powered by compressed air that sent scrolls shooting between offices, a rudimentary alert system based on pull-cords and bells, refrigeration that utilized ice stored beneath part of the complex, and more. Enough to indicate that Largess was only a step or two short of discovering and utilizing steam technology, and a few more from learning the benefits of electricity.

A union of Leeths that would qualify for associate membership in the Commonwealth would legalize outside assistance and greatly accelerate such development without damaging the social structure. Felelagh na Broon's calculated obfuscation could only delay that natural progression, not stop it. Unless, Flinx knew, the Hobak of

Minord managed to sway others and bring them around to his way of seeing things. Then the setback to Largess's development could prove far more serious, and the consequent loss to its naïve population more detrimental.

Guards at every entrance had plainly been instructed to prevent them from leaving. With Pip, Flinx could easily have forced an exit. But that would solve nothing, though an increasingly anxious Wiegl disagreed.

"We have come to find the Firstborn of Borusegahm," Flinx reminded his companion, "so we can return her to her family, and so put an end, to this obstruction by Minord."

"I know, I realize, I am aware," the guide muttered melodically, "though I would feel far better about our prospects, if you would put to use your magic, instead of crafty words."

Their efforts took a step in the right direction when they encountered Preedir ah nisa Leeh the following day. Flinx found it instructive that while he and Wiegl were allowed free run of the municipal complex, the Firstborn of Borusegahm was accompanied on her walk by four tall, well-armed guards, all of whom appeared to regard their assignment with the utmost seriousness. While outwardly appearing calm, collected, and in charge, emotionally they were tense and on edge.

Sighting Flinx, the Firstborn swerved and came right up to him. Having received orders not to prevent such a meeting but, in contrast, to take note of everything about one should it occur, her escort hung back and allowed the encounter to proceed.

"I am delighted to have the honor, to finally meet in person—" Flinx began in his best singspeech. He was not allowed to finish the melody.

"You are a human, who sings our language, like the walking offal, who brought me here."

"The language yes, the description no, as by any account"— eyeing the attentive but distant escort, he lowered his voice to a melodious whisper—"I and my friend, are here to rescue you."

She gestured curtly and made a show of looking long and deliberately past him. "While I approve of your sentiment, your methodology strikes me as lacking, as I see only two of you, and no army behind."

Plainly taken with the beauty and spirit of the Firstborn, Wiegl felt a need to contribute to the conversation. "There is no army, only just we two, as it was felt that an armed force, would too readily alert the Minordians, to our true intentions." He eyed his employer. "Or so it has been sung, by my companion here, he of many surprises and too many digits."

"No army, just two; you two, most unimpressive." Her gaze flicked from guide to human. "In place of offworld trickery, I would rather see swords and cannon in number, the better my freedom to secure, the better certain body parts here to remove."

Behind her words lay a host of emotions, easily accessible to Flinx. There was anger, and frustration, and barely suppressed fury. So much of it, in fact, that as they stood conversing, Pip reared her head from the mouth of the walking tube, yawned, looked around, and eventually focused on—the Firstborn.

Flinx had a moment of panic. Their jailer had emitted a mixture of curiosity and wariness: Pip had not reacted. The Hobak's chief assistant had evinced unease and concern: Pip had not reacted. Na Broon's confusion of feelings had swung between curiosity, amusement, boredom, and wariness: Pip had not reacted. Vashon, the cause of so much trouble, had been and remained an emotional blank. Pip had not reacted.

Now, in a moment of delicious but dangerous irony, the only individual they had encountered in Minord who had generated enough animosity in Flinx's direction to stimulate Pip defensively was the very one they had come to help.

A couple of hastily sung fawning sonnets praising her determination and perspicacity mollified the Firstborn's feelings sufficiently for Pip to withdraw back into the tube. With her brief appearance blocked by Flinx's body, the minidrag had not been noticed by the quartet of soldiers, who milled about nearby singing in low tones among themselves. On the heels of Flinx's flattery, Wiegl essayed a tune that further calmed the situation as well as the Firstborn's boiling emotions. While inaccurate, the guide's words offered up encouragement. Like Flinx, he kept his singspeech to a whisper.

"Though I am of similar mind, Firstborn, and would myself prefer to be backed by an army, we are not as helpless as we may appear, not as defenseless as others may think." He gestured in the direction of the walking tube. "You saw the head of the creature that sleeps within, whose venom is capable of killing the strongest of enemies, with a single spit. As for my companion and employer, he is no ordinary human, but an offworld magician, commanding powers great and strange."

Preedir turned a penetrating gaze on the taller Flinx. "Is there any truth, to what the servant babbles, and in that truth, some small chance of flight?"

There were times, Flinx knew, when an expeditious lie was more useful than an inconvenient truth. He could always explain later.

"Wiegl is my friend, and not a servant, whose company I respect, and whose skills are vital. It is true that I am a magician." Out of the corner of an eye, he could see the triumphant guide, whose expression and emotions both shouted the equivalent of "I knew it!" Flinx continued.

"But I am one whose abilities must for now remain veiled, as we must choose carefully, the moment of our leave-taking."

Satisfied with this explanation while not believing all of it, Preedir indicated her understanding. "I will rely then, on this unlikely claim, since in any case, I have no choice. Might there be a possibility, as we make our departure, of paying farewell to certain individuals, and dispatching them slowly? I have made promises to myself, promises I should like to keep, and need only a blade, with which to fulfill them."

Flinx swallowed. The Firstborn of Borusegahm was a barely contained cauldron of rage. He wondered if she was like this all the time, or if it was her abduction that rendered her (emotionally at least) borderline apoplectic. If she was elected Hobak of her Leeth (it was not a hereditary position), her energy would bode well for Largess's ascension. Provided it could be directed away from thoughts of general homicide and into more practical channels.

"I can make no promises," he sang carefully in reply, "since we can only respond, as the situation develops, and proceed from there."

Once again he was relieved to perceive that she quite understood. "I follow your reasoning, if with some disappointment, and will restrain myself, until such circumstances suggest otherwise. I will content myself, with inventive imagining, of how I might at the least, extract some small measure of retribution. Against those who have taken me, against those who threaten Borusegahm, against those who would, for reasons deranged and misguided, hold back the advance, of all Largess."

Flinx read her emotions, shuddered, and was glad he was not one of those individuals on the receiving end of the Firstborn's fantasies of revenge.

"Though one of my own kind, this visitor poses problems, that need to be resolved, as quickly as possible."

Light from the tall, thin, cast-iron oil lamps that lined the waterfront promenade burned with a warm glow that no modern photophilic material could replicate. They were not as bright and not even a fraction as efficient as the cheapest modern lighting, but they possessed a life no Commonwealth technology could easily duplicate.

"I have heard it soft-sung, that this human is a magician, and can defend himself, without physical weapons," Zkerig replied in response to Vashon's comment.

The long prehensile tongue of a *dadderig* shot out of the water off to their right and snatched a big-eared *skwyk* out of the mist-laden air. The *skwyk* didn't even have time to squeal. Human and Larian ignored the spontaneous predation.

"Firstly," Vashon replied, "saying one is a magician does not make him so, and secondly, there are no such things among my kind as true magicians. There are plenty of fake magicians; clever manipulators of reality and sight, who are ready to fool the credulous, and make money from their deceptions." Vashon aimed an irritable kick at a *nogabloat* squatting on the wooden plank in front of them, but the warty greenish lump of flesh expanded and propelled itself into the water before the tip of his boot could arrive.

The Tralltag's tail switched up and down as they walked, the human's footgear making a soft clatter on the wooden walkway while the Larian's leather-clad feet produced hardly any noise at all.

"From what I have heard, this one plays boldly, and with apparent confidence, considering that he is betting with his life." Black eyes regarded the brooding Vashon. "Why, it is said that he self-promoted, before the honored Hobak, a version of himself, to replace *you*. Imagine the audacity, that a stranger to Minord, and an offworlder no less, would have to muster, to make so bold a proposal! Surely you are not worried, the great and resourceful Vashon is not concerned, that this is a possibility, the Hobak might consider?"

Zkerig had spent enough time in the human's presence to learn the meaning of certain looks, gestures, movements, and reactions. As everything he observed now pointed to Vashon's genuine discomfort, the Tralltag was well pleased. He was not exactly the human's underling, more an appointee of equivalent but different rank. Only when the Hobak issued specific orders for him to follow Vashon's instructions was Zkerig compelled to assume the role of a subordinate. Such had been the case in the recent business of abducting the Firstborn of Borusegahm. That task accomplished, he and the human were now once again more or less equals.

It did him good to see the human so discomfited. He did not even have to exaggerate the awkwardness of the situation in which Vashon must now find himself. As if reading his thoughts, or perhaps merely the Tralltag's body language, Vashon glared at him through the mist.

"Who can say, with any confidence, what our noble Hobak, might do? If there is one constant to Felelagh na Broon, it is his unpredict-ability, and it is not inconceivable, that he might make a decision, that he might make a choice, that goes against the best interests of Minord, as well as himself."

Zkerig gazed up the inlet in the direction of the Kelleagh Shal-lows, a prime seafood-producing corner of the Ghaleargh Sea.

"It is the job of the Hobak," he replied, "to make such decisions, and while na Broon may seem odd, his thoughts are not bent, as is his body. The people trust him to do, what is right for Minord, as does the High Council—as do I, his Tralltag."

What Zkerig did not say was that he had long since grown tired of Vashon using every opportunity to lord it over him. Though he knew nothing of this new human, and might be doing no more than trading one offworld master and tormentor for another, he was will-ing to take the risk that might result from such a change.

"So you will not help me then," Vashon challenged him, "to deal with this nuisance, and save the Hobak, the trouble of doing so?"

Zkerig had about had enough of Vashon, not only this night, but in every way possible. The human's persistence, his whining if fluent singspeech, had grown wearying. The Tralltag decided he definitely would welcome a change, even if possibly for the worse. That did not prevent him from equivocating.

"The nuisance will resolve itself, through the decision of the Hobak, and whether it remains a nuisance, only time will tell, only days will say, only further acquaintance will dispel."

Vashon's lips tightened and he nodded. "I had hoped better of you, after all this time, had hoped a stronger alliance, had perhaps been forged. But I see it is not so, and yet I can understand, that your first loyalty is to the crazy one, and not to an offworlder."

Zkerig continued to gaze at the distant, mist-veiled Shallows as he sang an indifferent reply. "That should not be a surprise, to one who knows our ways as well, as you have come to know them, Vashon of the Commonwealth."

"Yes: I know those ways, as well as yourself," the human agreed without humility, "which is why I am here, on Largess, in Minord, beside your Hobak, to improve a lot, that in the Commonwealth is—strained." Without further word or song he reached for the neuronic pistol secured at his waist.

The holster was empty.

Zkerig had moved away from him. His flexible nostril was weaving slowly back and forth, his ears were pointed sharply forward, and his lips had pulled back from his teeth. The missing pistol was gripped firmly in his left hand.

"Did you think me half the fool, that you wished to believe, when we were working together, to bring back the Firstborn? That with your position here threatened, and a request to meet you tonight, on this lonely walk, I would not take precautions? Against possible treachery, against deception, against murder?" The Tralltag's tune had risen to a high pitch. His singspeech displayed the cadence of a conqueror. "Nothing you can do now, nothing you can say now, nothing you can threaten now, matters any longer!"

"It does matter, for I will deal with you now, as the nothing you are, and do so despite, your shameless thievery." Vashon took a step in the Larian's direction.

Zkerig tensed. His middle finger appeared comfortable on the pistol's trigger, while the other two just did manage to hold the alien weapon steady. "Stay your advance, duplicitous human, befouled offworlder, or die. My digit is longer, but I have watched closely, your use of this weapon, and only one finger, is needed to operate it. I can aim as well as you, or better, and though I know not how it works, I know full well what it does." Raising the pistol, he aimed the projection point directly at Vashon's chest. "At this range, even a novice with the device, cannot possibly miss, so lumbering a target."

"You might be surprised, you ignorant thug, at the speed I can move, when properly motivated." So saying, Vashon launched himself at his former ally.

Zkerig didn't hesitate. Holding the pistol exactly as he had seen Vashon do, he pulled the trigger. The damp night air clearly transmitted the brief crackling sound the weapon produced. This was accompanied by a flash of energy that enveloped the entire pistol. It flowed through the Tralltag's hand and partway up his arm before fading to nothingness in the vicinity of the Larian's elbow.

Twitching violently, Zkerig fell to the ground. A moment later his body was still. Vashon looked down at him for a moment, then walked over and crouched. Reaching out, he recovered and reholstered his pistol. The Tralltag's lidless eyes were vacant now, staring out into the darkness. With a sigh Vashon used both hands to roll the corpse a couple of times until it slid quietly into the dark water. Straightening, he tracked the dead body until the outgoing current had carried it away from the promenade and into the distance, toward the beckoning Shallows.

Then he turned and headed purposefully back toward the nearest paved street. There was no way the Tralltag could have known that both of Vashon's weapons were keyed to the human's personal electromagnetic field via the tiny rubidium sensor embedded in its grip. Anyone except their owner who attempted to use either pistol would induce only failure on the part of the projectile weapon. In the case of the neuronic pistol, there would be—a fatal backflash.

His work for the evening, however, was not quite finished.

As he made his way into the town proper and toward the City Hall complex, he doubted he would have any trouble dealing with the unwanted visitor. Just like the Commonwealth authorities, he thought, to send someone after him who would not carry or utilize advanced weaponry—because doing so would violate the same strictures that the one they sought to take into custody had already violated. Did the authorities expect their envoy, perhaps through the use of witty language, to persuade Vashon to give up everything he had worked for and return voluntarily to Borusegahm station for confiscation and prosecution? Or was he, Vashon, the one being naïve, and the authorities were more cunning than he believed? For example, what to make of this local prattle about the intruder being a "magician"?

It didn't matter what he was, Vashon knew. If the Commonwealth authorities had underestimated his own resolve and capabilities, it would be to this visitor's detriment. If they had not, then eliminating the problem might require a little more effort on his part. Either way, the end would be the same. At least now he no longer had Zkerig to trouble him.

As soon as the current irksome situation was resolved, he looked forward to working with a new Tralltag.

Locating the quarters that had been assigned to his fellow human was no problem. A brief bit of singspeech and a few coins were all that were necessary to secure the information. Though he was prepared to deal with any guards who might be posted outside the accommodation, there were none. It would all be over quickly: the principal infection removed, and then to be safe, the native guide. The Commonwealth authorities in Borusegahm would never know what had happened to their intrepid but woefully out-of-his-depth representative. After some time had passed, they would probably send another. Or perhaps several in a group, the use of a solitary agent having demonstrably failed. It wouldn't matter. Singly or several, Vashon would deal with them as required. He had the experience and the will necessary to do so.

He was not prepared for the bell that jingled when he quietly unlocked and then eased open the door, but the sound did not dissuade or slow him. Drawing the neuronic pistol as he rushed the bed located on the far side of the room, he jammed it against the linen-swathed shape lying there and unleashed a charge sufficient to immediately stop the heart of anyone, human or Larian. If anything, the unknowing agent ought to thank his assassin for delivering such a quick and relatively painless death.

He quickly saw that neither thanks nor death were in order. There was no one and nothing in the long, narrow Larian sleeping bunk save a cylindrical mass of artfully lumped padding.

"Over here."

The sound of curt terranglo was a shock, but Vashon was nothing if not resilient. Not wanting to make another mistake, he lowered the pistol as he turned.

Standing in the open doorway to a connecting chamber was a tall, olive-skinned figure. He had red hair, green eyes, and an air of insouciant conviction. Vashon tensed, then relaxed. Both of the younger man's hands were visible and neither held a weapon. Still, his attitude suggested either barefaced foolishness or supreme confidence. Until Vashon could be certain which was the more accurate description, he would hold back.

"It was necessary for me to learn very early on in my life," Flinx said conversationally, "how to sleep in different, sometimes uncomfortable places, and how always to be a light sleeper." He nodded in the direction of the doorway to the corridor, and to the bell mounted just above the inside. "That was enough to wake me, even in the other room."

Vashon nodded appreciatively. "It's a wise man who sleeps lightly." He started to bring up the pistol. "Soon now you'll sleep soundly, and without such cares."

"I wouldn't do that." Moving slightly to one side, the young man exposed his left shoulder, heretofore hidden behind the doorjamb. Vashon saw there was something on it. When it moved, he knew it was alive. When it spread wings of brilliant blue and pink, he knew it was dangerous.

While Vashon's emotional state remained an impenetrable, unperceivable void, Flinx's was not. Reading her master's concern and anxiety, if not that of his assailant, the minidrag rested on his shoulder, alert and fully awake.

"You may as well put down the gun," Flinx murmured. "If she senses a threat directed toward me, she'll respond immediately. She moves too fast to hit, and you'd only get off one shot before . . ." He shrugged. "I've been a spectator to the consequences too many times already in my life, and I'd just as soon not have to be one again."

"Beautiful, just *beautiful*." His voice full of genuine admiration, Vashon stared at Pip. "I've only seen one or two before, and then only as life-images. An Alaspinian minidrag."

The other man's response was not at all what Flinx had expected, and he was suddenly wary.

"You know what she is," he said slowly. "If you know that, then you know what she can do."

"Of course, of course! Such deadliness packed into such a graceful, perfect form! The lines of the creature, the evolution required to produce such a spectacular end product, the radiant colors: it is more beautiful in person than I could ever have imagined!"

While Pip was used to responding to an emotional threat directed toward her master, she detected none in the room in front of her or in the one behind her. Flinx continued to emit concern, and rising concern at that, but though her heightened senses repeatedly scanned the immediate vicinity, she could perceive nothing that could be construed as a danger. While unease oozed from Flinx, she could not sense a cause. Certainly not from the other human present, who emitted no emotions at all. Folding her wings against her sides, she settled down on Flinx's shoulder. Plainly, there was nothing *here* to be concerned about, her master's apprehension notwithstanding.

As soon as Pip collapsed her wings, and by extension any concern she might have for her master, Flinx retreated back into the secondary sleeping room, slamming and locking the door behind him. He had expected the flying snake to react, if necessary, to his own alarm. Or, failing that, to the first uncontrolled trappings of hostility from Vashon. But Vashon had not raised a weapon in his direction. He had only "attacked" an empty bed. It now struck Flinx that if he could not sense antagonism, or anything else from Vashon, then neither could Pip. She might sense her master's fear, but be unable to locate its cause.

Vashon's lack of perceptible emotion effectively neutralized her.

Bursting out into the lamplit corridor, he accelerated in the direction of the building's main entrance. Like much of the City Hall complex of interlinked structures, the section that was home to the quarters reserved for visiting dignitaries was constructed of finely worked stone. He knew he should find and alert Wiegl, but first he had to get away from Vashon. On his jouncing left shoulder, the rear third of her diamondback-patterned body curled securely around his upper arm, a sleepy Pip rode in evident contentment, kept awake only by Flinx's continued unease.

If he could just get clear of the visitors' building, across the small courtyard with its fountain of dancing *feynaks,* and into the Administration area, he would find company in the form of the Leeth's night shift. He had reason to doubt that Vashon, seeking to preserve his position beside the Hobak, would shoot him down in front of multiple witnesses. Especially after na Broon had shown interest in his new visitor's proposal. And it would give him time to think—in the face of Pip's striking lack of interest in Vashon, he needed time to *think.*

Too much thinking in concert with racing for the exit did not leave him with sufficient awareness to dodge the Larian coming around the near corner. Though more than adequate for the natives, who possessed much better night vision than humans, the hallway lighting was inadequate to reveal the female worker who was moving fast in his direction. The resulting collision sent both of them to the floor, limbs awkwardly entangled as a startled Pip struggled to unfold her wings and free herself.

From far up the corridor an angry Vashon struggled to compose a suitable command in singspeech strong enough to jolt the night worker out of his line of fire.

"Move away from him," Vashon sang, "and spare yourself, from my line of fire, at the intruder!"

At the singspeech, Pip's head came up. Her eyes locked on Vashon as her wings flared. Simultaneously and for the first time, a surge of enmity filled Flinx. It came from Vashon. The first emotion he had been able to perceive from the man.

Because, Flinx quickly determined, it had been released through the singspeaking.

He straightened. Unarmed but not undefended, he stared down the hallway at the other human. Nearby, the Larian with whom he had collided lay on her back, her eyes darting from one offworlder to the other.

Flinx could move fast, but not as fast as a burst from a neuronic pistol. The question was, could Pip move fast enough?

He had one chance. Taking a few steps toward Vashon, he began to singspeak.

"To bring you back, it was requested, preferably alive, but with alternatives open."

Vashon simply smiled and shook his head sadly. "Sending one was a foolish decision, a sad decision, one made without consideration, for my abilities. Now I will kill you, before another step you take, since unnecessary talking, is not my style." He started to take careful aim with the pistol.

The emotions and intentions writ plain in his singspeech were all Pip needed.

She sped toward him. In the confines of the corridor her room for maneuvering was limited. Vashon got off a single shot. It only grazed her left wing, but it was enough to destabilize her and send her fluttering to the floor.

Flinx slammed into him before Vashon could unleash a second, killing burst.

Though shorter, Vashon was heavy and muscular. In hand-to-hand combat he might have expected his experience to prevail. But Flinx had received training from Bran Tse-Mallory and was not about to be easily dispatched. One graceful move allowed him to disarm his emotionless opponent. At the same time, Vashon struck out with a knee that caught Flinx in the stomach, knocking the air out of him. This allowed Vashon to sidle sideways, grip the younger man's arm in both hands, and wrench. Pain lanced through Flinx as his shoulder was dislocated. Sensing victory, Vashon prepared to roll on top of his opponent and bring both linked hands down on Flinx's throat in a killing compression.

Down the corridor, the Larian with whom Flinx had collided rose to her feet. Her epidermal layer split wide open. Skin and fur fell away to left and right. What stood revealed as she drew her own weapon was a diminutive human female. She was completely hairless, down to her permanently depilated eyebrows. From neck to toe she was clad in a bodysuit of smooth, pure blackness interrupted only by the silver devices that shone on her belt and skullcap. These sported stylized skulls and crossbones.

Free now of the encumbering camouflage of the simsuit, the Qwarm came running toward the two entangled men while taking aim with her own weapon.

"Get clear of him, you idiot! I can't get a clean shot!"

17

■ ■ ■

It was the last thing Flinx might have expected to see, and it made no sense. *None.* How could the Assassins' Guild still be after him? *Why* would they still be after him? The Guild did not hold grudges. That he had escaped their attention previously should have no bearing any longer. Absolute professionals, they worked only for hire. Those who had originally hired them to kill him, the members of the Order of Null, were no more. They had been no more for some time now. So, if not the now-vanished Order, who would pay to see him dead? Not his half sister Mahnahmi, who as far as he knew still dwelled in an appropriate facility authorized to cope with her condition of infantile regression. Not the current AAnn government, with whose Emperor and imperial bureaucracy he had established an understanding and a formal relationship.

Then . . . who?

Still on the ground desperately grappling with Vashon, he thrust out at her with his talent and found, not unexpectedly, nothing. Among all the members of his kind that he had encountered, among all with whom he'd had dealings both benign and hostile, only the

Qwarm had the ability as a group to thoroughly mask their emotions. In the course of a previous encounter, that unexpected revelation had nearly cost him his life. Ironically, he had been saved by the intervention of the same thranx, Sylzenzuzex, who had persuaded him to take up his present task on Largess. But she wasn't here now, wasn't going to burst through a portal armed and ready to protect him. He had no other weapon with which to defend himself save a small Secun vibraknife and his unique ability, and the latter was utterly useless against someone devoid of emotion.

At the same time, the bulk of his attention was necessarily occupied by Vashon. The other man did not roll clear in response to the call from the assassin. Instead, ready to deliver a lethal blow himself, he glared down at Flinx, his eyes wide, preparing to kill.

It was, finally, the one feeling he was unable to suppress.

Leaping into the emotional gateway thus opened, Flinx struck out with everything he had. For an instant, Vashon's bunched-together fists hovered above his head. They trembled slightly as a storm of emotional discord raged through the man seated on Flinx's torso. Then, tormented beyond measure, assailed by such guilt and fear and nightmarish terror as he had never before experienced, Vashon fell backward and off the younger man. Blasted into a coma from which he would never recover, he lay whimpering on the stone floor.

His head throbbing from the effort, Flinx struggled to turn and direct another emotional blow against the Qwarm who had come up behind him. But she was completely controlled and evinced nothing in the way of feeling. There was no way in for him, no ready avenue of attack. And his head hurt, hurt worse than it had in years. The effort of putting Vashon down had exhausted him.

Turning, he looked over to where Pip was struggling to get airborne. Meeting his eyes, she came slithering toward him. He tried to urge her up, to at least raise her head, to fight on his behalf. To spit.

Pip ignored the Qwarm as she continued to come toward him.

Gazing down at him, the diminutive assassin looked peeved. His eyes widened as he recognized the weapon she was holding: a Hornet VI. At this range . . .

Goodbye, Clarity. No one escapes death forever. . . . At least if he could not be with her, he was with Pip.

"I told you to get out of the way. Didn't you hear me?"

Wait . . . what?

"I thought . . ." Reaching him, Pip slithered up his chest. Curling around his upper body and neck, she began to lick her partially paralyzed wing. Flinx continued to gape at the Qwarm.

"You're not . . . you're not here to kill me?"

Her expression . . . her emotionless expression . . . twisted. "Kill you? I don't even know who you are." With a nod she indicated Vashon, who had curled into a fetal ball, eyes open and staring blankly. "It seems you may have done my work for me, and without even being requested to assist. I am Chela Voh, a member of—"

Flinx kept his tone even as he replied. "I'm familiar with your organization." He did not add that he was familiar with it because in the past its membership had been hired to murder him. He shook his head slightly. "You're sure you're not here to kill me?"

Clearly taken aback, she frowned. "Why would I have been hired to do that?" Once again she indicated the motionless, alive-yet-dead-inside body lying nearby; the flickering light of the oil lamps that lined the walls glistened off the hairless face. "Vashon is—was—a defector from the Guild. I was chosen to deal with him. It took us some time to track him to this world." She turned back to Flinx. "I don't know what you did or how you did it, but . . . is his present condition permanent?"

"I believe it will be so. Judging from prior experience."

She holstered the deadly pistol. "That will, then, be sufficient to satisfy my needs."

A defector from the Guild, a relieved Flinx thought. That explained it. The assassin had not been hunting him, but Vashon.

Flinx looked thoughtful. "I imagine that he knew you would have found him soon enough on a developed Commonwealth world. So it made perfect sense for him to try to carve out a life on one that was not a member, but also not too primitive. Where he could establish himself without drawing attention to his activities, and where due to Commonwealth restrictions he presumably would have a better chance of survival."

She nodded. "To say that the Guild's activities skirt the aphelion of legality is to admit to nothing that is not already widely known." Her gaze, all the more penetrating for her lack of eyebrows, narrowed. "He apparently wanted *you* dead. Why?"

"I was asked by the authorities—the Church, actually—to try to bring him back alive. He participated in the abduction of an important member of the leading family of Borusegahm Leeth. In the process, he utilized advanced technology. On a Class IVb world."

"Serious violations of Commonwealth protocol. Not that that is any concern of mine." She gestured at the motionless body. "You can still bring him back, but not exactly alive. If it were up to me, I would leave him for the locals to wonder at."

He looked around. At this hour of the night the intersecting hallways were still deserted. Reflecting the nature of the weapon he had employed, the fight had been a comparatively quiet one.

"I have no choice. I still have to extricate this family member and get her back to her home Leeth. Also my guide, to whom I am indebted." He hesitated. "I could use your help."

She shook her head and started to turn away. "Your individual concerns and those of the Church or Commonwealth government are not mine."

He started to reach out to her but then decided against making physical contact. Thinking quickly, he said, "I'll pay you."

She considered the unexpected proposal. "An intriguing aside. But I can only accept payment on behalf of the Guild. No Guild member operates independently."

He smiled thinly. "I know that."

Once again she searched his face. "You are very young to be so knowledgeable about things that are closed to most people."

He was forthright in his response. "And you're very young to be a professional killer."

She pondered this, then—it was not exactly a smile, but as close to such as she could manage. "I like you. You're honest. You're direct. You're not afraid. Would you like to have sex?"

It was all a bit too much for one night. She was lively, attractive, lethal. Not unlike Pip, he thought. But he was safe with Pip. "Without wishing, believe me, in any way to offend you, I have to decline. I have a life-companion."

She didn't seem in the least nonplussed by his rejection. "Oh well, then. As to business: How much can you offer for my services—for the Guild's services? And who do you need me to kill?"

"Hopefully, I won't need you to kill anybody. What I need is transportation, which you must have, since I'm guessing that despite your excellent disguise you didn't arrive here on foot. Did you hire a brund?"

She shook her head. "Without the advantage of a local guide such as you apparently retained, I could not have followed so readily using local means. I have a skimmer, illicitly hired, hidden just across the main river and outside the city." She smiled humorlessly. "As easy to violate several Commonwealth edicts as one. The Qwarm are not a shuttle service, save occasionally for the dead. Still, I am allowed to make exceptions if it is of significant benefit to the Guild. I ask again: how much?"

Flinx thought; named a figure. She would have raised her eyebrows had she possessed any. "I venture to repeat myself: you look too young to have access to such an amount."

"You expressed surprise at my knowledge. You'd be even more surprised at the extent of my financial and personal resources. I'll make full payment as soon as we and the individual I have come to take back with me are safely within the boundaries of Borusegahm station."

"How do I know that once we are safely there you will comply with the agreed-upon terms? And not turn me in to the authorities?"

He met her gaze without flinching. "I have confidence in your resourcefulness. If I renege, you can always shoot me." The way the back of his head was throbbing at the moment, he wasn't sure he would mind if she did.

"More difficult to do inside the station, but not impossible. Very well. On behalf of the Guild, which is after all not a philanthropic organization, I accept your offer of temporary employment. You are certain you don't need me to kill anyone?"

"I'll let you know if the need arises," he said dryly. "Right now our task is to find my guide, an indigene by the name of Wiegl, and then locate a female Larian named Preedir ah nisa Leeh. Following that, we will extract her from this polity, preferably without drawing the attention of the locals or the ire of their Hobak." He turned, paused, and added, "And hopefully without having to kill *anybody*."

She did not appear disappointed. Nor did she seem eager. Neither of which was surprising, since a Qwarm is trained to evince no emotions.

Moving fast, they returned to his quarters to recover his pack. While there was little among the food concentrates and medicinals that would violate Commonwealth edicts, his Secun vibraknife was an exception he could not let fall into local hands. Meanwhile Pip slipped back into the metal walking tube. Pack on his back and minidrag comfortably settled in for travel, they hurried back out into the hall.

Wiegl had been assigned quarters in another corner of the visitors' section. As Flinx tried the guide's door gently, Voh looked puzzled.

"No guards?"

"There were two stationed outside my rooms as well," he told her. "As I'm sure there were here. Vashon had a lot of authority. I expect he ordered them all to take a little time off so he could conduct his private 'business.'" The unlocked door opened.

The bed was empty. The void was replaced by the sounds of clashing sing-shouting behind him.

"It's all right, my friend, as she is our ally now, to help us escape!"

Expecting a guard or other local, Wiegl had hidden behind the door opening with an eye toward fleeing out into the hallway. Instead, he had run right into Chela and now found himself on the floor with a knife at his throat. Flinx noted idly that it was a model different from the Secun he carried: smaller, simpler, and doubtless just as lethal.

Backing off, Chela let the guide up as she pocketed her weapon. Confused and uncertain but relieved to see Flinx, Wiegl eyed the new human warily.

"Fast this one moves, fast as a *hirgael* hunting its prey, so that I did not even see her, until my gaze was framed by the ceiling."

"Chela Voh, this is Wiegl. My guide and friend." That, he knew, would have to do for introductions. There was no telling when the guards who had been "relieved" by Vashon would determine it was time to resume their duty. Before they returned, he and his companions had to get the Firstborn out and away. And those watching Preedir ah nisa Leeh would still be on duty.

As they carefully and quietly made their way through the night-deserted corridors, Flinx explained what had transpired.

"The human Vashon is dead, or essentially thus, so we won't be bringing him back, to Borusegahm Leeth, to face Commonwealth justice." Flinx indicated the slender, wiry human who stood impassively by his side. "This is Chela Voh, another representative of my species, but not of my government, who has her own reasons for being here, for having stolen into Minord, for wanting now to leave quickly. Unlike you and I, she came by skimmer, a traveling device of the Commonwealth you have seen, whose presence here, outrages our laws. We will temper such outrage, at least until we return to

Borusegahm, where I will deal with the fallout, as circumstances require."

Casting a glance over a shoulder, he was relieved to see that the
lamplit corridor was still empty. But he knew that in spite of the
hour, sooner or later some nocturnal wanderer was going to stumble
across the mess in the corridor near his former quarters, find the
comatose body of the Hobak's human, and raise the alarm. Before
that happened, they needed to free the Firstborn and be on their way
southward.

As at his quarters and Wiegl's, two guards were stationed outside
her rooms. Flinx had expected more, but as his guide pointed out,
even had she managed to flee her quarters, there was nowhere for her
to run. The entire Leeth of Minord would have been alerted to her
escape.

Once Flinx and Chela had positioned themselves, Wiegl showed
himself in the corridor, sauntering nonchalantly toward the doorway and the guards who flanked it, a cheerful expression on his face.

"Though it is late, a visit I would make, to the Firstborn of my
Leeth, that I might comfort her, that I might reassure her of her forthcoming freedom, and imminent departure from this miserable land."

The ensuing fight was brief, though noisier than Flinx would have
wished. One of the guards managed to shout before Voh took him
down. They could only hope, Flinx knew, that in the silence of the
night it had not been heard. Leaving the Qwarm to stand watch over
the two now-unconscious guards, he and Wiegl entered the room.

The dinner service that came flying in Wiegl's direction hit hard.
At least it was devoid of content, the Firstborn not being one to
waste food and having already consumed it. Words were hastily sung
to reassure her that Flinx was her friend and not Vashon's, and that
in fact her human abductor would trouble her no more.

"I apologize, then, to your associate, whose head, I fear, I have
wantonly indented."

Feeling of the bruise on his forehead, Wiegl winced as he struggled to sing a reply.

"An honor it is, to be bashed by the Firstborn, whose apology I accept, whose bravery is striking, and whose aim is as notable as her reputation."

Outside in the hallway, Voh's attention was devoted to the still-deserted lamplit corridors. "Talking is for later, conversation for later still, as we cannot take for granted, the continuing peace."

"Yes," murmured Wiegl. "Time to go, time to flee, time to make use of what time has been granted us. Do you know, Firstborn, the way out, that we might reach the surrounding forest, unencumbered by pursuit?"

Before she could reply, Voh sang out again. "I entered quietly, and know the way back. Follow me now, and we will leave this place, to its dreamings."

Moving as fast as short Larian legs would allow, they followed the Qwarm as she retraced the route she had used to infiltrate the City Hall complex. It was only as they neared the south side and the wide stone courtyard located there that Flinx began to sense the emotional presence of others.

Many others. The shout by the one guard had been heard, and the alarm had been raised.

There was no point in retreating inside. Flight in the opposite direction would only lead them deeper into the municipal complex and eventually into the densely populated neighborhoods of Minord itself. In this direction lay the river, the surrounding heath and forest lands of the greater Leeth, and, according to the Qwarm, the place where she had concealed her exceedingly illegal but now highly desirable skimmer.

Carrying torches and lamps, between one and two hundred soldiers stood drawn up in double ranks in the center of the courtyard. Light gleamed off their armor and weapons. Several carried primitive long guns that in size fell somewhere between large rifles and small cannons. Wisps of smoke rose from their ready fuses. Scrutinizing the primitive projectile weapons from a distance, Flinx doubted their accuracy but not their effectiveness.

Standing a few steps forward of the exact center of the front rank of fighters was a badly bent figure who leaned sharply to his right. Only a wonderfully carved cane prevented its owner from falling over. Unlike the emotions of his neatly arrayed soldiers, which were relatively consistent with expectation and trepidation, Felelagh na Broon's feelings were mixed. In the flickering but ample light from lamps and torches, the Hobak squinted at the half-Larian, half-alien quartet. Coming upon the confrontation in the courtyard, the few citizens out for a very early morning walk hurriedly betook themselves elsewhere.

"Y-you you have acquired a new companion, one of y-your own kind, though by what means it came here, I-I cannot fathom."

Flinx cleared his throat. He wanted this singing to be as clear as his words. "By means you cannot fathom, is the truth indeed, and it is by the same such means, that we will now take our leave—sorry as we are, to have to forgo, the remainder of your hospitality."

Unable to draw his bent body up, na Broon straightened his head as best he could and stiffened his ears. "That will be decided, by m-myself and m-myself alone, as y-you are m-my 'guests' here, and cannot depart except when I-I say." He coughed, a strange hissing sound among the Larians. "By y-your singing, by y-your song, by y-your tune and by y-your melody, am I-I correct in assuming, y-your offer to replace the human Vashon in m-my service, is now withdrawn? As I-I am similarly assuming, y-you chose for reasons of y-your own, to leave h-him alive yet dead?"

Plainly, someone had already found Vashon's comatose form, Flinx realized, lying motionless in the hallway. Connecting it with the missing "guests" as well as the Firstborn would not have been difficult.

Behind their Hobak, soldiers shifted positions uneasily. Flinx could sense they were ready to carry out his orders, ready to fight, but less than eager to do so. Perhaps word that he was a magician had spread among them.

Could he otherwise turn that to his advantage? Certainly by projecting he could put down some of them, as he'd done to the unlucky Vashon. But there were far too many for him to influence all at once. When their comrades started to drop, surely the most alert among the rest would reasonably assume the strange visitors might be responsible, and would open fire. A metal slug might be a primal kind of projectile, but it could kill as readily as a neuronic pistol.

How to respond to the Hobak's sardonic query? What, he thought, if he used his ability to put down the Hobak? Would the soldiers then respond by opening fire? Or might he be able to "persuade" Felelagh without having to render him as insensible as he had Vashon? Reaching out, he tried to peel back the layers of the Hobak's emotions, tried hard to parse his feelings. He didn't have much time, and yet, and yet . . .

What he found, if he was correct in his reading, offered yet another possibility. One he had never contemplated before; one he had never acted on before.

He'd had no compunction about dropping Vashon, who had been on the verge of killing him and Wiegl. But Felelagh had done him no harm. Yes, he was about to, but for reasons that to him seemed right and just, and on behalf of his position and his Leeth. Wasn't there something that could be tried besides doing nothing and rendering the Hobak insensible? If Flinx's read of him was correct, there just might be.

It also might pose more danger to Flinx himself than to Minord's leader. But first and above all, he had to ask a question. The question itself might result in the assembled troops opening fire, but Flinx saw no way around the asking of it.

"I beg of you, before death is dealt," he said, "the reply to one question, to the satisfying of a singular curiosity, by whose content, I mean no disrespect."

"One question, y-you may ask," Felelagh replied magnanimously, "as I-I am in no rush, to seek the ending for y-you, the ending that is inevitable."

"Perhaps not so," Flinx continued as Wiegl gaped at him and

Preedir only stared, "if certain parameters can be established, whose knowing, might lead to your benefit."

The Hobak laughed, as did several of the ranked soldiers. "Might y-you presume to buy, y-your freedom from y-your situation, which is founded on treachery, and which y-you cannot possibly afford?"

"There is something I might offer, depending on your answer, to the question I would pose, that is worth more than coin, that is more valuable to you than a ransom."

"Ask away then, y-your last question, before I-I have y-your entrails, filigree the pavement." Black eyes regarded Flinx without humor or mercy.

Flinx took a deep breath and hoped his singing matched his directness. "Have you always, always have you, been like this . . . physically unsettled?"

It was not the question the Hobak had been expecting. Though unharmonious, the collective intake of air among the assembled soldiers and their officers was unmistakable. Even Wiegl and the First-born gasped, while Voh's right hand slid closer to her partially concealed pistol. The almost universal reaction caused Pip to stir within the walking tube.

All eyes turned to Felelagh na Broon. Three-fingered hands slid closer to the hilts of swords and the awkward triggers of clumsy long guns. Contrary to what everyone in the ranks expected, the Hobak did not give the command to fire or to attack. Quite unexpectedly, he answered.

"When I-I was young, so very young, came hither the Ureleak Horde, came down from the north, to pillage and to plunder. Came to Minord, with sword and fire, to kill and destroy, to take what they could." Murmurs of memories much rather forgotten rose from the senior officers among the assembled ranks of soldiers.

"Slain without pity, without thought or c-compassion, any who resisted, any who fought back. Among the latter was m-my family: father and mother, two elder brothers. One Ureleak held m-me and made m-me watch, while first m-my brothers, they slew before m-me. Held m-me close so that I-I would feel their blood, warm and salty, as it sprayed in m-my face. I-I screamed and fought, but could not break free, could not turn, from the slaughter before m-me. Then m-my father, brave but foolish, th-they cut h-his throat, and cast h-him aside. Lastly m-my mother, th-they held bent toward m-me, and when h-her throat was slit, h-h-her lifeblood m-my eyes blinded." He paused for a moment, recalling that which was best forgotten.

"Picked m-me up, did the one holding m-me, picked m-me up and threw m-me aside. Like garbage I-I slammed, into a wall unyielding, and lost all thinking, only to awake, as y-you see m-me now." Making a great effort, he raised the heavy cane and, tottering, used it to stab at Flinx.

"Now to y-your question, y-you have your answer, and before you die, I-I would have one to mine. What possible purpose could y-you have in the posing, of such a query, of such an intimate, of such an insulting line?"

In their encounters with the Hobak, several things had impressed themselves upon Flinx. Like everything else he noted when on another, new world, he had filed those observations without thinking he might ever make use of them. Now they might make the difference between life and death. Not only for him, but for Wiegl, the Firstborn Preedir ah nisa Leeh, and perhaps even for one who believed himself to be ruler of all he surveyed.

"I think," he sang quietly, "if you will let me, if you will trust me . . . that I can help you."

For a second time, murmurings of disbelief rose from the assembled. Only Wiegl remained entirely composed. Because nothing about his offworld friend surprised him. After all, was he not a magician?

He had better, the guide thought, *be a good one.*

Felelagh na Broon stared back at the tall visitor. "None can help me, for I-I am broken, broken as I-I explained, broken till comes m-my end."

Flinx shook his head despite knowing that the Hobak might not understand the meaning of the gesture. "I have watched you, and found it curious, that in certain moments, your breaking varies, your breaking shifts. This I think, is that you were shaken, not so much physically, as in your mind, as in your heart. That you are crippled, but not in body, so much as in mind, so much as in emotions, that twist your frame. I can fix that, maybe, possibly; if you will let me, I will try."

Once more, all eyes turned to the Hobak. Felelagh na Broon considered.

"I-I think you are mad, a mad magician, who from desperation, proposes miracles. Why should I-I trust you, why should I-I place, m-myself in y-your hands, or whatever y-you would use?"

"You might kill me," Flinx replied as calmly as he could manage, "and my friends here, but that would gain you, nothing worthwhile."

From the Hobak's throat rose the by-now-familiar barking Larian laugh. "Nothing worthwhile? Y-you underestimate, the pleasure to be gained, the satisfaction to enjoy."

"True to yourself, I cannot deny it," Flinx responded despite Wiegl tugging frantically at his coat, "yet still I offer, one chance fleeting, to help you where none here, anything can do. One chance fleeting," he concluded with a coda-like flourish. "I will not touch you, with my hands, not with my body, but with my being."

"Y-you speak nonsense," the Hobak sang back, "y-you who prattle, of things unthinkable, of ways impossible. Why should I-I think, y-you would not take, the opportunity presented, then to kill m-me?"

"If I wanted, to do that thing, to do it quickly, so none could stop me, I would already, perforce have done it."

The Hobak stood motionless, staring back at Flinx. Then he gestured understanding, slowly. "Y-you speak sense, y-you speak truth, if not wisdom, from y-your flat little mouth. Do y-your best then, try y-your utmost, and when y-you fail, I-I can kill y-you after."

Flinx nodded tersely. Then he reached out.

It was all there: coiling, writhing, raging within the Hobak. He winced as he perceived it. So much pain, so much anger and hurt, crying out for repair, for restoration. Would his talent function now? Could he do to the Hobak the emotional opposite of what he had done to Vashon?

Why not simply do what he had done to Vashon? a small voice prompted him. As he had briefly contemplated earlier, why not render the Hobak insensible, unable to give orders, unable even to respond? What would his troops do in the face of such an unnatural, otherwordly assault? They might flee in panic instead of attacking, allowing Flinx and his companions to escape. It was a definite possibility.

It was also one he considered only for an instant. Where his ability was concerned, he had long ago determined that whenever there was the slightest chance to use it to heal instead of to hurt, that was the way he would take. He began perceiving.

There the pain; from the memories, never shut away and always present. He pushed, he prodded, he did his best to soothe.

The back of his head started to throb.

Next the anger; poisoned serpents of emotion that burned and bent within the Hobak's mind. Flinx adjusted, he reassured, he strained to break the chains that fastened the crippling feelings to the Hobak's thoughts.

Pain lanced through his skull and he stumbled. Voh rushed to support him while Wiegl slipped under his arm on the other side. Yet another gasp of astonishment came from the ranked soldiers as the Hobak's right hand uncurled. The webbed digits straightened. Looking down at his hand as if seeing it for the first time, the leader of Minord beheld normal fingers. *His* fingers.

Now the hurt; the worst inflammation of all, filling the Hobak's whole being with an unforgotten, unimaginable desolation. Flinx mentally massaged it, pushing it away, aside, forcing it from the Larian's mind, until it was gone, all gone, like dark clouds on a rare sun-filled Largessian day.

Turning his torso to his left, Felelagh na Broon did something he had not done since he was an infant. He stood straight.

Cheers broke out from the soldiers. Larian cheers, full of whistling and barking, as they crowded around their Hobak, miraculously restored. The most senior officer among them, equivalent in rank to the missing Zkerig, could hardly speak as he addressed his liege.

"How is it, most noble, most high and respected, this wonder that the offworlder magician, has wrought in your body?"

Na Broon's nictitating membranes flashed. He looked down at his body, rotating and turning his arm, flexing his long webbed fingers. He was not yet sure how to answer and he certainly could not explain, but he did his best.

"Still lingers does the shock, of what has happened, and will take some time, to fully apprise. Yet one thing for certain, I . . . I . . . can tell you." He looked at the officer, then let his gaze rove over his overjoyed troops. "This strange sensation, that through me courses, it is quite shocking, to . . . normal . . . *feel*."

Looking on, Flinx smiled. Then the pain in his head became at last too much, and despite their support he slumped unconscious in the arms of the assassin and the guide while a concerned Preedir stood ready to offer what assistance she could. Meanwhile Pip zoomed out of the tube to hover anxiously above them all. Sensing the desire of the others trying to help, the minidrag stood off and waited, helpless in the absence of her master's guidance and any readily perceivable enemies.

Na Broon and his officers rushed over immediately. It was not until they reached the spot where Voh and Wiegl laid Flinx down on the ground that the Hobak realized he had left his cane behind. At the moment, he was too concerned for the condition of the human magician to wonder at subsidiary marvels.

"Is he dead or is he sleeping," he inquired anxiously, "the one who has restored me, who has returned to me a life?"

If there was one thing Chela Voh knew intimately, it was death. Kneeling and leaning forward, she put an ear to Flinx's chest, then straightened.

"He is not deceased but neither slumbers, but lies now in a state that needs attention. From others who know, better than I, how to treat, his present condition." She felt compelled to add, "He will live, if I am a judge, but it is possible, never awaken." Rising, she gestured toward the forest that came close to the east side of Minord.

"I ask your help, the magician to carry, to my transport, which in the woods lies waiting."

Quickly the Hobak sang instructions to his soldiers. Putting down their arms, a dozen of the strongest came to gently lift the motionless form of the offworlder, forcing themselves to overcome their nervousness at the presence of the winged shape resting on his chest. Wiegl walked by Flinx's side as they carried him out of the city.

Once in the forest, the Hobak let his soldiers marvel at the skimmer while he addressed the other human.

"You who come from worlds beyond the sky, you who would make of my world a single Leeth, know here that I, Felelagh na Broon, swear I will work, for the end you seek. To this I pledge, the new life I have been given, on behalf of your Commonwealth, for one who lies dreaming, in hopes he will awake."

Voh was distinctly uncomfortable. "I am something not a diplomat, in fact quite the contrary, yet your song I will convey, as best I am able, to those for whom its meaning, will be most welcome, will be well received."

Nearby, Preedir ah nisa Leeh eyed the Hobak of Minord, he who had taken her prisoner for his own ends, for his own purpose, and instead of anger and insults, found in her heart only pity. She said nothing, which, for her, constituted a kind of forgiveness.

Advised to step back, the soldiers watched in awe as the skimmer lifted off. Briefly visible against the cloud cover, it turned and accelerated toward the south. The soldiers watched it go, sing-chattering excitedly among themselves. In seeing the skimmer, they had been given a foretaste, however prohibited, of what offworld technology could do, and what it might bring even to far Minord. Only Felelagh na Broon, the grand, the powerful, master of all the lands and islands he surveyed, did not follow its departure with his eyes.

He was too busy contemplating the fluttering fingers of his right hand.

Utilizing the same masking technology she had employed to allow her to illicitly take a skimmer out of Borusegahm, Chela Voh steered them unseen back to the Leeth. A last exchange of credit between her and the unscrupulous merchant who had rented her the vehicle completed the forbidden transaction.

Asserting that it was better her true identity remain unknown to local Commonwealth authorities, she left it to Wiegl, Preedir, and the wagonmaster they hired, to convey the insensible Flinx to Church headquarters. There Padre Jonas took charge. Too relieved and delighted at the return of Borusegahm's Firstborn to ask too many questions, she focused her attention on the one who had somehow made Preedir's return possible.

Flinx lay unconscious for a week and a day. On that last day, he opened his eyes to find himself in the Commonwealth outpost hospital, surrounded by the gleaming whiteness of contemporary medical tech. After so many days spent jouncing about in a brund saddle and then in Minord, he . . .

Minord. What had happened? The last thing he remembered was easing the remaining painful memories from the mind of that Leeth's emotionally tormented Hobak, then . . . nothing.

Something warm and slender slithered down from the top of the bed to coil up on his chest. Pip eyed him for a moment, then promptly closed her eyes and went to sleep. It was as reassuring a sight as he could have wished for.

She could not supply answers to his questions, nor could the tech that surrounded him, but a certain semi-reputable local guide could. Easing himself forward off the supportive tripod composed of his legs and tail, an energized Wiegl brought curved black eyes close to Flinx.

"You live, I am glad to see, for final payment, I am now sure to receive!"

Flinx smiled. His head hurt, but not badly. Not anything like the sharp, cleaving pain that had shot through him when last he could remember anything.

"You'll certainly get the last of the money that's owed to you, because I suspect I wouldn't be here now, in this place, if not for you and—" At Wiegl's scrunched expression, Flinx hastened to re-form and singspeak his words. Then he remembered that the guide could understand and speak some terranglo. The pained look came not from the singspeech, but from Flinx's stressed rendition of it.

"You didn't get me safely back here," he continued, "just for the money."

"No, I not . . . did not." Wiegl confirmed Flinx's remembrance of the guide's linguistic ability. "Who else among the Larians can claim a magician as a friend? The greatest magician known? The coin can wait." He leaned forward. "What I would know, what would most please me," he said, reverting to the singspeech of his kind, "is the learning of the secret, the knowing of how, you transformed the Hobak Felelagh of Minord."

Flinx tried to raise his head, winced, and settled for lying back down and turning toward the guide. "Come closer and I'll tell you." Eagerly, Wiegl complied. Flinx whispered to him.

"I had a feeling. . . ."

Having been apprised of his arrival, Clarity was waiting for him when the skimmer sidled back up to the side of their floating home. After disembarking, he watched while its AI guided it aloft, sharply increasing the angle of ascent on its way back to the waiting *Teacher*.

Espying Scrap, Pip launched herself from his shoulder. He looked on while the two minidrags circled each other above the residence, dancing together in the clear blue sky. He stretched.

It was good, so good, to be warm again.

Warm also was the kiss Clarity bestowed on him. Stepping back, she searched his face and frowned slightly.

"I thought this little jaunt was going to be a simple one. Did the bug lie? And what have you done to your hair?"

Reaching up, he felt of his lingering chevron. "A, um, sign of appreciation from the locals of Largess. As for Sylzenzuzex, she told the truth . . . as well as she knew it."

"Equivocating again." Clarity shook her head. "Sometimes I think that as long as I live I'm never going to get a straight answer out of you."

"Here's a straight answer, and you don't have to be able to read my emotions to know it's true. I love you."

They kissed once more, longer this time. When she again stepped back, her eyelids fluttered.

"Okay, I'm convinced. Plenty of truth in that, for sure." Her tone turned serious. "What are you going to do now? How soon before I have to worry about you getting 'bored' again?"

"Not for a while, anyway," he assured her. "I think I'm going to try to exercise a different talent for a change."

She perked up. "You have a different talent?"

"Some would say so." Turning, he gazed out upon the endless ocean of Cachalot. They had friends here, swimming deep. "If they'll teach me, I think I'd like to learn whalesong."

ABOUT THE AUTHOR

ALAN DEAN FOSTER has written in a variety of genres, including hard science fiction, fantasy, horror, detective, western, historical, and contemporary fiction. He is the author of several *New York Times* bestsellers and the popular Pip & Flinx novels, as well as novelizations of numerous films, including *Transformers, Star Wars,* the first three *Alien* films, and the most recent one, *Alien: Covenant.* Foster and his wife, JoAnn Oxley, live in Prescott, Arizona, in a house built of brick that was salvaged from an early-twentieth-century miners' brothel. He is currently at work on several new novels and media projects.

alandeanfoster.com
Facebook.com/AlanDeanFoster

ABOUT THE TYPE

This book was set in Sabon, a typeface designed by the well-known German typographer Jan Tschichold (1902–74). Sabon's design is based upon the original letter forms of sixteenth-century French type designer Claude Garamond and was created specifically to be used for three sources: foundry type for hand composition, Linotype, and Monotype. Tschichold named his typeface for the famous Frankfurt typefounder Jacques Sabon (c. 1520–80).

How to Contact the Author

Please feel free to write to me with your own stories and suggestions.

Marianne Gilliam
c/o Eagle Brook
An Imprint of William Morrow and Company, Inc.
1350 Avenue of the Americas
New York, New York 10019

shoulders—not on disease theories, outside conditions, or character defects and how willpower and determination can be used to achieve sobriety. He summarizes the various treatment approaches and introduces the concept of Reality Therapy: "All the alcoholic is doing is trying to satisfy certain of his basic needs, needs that are shared by all human beings, but is doing so irresponsibly and needs to be taught more responsible ways. This book undertakes to teach those ways."

The book is available from:

Positive Attitudes, Publishers
91060 Nelson Mountain Rd.
Greenleaf, OR 97430
Tel: 503-964-3731

All of these various recovery programs and books offer different things for the different treatment needs of alcoholics. It is interesting that so many components of the different programs overlap, such as accepting full responsibility for our alcoholic behavior, changing our negative, self-defeating belief systems, and finding positive expressions for ourselves. I believe that the best recovery program of all is the one that addresses our own particular needs, validates us, and uplifts us. One that encourages us to take the tragedy of our addictive behavior and use it to construct a healthy, powerful, responsible life. In conclusion, I would like to leave you with the words of Charlotte Kasl: "And simply presenting people with choices to explore is empowering." May your own journey be one of empowerment.